HarperChoice

second
SIGHT

BETH AMOS

HarperPaperbacks
A Division of HarperCollins Publishers

HarperPaperbacks
A Division of HarperCollins*Publishers*
10 East 53rd Street, New York, NY 10022-5299

This is a work of fiction. The characters, incidents, and dialogues are products of the author's imagination and are not to be construed as real. Any resemblance to actual events or persons, living or dead, is entirely coincidental.

ISBN 0-06-101288-2

HarperCollins®, ■®, and HarperPaperbacks™ are trademarks of HarperCollins Publishers, Inc.

Cover composite © 1998 by Douglas Paul Designs

First paperback printing: November 1998

Printed in the United States of America

Visit HarperPaperbacks on the World Wide Web at
http://www.harpercollins.com

❖ 10 9 8 7 6 5 4 3 2 1

For Dad,
gone from my life
but not from my heart

ACKNOWLEDGMENTS

Though writing is often a solitary task, there are any number of names and faces behind the scenes who make it all possible by offering encouragement, support, love, and technical advice. To all of you—and you know who you are—my heartfelt thanks.

A special note to Damaris Dedulonus, whose name was used for one of the characters in this book in exchange for a generous donation to the Association for the Support of Childhood Cancer at a fund-raising auction. The cause is a heroic one; I hope you find your character to be the same.

second SIGHT

prologue

*I*t *looks just like the Haber Crematorium,* thought Marlie Kaplan as she stepped from the Jeep. The resemblance was uncanny. Though the building before her now was larger and sported a row of scratched and dirtied windows beneath its roof, it was, in all other regards, a dead ringer. The same square brick construction. The same air of abandonment. The same tapered smoke stack rising from one corner, its inner walls lined with the smoke and ash of an untold number of lives.

Even the setting was eerily similar: the bordering woods, the colorless light of a full moon, a smattering of weeds growing up through cracks in the concrete lot. Marlie could almost hear the whispered taunts of her childhood friends, daring her to move closer. She remembered the pulse-pounding excitement that had coursed through her veins as she took the dare one step further by not just approaching the crematorium, but entering it. The memory was so vivid, her nose wrinkled in remembrance of the odd, acrid odor that had hung in the air, still strong years after the last body had been burned there.

The building she faced now wasn't the Haber Crematorium but rather an abandoned warehouse that had recently served as a meat-processing plant. And this was the far end of a suburban Virginia industrial park, not an isolated backwoods section of upstate New York. Yet the feeling of anticipation, the knowledge that she was about to be tested, was the same.

Her fearless entrance into the crematorium had been a turning point for her some thirty years ago. From that night on her friends had treated her with awe and respect. It was a heady feeling, one she grew to not only like but need. Perhaps this feeling of déjà vu she had tonight was a premonition. Maybe this building would prove to be equally fortuitous, another turning point in her life, the stepping-stone to the story that would finally make her colleagues stand up and take notice.

She approached the chain-link fence surrounding the property, her dark hair, combined with the black slacks and sweater she wore, making her little more than a shadow in the night. Her hand hoisted the broken padlock that hung from the gate; then she let it drop and gazed at the building across the lot, still feeling as if she were caught up in some sort of time rift. She was seized by a momentary and vague sense of dread, a feeling that something wasn't quite right, but she shook it off, chalking it up to a mere case of nerves brought on by the resemblance of the building before her to the one from her childhood.

Turning, she waved her hand in a come-on gesture at the Jeep. The passenger door opened and Chris Young extracted his lanky body from within. Though he, too, was dressed in dark clothing, the knit cap he'd brought along was clutched in one hand and his blond hair shone like a beacon under the moonlight.

"The lock is broken," Marlie said when he reached her. "At least we won't have to climb the fence."

Chris reached over, cupping the padlock in his hand and twisting it in the moonlight. "Look how shiny this metal is near the hasp," he said. "Whoever broke this did it recently."

Marlie gave him a distracted nod, her gaze roving the property. "Why don't you hide the Jeep over there," she said, pointing toward the trees to their left. "I'm going to head for that door near the far end of the building and see if our luck holds out. If it's locked, I'll scout around the outside and see if there's another way in, or if we can find someplace to hide." Without waiting for Chris to answer, she pushed the gate open a foot or so, squeezed her way through the gap, and headed across the lot.

The door to the building wasn't locked, and Marlie pulled it open, propping her shoulder against its weight as it tried to close again. A narrow band of moonlight splashed across the floor, stretching and thinning her shadow until it resembled that of an extraterrestrial creature. She pulled a small flashlight from her pocket and aimed it straight ahead. A narrow beam of light shot forth, looking meager and pathetic as it cut a path through the interior gloom.

The room was littered with the detritus of the plant's closure: partially dismantled machinery, scraps of metal and wire, emptied steel bins, and an assortment of chains and gears that either hung from the walls and ceiling or snaked along the floor where they'd been dropped. Trash lay everywhere: empty soda cans, chunks of cardboard, dozens of papers, and a smattering of Styrofoam cups, one of which rocked slowly on its side not ten feet away, stirred by the faint breeze coming through the open door.

Off to her left were two large propane tanks, and she traced the pipes that ran from them—up the wall and across the ceiling—until they disappeared into the building's gloomy depths. Straight ahead, a series of long metal tracks hung suspended from the ceiling, the closest one sporting a thick dangling chain with a nasty-looking hook at its end. Dark stains mottled the floor beneath the tracks, and Marlie wrinkled her nose at the faint scents of blood, death, and fear still lingering in the air.

A hand clamped down on her shoulder, and Marlie whirled around, slapping one hand over her chest. "Jesus Christ, Chris!" she hissed. "You scared the shit out of me!"

"A little tense, are we?" His cap was now in place, obscuring most of his hair. A renegade cloud passed in front of the moon, casting his face in a mix of light and shadow and giving his head a skull-like appearance. He peered over Marlie's shoulder into the gloom, then gestured toward the video camera in his hand. "It's pretty dark in here. If someone does show up, I hope to hell there's a light source inside, or I'm not going to catch much. I'm willing to bet they didn't leave the power on when they left this place."

Marlie ran her flashlight down the wall beside the door until she found a light switch. She gave it a quick flick, but nothing happened. "Don't worry about it," she said. "Film would be great, of course, but I can get by without it." She patted the tape recorder tucked into the waistband of her pants. "Worse case scenario—we play the audiotape on air with some sort of picture montage."

Chris grimaced and wrinkled his nose. "Man, this place stinks."

"Get used to it. We're going to be here awhile. Let's find someplace to set up. We've got a little less than an hour." She handed the weight of the door off to Chris and stepped inside.

Shining her light to the right, Marlie saw several abandoned offices. An old metal desk sat in one, its surface littered with papers and dust. In the doorway of another, a metal filing cabinet lay on its side, two of its drawers missing. "We might be able to hide in those offices," she suggested, gesturing with the flashlight.

She then aimed the light to her left, peering into a seemingly endless expanse of darkness. "I can't imagine anyone venturing any deeper into this place than they have to," she said. "But just to be thorough, we should scout out that end of the building."

"I can't believe anyone would venture *anywhere* in this building," Chris said with distaste. "If I was a dirty cop, I'd sure as hell find someplace nicer than this to conduct my business. I still think your caller is sending you on a wild goose chase."

Marlie shot him a look of exasperation; she was rapidly tiring of this argument. "I think I've been doing this long enough to know the difference between a crank call and a serious one, Chris. This guy was for real."

"Then why doesn't he just go to Internal Affairs? Why all this subterfuge?"

Marlie rolled her eyes, her irritation showing. "You know how tight the brotherhood can be. Turn in a fellow cop and you're a pariah on the force. Doesn't matter what the dirty cop was doing. It's an unwritten rule. Breaking the code of silence can be fatal. Next thing you know, the whistle-blower ends up dead, supposedly the victim of a bust gone bad. Tipping us to the situation was a smart move. We investigate, the dirty cops are exposed on the evening news for all to see, and the whistle-blower remains anonymous and protected."

"And you get the story that will give you the career boost you've always wanted, right?" Chris said with a strong hint of sarcasm.

"And what's wrong with that?" Marlie asked, whipping her hand around so that the flashlight shone directly into his eyes. He reached out and gently pushed it aside.

"I just think you go too far sometimes," he said, his words carefully measured. "You take too many risks."

"I didn't get where I am today by playing it safe, Chris."

"There's a lot of space between playing it safe and acting recklessly. Even Granger thinks you go too far, and he's always eager to sniff out a good story. I'll bet he doesn't even know we're out here, does he?"

Marlie's expression gave him all the answer he needed.

Chris sighed heavily and shook his head. "He's going to be pissed," he said.

"He'll get over it. He always does, once I deliver the goods."

Chris studied her face a moment. "What about you? Will you get over it?"

"What's *that* supposed to mean?" Marlie asked tiredly.

"It means there's more to life than this career, or a slot on a national network, Marlie. Hell, this blind ambition of yours has already cost you your marriage. How much more are you willing to lose while you search for the perfect story?"

Marlie's eyes narrowed in anger. "My marriage is none of your business, Chris," she said, her teeth clenched. "And this is hardly the time or place for this discussion. I've got a story to sniff out here, and that's what I'm going to do. Either you're with me or you're not."

She whirled away from him and pushed off into the darkness to their left, waving her flashlight back and forth to avoid all the junk littering the floor. When she heard Chris ease the door closed and fall into step behind her, she smiled.

The mess of tracks, tables, and dismantled machinery trailed endlessly into the gloom. With each step, the smell worsened and the dark became more cloying. Marlie swung the beam of light up and down, back and forth, creating a ghostly dance of shifting shadows as they picked their way through the debris.

Her legs were straddling a wide wooden beam when she heard a sound from high up and to her right—a small, scraping noise. She paused and turned her light in the general direction of the sound, seeing nothing within the twenty or so feet illuminated by the light's path. In the shadows beyond, she could just make out a set of wooden stairs, leading to what appeared to be some sort of loft or catwalk. She stared into the darkness above, her eyes searching for anything that looked out of place.

"Did you hear something?" she whispered to Chris.

"Probably just a rat," Chris suggested, as if it were some sort of consolation.

Marlie played her light over the catwalk and thought she saw one of the shadows shift. Unsure if it was a trick of light, she froze the beam in that general direction, but it barely penetrated the distant gloom. Her heart skipped a beat, then picked up its tempo, thundering through her ears like river rapids. Her eyes darted back and forth as she tried to watch the shadows from the periphery of her vision; staring straight at them made them blend into invisibility.

She opened her mouth to tell Chris to turn the camera on, to be ready, just in case. But before she could get a word out, she heard a muffled pop, like the cork in a champagne bottle. In the same instant, she saw a tiny flash of light from the loft. The flashlight was ripped from her hand, its light instantly extinguished. The wall behind her splintered in a miniature explosion of brick dust and debris. Darkness fell like lead.

"Oh, shit," Chris hissed. From out of the darkness, his hand found and gripped her arm. "Are you all right?"

Marlie was too stunned and confused to answer right away. She became aware of a throbbing pain in her hand and felt a warm wetness running down her fingers. The darkness bore down on her, smothering and heavy. Fear edged its way in. She gulped in a mouthful of foul-tasting air. "Someone shot at us?" she said finally, with a mixture of disbelief and excitement.

Chris tugged at her arm. "Come on!" he whispered, his voice hoarse with dread. "Let's get the hell out of here."

It took a moment for Marlie's stunned mind to connect with her feet and start her moving. She had managed two tentative steps when she heard a second pop, followed by a metallic thud. An odd hissing sound filled the air, and seconds later, the smell of gas mingled with the aging stench.

Chris tugged even harder, dragging Marlie behind him, stumbling over the junk that littered the floor. Marlie thought of the tape recorder tucked in her pocket and fumbled with her good hand to get it out and flip it on. If she was lucky, maybe she could catch something that might be usable. Then something snagged at her foot and she fell, her arm yanking loose from Chris's grip, the tape recorder flying off into the air. Chris found her and again yanked on her arm, making Marlie wince in pain. She struggled to her feet but resisted Chris's pull for a moment, reluctant to leave the recorder behind.

"Dammit, Marlie. Move!" Chris hissed through his teeth.

The urgency and fear in his voice was unmistakable. A shiver of pure terror raced down Marlie's spine and kicked her legs into action. She stumbled blindly ahead, now at Chris's side. Her hand throbbed in time with the rapid pounding of her heart, and she knew the sticky wetness along her fingers was blood. She had no idea how badly she was wounded, and suddenly, staring death in the face, she didn't much care.

Aided by the tiny bit of moonlight that shone through the windows above, Marlie saw the hanging meat hook just ahead and knew the exit was close. Her eyes searched for the outline of the door and, when she found it, she felt a brief burgeoning of hope. Then Chris stumbled and fell to the floor with a loud grunt, his camera flying off to the side and smashing into several pieces.

Marlie whirled around, barely able to make out his shape in the dim moonlight. "No!" she yelled, thinking he had been shot. Then she saw his feet entwined in a pile of metal and wire. He kicked and thrashed at the entangling mess, trying to get free.

"Get out!" he shouted. "Go for the door! I'm right behind you."

Marlie hesitated only a second, until she was sure Chris's feet were free. Then she turned and ran the last few yards to the door, shoving at it with her hands, wincing as agony ripped through her injured arm. With her heart in her throat, she looked back toward Chris, to be sure he was following.

The next pop was louder than the first two, accompanied by the twangy whine of metal on metal. Along one of the pipes that ran down the wall to the propane tanks, Marlie saw the briefest flare of a spark—a millisecond before the darkness gave way in an explosion of fiery white-and-orange light. A deafening *whoosh* filled the air, and Marlie felt a searing rush of heat surge past her. She covered her face with her arm, hiding from the blinding light and scorching heat.

Chris screamed.

Marlie dropped her arm and saw Chris writhing on the floor, his body totally engulfed in flames, his hands clawing in frantic desperation at his face and clothing. Marlie opened her mouth to mirror his scream with one of her own, but a second explosion ripped the sound from her throat at the same time it ripped her feet from the floor. Her arms pinwheeled through the air, fighting the horrible force that pushed her as she tried to swim through the heat and fire toward Chris.

The last thing she saw before the blast blew her out the door was Chris's agonized face enveloped in flames, his hands reaching out to her, his tortured body slumping to the floor. The last thing she thought was that she'd been wrong all along—this *was* the crematorium.

And then there was nothing but darkness—a solid, enduring darkness that moved in to stay.

chapter 1

One year later . . .

Marlie moaned in her sleep, arms twitching, eyes watering, reliving the last moments of Chris's life. She stared in horror at the licking flames, reaching for him even as that terrifying force pushed her away. And then the pain slammed into her, leaving her flat and helpless on the concrete outside. The cool night air snaked its salacious fingers beneath her clothes, and the shroud of darkness above her began its slow descent. She thrashed about, trying to escape, but it came anyway, enveloping her, wrapping its corners firmly over her mind, shutting out all light, all joy, all hope.

She awoke then, stifling a scream, realizing with some distant part of her mind that this was only a dream. Yet the terror and anguish lingered, a wound as raw and tender as the day it was first inflicted.

It was an almost daily part of her life now, this nightmare. In the beginning, she had been desperate for it to cease, feeling as if she were trapped in a time warp, destined to live those horrible moments over and over again, on into eternity. But in time she had come to accept it as her penance—that, and the darkness that had moved in on that fateful night, making those final, horrifying moments the last images she would ever see.

She forced the tension from her body and struggled to reorient herself, but found her mind more muddled than usual. Something was different—the sounds, the smell, the coolness in the air. She began to tremble, her limbs shaking and twitching with a life of their own.

Then she felt a hand settle on her arm and heard a voice that was soothing, female, but unfamiliar. "Ms. Kaplan? The surgery is over. You're in recovery."

Marlie struggled to put a face with the voice, but failed. Tears of anguish and frustration welled, and she tried to blink them away, only to be momentarily puzzled by the obstructing weight on her lids. And then the words of that soothing voice sunk in. The hospital. The surgery. The hope.

Oh, God, the hope.

She felt a small tug at her arm and heard the ripping of a blood-pressure cuff. "Dr. Winslow said to tell you he's very optimistic," the nurse said.

Marlie thought she knew now what the weight on her eyes was. Fighting the drug-induced fog that gripped her mind, she tried to remember what the doctor had told her to expect. "Do I have bandages on my eyes?" she asked. Her throat was dry and raspy, almost as if the superheated air in her dream had been real.

"Yes," the voice told her. "Dr. Winslow doesn't want you to try to use them until he can control the conditions. Since you're the first person he's ever performed this procedure on, he's not sure how intense the visual input may be. Though we won't know the final outcome until the bandages come off, Dr. Winslow said everything went well and the odds are about ninety percent that you'll regain some vision. Just how much is the question."

Ninety percent. Marlie felt a small surge of hope, but immediately quelled it. Too many times lately her hopes had been raised, only to be dashed to bits. No sense getting worked up again until she knew something for sure.

"It's pretty exciting," the nurse went on. "I mean this computer chip, if it works . . . just think what it could mean to thousands of blind people."

Marlie knew the nurse was trying to sound encouraging, but all she could focus on were the words "If it works . . ."

"We'll see," Marlie said, and then she coughed out a tiny, humorless laugh at the irony of the statement.

The nurse gave Marlie a pat on the arm. "We'll be taking you to your room soon. In the meantime, try to rest. Even though everything looks fine, brain surgery is no cake walk."

Marlie felt a tiny rush of air and knew the nurse had walked away. She lay there in the now familiar darkness, struggling with the flame of hope that burned inside her chest, trying to keep it from growing into a full-fledged fire.

"Just a little more to go," Dr. Winslow said as he unwrapped the gauze that held Marlie's bandages in place. "I want you to keep your eyes closed. Don't open them until I tell you to."

Marlie started to nod, then, feeling the doctor's

hands still the movement of her head, she mumbled her understanding instead. Her heart pounded in her chest, the rush of blood through her ears almost deafening. So much was riding on the next few minutes. Part of her wanted to urge the doctor along, to hurry the unwrapping, so she would know once and for all. But another part of her wanted it to take forever, forestalling the moment of truth for eternity. At least then there would always be some meager bit of hope to keep her going. Failure now would sound the death knell for her future, plunging her into a despair even greater than before. Hope could be so cruel.

She heard the doctor instruct Nurse Pacinski to dim the lights and felt the last of the gauze wrapping give way. Now, only the doctor's hands holding the eye pads in place stood between her and the future. She tried to swallow, found she couldn't, and sucked in a deep breath instead, holding it.

The doctor let go.

Marlie kept her eyes squeezed tightly closed, her heart pounding even faster. She eased her breath out and uttered a silent prayer—not that she believed in God anymore, but she figured she might as well hedge all bets.

"Okay," Dr. Winslow said, and Marlie could hear the anticipation in his voice. Was his own anxiety a good sign or a bad one? "Open your eyes slowly. You probably won't be able to see much at first, but some light should be visible."

Marlie gripped the side rail of the bed with one hand and twisted a handful of covers with the other. The tension in the room was palpable, audible—she could hear everyone else's breathing, tentative and expectant. She tried to open her eyes, and felt a moment's panic when her lids refused to obey. But then they lifted—slowly, stiffly—weakened from their many hours beneath the bandages.

She gazed into the same black void that had been her constant companion for the past year.

A wave of intense disappointment washed over her. She let out a little cry of dismay, then, embarrassed by her emotion, covered her face with her hands. When she felt she had herself composed, she dropped her hands and turned in the direction of the doctor's voice, prepared to deliver the bad news.

The words froze in her throat.

There! Off to the right. A rectangle of light gray against a background of darker shades. She stared at it, watching it blur as tears welled in her eyes. And then the rectangle all but disappeared, replaced by a rounder shape that was even lighter in color: a head.

"Well?" Dr. Winslow asked, and Marlie could feel the warmth of his breath on her face.

"Oh, my God!" Marlie clamped her hand over her mouth and continued to stare, afraid to blink, afraid the shape would disappear if her eyes left it for even an instant. When she could hold out no longer, she blinked quickly, sending a pool of tears cascading down her cheeks in hot, wet streams. She looked again. The shape was still there—blurred and indistinct, but there nonetheless.

"I . . . I can see you," Marlie said, her voice breaking with emotion. "Or at least the shape of you. And there was something else, over there." She released the death grip she had on her blanket and pointed toward where she'd seen the light-colored rectangle.

Dr. Winslow raised up and looked across the room.

"That's the window," he told her. Marlie could hear excitement and something else—was it relief?—in his tone. "It's evening, so the light outside is dim."

Marlie rolled her head on the pillow, bringing the doctor's shape back into view. He was little more than a beige blob, but she drank it in with the desperation of an alcoholic in DTs. Excitement quivered within her breast. A smile broke out on her face. She risked another blink and still he was there . . . and . . . was it possible? Already he seemed lighter than before. Then she realized it wasn't him that was lighter, but rather the air around him. An undulating golden-white glow hugged the perimeter of his body.

"Is there a light behind you?" Marlie asked.

She saw the doctor turn his head over his shoulder. "No. Why?"

"There's this circle of light around you, all gold and white."

"The only light in the room is the dimmed one in the ceiling above you."

Marlie glanced up and saw a faint rectangle. It was colorless and static, just a lighter shade of gray than the surrounding ceiling. She looked back toward Dr. Winslow and saw that the light encircling him had narrowed, taking on a more yellowish hue. The whole thing was swirling, like a slow-moving hurricane viewed from above.

"It's more yellow now," Marlie said. "And shrinking."

"I'm not sure what you're seeing," Winslow said,

his voice sounding perplexed but not worried. "It might be some sort of neural quirk, created by your optic nerve adjusting to the computer-enhanced image. The chip we implanted in your brain works like a tiny processor, not much different than a computer and monitor. It may take some time for you to adjust to its interpretations."

Marlie frowned, but only briefly. Sight, of any sort, was something to be thankful for. If it was something less than perfection, it was still leagues ahead of the void she'd had before.

Someone stepped up to the bed beside Dr. Winslow. A nimbus of light surrounded this person as well, though in shades of pink—large, warm, and glowing. Marlie knew both her mother and Nurse Pacinski were in the room, but the shape was too indistinct for her to tell who it might be. Then she caught a whiff of perfume and knew it was her mother.

"Oh, Marlie," her mother said in a near whisper. "It worked! You can see!" She reached out and pulled Marlie to her, hugging her fiercely. Marlie squeezed her eyes closed, no longer afraid her vision might dissipate. Though she couldn't see the strange light around her mother any longer, she swore she could feel it—warm and pleasant, like love itself.

Her mother finally let go and stepped back, taking the warm light with her. But she grasped Marlie's hand, giving it a gentle squeeze and holding it tightly. Marlie used her other hand to swipe at the tears itching on her cheeks.

Dr. Winslow cleared his throat, and Marlie knew he, too, had been touched by the powerful emotions in the room. "I'm going to have the nurses keep the light in here dimmed until morning," he said. "Your eyes will need some time to adjust. Tomorrow we'll brighten things up some and see what happens." He turned to Marlie's mother and, with a brief nod, said, "Roberta, good to see you again as always."

As he started to walk away, Marlie snatched her hand from her mother's grasp and groped for him, managing to snag his sleeve. She gazed up at the blur of his face and flashed him a smile of warm gratitude. "Thank you," she said.

Dr. Winslow gave her arm a pat, and the glow surrounding him flared brightly. "You're welcome. I'll see you in the morning. If there's anything you need tonight, just ask the nurses."

As Winslow took his leave, the third figure in the room fell into step behind him. Marlie knew this had to be Nurse Pacinski and was surprised to see that she, too, had a cloud of light around her, only in a vibrant shade of red.

Marlie looked back toward her mother, who was still a glowing mist of rose-colored warmth.

"You're all pink," Marlie told her.

"I'm what?"

"The air all around you is filled with this wonderfully warm pink light. And the nurse was surrounded in red."

"Well, as Dr. Winslow said, it's probably some sort of neural synapse that's either misfiring or a bit overloaded. The neurons and ganglia have been at rest so long they—"

Marlie held up her hand. "Okay, okay, enough Dr. Gallaway. You *are* retired, remember? And this is me you're talking to, not one of your medical colleagues. Pretend I'm one of your pediatric patients and explain it to me in their terms."

Roberta laughed. "Sorry," she said. "I guess it's my excitement coming through. I'm just so happy for you, Marlie. This is . . . it's a miracle."

Marlie nodded and smiled in turn, though deep down she wondered if her current level of vision was all she would ever have. Then she quickly gave herself a mental kick for the thought, knowing she should be grateful for any improvement. "You're right," she said with more optimism than she felt.

Roberta cocked her head and stared at her daughter. "Okay, what's wrong?" she asked.

"Nothing's wrong."

"Horsepuckey."

Marlie couldn't help but smile.

"Come on, out with it," Roberta urged.

"I don't know," Marlie said with a sigh and a shrug. "I guess I was hoping for something more . . . dramatic. Don't get me wrong, I'm delighted to be able to see anything at all, but it's all so blurred and indistinct. I had thought . . . hoped it would be more."

"I'm sure your eyes need some time to adjust. Be patient. Give it time."

Marlie let out a derisive snort. "Yeah, sure. Give it time. Guess I don't have much choice, do I?" She regretted the words almost as soon as she uttered them. Not the words so much as the bitterness that tinged them. Sometimes she hated what she had become. Suspecting she was about to get another of her mother's seemingly endless pity-pot lectures, she hurriedly changed the subject. "Have you heard from Kristen yet?"

Roberta hesitated the merest fraction of a second before answering. "No. But William said he'd bring her by at some point. He just wasn't specific about when."

"I wish Kristen could have been here for this," Marlie said, her brow wrinkling into a frown. "I'm so anxious to see her. Literally," she added with half a smile.

"I'm sure she's anxious to see you, too," Roberta said.

Marlie wasn't so sure. Her daughter was at that awkward teen stage, where any variation on normalcy, any perceived deficiency, embarrassed her.

"She's growing up so fast," Marlie said wistfully. "In the past year alone she's shot up so much, she's nearly as tall as I am." Her hand fluttered, rising in the air in remembrance of the last time she had reached out for her daughter's shoulder and been surprised to find it so high. Tears stung at her eyes and the image of her mother's shape blurred. "My little girl is turning into a young woman and I don't want to miss it. I want to *see* it. I want to see *her*."

"You will," Roberta said with conviction. "You'll see it with your own eyes."

The words made Marlie's heart flutter with hope. Not only hadn't she been able to see the changes in Kristen over the past year, lately she was having trouble conjuring up Kristen's image in her mind. And that scared the hell out of her.

"I hope you're right, Mom," Marlie said. "Assuming this computer thing they've stuck in my head really works. And," she added after some thought, "assuming William lets me see her at all."

chapter 2

As Marlie rose from the depths of her slumber the next morning, it was, for a moment, as if the past year had never been. Not only could she feel the morning light warm upon her face, she could *see* it, like thousands of mornings gone before. Then she remembered the surgery and the eternal night she'd awakened to every day for the past year. Eagerly, she rolled onto her back and sat up straight in the bed, looking around the room, wondering if there had been any improvement overnight.

The room was certainly brighter, thanks to the morning sunlight streaming through the window. She blinked to clear the sleep from her eyes, then fixed her stare on the table beside the bed. But no matter how hard she focused, it remained blurred and indistinct, mere shapes and shades of gray and brown. Frustrated, she switched her gaze to the window itself, but it, too, was blurred, though incredibly bright, like some celestial portal. She fought down her disappointment, telling herself it was simply too soon.

Though far from perfect, her vision was enough to allow her to negotiate her way to the bathroom on sight alone, giving her a small sense of accomplishment. Once there, she stared at the dim shape of herself in the mirror.

As with everyone else she had seen thus far, a

corona of light hugged her body. Yellowish gold in color, it vibrated slowly, rising and falling like the chest of a sleeping child. She watched it awhile, reminded of the night-light that had sat next to her bed when she was a child. Modeled after the good witch in the Wizard of Oz, the night-light was little more than a doll's head atop a long, bell-shaped plastic gown. But beneath the gown was magic in the form of a rotating tube with various colored slits in it and a light at its core. As the tube revolved, different colors of light shone from beneath the gown, faintly illuminating the room. Once, when a friend had been spending the night, she and Marlie had gotten into a debate over what to call the light emanating from that gown. Marlie called it a glow, her friend said it was more of a radiance. In the end, they had settled this childish argument with a grown-up compromise by developing a term all their own, declaring the light a glowance. To Marlie, these colored clouds that seemed to hover around everyone she saw were just like the light from that gown, a glowance.

She finally tuned out the halo of light and focused on the outline of her shape instead. After lying in bed for so long, her curly hair was wild, making her head look huge even without the corona of light that surrounded it. When she turned a bit to the right, she could see where her hair took a sharp dent inward just above her right temple. Her hand reached up and gingerly prodded the bald spot, feeling the stiff thread of the sutures among the fine bristles of her scalp. She grimaced, wondering if the spot made her look as Frankensteinish as she felt.

She played with the surrounding curls awhile,

tugging and pulling at them in an effort to cover the bald spot. When she realized that wouldn't work, she turned her attention to the sink, sorting through the few darkened shapes that sat along its edge. Zeroing in on the one she thought was her hairbrush, she smiled when her hand confirmed her choice. Carefully, she worked it through her hair, wincing whenever she came too close to the suture line.

Once she felt she had tamed the mass of curls as best she could, she brushed her teeth, finding the toothbrush on sight alone but having to grope around the sink's perimeter for the toothpaste, which she then measured out with her finger.

Back in bed, she sat a long while staring toward the window, contemplating her future. She finally admitted to herself that she had invested a good deal of hope in this little computer chip now resting in her brain. She hadn't wanted to; there had been too many disappointments in her life of late and she didn't know how many more she could take. The surgery was a gamble—she'd known that when she'd agreed to it. But without it, without her sight, she had nothing. No daughter, no job, no life. The total dependence that had been thrust upon her with this sudden blindness had been devastating. One minute she was an up-and-coming TV news journalist on the fast track to a bigger network station, the next she was a helpless cripple who couldn't even get to the bathroom under her own power.

Adding to her misery was the knowledge that her selfish lust for the ultimate story, her need to prove herself in a business filled with cutthroat competition, had led to Chris's untimely death.

I think you go too far sometimes. You take too many risks.

She could still hear his words, uttered that night in the dark. They were burned into her brain forever, stored away, taken out periodically and used like a lash.

Her job was gone, of course—not that they'd fired her, but it didn't take a rocket scientist to figure out they'd have little use for a blind and totally dependent TV journalist. The station had made a token effort by offering her a position editing some audiotapes, but Marlie knew it had sprung more from pity—and perhaps a fear of her filing suit against them—than anything else, and she swiftly rejected the offer. Then, of course, there was the fact that everyone at the station undoubtedly blamed her for Chris's death. She could just imagine the unseen stares of condemnation that would follow her if she ever ventured back there.

The final blow, however, the one that robbed her of any remaining self-respect and hope for the future, was the custody hearing William initiated little more than a month after the explosion. Even though their divorce had been marked by rancor, the very viciousness of William's actions rocked Marlie. She felt as if Kristen was the only good thing left in her life. Determined not to lose that, too, she had gone to the hearing, still battered both physically and emotionally, but strengthened by her fear and desperation. She tolerated the humility of having her mother lead her through every step, steering her along like some reluctant dog on a leash. She tried to ignore the heavy silence in the courtroom as they entered, knowing all eyes were upon her. And though she sensed the overwhelming pity in the air, she struggled to keep it from carving away what little self-respect she had left, holding her head high and keeping both her expression and demeanor as dignified as possible. She knew appearing self-assured and confident was crucial to any chance she had of winning.

Despite her best efforts, Marlie sensed early on she was losing. William's arguments were convincing and compelling, befitting the defense lawyer he was. And in her heart Marlie knew she must seem pathetic in the eyes of the judge and, perhaps, in the eyes of her daughter as well. The thought of losing Kristen tore at her guts, leaving her feeling empty, hollow, and panicked.

Even though she knew it was coming, the judge's verdict hit her like a sledgehammer. Both her mind and heart screamed in denial, and she shot up from her chair, desperate to make one final appeal. But one of the more frustrating aspects of her newly inflicted blindness was the effect it had on her sense of balance. She felt herself tottering before she had fully risen to her feet. She made a frantic grab for the table to steady herself, knocking over a glass of ice water and flailing wildly as she realized she was going down whether she wanted to or not. The chair tipped too, crashing down on top of her as the water from the glass coursed its way across the tabletop and rained down upon her head.

A hot flush of humiliation surged up her neck as she heard gasps and sniggers from around the room.

Tears burned in her eyes, mingling with the icy cold rivulets of water from the glass. Roberta reached for her, but Marlie slapped her mother's hand away in anger as she struggled to disentangle herself from the chair. She swiped irritably at the water dripping from her brow and reached for the table's edge to pull herself back up, thinking crazily that she might yet be able to salvage the situation. But deep down inside she knew her bumbling inadequacy had indelibly sealed her fate, and in the end, her despair had been too great. It sucked away the last of her energy and hope, leaving her limp and helpless. Collapsing into a heap on the floor, she sobbed.

After the custody-hearing fiasco, loss and humiliation drove Marlie deeper into herself. She shut everyone and everything out of her life, closing herself inside her rambling country home, some days never bothering to even get out of bed. On those days she did rise, it was often to wander about the house, feeling her way amongst the treasured belongings she would never see again, pulling her cloak of misery and self-pity tighter around her. She had few friends beyond those she'd worked with, and the handful who made any effort to contact her were met with swift rejection. It didn't take long for them to get the message, and soon most of them didn't bother anymore.

The only person who had stuck by her was Roberta. And Marlie hadn't made it easy, first heaping all her anger and frustration on the woman and then ignoring every suggestion for rehabilitation. For months they engaged in a battle of wills: Roberta determined to help her daughter establish a new life,

Marlie equally as determined to crawl into a corner and dwell in the past. In the end they reached a sort of silent compromise when Marlie, tired of both the nothingness of her existence and her complete dependence on others, gave in and agreed to learn a few basic adaptive skills. She learned only what she had to in order to establish some semblance of self-sufficiency. Beyond that, she kept herself firmly wrapped in her cocoon of depression, shut away from the rest of the world.

It was Roberta who first learned about the computer chip. Marlie's initial reaction had been pessimism: The procedure was still experimental, only a handful of surgeons around the country had done it, and it involved delicate brain surgery. One patient had died during the operation, and among those who survived, the results had been mixed.

But someone with Marlie's type of blindness—induced by brain injury and trauma to the optic nerves—was thought to be an ideal candidate. The fact that a surgeon nearby in Georgetown had recently learned the procedure clinched the decision for Marlie. That, and a sense of desperation.

And here she was, walking a tightrope of hope, trying to avoid yet another defeat, her emotions in precarious balance. The surgery had to work. It had to. She could accept no other outcome.

With that thought, she climbed out of bed and made her way to the window. The sunlight outside felt warm on her face, but it also blurred much of the detail beyond—the very light she had so hoped to see again now blinding her. Yet even with her limited ability to see, she felt the world around her had changed somehow, shifting into another dimension. It felt different, looked different, even smelled different. The flame on the candle of hope Dr. Winslow had given her guttered beneath her disappointment, but it didn't die out.

As she turned back toward the bed, she was momentarily terror stricken when she realized the room had grown darker, the shapes and shadows even less distinct than before. But then it began to lighten, and she realized it was only her eyes adjusting from the brightness of the sunshine outside.

She was an arm's reach from the bed when she noticed the smell: fresh-cut flowers. Something different from the scent of those already in the room. She looked toward the door and realized she was no longer alone. A figure stood there, as indistinct as all the others had been and, like all the others, surrounded by a glowance.

"Who's there?" Marlie asked, clutching at the top of her robe.

"It's me. Cindy."

Marlie relaxed and smiled. Cindy Lynch was the administrative assistant for Joe Granger—Marlie's one-time boss and the station manager at WKAL. Despite her innocuous title and behind-the-scenes position, Cindy was one of the most powerful people at the station. She knew all the dirty secrets, knew what closets held the skeletons, and knew more about the overall operation of the place than any other person, including Granger himself. Plus, she had a reputation for being able to exert an exceptional amount of influence over Granger. Early in her career, Marlie had recognized the importance of being on Cindy's good side and set out to establish a friendship with the woman. While the initial motivation may have been suspect, the camaraderie that eventually developed was genuine. And the relationship had proven to be a valuable one—Cindy had saved Marlie's ass on many an occasion.

But not even Cindy could fix Marlie's last mistake.

Staring at the blur of color in Cindy's hands, Marlie said, "You brought flowers."

"Yes. You can see them?"

"I can smell them better than I can see them, but I can tell they are there."

"That's wonderful! This thing really worked then?"

Marlie shrugged. "Not the way I had hoped. At least not yet. But I can distinguish shapes and colors." She frowned as she said this, noting the waffling, golden-white glowance surrounding Cindy. These clouds of light were starting to get annoying, and she hoped they would disappear soon. "How did you find out about the surgery?" Marlie asked as she climbed back into the bed.

"How do you think?"

"Had to have been my mother," Marlie said, knowing that over the past year Roberta had struck up a friendship with Cindy that rivaled Marlie's own.

"Good guess." Cindy walked over and placed the flowers on the bedside stand, pausing a moment to rearrange the blooms.

"So I suppose everyone at the station knows about the surgery," Marlie said.

Cindy shrugged. "You know how the grapevine

works."

"All too well. Let me guess. They stuck you with the job of official flower bearer so you could come by and get the latest scoop. Right?"

Cindy smiled and settled into a chair beside the bed. "Actually, I volunteered. For two reasons. One, I wanted to see how you were doing and figured you'd be less likely to slam the door in my face while you were here in the hospital. I imagine you can guess the other reason."

"Michael?"

Cindy nodded.

Michael was Cindy's twelve-year-old nephew, who had been blind since birth. During the first few months after the explosion, Cindy had come by the house with Michael several times under the pretense of visiting Marlie to see how she was doing. But Marlie knew better. Cindy's visits were just one more weapon in Dr. Gallaway's arsenal of tricks, designed to get Marlie back on her feet again. Unfortunately, the plan had backfired. Michael was a neat kid, and Marlie had met him a time or two before the accident. But after the fact, his level of independence and his seemingly placid acceptance of his limitations only served to irritate her. Besides, it was different for Michael. He'd never known sight and had no idea what he was missing. The void was the only world he'd ever known.

"Do you think Michael might be a candidate for the surgery?"

"Unfortunately no. At least not yet." The disappointment in Cindy's voice was plain to hear. A moment later, Marlie had the odd thought that it was plain to *see* as well as she watched the glowance around Cindy shrink and fade until it was almost nonexistent.

"I ran into this Dr. Winslow out in the hallway just before I came in here and explained Michael's situation to him," Cindy went on. "The procedure you had replaces the nerves leading to the eyes and the area of the brain where the visual input is processed. But Michael's blindness is a problem with the eye itself and there's nothing available yet to fix that."

"I'm sorry."

"Me too. There is a glimmer of hope though. Apparently the same guys who invented the microchip used on you are working on a replacement for the eye itself. Dr. Winslow says maybe in the next year or so . . ." Her voice trailed off and Marlie chewed her lip, trying to think of something more to say.

"Well," Cindy said, slapping the arms of her chair and pushing herself to a standing position. "I should be going." She took a couple of steps toward the door, then stopped and turned back. "By the way, Granger thinks this surgery of yours might make a good story. I think he's going to ask Ronni to look into it, assuming, of course, that you agree."

Marlie stared at Cindy, a half-smile on her face. "You're kidding, right?"

"I'm afraid not."

Marlie's smile faded. "Granger wants Ronni to do a story on *me*? Is he nuts?"

"Is that a no?"

"Damn right it's a no! If I was willing to let anyone do a story on me, which I'm not," she added with emphasis, "Ronni is the last person I'd pick. You know that, and so does Granger. Besides, this is a personal, private thing. I don't want my life splashed all over the screen for thousands of people to see."

"Privacy never seemed to be much of an issue when you were the reporter."

Marlie scowled, an objection perched on her lips, but at the last second she bit it back. Cindy had a point, damn her. Frustrated, she folded her arms over her chest and thrust her chin out in defiance. "Tell Granger to forget it, because I won't give Ronni the time of day, much less an interview. Hell, I'd do the story myself before I'd ever let Ronni touch it."

Cindy scoffed. "Yeah, right," she said, once again heading for the door.

"Wait a minute!" Marlie yelled after her. "What do you mean, *Yeah, right?*"

Cindy kept walking.

"Damn it, Cindy. Answer me!"

Cindy paused, sighed, and turned back toward the bed. "Face it, Marlie. The idea of you doing a story of any sort at this stage in your life is pretty ludicrous. You were good once, but now it's time to let the real pros, like Ronni, take over."

Marlie couldn't believe her ears. Ronni a pro? That was a joke! She tried to laugh the whole thing off, but Cindy's words had stung deep. Her face flushed so fast she could feel her heart beating in the incision on her scalp.

"It was good seeing you again," Cindy said as she turned to head out the door. "I'm sure Ronni will be in touch."

Marlie leaned forward in the bed, her hands balled into fists. "She better not be, Cindy. I mean it! I don't want that woman anywhere near me! Or anyone else either! Do you understand?"

Cindy exited the room, shutting the door softly behind her.

"Dammit!" Marlie flung herself back against the pillow and pummeled the mattress with both hands. "Dammit, dammit, dammit!" She folded her arms angrily over her chest. "Just because I'm blind they think Ronni is better than me?" she muttered. "Hell, I could outreport her if I was blind *and* deaf."

Her foot tapped the air with angry agitation. Her eyes wandered over to the colorful blur of the flowers Cindy had left on the bedside stand. She reached for them, nearly tipping the vase as her hand overestimated the distance. Holding the flowers in front of her, she concentrated on their shape and form, fondling the petals as if that would somehow help her eyes bring them into focus. She imagined the flowers were a person, someone sitting across from her, being interviewed. One of her greatest talents as an interviewer had been her ability to read faces, to determine through the subtle gestures and expressions of the person before her whether or not they were lying or truthful, anxious or relaxed, nervous or calm. Often it was the merest shift of a gaze that told her she was zeroing in on a sore spot, closing in for the kill.

Now, she tried to imagine these petals were those expressions, those shifting eyes. She squinted, her face screwed up in determination as she willed herself to see the blossoms more clearly. But try as she might, they remained nothing more than a shapeless blur of color.

"Goddammit!" she hissed. Then she reared back and flung the flowers, vase and all, across the room.

chapter 3

Marlie heard Dr. Winslow's voice outside in the hallway and straightened up in her chair. Today he would discharge her, and she was dressed, packed, and ready to go as soon as Roberta arrived to pick her up. She was relieved to be going home, but oddly reluctant as well. There was a certain level of security here in this antiseptic hospital room, whose four corners she had come to know well over the past seven days. Although her vision had improved little, if any, since the surgery, her knowledge of this room and its different shapes and shadows allowed her a pretense of vision that far exceeded reality. She feared exposure to the rest of the world would return her to the bumbling creature she had been before. Still, she knew Dr. Winslow was pleased with her progress, and she had no wish to disappoint him. Bracing her shoulders, she put on her best smile, determined to hide her fear and doubt.

"Well, well. My favorite patient," Dr. Winslow greeted as he strode through the door. "How's the sight today?" It was a question he asked every morning, and every morning, Marlie gave him the same answer.

"Maybe a little better," she lied, trying to keep her tone as cheery as his own. "Mostly it's just shadows—shapes and shades of gray."

"Well, it's still early yet. Don't give up hope."

"I think I could see better—clearer anyway—if these weird lights would go away." The strange glowances were the only part of her vision that had shown any noticeable improvement. They were clearer and brighter now than ever before. It was an improvement she could have done without. "They're very distracting," she said.

Winslow raised his hand and rubbed his chin, the shimmering color around his fingers washing over his face. "I'm still not sure what's causing that," he said. "I don't recall reading or hearing anything of this nature among the other patients but I'll make some inquiries. I suspect it's a temporary thing. Your brain needs to adjust to the new feedback. This is a different signal than what it's used to."

The door to Marlie's room opened, and another figure entered the room. The way the person's glowance quickly turned red told Marlie it was probably Nurse Pacinski—or Sally, as the woman had insisted Marlie call her. For some reason, Sally's glowance turned a vibrant shade of crimson every time she was in the company of Dr. Winslow. Yet whenever she was in the room by herself, it was a calming mix of gold and pink.

Dr. Winslow acknowledged the nurse with a nod of his head, then stepped up in front of Marlie to perform his morning ritual. Quickly, he shone a flashlight into Marlie's left eye, then the right one. Marlie had come to dread this daily routine because the intensity of the light created an aggravating spasm inside her head. Yet a part of her reveled in the pain, tickled she could see the light at all.

Winslow stepped back and shoved the flashlight into the pocket of his lab coat, a misty trail of yellow light following his hand. "Let's give it a little longer," he said. "As you know, there aren't many patients who have undergone this procedure yet, so it's hard to predict the outcome. But I'm optimistic. I think we'll continue to see some improvement, though it may be slow in coming. I know that one of the first patients required several months before he could see with any clarity."

Several months. Marlie found herself torn over that prediction. On the one hand, it meant there was still hope for improvement. On the other, it meant she might have to set aside her hopes for the future for a while.

"Okay," she said with little enthusiasm. She instantly regretted the tone of her words as well as the sigh that followed. Feeling as if she had let Dr. Winslow down somehow, she dropped her head and stared at her hands, which were clenched in her lap. Her own glowance had narrowed and lost much of its color, barely visible along her arms.

"Look, Marlie," Winslow said. "I know how badly you want this to work. So do I. But we can't get ahead of ourselves. You need to be patient and not lose hope, okay?"

Marlie made herself look back up at him and forced a smile to her lips. She hoped it looked more natural than it felt. "I'll try," she said.

"Attagirl." Winslow reached over and gave her shoulder a squeeze. "Make an appointment with my office to see me in the next couple of days. By then, we can get those stitches out and, hopefully, we'll see more improvement. If you have any questions in the meantime, call me, okay?"

"Okay. Thanks."

Winslow turned away, then stopped and looked back at her, as if he had something more to say. But instead, it was Sally he spoke to. "Nurse Pacinski, will you assist Ms. Kaplan with her discharge?"

The nurse's response was a crisp and professional, "Of course, Doctor."

Marlie watched with fascination as the nurse's glowance flared an even brighter red. Something about it niggled at her mind, some knowledge or understanding that lurked just beyond the edges of conscious thought. But as Sally walked out of the room behind Dr. Winslow, taking her glowance with her, Marlie let the thought slip away.

Marlie stared out the car window, watching blurs of color rush by. The day was bright and sunny, the light warm on her face but doing little to enhance what she could see. Her hands wrung themselves in her lap.

"What's wrong?" Roberta asked from the driver's seat.

Marlie smiled, though it looked more like a grimace. Her mother's unfailing radar was at work once again. "I'm a little nervous," she said slowly. "About Kristen."

"What about her?"

Marlie shrugged. "I don't know. I guess I'm afraid she'll be disappointed. That she's expecting more."

"I don't think you're giving her enough credit. She's your daughter. She loves you. Do you really think her love is contingent upon your ability to see?"

"Yes," Marlie snapped, feeling an odd flare of anger. Then, "No . . . maybe . . ." She threw her hands up in frustration. "Hell, I don't know. Ever since the accident, our relationship has been so strained. And all wrong. It's almost as if she's the parent and I'm the child. Every time we're together, she runs around getting things for me, doing things for me. And I know I'm an embarrassment to her."

"I think she's adapted quite well. But you have to keep in mind that she's a teenager, Marlie. And teenagers are notoriously self-centered creatures, very sensitive to appearances. Peer pressure is everything at her age."

"I know what age my daughter is," Marlie shot back. She felt rather than saw her mother's gaze turn toward her.

"I wasn't implying you didn't," Roberta said carefully. "But I do think you could be a bit more sensitive to her needs and try to see things from her perspective."

Marlie leaned back against the headrest, staring up at the gray blur of the car's ceiling. There was some truth to her mother's words; there were many things about Kristen Marlie didn't know. And their relationship over the past year or so hadn't exactly flourished.

Roberta reached over and patted her daughter's leg. "This has been a rough time for both of you, but Kristen does love you, Marlie. Don't ever doubt that.

This hasn't been easy for her. Everything that's happened—the divorce, your accident, the custody hearing—is bound to be confusing for her. Give it time."

"Like it's been easy for me," Marlie mumbled. "Give it time," she mimicked sarcastically. "Everyone says to give it time. First Winslow, now you. What is this, the advice du jour?"

The car swerved suddenly to the right, and Marlie flung one arm toward the dashboard to brace herself, then whipped her head around to give her mother a panicked look. The car lurched to an awkward halt, spitting up a miniature tornado of gravel along the road's shoulder.

Roberta slammed the car into park, then turned to face her daughter, one arm thrown over the seat behind her. Her glowance had turned dark and heavy, angry spikes emanating from its core. "Look," she said, her voice tight. "You're my daughter and my only child. I love you like life itself and I'll support you in anything you do. But I am *not* going to sit by any longer and watch you wallow in this pond of self-pity you've built for yourself. Life doesn't come with any guarantees, Marlie. You make the best of it you can, something you used to be good at. But somewhere along the way you lost it."

Marlie stared at her mother, stunned by the outburst.

"You've turned into this sniveling and pathetic creature who is so caught up in her own misery that she has no time and no space in her heart for anyone else," Roberta went on. "And frankly, I'm sick and tired of it. In all my years of practice I've treated dozens of patients—young children—who had far greater problems than you. And they faced them with courage and laughter and hope. Even when there was no hope. You insult them . . . hell, you insult me, not to mention everyone else who cares about you with this sullen, 'poor-me' attitude of yours. So knock it off. Because I'm not going to tolerate it any longer."

Marlie was speechless. She couldn't have been more surprised if Roberta had suddenly sprouted horns and a tail and declared she was the devil himself. Roberta Gallaway was the kindest, most patient person Marlie had ever known. Never, in all their years together had the woman laid a hand on her. Rare was the occasion when she so much as raised her voice. Now this. Marlie felt confused and betrayed. She struggled for something to say, searching the ball of angry hurt burning within her chest, waiting for it to give birth to some scathing and nasty retort.

But the burn gave way to shame. Marlie hung her head and stared at her lap, not knowing what she should or could do to make things right between them. She felt as if she were five years old again, trying desperately to please her parents and knowing she had somehow failed.

Roberta shifted the car back into gear and pulled out onto the road, severing the taut string of tension between them. For a moment, Marlie thought her mother might apologize for her sudden and surprising outburst, taking back the cruel words she'd so carelessly flung across the seat. But it didn't happen. In fact, they passed the remainder of the trip in total silence, broken only by the quiet hum of the car's engine and the occasional *whoosh* of air as another car passed them on the road.

chapter 4

As Roberta pulled up in front of the house, Marlie's eyes scanned its facade, her memory filling in the details that remained blurred by her sight. One of a dozen or so houses along Holliman Road, a narrow two-lane country route that meandered for some five miles through a rural area west of the sprawling suburban developments outside Washington, DC, the house dated back to the Civil War. Though it had a certain historic majesty about it, Marlie knew it showed its age. She had bought the place only a few months before the warehouse explosion and had instantly fallen in love with its quirky charm. It had been on the market a long time, plagued by rumors it was haunted. Marlie guessed the rumors had something to do with the maze of tunnels—part of the Underground Railroad used during the Civil War—that ran beneath the house.

The existence of the tunnels was something Marlie had uncovered by accident. There was no mention of them when she bought the house, but in researching its history, she had run across an old plat map from seventy-five years ago that had "underground passage" marked on it as an offshoot of the basement. Curious, she had investigated the cellar and had eventually discovered that an old cabinet, which appeared to be built into the wall, was actually a cleverly structured doorway to the tunnels' entrance.

She had ventured into the tunnels then, but hadn't gone far, as they were a mazelike path of twists, turns, and dead ends. Realizing she would need to better prepare, Marlie postponed her exploration for a later date. The idea of getting lost down there wasn't a particularly pleasant one. Carved through the subterranean dirt and rock, the tunnels oozed with dampness and never grew warmer than about fifty degrees. A musty smell of age and decay permeated the air, and the walls seemed to swallow sound and nibble away at the edges of even the most powerful flashlight beam.

Despite that, she had never felt as if they were haunted. Marlie saw the tunnels for what they were: a well-preserved remnant from a fascinating period in history. She had even entertained doing a news piece on them, tying them in to some historically significant date.

Perhaps it was the main part of the house that inspired all the ghost lore, for its plank wood floors, stone fireplaces, mullioned windows, and old-fashioned wainscoting spoke of a time long past. Unfortunately, so did the plumbing and wiring, which were about as trustworthy as a con man.

On the outside, the front of the house boasted a pillared verandah, the roof a good-sized widow's walk. But the paint was old and peeling, the wood crumbling and rotten in places. It had been her intent to give the place a major face-lift, restoring its stately beauty and functionality while preserving its air of historic dignity. But after her accident she had lost all interest in the project, and with no steady source of income in the foreseeable future, it became economically unfeasible.

The run-down condition of the house was a constant source of irritation to William, who hated the place with a surprising vehemence. According to him, it was nothing more than a money-sucking death trap. Marlie suspected his passionate dislike of the place stemmed less from its condition than it did from the symbolism of her purchase, which represented one more nail in the coffin of their marriage.

Hearing the crunch of tires on gravel, Marlie twisted around in her seat to look out the back window. A sleek black vehicle pulled up behind them, and even with her limited vision, Marlie knew it was William's Porsche. She'd know the sound of that engine anywhere.

As if to confirm, Roberta said, "There they are. Right on time."

Marlie faced front again and took a moment to collect herself, thrilled her daughter was finally here, but also nervous about seeing her for the first time since the surgery. She knew her blindness had been a source of some embarrassment for Kristen. Teenagers wanted to have parents who were perceived by their friends as "normal" at the very least, although "cool" would be even better. Marlie wasn't sure the results of her surgery would qualify her for either.

She braced herself with a deep breath, climbed out of the car, and turned toward the Porsche, her eyes hungrily searching for their first glimpse of her daughter in over a year. Both William and Kristen had already exited the car and stood side by side near the hood. Unable to distinguish any details, Marlie looked for the shorter of the two, assuming that would be Kristen. But to her surprise, both figures were the same height. Further confusing the issue was the fact that both figures were surrounded by a glowance, one of them a dark greenish brown color that clung tight to the body, the other a white-gold cloud that vibrated with excitement.

Roberta approached the golden-white glowance and wrapped her arms about its owner, something Marlie knew her mother would never do to William. Impatient and excited now that she knew which of the figures was Kristen, Marlie moved closer, trying to study Kristen's face over Roberta's shoulder, hoping to be able to make out any detail, no matter how vague.

Roberta finally released Kristen and stepped aside, giving Marlie a close and unobstructed view of her daughter. What she saw took her breath away. The disparity between the image Marlie had carried in her mind for the past year and the reality of the young woman standing before her was startling. When Marlie had last seen her, Kristen's hair had been a dark wavy waterfall hanging halfway to her waist. Now, it was short and cropped, a tousled cap of curls atop her head. And though she'd known Kristen had grown, the enormity of the physical changes that had occurred over the past year came as something of a shock. The Kristen Marlie remembered was short and slightly pudgy, vestiges of baby fat clinging to her bones. The Kristen standing before her now was a lithesome, graceful creature with the stature and bearing of an adult. No longer a child by any stretch of the imagination.

"My God," Marlie choked out, her throat feeling as if it were in an ever-tightening stranglehold. "Look at you!" She extended her arms, inviting a hug.

Kristen took a tentative step forward, then hesitated. She cocked her head to the side. "Can you see me?" she asked, her tone a mix of curiosity and hope.

Marlie wanted to say yes—she wanted to say a lot of things—but emotion lodged in her throat like a too-large pill swallowed dry. And what little she could see was blurred more than usual as she tried to look past a wall of burgeoning tears. So she nodded instead.

"That is so cool," Kristen said excitedly, and she finally closed the gap between them, giving her mother a brief but powerful hug.

As soon as Kristen released her, Marlie grabbed her daughter by the shoulders and held her at arms' length, shaking her head in wonder. "Let me get a good look at you," she said, her voice shaky, but there. "I can't believe how much you've grown. My little girl isn't so little anymore."

"Not hardly," Kristen said. "In fact, I'm now taller than most of the boys at school."

Judging from the tone, Marlie guessed Kristen's feelings on this issue were mixed. "Don't worry, honey," she said. "They'll catch up to you soon enough. And I'd wager most of them will be chasing after you before long."

Kristen's glowance flared brighter, taking on hues of pink and red. "You really can see," she said with some wonderment. "I mean, you can see like you did before, right?"

Marlie hesitated a fraction of a second. She was so tickled with Kristen's reaction that she was reluctant to tell her the truth—that her sight was still far from perfect. But from the first time Kristen was old enough to understand what honesty was, Marlie had been hammering home its importance. Now was no time to start lying; she had to practice what she'd preached.

"Well, it's not perfect," she admitted. "I can't make out much detail yet, but I can see shapes and color. Like your hair. When did you get it cut?"

"Last week." She reached up and raked both hands through the curls. "Do you like it?"

"I do. It's very chic. Very sophisticated." Off to the side, William let out a derisive grunt.

"I see you have a different . . . um . . . style yourself," Kristen said.

Marlie cursed to herself. With all the anticipation and emotion of her homecoming, she had completely forgotten about her bald spot. She'd been so worried about her less-than-perfect sight that she failed to consider how her daughter might feel about her freakish appearance. Now, her face flushed hot as she fought back an urge to fuss with her hair in an effort to cover the flaw.

"It will grow back," Marlie said with a shrug, hoping she looked and sounded more nonchalant than she felt. She forced a smile to her lips. "And in the meantime, I fit in well with the punk crowd, don't you think?" Eager to change the subject, she draped an arm over Kristen's shoulders. "Let's go inside. I want to hear all about what's going on with you."

Marlie led the way, her eyes scanning the shapes and shadows that lay before her. The interior of the house had ceased to be a visual memory some time ago, replaced by a tactile map Marlie held in her head. Now, the memories surged back as Marlie remembered the layout, the furnishings, the warm glow of afternoon light reflecting off the wood floors.

Roberta went into the kitchen to fix some drinks, and William, apparently impatient behind Marlie's meandering gait, pushed his way past her and Kristen to claim the living room sofa. Ever since the custody hearing, he had been reluctant to leave Marlie alone with Kristen for any length of time and had even managed to make Marlie's visitation contingent upon the presence of another supervising adult. Marlie couldn't help but wonder if his quick acquisition of the couch—the only piece of furniture in the room that could sit more than one person— had been calculated to keep her and Kristen as far apart as possible.

Determined to keep things light, Marlie swallowed down her annoyance and settled into a chair, smiling as Kristen bypassed the couch and her father, taking the chair beside her mother instead.

"So how's school?" Marlie asked. "You're almost finished for the year, right?"

"Just another two weeks to go."

"Have any special plans for the summer?"

Kristen shrugged and shot a worried glance toward her father. "Maybe," she said. "Brittany's family has invited me to go camping with them the last two weeks in July."

"I see," Marlie said, smiling knowingly. Brittany was Kristen's closest friend, and Brittany's older brother, Mark, had been the subject of Kristen's smitten attention for the past two years. Thus far, Mark had barely acknowledged Kristen's existence. But as Marlie considered the remarkable changes that had occurred in her daughter over the past year, she suspected the boy might soon take closer notice of his little sister's friend. "That sounds like fun," she said. "Where are they going?"

"The Poconos."

"Is the whole family going?"

"Yep."

Kristen tried to sound nonchalant, but Marlie could hear the excitement in her daughter's voice. And oddly, the glowance around her began to waver with shimmers of red, much like Nurse Pacinski's had. Marlie again felt a nudge of dawning, some bit of enlightenment lurking just beyond her grasp. But before she could pursue it, a realization struck. The last two weeks in July were Marlie's scheduled visitation time.

Her first impulse was to protest. Mark or no Mark, she didn't want to sacrifice the few precious opportunities she had to spend time with her daughter. But she stopped and thought things through. She knew how much this trip would mean to Kristen. Nixing it would only serve to alienate her. Besides, it wasn't as if she herself was locked into any schedule. They could simply change the visitation plans.

"Listen, I have an idea," Marlie suggested. "Now that I have some sight back, I'd like to do a little shopping, add some color to my life. You know, get some new clothes and pick out a few things to spruce up the house."

William snorted. "It will take more than a few things to brighten up this dump," he mumbled.

Marlie ignored him. "So, how would you like to spend a week or two here once school is out and help me shop?"

Before Kristen could answer, William leaned forward on the couch and said, "That won't be possible."

Marlie sighed, assuming an expression of weary patience. Reluctantly, she turned toward William, whose glowance swirled with an ugly dirt green color that made her almost pull back in disgust. "Why not?" she asked, her voice tight.

"We've already made plans for that time," William told her. "We're going to Florida to visit my folks for two weeks."

Marlie gritted her teeth, then quickly relaxed her jaw when she felt the tension pull painfully at the stitches in her scalp. "Fine," she said, the word short and clipped. "Then we'll do it when you return, early in July."

William looked toward Kristen and gave a sideways nod of his head. "Why don't you go out to the kitchen and give your grandmother a hand," he suggested.

Kristen let out an exaggerated sigh of impatience, rolling her eyes. "There are only four of us," she said in her best "how can you be so stupid?" tone. "I don't think it takes two people to fix four drinks."

Marlie winced. This argumentative side of Kristen was something that had appeared over the past year. It was a trait she knew aggravated William to no end, and if he was in a foul mood already, this wasn't going to help.

"Do it, Kristen." William's tone was deathly quiet, but it was a deceptive calm. Kristen knew it and hesitated only a second before flinging herself from the chair and stomping from the room.

Marlie was furious, with both William and Kristen. But she laid most of the blame at William's feet, irritated that he had turned her homecoming into yet another war of the wills. If history was any indication, she knew the next few minutes would be intense. Bracing herself, she said, "What the hell was that all about?"

"You know full well the conditions of the custody agreement, Marlie. Kristen's time with you is the last two weeks in July. And then, only if your mother is here."

"But she'll be gone for those two weeks. So we adjust the schedule."

"There will be no adjusting. Those are your two weeks. If Kristen chooses to do something else during that time, that's her option."

Marlie felt her stomach knot. "Surely you don't expect to make her choose between the two, William. That's hardly fair to her. Or me."

"She's already chosen," William said with irritating calm. "She knows what those two weeks are and she wants to go to the Poconos."

"Then we set up another time for her visitation with me," Marlie snapped. "It's not that big a deal."

"We already have plans for the rest of the summer."

"Then change them, dammit! She's my daughter, too, William. I have as much right to see her as you do. And at the age she's at, she needs her mother now more than ever."

"She's doing just fine without you," William said, his words like arrows slamming into her heart. "And where the hell does this sudden maternal concern come from? You didn't seem too worried about Kristen's need for a mother when you were stupid enough to go into that damned warehouse and nearly get yourself killed."

"Oh, puh-lease," Marlie moaned, smacking her hands on the arms of her chair. "Don't tell me we're going to dredge up *that* old argument." She closed her eyes, feeling the muscles in her head tighten again. The stitches in her scalp pulled painfully, a stinging addition to the headache that was now building. She reached up and massaged her temples, trying to force the muscles to relax. "We've been through all this before, William," she said tiredly. "It was my job. Having a job doesn't make me an unfit parent."

"Well, that's not what the judge thought, is it?" He pushed himself off the couch and paced back and forth in front of her. "You just don't get it, do you? Your behavior was reckless and foolhardy. And finally there was a judge with enough sense to recognize that. A good wife and mother doesn't put her job ahead of the needs of her family, Marlie. But you showed time and again that your job came first— ahead of me, and ahead of Kristen. You should have stayed at home like I asked you to. That's where a wife and mother belong."

"If I was such an unfit parent, why did the judge give me primary custody of Kristen when we first divorced?" Marlie shot back.

William stopped pacing, folded his arms over his chest, and looked down his nose at her. "Well, you don't have her now, do you?" he said in his most mocking tone.

"The only reason I don't is because of that custody hearing you instigated after the explosion. That was low, William. Even for you."

"And just what the hell was I supposed to do? You were in no shape to take care of her. Christ, you could hardly take care of yourself."

"You didn't do it out of concern for Kristen or me, William, and you know it. You did it to be spiteful, to massage your wounded little ego. You took advantage of me."

"I did what I thought was best for us."

Marlie shook her head in dismay. "There is no 'us' anymore, William. And all you did for Kristen was deprive her of her mother at a time in her life when she needs one the most."

"You get visitation."

"It's not the same, and you know it. Besides, you're trying to take that away from me, too."

William's hand raised up toward his head, and Marlie knew from nearly sixteen years of living with him that he was raking his fingers through his dark hair. "Come back to me, Marlie," he said. "Let's be a family again. That's what Kristen really needs."

Marlie shook her head in disbelief. "No,

William. That's not what any of us needs. Kristen doesn't want to see her parents fighting like cats and dogs all the time, and neither of us wants a life where we're constantly walking on eggshells. Face it, William, we weren't meant to be together. You want a housewife, someone to fix your meals and darn your socks and have a drink waiting for you when you come home."

"And what's so awful about that?"

"There's nothing awful about it. It's just not me. You know how much my career means to me."

"And look where it got you." He laughed then, a decidedly unhumorous sound. "Why are we even talking about your career? It's not like you have one anymore. Hell, you barely have a life, Marlie. You stay holed up in this decrepit old house, day in and day out, totally absorbed in your own self-pity."

Marlie reeled from his words as if she'd been slapped. If his intent had been to hurt her, to undermine her confidence, then he'd certainly succeeded. What the hell was this, pick-on-Marlie day?

A bolt of anger, like an electrical surge, coursed through her. The tips of her fingers tingled, the muscles in her body twitched. The ache in her head grew more intense, a throbbing, living thing. She channeled the pain toward her anger, letting it fuel the flames even higher. Thrusting herself from the chair, she was right in William's face in two steps, trying not to be repulsed by the sickening green light that swirled around him.

"If you think I'm going to let you walk all over me, or take my daughter from me, you are sadly mistaken," she seethed. "You're a petty, jealous man,

William. So much so that you can't get past your own ego long enough to see what's best for Kristen. I've had it with your selfish, bullying attitude and I'm not going to take it anymore. I'm not the meek and helpless little woman you seem to think I am. I can fight just as dirty as you can. Watch me."

She stood there, almost nose to nose with him, waiting for him to snap, to totally lose control and lash out at her. But instead, he merely chuckled.

"You are so pathetic," he said, shaking his head. "Just because you have a tiny bit of sight back, you think you can conquer the world? Obviously, you haven't learned your lesson, Marlie. I guess it isn't enough that you've already caused one man's death with your reckless behavior, eh?"

Marlie stared at him, stunned momentarily speechless by the cruelty of his words.

"Tell Kristen I'm waiting for her in the car," he said. Then he whirled away from her and stomped from the room. A second later, the front door slammed.

Marlie squeezed her eyes shut and dropped her head onto her chest. Her headache was pounding with the force of a hurricane surf.

"Why do you guys always have to fight?"

Marlie's head snapped up, and she saw Kristen standing in the doorway to the living room, her glowance narrow and dark, a slowly churning turbulence at its core.

"Kristen, I—"

"Why do you do that?" Kristen asked with a whine.

"Pardon me?"

"You're always picking fights with him. Why do you have to make things so difficult?" The whine was verging on hysteria now. "You're always pushing him, trying to make him mad. You ruined everything before, and you're still doing it."

"No, no," Marlie said, shaking her head and taking a step toward her daughter. When Kristen backed away, Marlie froze, a wounded expression on her face. "Kristen, *he's* the one doing the pushing. He wants to control me, to control you. He always has. I can't—"

"Oh just forget it!" Kristen whirled away and stomped along her father's path to the front door. She managed a final parting shot before she slammed it behind her. "You just don't understand. And you never will!"

Marlie held her head in her hands, feeling pain pulse along her scalp and down her neck. She turned around and headed back for her chair, dropping into it. Leaning back, she stared up at the ceiling. "Shit," she mumbled.

And then she cried.

chapter 5

Desperate to prove her independence after the showdown with William, Marlie insisted her mother go home for the night. After a brief argument, Roberta gave in, but she stayed on until after eleven and then said she would be back bright and early the next morning. No sooner had Roberta left than Marlie began to have second thoughts about the whole idea. Her first night alone with her new vision was proving to be just as terrifying as her first night alone after being stricken blind. Only rather than being frightened by all she couldn't see, she quickly discovered that what she *could* see was just as scary. Everywhere she looked dusky shapes and shifting shadows loomed out of the half darkness. She worked her way through the house turning on every light she could find, hoping to banish the shadows, or at the very least lessen their depths. Lights had been of little use or importance to her for the past year; now they were her companion and savior. She said a silent prayer that the unreliable wiring in the old house wouldn't give out anytime soon.

When she turned on the light in the spare bedroom that served as her home office, something caught her eye. Along with several file cabinets, two desks, a credenza, and all the usual office equipment, the room was furnished with a bookcase that stood against the far wall. Its shelves were lined with a variety of papers, books, and videos, as well as a few pieces of memorabilia. The most notable were three trophies Marlie had been awarded over the years, each one given in commemoration of a particularly outstanding piece of TV journalism.

Marlie was incredibly proud of those trophies, and during the early months of her blindness, the office had become something of a shrine for her, a monument to the best time of her life. While she and Roberta generally shared the chores throughout the rest of the house, sweeping and dusting this room was solely Marlie's responsibility. She had a routine she followed, always saving the best—the trophies—until last. When she finally came to them, she would take each one down and buff it to what she hoped was a glistening shine. She would run her hands lovingly over their surfaces, momentarily forgetting the misery of her current life while she indulged instead in the glories of her past.

As gratifying as it was to hold and fondle the trophies, Marlie was unprepared for the emotional onslaught of actually seeing them again. Turning on the light cast most of the room in a maze of shapes and shadows, but the three trophies gleamed brightly from their shelves, the light from their burnished gold surfaces cutting through the air like lighthouse beacons. Tears welled in Marlie's eyes: tears of joy at seeing them again, tears of sadness at all she had lost. She stood there a long time, barely blinking, barely breathing, drinking in the sight.

Eventually she moved on, until she had the house as close to daylight as artificial light could get it. Then she settled on the couch and flipped on the TV, grateful for the background noise. But rather than listening to Jay Leno and his guests, her thoughts wandered back to the afternoon and her fight with William.

Their relationship had always been marked by conflict, even when things were relatively good between them. In the beginning, that conflict had been exciting, the spark igniting their passionate fire. But over time the heat of those flames had dwindled, leaving behind the cold ashes of a dying relationship and an emotional rancor that too often turned malicious—as it had that afternoon.

William's words had wounded her more than she cared to admit. Maybe he was right—she *was* pathetic. Here she was, sitting in a circle of blazing light like some frightened child too afraid of the dark to sleep. Though the surgery seemed to have been some small success, the only thing she could see worth a damn were those annoying clouds of color. She had hoped the glowances were temporary, an aberration that would soon disappear or at least fade. Instead, they seemed to grow more vivid with each passing day, further obscuring the other details around her. Meanwhile, the rest of her vision had shown little improvement.

Depressed and disconsolate, she finally went to bed in the wee hours of the morning, hoping the light of a new day would expunge both the shadows in the house and those on her soul. Mother Nature, however, refused to cooperate. The morning had dawned gray and gloomy, the skies overcast and weepy—a perfect match to Marlie's mood.

*   *   *

The weather had remained gloomy for an entire week, and each morning Marlie fought the urge to simply snuggle down and pull the covers over her head. But then she would remember her mother's startling outburst in the car on the way home from the hospital, and muttering a halfhearted curse, she would fling back the covers and climb out of bed.

This morning was no different. Slipping on her robe, she dragged herself across the hallway and stopped in the doorway to her office to stare at the trophies for a few minutes, a sojourn that had become something of a daily ritual. While she had grown comfortable enough with the house's many shadows over the past week to turn off some of the lights, the one in her office blazed away twenty-four hours a day, a substitute for the sun that refused to put in an appearance.

When she was through with her daily dose of what she laughingly referred to as her "trophy fix," she moved on toward the kitchen. Each day she had made this trek a little faster, delighted with her ability to negotiate the path almost as easily as a normally sighted person. Today she hesitated, however, sensing something different about the house. A moment later she knew what it was. Every day for the past week Roberta had arrived bright and early in the morning, and by the time Marlie got out of bed, her mother was in the kitchen with the radio on and the coffee brewed. The accompanying sounds and smells were like a radar beam, guiding Marlie along to their source. But this morning Roberta wasn't there because of some prior commitment, and the only noises Marlie could hear were the occasional creaks and groans of the house, the only smell the slightly musty odor that seemed to permeate the place whenever it rained.

Making her way to the kitchen, Marlie hunted down the coffee and filters using her sight alone. By the time she managed to set up the coffeemaker, pour the water in without spilling a drop, and start the coffee brewing, her mood had lightened some, as much from her success as from the heavenly aroma that quickly filled the kitchen. When the coffee was ready, she poured herself a mug and leaned against the counter, nursing the brew and contemplating the hours ahead. She missed Roberta. Sometimes, the days seemed endless, and she often found herself with little or nothing to do. At least when her mother was here, she had someone to chat with and keep her company.

She heard the crunch of tires on the drive outside and felt an almost instant sense of relief thinking Roberta had decided to come after all or had finished with whatever it was she had to do. Walking over to the window, Marlie pushed the curtain aside, peering out into the grayness of the day.

The car outside was barely discernible, its color and shape blending with the overcast skies. Marlie knew her mother's car was a bright cherry red, a little sporty thing. And William's Porsche was low-slung and black. This car, however, looked boxy and square. And whatever its color, it was neither red nor black. Marlie caught movement from the corner of her eye and saw a faint glowance of yellow light step onto the front porch.

She backed away from the window, her pulse quickening. When she'd bought this house, one of its primary attractions was its location—far out in the countryside, away from everyone and everything. Back then, privacy and space had been her main priorities. Now, she was keenly aware of how isolated she was—isolated and vulnerable. Why did her mother have to pick today of all days to make plans to be elsewhere?

The doorbell rang and she jumped, her heart fluttering birdlike inside her chest. She set her coffee cup on the counter and nibbled at her thumbnail while she tried to decide what to do. Glancing toward the phone, she walked through the steps in her mind. *Lift the receiver, punch 911, ask for help.*

The bell rang a second time.

She realized how ridiculous she was being. Plenty of times during her blindness she'd heard a car pull up outside and it never frightened her like this. While it was true she rarely had visitors, it wasn't unheard of. And if the person out there meant her harm, it was highly unlikely he would announce his presence by ringing the doorbell. If it even was a he. It might be Mrs. Henderson, who lived a mile or so down the road and who often stopped by to share a muffin and some coffee with Roberta.

Marlie imagined how embarrassing it would be to have the police respond to her call, only to find sweet old Mrs. Henderson standing on the porch. And then she thought about William and what he would do if he found out, twisting and turning the facts to make her look paranoid and helpless. That image clinched it. Squaring her shoulders, she marched to the front door, flung it open, and stared at the figure on the porch.

Judging from the broad squareness of the shoulders, the height and general build, Marlie was fairly certain it was a man. And just as certain it wasn't William. She and William were roughly the same height, whereas this person towered over her by several inches. She stared at his face, trying to distinguish the features, but it remained a frustrating blur. She searched her memory for someone whose general shape matched that of the figure before her but came up empty. To make matters worse, the man's glowance was oddly disturbing. The yellow she had seen a moment ago was gone. In its place was a narrow band of gray, barely there and nearly colorless, tightly drawn around his shape. The sight of it made her uncomfortable, and she clutched the top of her robe closed. It didn't help any that the man said nothing; he just stood there staring at her. The panic she had just managed to swallow down crawled back up her throat.

"May I help you?" she said. Her chin thrust up in a gesture of fearless defiance, though inside, her guts were quaking.

"It's me, Marlie."

A smile broke out on Marlie's face and her shoulders sagged with relief. "Detective Carvelle," she said, releasing the death grip she had on her robe. "I wasn't expecting you." She stepped aside. "Please, come in."

He hesitated a moment, then moved past her and headed toward the living room. Marlie pushed the door closed and followed, her eyes eagerly studying his back and overall physique. It was with some reluctance that she finally tore her eyes away to find a chair. Settling in, she leaned back with what she hoped was an air of relaxed confidence, though she felt unaccountably anxious. He sat on the couch across from her, perched on the edge, his gaze once again fixed on her.

For a long moment, no one spoke; they simply both stared. Then Carvelle turned away, clearing his throat and looking around the room. Marlie suddenly remembered that she had yet to run a brush through her hair, and that, in fact, a good chunk of it was missing. Even though her fingers told her there was nearly half an inch of new growth around the incision site, she knew from the shape of her image in the mirror that the flaw was still obvious. Her hand fluttered up toward the spot, and she made a futile attempt to cover it with the surrounding hair.

"I guess I must look a sight," she said, her voice close to a titter.

"You look fine," Carvelle said without looking at her.

The words were spoken rather matter-of-factly, as if the way she looked was of little consequence to him, something Marlie found disturbing, as she was incredibly curious about how *he* looked. She had conjured up a mental image long ago based on the deep rumble of his voice and the sneak peeks she'd had into his personality. Now, confronted with the physical reality of the man, she was anxious to compare it to her imaginings.

"So, what brings you here today, Detective?" she asked. "Don't tell me you've finally managed to make some actual progress with the warehouse investigation." She winced as she heard the snide tone in her voice and cursed to herself. She had learned long ago that whenever she felt vulnerable or defensive, her first impulse was to go on the offense. It was a trait that had served her well in her job but was something of a handicap in any social situation. She knew Carvelle hadn't missed the cruelty in her tone when he reeled back a few inches, as if she'd swung at him.

"I just wanted to see how you were," he said, his voice tight. "To see how the surgery went."

His statement hung in the air between them, supported by an awkward silence. Marlie struggled for something to say to make amends, to soften the blow she'd never meant to deliver. But before she could come up with anything, Carvelle abruptly stood and headed for the door.

"I should have called first," he muttered. "I'm sorry."

Seized with a sudden inexplicable panic, Marlie jumped to her feet and propelled herself along behind him. "Detective, wait."

One of the more frustrating effects of her new vision was a severely skewed depth perception. Thus she almost ran into Carvelle before she realized he'd stopped. He spun around, and Marlie found herself inches away from an impressive expanse of chest. He was so close, the smell she had come to associate with him filled her head, and his breath was warm on her cheek. Her gaze crawled upward, and she tried desperately to make some sense of the blur that was his face. Another blanket of rough silence wrapped around them.

"Can you see me?" he asked suddenly. It came out little more than a whisper, yet crackled with a nervous tension Marlie found puzzling.

She took a step back, widening the distance between them. "Not really," she said. "I can see a vague outline, just your shape more or less. No details."

"Oh."

Marlie saw his head drop and his shoulders slump. She wondered if it was disappointment or relief that had changed his posture. "It's not much now," she went on, making a concerted effort to sound cheerful and perhaps undo the damage she had wrought earlier, "but the doctor says it may well improve. I just need to give it some time." Suddenly she burst out laughing.

"What?" Carvelle grumbled. "What's so funny?"

Marlie wrapped her arms around herself, shook her head, and looked up toward the ceiling. "Just a bit of irony," she told him. "'Give it more time' is what everyone else has been telling me, hoping to cheer me up. Now, here I am saying the same thing to you, trying to cheer you up."

"Cheer *me* up? What the hell for?"

Marlie looked at him, noting how the tight gray of his glowance had widened some. "Well, you seem a little down, Detective. I thought perhaps you were disappointed that I hadn't become some sort of Wonder Woman with X-ray vision."

"Disappointed?" Carvelle scoffed. "You think *I'm* disappointed with *you*?"

Marlie shrugged.

"It would take more than that for me to be disappointed with you, Marlie," he said, his voice softer. His glowance sparkled with the barest hints of pink and gold. "I mean, I'm sorry you don't have perfect vision yet, but I think the fact that you can see anything at all is good. Isn't it?"

"It is," Marlie agreed.

"But you were hoping for something more . . ."

"More dramatic," Marlie finished for him. "Yes, I suppose I was." She smiled warmly at Carvelle's blur of a face, trying to tune out the annoying glowance so she could make out more of the details. But after only a few seconds, Carvelle dropped his gaze to the floor, shuffling his feet.

"Well," he said, coughing a little to clear his throat, "I can't stay. I have a ton of paperwork to catch up on." He moved quickly for the door and opened it. "I just wanted to stop by to say hello and make sure you were okay," he said over his shoulder.

"I appreciate it," Marlie said. "I'm fine. Really I am. Thanks for stopping by."

"No problem." Carvelle pulled the door closed and was gone.

Marlie stood in the foyer, a frown furrowing her brow. She and Carvelle had always shared a comfortable camaraderie, and he was normally relaxed and laid back in her company. Yet today he seemed jumpy and nervous, for reasons she didn't understand. Letting him leave on that note seemed wrong somehow. She reached over and yanked the door open. "Detective?" she yelled. It took her a second to zero in on his shape in the uniform grayness that colored the outside world. He was just about to climb into his car, and he paused, looking back at her.

"Yes?"

She could think of nothing to say. The seconds ticked by as she stood there, feeling incredibly stupid and cursing the impulse that had made her grab for the door in the first place.

Carvelle waited.

Then Marlie remembered the snide remark she had made to him moments earlier, in the living room. "Um, I'm sorry for being rude earlier. I didn't mean it."

Carvelle's glowance brightened suddenly, broadening and taking on a distinctly pinkish tinge. "Don't worry about it," he called back to her. "You always do that when you're feeling threatened. I'm used to it by now."

After watching Carvelle's car disappear down the driveway, Marlie went back to the kitchen and poured a fresh cup of coffee. Settling in at the kitchen table, she replayed Carvelle's visit in her mind. As the detective assigned to investigate the warehouse explosion, Carvelle was one of the first people Marlie had encountered upon waking in the hospital. It was the first of many visits, both there and, in the months that followed, at her home. Though he certainly wasn't pursuing the investigation now with the vigor he had initially, it remained open for two reasons. One was Marlie's reluctance to tell him what had led her and Chris to the warehouse in the first place. The fact that the anonymous caller had hinted at police corruption made Marlie wary of anyone associated with the force. Whenever Carvelle asked, she claimed amnesia, stating she couldn't recall what made her go there that night. The other reason the investigation was still open was that the body of the shooter had yet to be identified. The fire, sparked when a bullet ruptured one of the gas lines, and fueled by the propane left behind in the tanks, had burned hot and intense for several hours, destroying the building and leaving nothing of the shooter's body other than some charred teeth and bones. So far, these remnants had yet to be matched to any records.

In a way, Marlie was glad the case hadn't been solved. Carvelle's visits were something she had come to look forward to. For one thing, he never showed any pity toward her. But the other thing, the one that mattered most to Marlie, was that he hadn't known her before the accident. Having transferred to the area only months before the explosion, Carvelle had no knowledge of who she had been or what her life was like. The only Marlie he knew was the blind one. That fact gave her a certain level of comfortable acceptance with him that she felt with no one else.

It was several months before Marlie admitted she might be attracted to Carvelle, and when she did, she laughed. She had no idea what he looked like, no idea where he came from. Her sole knowledge of the man came from the way he smelled, the sound of his voice, and the things he revealed about himself in conversation—which wasn't much. When she asked him about his life prior to joining the local force, he was annoyingly vague with his answers and frequently changed the subject. During one conversation he revealed the rather startling fact that the partner he'd been paired with upon first joining the local force had been killed in the line of duty. Marlie vaguely remembered the incident, but since it hadn't been her story to cover, she didn't know many of the details. And Carvelle always managed to avoid providing them.

Despite her lingering doubts about him, Marlie liked Carvelle. A lot. He was arguably the only person left in her life she could call a friend. Until this morning, she had always thought that friendship was mutual.

Now, she wondered.

chapter 6

Roberta still hadn't shown up by ten o'clock, and Marlie found herself both bored and irritated. The more she thought about Carvelle's strange behavior, the more convinced she became that it hadn't been strange at all. Maybe she had been reading things into their relationship all along that had never been there, deluding herself. The idea made her feel stupid and gullible. Consequently, she wasn't in the best frame of mind when the phone rang.

"Hello?" she said, none too cheerfully.

"Could I speak with Marlie Kaplan, please?" asked a voice with a hint of a New England twang.

"Speaking," she said impatiently, figuring it was a telemarketer, though the voice seemed vaguely familiar.

"Ms. Kaplan, this is Roger Garrity. I work with Senator Richard Waring."

"Ah, yes," Marlie said, her tone lightening. Garrity was a public relations person and campaign manager for one of the state's senators. She had dealt with him several times in the past, back when she was still reporting, and had always found him to be uppity and obnoxious. If he had worked for anyone else, she would have told him where to stick it a long time ago. But his boss, Richard Waring, was an up-and-coming state politician, purported to be the next gubernatorial hopeful, and one of the hottest news items around. Waring's popularity stemmed as much from his dark good looks, casual sophistication, and very single marital status as it did from his politics. The fact that the cameras loved him and that his background included several heart-tugging stories didn't hurt either.

"Ms. Kaplan, we spoke a year or so ago when you contacted the senator's office about doing an interview, a personal profile I believe it was."

"Yes, I remember," Marlie said. It was one of several stories she had been working on at the time of the warehouse explosion. Her brow furrowed in puzzlement, wondering where this conversation was leading. "You turned me down, as I recall."

"That is correct," Garrity said, and the officious, stilted tone of his voice made Marlie picture him in her mind with a broomstick up his ass. She stifled a giggle. "As I think you know," Garrity went on, "the senator is a very private man. While he understands the need for his political activities to be televised and reported upon, he prefers to keep his private life separate."

Tell me something I don't know, Marlie thought with a roll of her eyes. Waring's steadfast avoidance of the press on any matter other than his political activities was legendary. Ironically, it only made the press that much hungrier.

"However, Ms. Kaplan, the reason I'm calling you today is to let you know the senator has reconsidered your request."

Marlie reeled back, holding the phone away from her ear for a second and staring at it as if it had just bitten her. "Reconsidered? Mr. Garrity, I don't mean to be rude, but that request was made well over a year ago. And besides, while I appreciate the thought, I no longer work for WKAL. Or for anyone, for that matter. Perhaps you aren't aware—"

"I am well aware of your history, Ms. Kaplan. As is the senator. Frankly, that's one of the reasons he is willing to let you do the interview."

Marlie shook her head in confusion. "I don't think you understand, Mr. Garrity. I'm not a reporter any longer. I don't work for any TV station."

"Yes, I know. As I recall, you had some sort of accident that blinded you and you were forced to take a leave of absence, correct?"

"That's more or less correct, Mr. Garrity," Marlie said irritably.

"But I understand you recently had some surgery which has corrected that problem?"

"How do you know about that?"

"Perhaps you've forgotten, Ms. Kaplan, that Senator Waring is chairman of the Senate Education and Health Committee and, as such, is often aware of the very latest advances in health care."

Again Marlie rolled her eyes. God, the man could be condescending. "Look, Mr. Garrity," she said. "I'm hardly the person you want to have conducting any sort of interview with the senator. While it's true that I've had some corrective surgery, the results are . . . well . . . less than perfect. My vision is still quite poor. I'm sure there are plenty of other reporters who are more than qualified and who would love the opportunity."

"Frankly, Ms. Kaplan, the senator would prefer

to have this done by someone whose work and reputation he knows. Someone of a . . . shall we say, high ethical and professional caliber. He's not particularly enthused about doing the interview in the first place, but if he must, he would rather do it with someone he feels he can trust."

"I'm flattered," Marlie said with no small amount of sarcasm.

"As well you should be. The senator is quite impressed with your background and credits."

Sarcasm was obviously wasted on this man. "Tell me something, Mr. Garrity. Senator Waring's avoidance of any sort of personal interview is well known among those of us in the field. And from what you tell me, he still finds the prospect a distasteful one. So why the sudden change of heart?"

"Surely you realize the importance of the senator's work. He maintains a strong voice on many critical issues and his record of success speaks for itself. However, while his current role has enabled him to achieve many of his goals, he realizes how much more he might accomplish if he were to attain a more influential position within the government."

"And that position would be as the governor, I presume," Marlie said. Now things were making a little more sense.

"That's correct. The party recently indicated its intent to nominate Senator Waring as their candidate. Given that fact, we now see where it might benefit the senator's future goals if we were to present a more personalized face to the public."

"I understand your situation," Marlie said. "But I'm afraid I can't help you. I don't have the connections necessary to do this interview, and frankly I'm not sure I have the right . . . uh . . . physical presentation either. I am still legally blind, Mr. Garrity."

"I am well aware of that, Ms. Kaplan," Garrity said a bit gruffly. Marlie suspected the man wasn't used to having his requests denied. "I, however, see your limitations as an asset. I don't know if you are aware of this or not, but many of Senator Waring's successes at the General Assembly earlier this year had to do with legislation that protected or enhanced the rights of both women and handicapped persons, particularly in a work environment."

It took a second for Marlie to understand what the hell Garrity was talking about. When it finally hit her why Garrity was calling *her* for the interview, she was furious. "You want to use me as a prop," she said, her voice incredulous. "You want me to be Waring's campaign poster child so people can say, 'Oh, look, isn't that nice. The senator practices what he preaches and works with those poor handicapped people.'"

"Well, I think you're making this sound more calculated than it really is, Ms. Kaplan."

"Am I?" Marlie snapped back.

"Ms. Kaplan, our primary reason for requesting you is based on your journalistic abilities and your reputation in the industry as a—"

"Don't bullshit me, Garrity. I know exactly why you want me and it has far less to do with my abilities than my disabilities. Thanks, but no thanks. Find yourself another poster child."

"But—"

"I've said all I have to say on the subject, Mr. Garrity. It's been wonderful talking with you again," she said in a tone that suggested just the opposite. "Good day!"

She slammed the phone back in the cradle before she could hear any more of Garrity's arguments, then stood there tapping her foot in anger. Of all the nerve! Garrity wasn't interested in her for her talents as a reporter, but rather for her token value as a handicapped woman. His request was a media ploy, a PR stunt designed to use her to make Waring look good. She'd always known Garrity was something of a weasel, but this was a new low, even for him.

She couldn't help but wonder how much of this Waring was aware of. From what she knew of the man, he was forthright, honest, and straightforward. Unlike some of his counterparts who were fervent publicity hounds, he seemed solely interested in doing his job and doing it well. While he tolerated the inevitable publicity that accompanied his political duties, he was content to leave it at that. Marlie had followed his career—as had almost every other journalist in the area—and in the process had come to have a great deal of respect for the man, not only for his political beliefs and accomplishments but for his general comportment, as well. As soon as the first rumors began to leak out that he was likely to be the next Republican gubernatorial candidate, Marlie had begun putting together information with the intent of doing a profile, hoping to eventually get the very interview Garrity was now offering her.

But then life—and death—had gotten in the way.

The phone rang again and, thinking it was Garrity calling back, Marlie snatched it up and answered with a terse and impatient, "Hello." But it was much worse than Garrity. It was Ronni.

"Marlie! How good it is to hear your voice. It's been a long time."

Marlie didn't buy into Ronni's feigned sweetness for a minute. And after her conversation with Garrity, she was in no mood to play along. "What the hell do *you* want, Ronni?"

"Well, *that's* not a very nice way to greet an old friend," Ronni said, sounding wounded. "Did I catch you at a bad time?"

"Something like that," Marlie said, thinking there was no such thing as a good time to be caught by Ronni.

"Oh, I'm sorry. I just wanted to call and congratulate you on the success of your surgery. Cindy tells us you have some sight back. That's wonderful! You must be thrilled."

Marlie grunted.

"You know," Ronni went on, her tone annoyingly cheerful, "Granger thought this whole surgery thing would make a great story. The miracles of modern medicine and all that. He's assigned me to cover it."

The muscles in Marlie's jaw twitched. "So I've heard," she grumbled.

"Did you? That's great! So let me bring you up to speed. I was thinking we could start off with a personal profile of you as one of the patients, segue to the scientific stuff, and then go back to you."

"Ronni, I don't want—"

"We can hit on some of your career highlights, the effects of the accident, and then show how this wondrous new surgery has changed your life. I think that will give the whole piece a more personal touch, which we know the viewers love, and we can sneak in some good PR for the station while we're at it."

"I'm not—"

"I've been going through some of your old files and clips, and there's some great stuff in there, Marlie. It's going to be tough choosing which—"

"Dammit, Ronni!" Marlie yelled. "Hold up." To her relief, Ronni finally stopped and took a breath. "Apparently Cindy forgot to tell you that I have no interest in being any part of this story. I will not have my private life smeared all over the tube to titillate the public. So forget it."

"Marlie, you can't mean that," Ronni whined. "Think about how groundbreaking this surgery is. Put your reporter's hat on for a minute and try to see—"

"I've given you my answer, Ronni," Marlie snapped. "If you want to do a story on the microchip, fine. But you're doing it without me."

"But—"

For the second time that morning, Marlie slammed the phone down. "Damn!" she muttered, her fingers drumming with annoyance on the countertop. This was rapidly turning into one shitty day. First Garrity, now Ronni. Everyone wanted to take advantage of her situation, to use her for their own goals. She was down and out and the buzzards were circling low. Garrity, she thought, was at least smart enough to take no for an answer, even if he didn't like it. Ronni, on the other hand, wasn't likely to give up that easily.

She picked up the phone, felt along the number pad, and dialed the station, asking for Cindy's extension. When Cindy answered, Marlie exchanged a few perfunctory greetings and thanked her for the flowers she had brought to the hospital. Then she said, "I just got a call from Ronni."

"Let me guess. She hit you up for the story?"

"She did. And I told her the same thing I told you. You have to call her off, Cindy. Otherwise she'll drive me crazy with this thing."

"I passed on to her what you said in the hospital, but you know Ronni. She doesn't let go easily."

"Don't I know it."

"You should. You two are a lot alike, you know."

"Come again?"

"Well, you are. You're both driven, thorough, and stubborn as hell. Or at least you used to be."

Marlie was appalled. "You can't be serious," she said. "How can you possibly compare me to Ronni? Sure, she gets the stories, but her methods certainly leave something to be desired. I may have been as tenacious as she is, but at least I was scrupulous. I still can't believe someone hasn't nailed her for all those illegal tapes she's made over the years. Hell, she probably taped the conversation we just had."

"She probably did," Cindy agreed.

Marlie chewed her lower lip in frustration. "Why the hell did Granger assign her this story in the first place? He knows there's no love lost between me and Ronni. If he really wanted the story, why didn't he give it to someone else?"

"Actually, I think he *should* assign it to someone else."

Marlie waited for Cindy to tell her who, then realized she wouldn't unless Marlie asked. At the rate her morning was going, it might be better if she didn't know. But her curiosity got the better of her. "All right. I'll bite. Who?"

Cindy chuckled. "I knew you couldn't let it go. Your reporter instincts are still there. Which is a good thing, because I think *you* should do the story."

"Me?" Marlie couldn't have been more stunned.

"Sure. Who better?" Cindy said. "Think about it."

"That's crazy, Cindy. Granger would never let me come back."

"Well, you'll never know if you don't ask. Why not run it by him? All he can do is say no."

"I don't need the humiliation right now," Marlie snapped. "But thanks anyway." She instantly regretted the tone of her words. Cindy had been a good friend and deserved better. "I'm sorry, Cindy. I didn't mean to take it out on you. It's just that even if Granger was willing to let me do some of the legwork on the story, I'd just have to turn it all over to Ronni or someone else. It's not like I can get in front of a camera again."

"Why not?"

"Well, for one thing, I'm missing half my hair," Marlie said irritably.

"Buy a wig."

"You're not serious."

"I'm always serious, Marlie. You know that."

One of the things Marlie had always liked best

about Cindy was her no-nonsense way of cutting straight to the core of a matter. It was a trait she had admired and valued when Cindy was fighting on her side. Now, with the tables turned, Marlie saw just how effective—and annoying—Cindy's talents could be.

"Look, Marlie," Cindy went on. "Why don't you come by the office and just talk to Granger. See what he has to say. I think you can convince him. And if you don't, you're no worse off than you are now. In fact, you might find that taking charge of your life will do a world of good for your state of mind."

Gee, Marlie thought. *Where have I heard that before?* Apparently, Cindy and Roberta had been comparing notes again. Then a realization hit her.

"Cindy, when you came to see me in the hospital the other day, you were trying to piss me off, weren't you?"

"What do you mean?"

"Of course!" Marlie said. "Man, I can't believe I didn't see it then. You were acting as if the idea of me doing a story was laughable just to get me angry enough to want to prove you wrong, weren't you?" Her eyes narrowed with suspicion. "Did my mother put you up to this?"

There followed a long silence, which as far as Marlie was concerned was as good as an admission of guilt.

Finally Cindy said, "You know, Marlie, life is what you make of it. It's in your control. Play the hand you've been dealt, and play to win."

There was no anger, no condescension in Cindy's voice. Just a simple statement from a woman Marlie had grown to like and respect.

"Hey, I gotta go," Cindy said. "Granger's buzzing me. Holler if I can do anything."

Marlie started to say thanks, but realized Cindy had already hung up. She did the same, then went in search of some aspirin. Her head felt like it was about to explode.

chapter 7

D r. Winslow flashed his light in Marlie's eyes, momentarily obliterating everything else. She winced, expecting the same tug of pain she had felt during this exercise both in the hospital and on her last visit, but to her delight, nothing happened.

"Everything looks good," Winslow said, standing back and giving Marlie a critical eye. "How's the vision doing?"

"It's better," Marlie told him, thrilled to be speaking the truth. "The shadows are still all I see primarily, though they're more distinct now, a bit sharper around the edges."

"Good!" Winslow said, smiling. "That means we're making progress. Slow progress, perhaps, but moving in the right direction."

"Yes, I suppose so," Marlie said with a sigh.

Winslow cocked his head to one side. "There's a 'but' here, isn't there?"

Marlie gave him a weak smile. "There is," she admitted. "I hesitate to complain because I don't want to seem ungrateful for what you've done. Believe me, any sight at all at this point is a precious gift."

"But?"

"But . . . it's these colors."

"Colors?"

"You know, the clouds of light or whatever they are. I've mentioned them before."

Winslow nodded his remembrance.

"They surround everything . . . or at least every-*one*, I encounter. You, for instance, had a warm golden-white color around you when you first came in here. A moment ago, it began to undulate or vibrate, and now it's changed to a sort of twirling yellow cloud. It's very distracting, not to mention annoying. They've been there ever since the day of the surgery and it's been three weeks now. I hoped they would go away, but if anything they're brighter than ever."

Winslow settled onto a nearby stool and pulled thoughtfully at his chin. "I'm sorry, Marlie, but I don't know what they are or what's causing them. Though I suppose it might be some form of synesthesia."

"Syne-what?"

"Synesthesia," he said more slowly. "Basically it's a short circuit, or blending, of one's sensory perception. People who have it may hear colors, see sounds, or taste shapes . . . that sort of thing. I consulted on a woman a few years ago who saw colors in various shapes every time she heard a loud noise. If a car beeped, she saw green triangles; if a phone rang, she saw wavy yellow lines."

"I see," Marlie said. "Is it something that can be cured? Or at least controlled?"

Winslow shook his head. "Not really. At least not that I'm aware of. Besides, I'm not convinced that's what this is. Understand that synesthesia is a naturally occurring, inherited phenomenon. We're not sure of its genesis, but the people who have it have been aware of it since their earliest childhood memories. It's an involuntary response, though an elicited one. And if I recall correctly, most synesthetes' perceptions remain consistent."

"What do you mean by consistent?"

"Well, if a synesthete perceives the ring of a telephone as green with white spots, they will always perceive it that way. It doesn't change. But from what you're telling me, these colors you see vary not only from one person to another, but with each individual."

Marlie nodded.

"Obviously, your experience is different from that of a typical synesthete, if in fact that's even what it is." He shrugged. "I suppose it's possible the microchip we put in your brain could trigger a synesthetic type of experience, but I can't be sure."

"If it is the microchip that's causing this, do you think it will go away in time?"

Winslow sighed. "I'm sorry, Marlie, but I just don't know. I'm not aware of anyone else who has had the surgery experiencing anything like this, though I'll make some calls and check around. I doubt we'll find much. A side effect that significant is bound to have been reported and I don't recall ever hearing of such a thing."

Marlie frowned. This wasn't the news she'd been hoping for.

"In the meantime, I have a suggestion. I know a neurologist here in DC who has done a fair amount of research into synesthesia. His name is Richard Nascott. I doubt he's had any experience with a case quite like yours, but if what you're experiencing *is* a form of synesthesia, he may be able to help you. I can set up an appointment with him if you'd like."

Marlie's frown deepened. More doctors, more tests, and more probing wasn't high on her list of priorities.

Sensing her hesitation, Winslow said, "Hey, maybe he won't be able to help you. But what have you got to lose? Nothing ventured, nothing gained."

Marlie gave him an ironic smile. In the past, she'd used that very same platitude more times than she could count when justifying some of her journalistic exploits to Granger.

"Okay," she agreed. "Set it up."

Dr. Richard Nascott's first opening was a week away, and Marlie found herself facing another series of endless, boring days. The one thing she had to look forward to was Kristen's scheduled visitation this coming weekend. Monday, Kristen and William were leaving for their trip to Florida, and Marlie was determined to start her daughter's summer vacation off on the right note. She had spoken with Kristen several times on the phone during the past week, and things seemed to be back to normal, that horrible scene the day of Marlie's homecoming either forgotten or pushed aside. They planned their weekend, intending to hit the mall for some serious clothes shopping for Kristen's trip. Given Marlie's newfound ability to navigate on her own, Roberta offered to drive them there, drop them off, and return later to pick them up. Marlie quickly agreed, overjoyed at the prospect of finally having some time alone with her daughter.

In preparation for Kristen's arrival, Marlie was in the kitchen Friday afternoon, baking up a batch of the blond brownies that were her daughter's favorite. She had the recipe memorized, having baked them hundreds of times while Kristen was growing up, though for the past year, Roberta was the only one who made them. Now, Marlie thought she could see well enough to measure out and mix the ingredients on her own. It was slow going, but between her limited eyesight and her sense of touch, she had succeeded. The batter tasted normal, and she was about to pop them into the oven when William called.

"I'm sorry to do this, Marlie," he said, sounding not sorry at all. "But Kristen and I are leaving for Florida tomorrow instead of Monday, so she won't be able to come for the weekend."

Marlie's fury was instantaneous. "No way, William! You can't do that. This is *my* weekend. And in case you've forgotten, there is a court order that says I have every right to have her here."

"Even if she doesn't want to come?"

That made Marlie pause. "She doesn't want to come?"

"No, she doesn't," William said, his tone smug.

"Bullshit, William. I don't believe you." He was bluffing, she was sure of it. Using his lawyerly tricks on her. Well, she wasn't going to let him get away with it. She'd call that bluff, dammit. Then William sucked all the wind from her sails.

"Hold on," he said. "I'll let her tell you herself."

He dropped the phone and hollered for Kristen. Marlie gnawed on her fingernails while she tried to figure out what the hell was going on. When she heard Kristen's approaching footsteps, her heart seemed to thud with the same rhythm. Then she swore it stopped altogether when she heard Kristen pick up the phone.

"Hi, Mom."

"Kristen, honey. Hi," Marlie said, putting on her best cheery voice. "Um . . . is everything okay? Your father said you don't want to come here this weekend. Is that true?"

"I'm sorry, Mom. I know you had a lot of stuff planned, but I'm just not in the mood for shopping this weekend."

"That's fine, honey. We don't have to shop. We'll do whatever you want. Just name it."

Kristen hesitated. "What I want is to go to Florida. Dad says if we go early we'll be able to spend more time at Disney World. And all my friends say you need a lot of time there to see everything."

"I see," Marlie said. And she did. William had screwed her over once again. She was seething but determined not to take it out on Kristen. More than anything, she wanted to repair the damage that had been done the last time they were together. Still, she had to hand it to William. He was a master manipulator and schemer. If she objected to the trip, it would only anger and frustrate Kristen, putting a damper on both the coming weekend and their relationship.

"Well then," Marlie said, struggling to hide her

anger and disappointment. "I guess you best get on down there. It sounds like you'll have a lot of fun. And you and I can go shopping some other time."

"Thanks, Mom. I knew you'd understand. Hugs and kisses."

"Hugs and kisses back at ya," Marlie said, trying not to cry—or scream. "Have a good time and take notes so you can give me a full report when you get back."

"I will."

"Put your father back on the phone, please."

"Okay. Bye."

Marlie tapped her foot with impatience, her now ragged fingernails beating out a staccato rhythm on the countertop.

"Are you satisfied now?" William said.

"You bastard."

"Hey, don't take it out on me. It's your own damned fault."

"*My* fault? How the hell do you figure that?"

"Kristen said you and she were going to the mall this weekend."

"So?"

"Alone, just the two of you."

"Is that a crime?" Marlie snapped.

"Technically, yes," William shot back. "According to our agreement, there must be another adult present whenever you're with Kristen."

"Dammit, William! You know the rationale behind that. That order was written when I was totally blind. I can see now. There is absolutely no reason why I can't be alone with my daughter. Not that there ever was."

"*Our* daughter," William reminded her. "And if you want the conditions of the custody agreement amended, take me to court."

"I will, you son of a bitch."

"See you there." And with a chuckle, he hung up the phone.

Marlie slammed the receiver back in place so hard the entire phone unit fell off the wall, dangling by its cord. That only incensed her even more, and she grabbed the receiver again and beat the phone until it finally cut loose from its umbilical and crashed all the way to the floor. She kicked it into the counter, then picked up the pan of brownie mix and scraped it down the garbage disposal.

Roberta, bless her, made no comment and asked no questions about the mangled phone. In typical form, she calmly picked the pieces off the floor and tossed them into the trash. The next day, a new phone appeared on the wall. She asked Marlie about Kristen's whereabouts, and Marlie said only that there had been a change in plans. Roberta pushed no further, knowing Marlie would fill her in when she was ready. That moment came a week later, in the car on the way to Dr. Nascott's office.

"Well, it was pretty low, what he did," Roberta commented when Marlie was done telling the story. "But technically, he's right. The conditions of your visitation do require another adult present."

"But that's ridiculous, Mother. It was ridiculous when I was blind, and it's just plain ludicrous now."

"I agree. But legally—"

"He's going to keep pulling this shit," Marlie said, staring out the side window, her brow furrowed in frustration. "How the hell can I stop him?"

"Take him up on his challenge and go back to court."

Marlie looked over at her mother. "Do you really think they'll consider a change, given the surgery and all?"

Roberta shrugged. "By itself, that might be enough. But if you really want to impress the judge, I think you'll need to do more."

"Such as?"

"You're going to have to demonstrate that you have some sense of responsibility, some independence."

"I'm reasonably independent," Marlie argued.

Roberta sighed. "Marlie, you know as well as I do that William will use every dirty trick he knows and do all he can to put you in the worst light possible. Think about it a minute. When he gets up in front of the judge and points out that you have no job, no real responsibilities, no hobbies, no nothing, what do you think the judge will do?"

Marlie didn't answer. She pouted instead.

"Look at your life, Marlie. Yes, you can see some now. But what are you doing with it? You still sit around the house, day after day, listening to TV shows or the radio. I spent several thousand dollars to have your computer modified so you could work on it, but it's been collecting dust ever since the day you finished your classes. You don't go anywhere, you don't socialize. You have all the classic signs of depression. That doesn't exactly make you a stellar candidate for motherhood."

"You know, I'm getting a little sick and tired of this constant harping about how I'm wasting my life," Marlie grouched. "What the hell do you expect from me? Yes, I can see a little now. But it's hardly an earth-shattering improvement. Legally, I'm still blind."

"Fine," Roberta said with irritating calm. "If that's the attitude you're going to take, then you'll just have to accept all the repercussions that go with it."

Marlie fumed, her arms folded tightly over her chest, her breathing harsh and rapid-fire. She wanted to yell at her mother, to yell at the whole frigging world for that matter. But she said nothing.

Deep down inside, she knew that much of what her mother said was true.

chapter

8

D
r. Richard Nascott was a short man, several inches below Marlie's own height. Though she couldn't make out the details of his features, she could tell his hair was blond and his build slight. The frames on his glasses were so large Marlie thought he looked like a bug. In stark contrast to his almost childlike stature, his voice was deep, mellifluous, and soothing. He greeted Marlie warmly, giving her hand a firm but friendly shake. Rather than sitting or standing before her, he hoisted himself onto the exam table beside her, bracing himself with his arms and leaning forward to look into her face.

"So," he said. "Tell me about yourself."

Something about the man's demeanor gave Marlie the impression he had all the time in the world to just sit and listen. She supposed it was part of a bedside manner he had honed over the years to put his patients at ease. If so, it worked. She began by giving him a brief synopsis of the night at the warehouse, then was surprised to find herself sharing some of the emotional and mental traumas of the past year, including her battles with William. Eventually she got to the recent surgery and the odd clouds of color she was now experiencing.

"And that's how I came to see you. Dr. Winslow

said he thought this microchip I have in my head might be causing a sort of synesthesia, and that you are the area expert on the phenomenon."

Dr. Nascott nodded. "Fascinating," he murmured. "Tell me, do you see one of these colored clouds around me?"

"I do. It's a nice shade of pinkish gold. Very calming," Marlie said.

"Calming?" Nascott repeated. "Interesting choice of description."

"Well, the colors do seem to have an effect on me in a way. In fact, sometimes I can almost feel the light, as if it's a manifestation of emotion. Like with my mother. Her light at the hospital when she hugged me felt warm and comforting. Though I suppose that may be nothing more than an extrapolation of the emotion I was feeling at the time."

"Could be," Nascott said. "Then again . . ." He hopped off the exam table and started to pace inside the tiny room. Marlie waited.

"Let me tell you a few things about synesthesia," he said finally. "It's been a recognized phenomenon for at least three centuries, though certainly it was less discussed in the past, as the sort of idiosyncratic perceptions these people experience were often associated with witchcraft or insanity. It appears to be a familial trait, often being passed down from one generation to another. It's anywhere from three to eight times more common in women than in men. And most synesthetes are left-handed."

He paused in his pacing and looked at her, his eyebrows raised in question. Then, remembering Marlie was probably unable to distinguish such a subtle facial expression, he asked, "Are you left-handed?"

Marlie shook her head. "Not even ambidextrous," she said.

Dr. Nascott resumed his pacing. "Doesn't prove or disprove anything."

Marlie noted that his glowance had changed, taking on a deep yellow color. She thought about mentioning the fact but sensed the doctor was deep into some thought process she shouldn't interrupt. So she waited quietly, watching him amble back and forth in front of her.

"Have you ever had, or do you now have any unusual sensory responses, other than these colored clouds you've described?"

"No," Marlie said, shaking her head. "Nothing like that."

"Tell me about your memory."

"My memory?"

"Yes, do you have a good memory, do you think? Or do you tend to be absentminded?"

Marlie thought a moment, then shrugged. "I guess my memory is pretty good. I was a compulsive list maker until my blindness sort of eliminated the usefulness of that habit. But I found I can do well enough without them. I used to be particularly good with faces and names, something I think stems from my years of working as a reporter. Now it's more voices than anything. Since writing is of no use, I find I need to memorize things like phone numbers and such. Generally, if I repeat them to myself a few times, I can recall them later without any problem."

"Ever had any sort of paranormal experiences? Clairvoyance? Precognition? The feeling of another presence?"

Marlie's eyebrows drew down in puzzled amusement. "No, can't say that I have. Why?"

Nascott laughed. "Don't worry. I'm not playing witch doctor here. It's just that many of the synesthetes I've worked with have such abilities, or at least claim to. Most have excellent memory skills as well, primarily as a direct result of their synesthesia."

To Marlie's relief, he finally stopped pacing. "Obviously, it's hard to diagnose something like synesthesia since it's a projected perception experienced solely by the affected person. There are no objective criteria to evaluate it . . . except . . ."

"Except what?"

"Well, there is one diagnostic test I've used, but it seems a bit extreme for you under the circumstances. And with your recent brain surgery, I'm not sure it would be wise. We've performed blood-flow studies on some of these patients by injecting dye into an artery and watching its flow through the brain. It's a way of measuring cerebral activity. Normally, cortical metabolism increases with any sort of brain stimulus, but in synesthetes, their cortical activity, at least in the left hemisphere, *decreases* with a synesthetic experience. In fact, I had one patient whose left hemisphere flows were unusually low to begin with, and during a synesthetic episode, they dropped to a level that we can't obtain in a normal person, even with the use of drugs. By all rights, she should have been blinded, paralyzed, or shown some other level of brain impairment. Yet her thinking and neurological function were perfectly normal."

Marlie struggled to follow the man's explanation, but thought she got the gist of it. Years of listening to her mother discuss various aspects of medicine helped.

"This whole cortical reaction in synesthetes is puzzling and perhaps troubling to most of the traditionalists," Nascott went on. "They tend to think of the cortex as a more highly evolved portion of the brain with the capacity for analytical reasoning, whereas the more primitive limbic system that encircles the brain stem is generally connected with the so-called lower functions, such as memory, emotion, and such."

"Tell me something," she said quickly, hoping to halt his lecture. "If these colors I see *are* some form of synesthesia, is there any way to cure it?"

Dr. Nascott stared at her a moment before he answered. "No." He sighed. "I don't think there is any way to eliminate or control it, unless you were to have the microchip removed."

"That's obviously not an option."

"Of course not."

"So I'm just stuck with it?"

"That would be my guess. Synesthesia has been induced in patients who were not previously known to be synesthetes by triggering a seizure in the hippocampus of the brain. In their cases, however, the experience is only temporary. If it's the microchip that's causing this phenomenon in you, functioning much the same way as a seizure, then I'm afraid the condition will remain as long as the chip is there."

"I see." Marlie's disappointment was obvious.

"Listen," Nascott said. "Don't lose faith. First of all, we're not even sure that what you are experiencing *is* synesthesia. Your visual perceptions are not at all typical. It almost sounds as if what you are seeing is some sort of human aura. Like the emanation of an individual's soul or life force."

Marlie gave him a dubious look.

"Don't be so quick to dismiss," Nascott said. "The human brain is capable of many surprising things. Did you know that the average person only utilizes about one-third of the brain's potential?"

"Yes, as a matter of fact I—"

"I've seen some amazing things in the course of my practice. Things that can't be explained. In fact . . ."

He paused, lost in thought. Marlie waited, almost afraid to hear what was going to come next but doubtful she'd get a word in edgewise if she tried.

"I have an idea," he said finally. "There's a psychologist here in the area who has done a lot of research with auras. In fact, she teaches a relaxation class where she endeavors to help people visualize their own auras, sort of a different twist on biofeedback techniques. Hold on a minute." He turned, flung open the door to the exam room, and disappeared. A moment later, he was back.

"Here," he said, taking her hand and placing a piece of paper in it. "Her name is Dr. Bosher, Linda Bosher. I've written her address and phone number on the back of this card. Should I read it to you, or can someone else do that?"

"I have someone else," Marlie said tiredly.

"Good," Nascott said. "Give her a call. I've never worked directly with her, but she's fairly well respected as a psychologist and I've heard some positive things about this aura relaxation technique of hers."

Marlie shook her head in disbelief, holding up the card Nascott had given her. "This is a joke, right? You're not serious."

"I understand your skepticism," he said. "I'm not thoroughly convinced this aura thing is legitimate myself, but I can't deny the results she's achieved with her patients."

"But I don't need a relaxation class," Marlie whined. "Nor do I want to learn about auras, if that's even what they are. All I want is the best level of vision I can get. And these damned colored clouds aren't helping. I just want them to go away. Is this New Age voodoo all you have to offer?"

"I'm afraid it is."

Marlie felt a surge of anger and crumpled the card in her hand. She climbed down from the exam table and flashed Dr. Nascott a sarcastic smile. "Thanks for nothing," she said. She half walked, half stomped her way past him into the hallway, anxious to get the hell out of his office. Outside the exam room she paused, momentarily confused by all the shadows and unsure of which way to go. She looked about frantically, trying to remember the route she had taken from the waiting room to the exam room.

Before she could orient herself, Nascott cupped her elbow and gently steered her in the right direction. "This way," he said.

"I've got it," Marlie snapped, snatching her arm away and heading off. When she finally reached the reception area, she zeroed in on the lighted rectangle she knew was the exit and headed for it at a rapid clip, not bothering to find Roberta among the few faces in the waiting room. Once she hit the parking lot, she stopped and looked about helplessly, unable to find the shiny red shape of her mother's car.

A breathless Roberta caught up with her a moment later. "What on earth is wrong?" she asked.

"Nothing," Marlie said irritably. "Let's go home. Where the hell is the car?"

Roberta grabbed Marlie's shoulders and turned her to the right. "It's over here," she said. "Behind a van. That's why you can't see it."

After allowing Roberta to lead the way, Marlie climbed into the passenger seat of the car and closed the door with a resounding slam. As soon as Roberta started the engine, Marlie groped for a button on her armrest to lower the window, hit the automatic lock first, then finally succeeded in getting the window to glide down. As Roberta backed the car out of its parking space, Marlie reached up and tossed the crumpled card she held in her hand out onto the parking lot.

chapter
9

"I take it things didn't go well," Roberta ventured once they were on the road.

"You could say that."

"Are you going to tell me what he said, or just sit and sulk all the way home?"

Marlie shot her mother a nasty look, then shook her head in disgust. "What a waste of time and money. This guy thinks I'm seeing spirits or something."

"Spirits? You mean like ghosts?"

"No-o-o," Marlie said, drawing the word out with sarcasm. "Not ghosts. Auras. He thinks I'm seeing people's souls. Or some such crap. He suggested I go see this shrink he knows who does some sort of aura class." She laughed harshly. "Have you ever heard of anything so ridiculous?"

Roberta remained silent.

Marlie turned and looked at her. "Don't tell me you think there's anything to this," she said, her tone incredulous.

"I've heard crazier things," Roberta said carefully. "Much of medicine is deeply rooted in hard science, but there's plenty of stuff out there that falls somewhere in between the scientific realm and reality as we know it."

Marlie scoffed. "Great," she said. "Not you, too."

"Did he give you the name of this psychiatrist he wants you to see?"

"She's a psychologist, not a psychiatrist," Marlie explained. "And yes, he gave me a name, but I don't remember it."

"Was it Linda Bosher?"

Marlie gave her mother a stunned look. "I believe it was," she said. "You know her?"

"I've heard of her. And her work."

Marlie sighed and massaged her temples. Another vicious headache was on the way. "Please don't tell me you lend any credence to this aura crap."

"Well then, tell me what *you* think it is."

"I don't *know* what it is," Marlie shot back, her voice rising. "Why do you think I went to this guy in the first place? I wanted some answers, damn it! But all I got was a bunch of mumbo-jumbo about souls and auras." She punched her thigh in frustration. "Hell, I might as well have gone to a palm reader."

They rode in silence for several minutes, the tension hovering between them like thunderheads.

"You know," Roberta said finally, "back when I was in medical school, there was a student in our class named David Albright who we all agreed was one of the best diagnosticians ever. Everyone in our class was amazed by his ability to pinpoint a diagnosis based on little more than a cursory exam of the patient. Amazed and perhaps a little envious."

Marlie gazed out the side window of the car, only half listening. It was a habit she'd developed years ago. Roberta's lifelong method for dealing with stressful situations was to simply change the subject and babble on as if nothing had ever happened.

"Anyway," Roberta continued, "we were impressed by his abilities, but never more so than when he told one of our fellow students to see his personal physician immediately and demand a complete work-up. The student in question laughed it off at first, claiming he felt fit as a fiddle and had no reason to see a doctor. But I guess the whole thing finally spooked him enough that he did do just that. They found out he had an early stage of leukemia. He underwent treatment and did fine, although the doctors told him that had he not been diagnosed when he was, the outcome would have likely been far more grim.

"We badgered David for weeks over the whole thing, demanding to know how he'd known. But all he would say was that he'd had a hunch, or a feeling. A year or so later, he and I were on call together during a particularly hectic night and we collapsed in the doctor's lounge around five in the morning, both of us exhausted and a little punchy. We were talking, and eventually the subject got around to that med student. I again asked David how he'd known. And he finally told me the truth."

Marlie was caught up in her mother's story at this point. "What was his answer?" she asked.

"Auras," Roberta said simply.

Marlie smiled and rolled her eyes. She should have known better than to underestimate Roberta.

"David claimed that not only did everyone have one, but he could see them. And he had learned to interpret them to some extent. He said that illness created holes, or defects in the auras, generally in the area of the body where the illness was located. In the case of this one med student, the entire aura was affected, letting David know that the disease was a systemic one of some sort."

"Did you believe him?" Marlie asked, figuring that as long as she had been suckered in, she might as well play along and see just where Roberta intended to go with this.

"No. Not right away anyway. But eventually I changed my mind. I had already seen some of the amazing things David had done and knew he had something, some ability, the rest of us lacked. And after that night I tested him several times, asking him to diagnose a few of the more difficult and challenging cases and describe for me these auras he claimed to see. Every time, he zeroed right in on the problem, including a few obscure cases that had thus far eluded all the best medical experts and tests."

"Where is he now?"

"Dead. He was killed in a car accident about five years after we finished our residencies. What a waste," Roberta added, shaking her head sadly.

Marlie watched the color surrounding her mother shrink and turn a pale bluish pink color. "You really liked him, didn't you?" she said.

Roberta smiled. "I almost married him."

"Really?" Marlie said, both surprised and amused.

"Yes, really. But by the time he asked, I'd already met your father and I knew we had something special. Still, it wasn't easy to tell David no."

"Amazing," Marlie said, fascinated by this glimpse into her mother's past. "So, are you saying you believe there really are auras? That they actually exist?"

"I'm saying I believe something is there. An energy perhaps? Or maybe it's some sort of life force."

"Life force," Marlie repeated. "That's what Dr. Nascott called it."

Roberta reached over and patted her daughter's knee. "I don't know what it is exactly, but I *do* know that one of your greatest talents in life has been finding the answers, no matter how challenging the questions may be. That's what made you such a success as a reporter. I would think, given your personal stake here, that this would be a good time to utilize that talent and see what you can find out."

Well, I walked right into that one.

Marlie knew she was being manipulated, but what her mother said made some sense. And the whole story of this David guy was admittedly intriguing. Marlie knew her mother was a logical person, soundly grounded in scientific belief. If she was willing to even consider the idea that David could really see something—or that there was something to be seen—then perhaps it was worth looking into.

"Think about it," Roberta said.

Marlie did.

Roberta dropped Marlie off at the house with a promise to return the following morning. Though Marlie had felt drained and exhausted when she left Dr. Nascott's office, by the time she arrived home she was imbued with a restless energy. She fixed herself a sandwich and settled in the living room to eat it, mulling over the conversation in the car.

Coming from anyone else, Marlie wasn't sure

she would have believed the David Albright story. But this was Roberta telling it—her down-to-earth, practical, honest mother. Though the ulterior motive had been obvious, Marlie didn't doubt the veracity of Roberta's tale. Fabrication wasn't one of her strong suits.

So, did these auras really exist? And if so, is that what the glowances were? Was she actually getting a glimpse at people's souls? The possibility both fascinated and frightened her. White lies and private thoughts were important to maintaining a social balance and some semblance of civility. She had once entertained the idea of how much fun it would be if she could read people's minds, how such an ability could strengthen her skills as an interviewer. But after she thought about it a while, she decided it might not be so great after all. Knowing what someone was really thinking could be shocking, depressing, and unsettling. She sure as hell wouldn't want someone peeking into the corners of her mind; it would be the ultimate invasion of privacy.

Still, the idea that she might have an ability to read people to such a degree was intriguing. She thought back to the hospital, to the warm rosy glow that surrounded her mother, and the fiery red that seemed to take over Nurse Pacinski whenever Dr. Winslow was around. Where else had she seen that red? It took her a moment before she remembered: Kristen. The light around Kristen had taken on that same scarlet shade when she talked about Mark, the boy she had a major crush on. Red, the color of passion. Pink, the color of love. Then there had been that sickly greenish brown shade that clung to William the day she came home from the hospital. Green, the color of envy, jealousy. The reds and pinks had been large, vibrant, enthusiastic. William's nasty brownish green had been tight, closed in, like his emotions. Could that be it? Were the glowances a reflection of emotion?

Marlie shook her head. It was a bit of a leap. Yet she couldn't help but wonder where these color associations came from in the first place. Why was red the color of passion? Why did people think of jealousy as green? Was it possible such ideas evolved from an ancient person's ability to see auras, an idea carried down through the ages and reinforced by others who could also see?

In her mind, she heard her mother's words, spoken in the car: *One of your greatest talents in life has been finding the answers, no matter how challenging the questions may be.*

Marlie pushed herself out of her chair and headed back to the kitchen, her mind whirling, spinning with the possibilities. She set her plate in the sink, then stood a moment staring at the phone, considering what she was about to do. *What the hell,* she thought with a shrug. *What do I have to lose?* She snatched the phone off the wall, punched in 411, and asked for the number of the hospital. When she finally reached the neurosurgery unit, she asked for Nurse Pacinski, then waited several minutes for her to come to the phone.

"Hello?"

"Nurse Pacinski? Sally?"

"Yes, this is she."

"This is Marlie Kaplan. Do you remember me?"

"Of course I do! How are you?"

"I'm doing well. Thanks for asking. Listen, I've got a strange question to ask you, one that's rather personal. If you think I'm out of line, just say so. But your answer to this question could help me a great deal in figuring something out."

"Okay." This said slowly, warily.

"Is there anything going on between you and Dr. Winslow?"

"Going on? What do you mean?" There was the faintest hint of panic in her tone, and Marlie felt a little trill of excitement, sensing she was onto something.

"I mean in a romantic sense. There is, isn't there?"

Sally didn't answer.

"Look, I know this is very personal, and I've got no right to even ask. But I swear to you I won't tell a soul, regardless of your answer."

"There is nothing 'going on,' as you put it."

"But you'd like there to be, wouldn't you?"

"I'm sorry, but I don't think I can continue this discussion. I'm glad you're doing well and wish you the best of luck."

"Wait!" Marlie yelled, sensing the woman was about to hang up. "Please?" She used her most imploring voice, and while Sally didn't say anything more, she didn't hang up either. "Just answer this. You're attracted to him, aren't you?"

"He's married," Sally said.

"Oh. I see. And I understand. I'm sorry."

"Can I go now?"

"Sure. I'm sorry to have bothered you, but you've been a big help to me."

"Good-bye, Ms. Kaplan." This time, she did hang up.

Marlie replaced the phone, chewing on her lip thoughtfully. Though Sally had never come right out and said so, Marlie was certain the woman had it bad for Dr. Winslow. That explained why her glowance turned that vivid shade of red whenever the two of them were together.

Or was she jumping to conclusions? Maybe these colors she saw were a form of that synesthesia thing. Rather than the colors being inherent to the person or the emotion, they were her own interpretation of those emotions. Emotions she sensed through other means.

It was then she felt it—an odd tingling sensation, as if every nerve in her body had been stimulated. It was a feeling she hadn't had for over a year, but she remembered it well. It was the thrill of the hunt, the adventure of investigation, the pulling together of a story. She had forgotten just how heady the feeling could be.

Her mind kicked into work mode as if it were still a daily thing, as if she hadn't spent the past year mired in withdrawal, isolation, and depression. She ticked off a mental list of questions, identified the areas she would need to research, and built a loose story outline in her head. She even conjured up a possible accompanying film clip—shadowy silhouettes surrounded by colorful coronas of light—her imagination visualizing it with a clarity her eyes might never produce.

Then her mind added in the voice-over and her expression rapidly changed from one of excited anticipation to irritation. For the voice she heard was Ronni's, not her own. A spark of anger and something else—possessiveness? competition maybe?—fired in her gut. *No way,* she thought. *I'll do it myself first.*

But could she?

She took a moment to weigh the facts. On the one hand, she was totally dependent upon others for certain things, like driving back and forth, since there was no public transportation available out here in the country. But she knew she could work around most of those obstacles with Roberta's help. Research might be difficult, although if she had an assistant of some sort, that could probably be handled easily enough. She wouldn't be able to see any film clips very well at this point, but if someone took the time to describe them to her she could still have a say in the editing process. As for being in front of the camera, with a little guidance, she could pull that off too. Writing was no problem, thanks to the modifications Roberta had provided for her on the computer. She could even approach Granger with several stories in hand. There was the one on her surgery, if Ronni hadn't already gone ahead and done it without Marlie's participation. Even if she had, Marlie might be able to put a different spin on it with this aura concept. Then there was Garrity and the piece on Senator Waring. Had he found someone else yet, she wondered? Beyond those, she would have to bone up on current events to get back into the swing of things. It would take some time, but it was doable.

The big question was whether or not Granger

would see it that way. But as Cindy had so succinctly pointed out, what did she have to lose? All Granger could do was say no. That wasn't the end of the world; there were other stations. Still, the thought of the humiliation she would feel if Granger turned her away was humbling.

She had to try. And she had to do it now because she knew if she waited any longer she would talk herself out of the whole idea. Reaching for the phone, she dialed her mother's number.

"Hi, Mom," she said when Roberta answered. "I was wondering if I could ask you for a couple of favors."

"Sure."

"Do you know this Dr. Bosher well enough to arrange for me to meet with her?"

"I don't know her personally, but I have connections with some folks who do. I'll be happy to give it a shot."

"Would you? I'd appreciate it."

"No problem. I'll get on it right away."

"Thanks. I was also wondering if you might have time tomorrow to take me somewhere for a haircut. I've got a good inch of growth near the incision now, and I was thinking that if I cut the rest of it really short, it wouldn't be so noticeable."

"I know the perfect place," Roberta said. "I'll call and make you an appointment."

"And after that, I was hoping you could drive me over to the TV station. I want to talk to Granger."

There were a few seconds of startled silence before Roberta said, "Consider me your chauffeur for the day. What time do you want to get started?"

chapter 10

P arked outside the TV station, Roberta fussed with Marlie's hair one last time, fluffing it with her fingers, arranging a curl here and there. "You should have had it cut this short a long time ago," she said. "It's very flattering. You look just like that cute little actress, Winona Ryder."

Any other time, Marlie might have objected to such fussing, but today she tolerated it in good humor. She ran her hands over her ears and down her neck, still a little startled to find everything so bare. Folding down the visor, she tried to get a glimpse of herself in the mirror, but things were still too blurred to give her any idea if the haircut was truly as flattering as Roberta claimed, or if her mother was merely trying to boost her confidence. At least there wasn't an obvious indentation where the bald spot had been.

It was a source of some surprise—and a lot of frustration—when Marlie realized that the return of her sight had triggered a renewed interest in her appearance. When she was blind she rarely cared or thought about how she looked, although she had made some token efforts whenever she knew Carvelle was coming by. But this morning she had worried about her appearance almost to the point of obsession, standing before the mirror, trying desperately to focus on her face, her hair, her skin. The fact that everything remained blurred beyond distinction was maddening. Roberta, sensing her anxiety, had treated her to the works at the beauty salon: shampoo, cut, style (though there was little to actually style), manicure, and makeup.

Marlie shoved the visor back into place and turned toward Roberta with a worried expression. "I look okay, right? They didn't overdo the makeup? I don't want to go in there looking like some adolescent girl who's just discovered cosmetics."

Roberta laughed. "You look great. And I'm not just saying that because I'm your mother."

"You swear?"

"Cross my heart."

"Okay then." Marlie stared out the front window, trying to muster up the courage to go inside. Yesterday this had seemed so simple, so easy. Now she was petrified.

"Shall we go?" Roberta urged. Not waiting for an answer, she opened her door and prepared to climb out.

Marlie reached over and put a staying hand on her mother's arm. "Mom, if you don't mind, I want to do this on my own. Would you mind waiting here for me? I think it will go over better if I show up under my own power, rather than with my mommy in tow."

Roberta froze, half in, half out of the car. Her glowance, which a moment ago had been a broad band of golden-white color, rapidly narrowed down to a closed-in circle of pale blue and yellow. "I suppose," she said. "If you're sure that's how you want to do it."

"I'm sure."

Roberta pulled herself back into the car and closed the door. Marlie opened hers and climbed out. "Back in a jiffy," she said with far more confidence than she felt. She straightened her shoulders, squinted at the layout of the parking lot, and carefully made her way to the station's main entrance.

As she entered the lobby, the first thing Marlie noticed was the smell: a mix of floor wax and the faint lemony scent of the dust spray used by the cleaning crew. Sounds quickly followed: the chirping of the phones, the low murmur of voices, the background noise of the television monitor that hung behind the reception desk. It was like a ride in a time machine. The year she'd been gone was instantly erased, and she felt the tingle of excitement, the sense of anticipation and joy that had accompanied nearly every day of her working life. She stood just inside the door, taking a moment to absorb it all, a hypnotic smile on her face.

"Marlie!"

Marlie shifted her attention to three shadowy figures standing behind the reception desk. The voice that had called her name was one she knew—Debbie Kincer, the station's main receptionist for the past ten years. But she couldn't tell which of the three figures was her until one of them stepped from behind the desk and quickly crossed the lobby toward her. Marlie gave her palms a quick swipe on her skirt, then offered a hand to Debbie, who sandwiched it between both of hers.

"Hi, Deb. Long time, no see." Realizing what she had said, Marlie stopped, grimaced, and shook her head. "And I mean that in the most literal sense," she added.

Debbie let out a low chuckle and gave Marlie's hand a vigorous squeeze. "Haven't lost that wicked sense of humor, I see." She cocked her head to one side, giving Marlie a quick perusal. "Wow! You look great! Love your hair."

"Thanks."

"I heard about your surgery. You have your sight back?"

"Sort of," Marlie answered, repeating the usual explanation of her limitations, though this time she downplayed them a bit.

"Well, that's a start," Debbie said. "Man, we've really missed you around here. Ever since you left, Ronni thinks she's the queen bee. If you thought she was bossy before, you ought to catch her act now. I think you were the only thing that kept her in check."

Marlie chuckled. Ronni was no one's favorite person at the station, but she and Debbie had shared a particularly rocky relationship.

"Please tell me you're coming back to work," Debbie went on. "Otherwise, I'm going to kill that woman."

Marlie laughed. "I don't know. I'm thinking about it."

"Well, think hard," Debbie said. She then turned around and gestured toward the other two figures behind the reception desk. "Let me introduce you to a couple of new faces. Susan, Damaris, this is Marlie Kaplan, one of WKAL's top reporters." Debbie turned back toward Marlie. "Damaris is our student intern for the year and Susan is the new evening receptionist. She's just getting oriented."

"It's a pleasure to meet you both," Marlie said, unsure which was which. The two women murmured back greetings of their own, their stares never wavering.

Marlie tuned them out, turning back to Debbie. "I thought I'd go upstairs and pop in on Granger," she said. "Is he here?"

"He is," Debbie answered, spinning around on her heel and heading back toward the desk. "I'll just call up and let him know you're coming."

"No," Marlie said quickly. "Don't. I want to surprise him. If you don't mind."

Debbie shrugged. "Sure. You know the way. Need me to key the elevator for you?" she asked, referring to the security lock that required a special key in order to make the elevator work.

"I'll just take the stairs," Marlie said. "The code on the button panel hasn't changed, has it?"

"It's the same," Debbie said. Two of the phone lines rang simultaneously, and Debbie held one finger up as a signal for Marlie to wait. Instead, Marlie took it as an opportunity to escape. She moved over to the door, fumbled with the keypad, and punched in the four-digit code that had been in place for over five years. When she heard the click that announced her success, she grabbed the door, tossed a "Catch ya later" over her shoulder, and stepped inside.

The door eased itself closed, and Marlie leaned against the wall, shut her eyes, and blew out a breath of relief. She'd made it past the first hurdle, but the worst was yet to come. Shaking her arms to rid her-

self of tension, she tried to focus on the meeting still
ahead. She'd been rehearsing what she would say to
Granger all morning, and she ran it through her
mind once again.

"You can do this, Kaplan," she whispered.

When she was ready, she opened her eyes and
moved to the stairs. Slowly, she worked her way
upward, her sweaty palm sliding along the handrail,
the pounding of her heart increasing with every
step. By the time she reached the top, her heart was
like a bass drum, crashing through her ears, pulsing
in her throat. She paused to gather her wits and gar-
ner her strength, then pushed through the door into
the hallway beyond.

It was surprisingly quiet. Though several offices
were on this floor, the entire stretch of hallway, from
where Marlie stood to Granger's office at the other
end, was empty. There were more offices, smaller
ones, on the next floor up and above that, the newsroom and studio. Most of the people involved with
the actual production were located on those floors,
and there, Marlie knew, things would be bustling.

Part of the pecking order at WKAL included
moving into the larger office suites on the second
floor as one gained seniority and earned promo-
tions, resulting in a standing joke among the crew
about moving *down* the corporate ladder. Only the
top reporters had these offices, and most of them
were likely out on assignment or digging up stories.
It was the sort of hard work and ambition that
earned them these offices in the first place. By the
time of the warehouse incident, Marlie had been in
a second-floor office for nearly two years.

The air of desertion was oddly disturbing, and Marlie quickly moved toward the only sound she could hear—a muffled female voice coming from somewhere ahead. As she drew closer, she recognized the voice as Ronni's. Judging from the general cadence of her speech and the lack of any audible response from someone else, Marlie assumed Ronni was talking on the phone. Then she realized *where* the voice was coming from and froze, a deepening frown marking her face. She turned and looked back the way she had come, counting the doorways to be sure. She was right. Ronni was in what had once been Marlie's office. The revelation carried a surprising sting.

Lightening her step, Marlie worked her way just to the left of the doorframe and stopped. The door itself was closed, but its upper half was an opaque glass window. Above that was a transom window, which was cracked open several inches. After glancing around to be sure the hallway was still deserted, Marlie cocked her head and listened.

"I intend to expose everything I know," Ronni said, her tone smug and confident. "I'm offering you the opportunity to present your side, should you care to, but the story will air regardless." There was a pause, then, "I'll be happy to meet with you, but understand, it's not going to change things. The public has a right to know. I'm extending a courtesy to you by telling you about it ahead of time."

Ronni's voice was low, but there was a hard-edged excitement to it that Marlie knew well.

"Agreed," Ronni said. "No cameras, no one else. Just you and me this time. If you decide you want to go with a rebuttal of some sort, we can do it live or film it later. Though personally, I don't see how you can possibly defend any of this." She paused again, then laughed, a mean-spirited sound. "Oh, trust me. I have proof aplenty. And it's solid. You'll see."

Marlie felt a twinge of jealousy. Whatever Ronni had happened onto, it was big. Marlie remembered how it felt, that current of excitement that coursed through her body whenever she was reeling in a big one. It was like a fix to a junkie, and hearing Ronni now threw her into a state of acute withdrawal.

"That will be fine," Ronni said. "I'll see you there." Marlie heard Ronni hang up the phone, and a second later she heard a faint click followed by a slight scraping sound. In her many years of working with Ronni, Marlie had heard that sound dozens of times before. *Some things never change,* she thought shaking her head.

A visit with Ronni certainly wasn't on Marlie's agenda, but the conversation she had overheard piqued her curiosity. She stepped in front of the door and raised her hand to knock, but when she caught sight of Ronni through the opaque glass, she hesitated. Ronni's shape was an indistinct blur moving about inside the office, almost pacing it seemed. But it wasn't her motion that intrigued Marlie, it was her glowance. It radiated light like the sun itself, golden white and undulating as if it were breathing heavily. Clearly visible through the milky glass, Marlie watched in fascination as pieces of it trailed behind Ronni like a comet's tail.

Suddenly Ronni stopped, and Marlie wondered if she had seen her through the glass. But then she took off again, more directed this time, until she reached what Marlie guessed was the far wall. There she stopped, her glowance wafting around her like some celestial blanket. Another sound traveled out over the transom, a rattling sort of hollow clatter.

Not wanting to be caught standing outside the door peering through the window, Marlie finally reached up and rapped lightly on the glass. Ronni's reaction was swift and startling. Her glowance shrunk down like a starved gas flame, its color turning first to yellow, then to gray, becoming almost transparent. She took a hesitant step toward the door, paused, then quickly covered the rest of the distance. She flung the door open, and for several long moments the two women stared at one another.

"Marlie!" Ronni said, finally breaking the silence. "My goodness, I almost didn't recognize you with your hair that short."

Marlie reached up and wrapped a self-conscious hand around her bare neck. What she could see of Ronni looked much as she remembered: shoulder-length dark blond hair and a build so slight she looked as if she'd topple over in a strong wind. Marlie knew that air of fragility was dangerously deceptive.

"I must say, this is quite a surprise," Ronni went on. "Does this mean you've reconsidered doing the piece on your surgery?"

Marlie dropped her hand to her side and straightened to her full height, squaring her shoulders. "Something like that," she said, more irritably than she intended. She was still smarting from the fact that Ronni had taken over her old office. "Although not the story you think."

"Really?" Ronni leaned against the doorframe and folded her arms over her chest. "You have another idea? A different twist to put on it?"

"Actually, I was thinking of asking Granger if *I* could do the story."

She waited for Ronni's reaction, expecting a derisive laugh at best, god-only-knew-what at worst, and wondering why on earth she was doing this. Telling Ronni ahead of time was suicidal. But then, maybe that was what she wanted—let Ronni kill the story now or undermine her confidence enough that she could avoid the agony of facing Granger at all.

"*You* do the story? The whole thing?" Ronni said.

"Yes," Marlie said, the slightest jut of defiance to her chin. "What's wrong with that?"

"Wrong with it? Absolutely nothing. In fact, Kaplan, it's brilliant. What a great idea! It will be much more powerful that way. Frankly, I don't see how Granger can say no."

Marlie's jaw dropped halfway to the floor.

Ronni laughed. "What's the matter, Kaplan?"

"That isn't quite the response I expected," Marlie said slowly, eyeing Ronni as if she might be a pod person. "You're not exactly known for letting stories go without a hell of a fight."

Ronni shrugged. "In this case, I don't mind. It's more or less a fluff piece anyway. Besides, I've just hooked into something big—*really* big, and I'd rather focus on that for now."

"Care to share?"

"Don't push your luck."

"Now, *that's* the Ronni Cumberland I know and love."

Ronni chuckled, then reached over and gave Marlie's shoulder a little squeeze. Marlie couldn't have been more stunned had the woman hugged her.

"You know, I'm really glad to see you back here, Kaplan. I know you and I have been pretty competitive in the past, and that we've butted heads on occasion—"

"That's an understatement."

"But despite all that, I've actually missed you around here. You were good for me, kept me on my toes, gave me drive. Trying to stay one step ahead of you was probably the best career boost I could have ever had. You're a good reporter, Kaplan. One of the best."

Marlie was speechless. It was as if Ronni had had a personality transplant or something.

"Don't look so shocked," Ronni said, laughing again. "It's the truth and you know it." She leaned forward then, close to Marlie's ear, dropping her voice to just above a whisper. "But if you tell anyone I said it, I'll deny it with my dying breath. I do have a ruthless reputation to maintain, you know."

Marlie flashed her a wry grin. "That's more like it," she said. "I confess, you had me worried there for a second." Truth was, she was *still* worried, or at the least very confused, but she'd be damned if she'd let Ronni know it.

"Trust me, I still have the Wicked Witch title firmly in my possession. Ask anyone."

Marlie gazed past Ronni's shoulder into the office, a wistful expression on her face. "So tell me, if Granger lets me come back to work, can I have my office back?"

"Not a chance." Ronni raised her arm and glanced at her watch. "Look, I've got to go meet someone in a few minutes. Sorry to cut things short, but if I don't get moving I'll be late. It really was good to see you again, Kaplan. Go give Granger some hell for me." With that, she stepped back into the office, shutting the door in Marlie's face.

Marlie took a step back, cocked her head, and mumbled, "Ah. Back to normal."

Turning away from the door, she gazed down the hall toward Granger's office. So far, things were going far better than she had hoped. But she had one more hurdle to clear—the biggest one.

"Here goes nothing," she said, and pushed on toward her future.

chapter 11

Though Marlie had intended for her visit to Granger to be a surprise, Cindy greeted her with an "Ah, *there* you are" as soon as she walked through the door.

Marlie shook her head in disgust. "Shit, Cindy. Does my mother tell you everything?"

"Not everything. Just the important stuff."

"Did you tell Granger I was coming?"

"Nope."

"Good. Is he in?"

"He is. He's on the phone at the moment, but I don't think he'll be long. Have a seat. Love the haircut, by the way. It's cute and makes you look five years younger."

"Thanks," Marlie said, easing herself into a chair and wondering if cute and younger-looking was an advantage at this point. She gave a nod toward Granger's door. "What kind of mood is he in?"

"I'm not sure. We took a hit on the ratings this week, but the budget came through without any cuts. I'm not sure which one is coloring his temperament more at this point. He's been holed up in there all morning."

Marlie smiled at Cindy's use of the phrase "coloring his temperament." If only she knew.

"Uh, there we go," Cindy said, picking up the

phone. "He just hung up. Let me tell him you're here."

A sudden panic burned its way up Marlie's throat, and one leg started to jump, the muscles in her thigh doing the herky-jerky. This was it, the moment of truth. She tried to still her leg with one hand while she nibbled the nails of the other and listened to Cindy's end of the conversation with Granger. But all Cindy contributed was an occasional "uh-huh" and then finally an "okay" before hanging up. Whatever Granger had said, it's effect on Cindy was to turn her glowance from a restful haze of pink and gold to a swirling mass of turbulent yellow.

"Go on in," Cindy said, her voice perfectly even. "He's waiting for you."

Marlie stood up, smoothed her skirt, and chewed on her lip. She gave a last, longing glance toward the door to the hallway before heading into Granger's office with all the enthusiasm of a death-row inmate walking the last mile.

The lighting in the office was dim, making everything blend into varying shades of gray. Marlie paused inside the door, giving her eyes time to adjust, hoping to God they would. From out of the grayness, Granger came bounding toward her with open arms, his glowance gauzy and white like some spectral figure.

"Marlie! What a wonderful surprise!" He covered the distance between them in three huge steps and wrapped her in a giant bear hug.

Marlie stood stunned and wooden a moment before she managed to bring her own arms up and return the hug, though with less vigor than Granger's.

She was glad when he released her, but he then grabbed her shoulders and, holding her at arms' length, eyed her from head to toe. "You look fabulous. I'm impressed. Especially considering what you've just been through."

"Thanks." Marlie flashed him a nervous smile.

"Come on in," Granger said. "Have a seat. Can you see well enough to find your way?"

Marlie knew any hesitancy, any sign of weakness on her part, would dilute her chances of convincing Granger to let her work. Panic rose again, a vise squeezing her throat and chest. But as Granger stepped back and opened Marlie's view to the rest of the room, she saw she could now make out the dim outline of the office furniture.

"I'm fine," she said, walking as boldly as she dared toward a chair. She made it without incident and dropped gratefully into its seat, shifting around in an effort to get comfortable. She concentrated on looking relaxed, trying to ignore the tickle of sweat weaving down her back and the trip-hammer thrum of her heart.

Granger took a seat behind the desk and leaned forward eagerly. "So to what do I owe the pleasure of this visit?" he asked.

"I, uh, thought I'd stop by and see how things were going." She shifted some more in the chair, dropped both her hands and her gaze toward her lap, then decided that looked too humbled and self-conscious. Her hands moved to the arms of the chair, and she leveled her gaze directly at Granger, or at least what she could see of him. There was something different about him, she realized. Then it hit her—his hair. Where before it had been mostly dark with a feathering of frost along the temples, he now had a head capped in snowy white.

"It looks like you've acquired a lot more snow on the mountain," she said with a smile.

It took Granger a moment to respond, and Marlie feared she had somehow offended him. But then he laughed, and she saw his hand go up and rake through his hair. "Oh, you mean this," he said good-naturedly. "My wife says I look more like Colonel Sanders every day. That's what a career in TV will get you."

"So you're blaming it on stress?"

"Beats admitting I'm turning into an old fogy."

So far so good, Marlie thought. This was the same sort of teasing banter she and Granger had often indulged in before. "So how have things been going?" she asked.

"Not bad. The place has been hopping. Our ratings have done well overall, although there's been a bit of a slip the past few weeks."

"Any idea why?"

"I'm not sure, although I'm tempted to blame it on that hunky new anchorman Channel Seven just hired."

Marlie smiled. "A looker, eh?"

"You could say so," Granger said with disgust. "The guy can't deliver a single night's news without tripping over his tongue, and I think he's got the IQ of a slug. But when he bats them baby blues at the camera, it's like magic. Makes me sick."

"That you didn't get him first?"

Granger chuckled. "You know me too well." He drew silent a moment, and Marlie could feel his gaze, studying her. "I have to admit, Kaplan," he said finally, "I've missed you around here."

This was her chance; she couldn't ask for a better opening. She bit her lip and leaned forward. "Well, that's part of why I'm here today. I've been talking with Cindy and Ronni. I understand there's a suggestion afoot that you do a story about my surgery."

"We've tossed it around," Granger said. "I think it would make a great human-interest piece as well as the fact that it's groundbreaking science."

"And you assigned it to Ronni?"

"I did," Granger admitted. "Look, I know the two of you haven't always gotten along, but I think Ronni is the best person here for the job. She knows you well, knows the story of what happened, and has enough understanding of the medical aspects to give an intelligent report. I simply couldn't think of anyone else as qualified to do it."

"What about me?"

The silence that followed was so complete, so enveloping, Marlie panicked, thinking she had suddenly lost her hearing as well as her sight. Then she heard Granger clear his throat.

"You," he said simply, as if he were tasting the idea. "You're suggesting that *you* should do this story?"

"I am. Who could understand the situation better than I? You know I've got the skills, Granger. And just imagine how much stronger the human-interest aspect will be if one of the patients who underwent this procedure is the person reporting the story."

Granger didn't respond, but his glowance had shrunk down to a thin blue corona that hugged his body.

"I want to do it," Marlie said firmly. Granger's hesitation worried her, but she was determined not to back down.

"I don't know, Marlie," Granger said, slowly shaking his head. He rose from his chair and walked over to the window, parting the blinds and peering out. "I know you're doing better since this operation you had, but do you think you're ready to climb back into the saddle again?"

"I do," she said without hesitation.

He turned from the window and walked back to the desk. "I'll take it under consideration, Marlie. But frankly, I don't see how we can do it at this point. I have a full staff already and the budget just came back with a bunch of cuts. I'm going to have to do some trimming, so I don't see how I can afford to take someone else on right now."

Marlie opened her mouth to suggest she would do this one story gratis, just to show she could. But then she realized what Granger's last words had been: *budget cuts.* Yet Cindy had told her the budget *hadn't* been cut. That could mean only one thing. Granger didn't want her back, and he was using the budget—lying about it—as an excuse. Hot blood flooded her cheeks, and her leg started trembling again.

"I see," she said. She had known this might happen. In her mind she had played it out with calm dignity, accepting the blow with grace and humor.

But as the sting of humiliation washed over her and tears burned in her eyes, she knew she had underestimated the impact it would have. She pushed herself out of the chair and quickly headed for the office door, hoping to escape while she still had a modicum of self-respect left.

"I'm sorry, Marlie," Granger said after her.

Marlie didn't stop or turn back. She dismissed his apology with a wave of a hand. "No problem, Granger," she said. "I understand. Just thought it couldn't hurt to ask. Thanks for your time."

She pulled the door open and walked across the reception area at a rapid clip, heedless of the fact she could barely see through the welling of tears. Cindy called out for her to wait, but Marlie ignored her and kept moving—down the hallway, past the closed and darkened door to Ronni's office, and into the stairwell. There she finally stopped, leaning against the cold cinderblock wall and staring up at the ceiling. Tears burned hot tracks down her cheeks and neck.

"What an *idiot* I am!" she muttered, stomping her foot. It echoed loudly inside the stairwell, reverberating off the concrete floor and walls. "Stupid, stupid, stupid! When are you going to learn, Kaplan?"

After making an angry swipe at her tears, she pushed away from the wall and groped about for the stair railing. She descended the steps considerably faster than she had climbed them a short while ago, aware she was behaving recklessly but too wounded at this point to care. Physical injury was the furthest thing from her mind. Her primary goal was escape.

She pushed through the door into the lobby and strode purposefully toward the door, hoping to avoid any further conversation. She knew Debbie Kincer might think her rude for leaving without a good-bye; at the moment she didn't care.

She made it back to the car, climbed in, and closed the door, staring straight ahead. "Take me home," she told her mother.

Roberta started the engine and backed out, one eye on her daughter. "Want to talk about it?"

"No, I don't."

Roberta nodded slowly and steered the car out of the parking lot, easing into the flow of traffic. "Did you see Granger?" she tried after a few minutes of silence.

"I told you, I don't want to discuss it," Marlie said, her jaw tight. "I just want to go home."

"Okay," Roberta said carefully. She didn't try again until forty-five minutes later when she pulled up in front of Marlie's house. "Look," she said, shifting the car into park and turning to face her daughter. "No one ever said this would be easy. You've had to prove yourself before, you can do it again."

Marlie rolled her eyes, opened the door, and climbed out of the car. "Go home, Mother," she said.

She slammed the door and stomped off toward the house, keenly aware of Roberta parked behind her with the engine running, watching her every move. Once inside, she slid down the inside of the door, huddling on the floor like some wounded animal. Finally, she gave her tears full release, the sobs continuing long after she heard her mother shift the car into gear and drive away.

chapter
12

The crying cleared Marlie's head. Feeling spent, but somehow cleansed, she tucked her knees up under her chin and sat on the floor thinking. She was extremely annoyed with herself. To start with, the way she had treated her mother was abominable. Taking her anger out on Roberta was unfair and misguided, for the person she was really angry with was herself, not her mother, not even Granger. What did she expect? That after being gone for a year she could just waltz back into her old job and pick up where she left off, particularly given her current limitations? Such an assumption would be unreasonable for someone with normal abilities, much less for her. Granger was just doing his job. If she were in his shoes, she, too, would be hesitant to hire someone like herself, at least without some proof of ability.

If she had any hope at all of ever returning to work, she knew she was going to have to harden herself. There was a time when a simple "no" was like a switch, turning on her determination and making her even more persistent. Yet today, Granger's refusal had easily shattered her ego, scattering the seeds of her newfound confidence like a puffball on the wind. She could kick herself for giving in so easily, for simply accepting Granger's decision without a fight. And she knew what she had to do.

Somehow, she had to show Granger she could still do the job, albeit with a few modifications here and there.

Modifications.

She pushed herself off the floor and headed down the hall to her office. For a moment, she stood in the doorway, taking in the sight of her trophies on the far wall. The sight of them boosted her morale, bolstered her self-confidence, and reinforced her decision. She had been damned good at what she did once, and she could be again.

She moved over to the desk and pulled the dust cover off the computer. Her fingers played over the front surface, found the power button, and pushed it, then did the same for the monitor. As the machine whined through its boot-up, Marlie pulled the chair out from under the desk and settled in. Seconds later, Ralph greeted her with his monotone, "Welcome, Marlie."

Ralph was the name Marlie had given the voice that accompanied her synthesizer, part of the package of modifications Roberta had installed on the computer after the accident. Marlie had been reasonably computer savvy prior to her blindness, but she had relied totally on her eyes and a mouse for navigating around the Windows-based environment. When she found herself unable to use either, she had given up all hope of ever using a computer again.

Roberta, however, had other plans. She harped for weeks until Marlie finally gave in and agreed to the computer modifications as well as the classes necessary to learn how to use them. It did make it possible for her to use a computer again, but it wasn't easy. Without a mouse, accessing the various software programs meant learning lengthy combinations of keystrokes while Ralph served as her seeing-eye cyberdog. While Marlie had always prided herself on her ability to learn and memorize, she was constantly getting the combinations mixed up, forgetting a necessary keystroke or using the wrong one. And since she had never been much of a touch typist, her frustrations were further compounded whenever her fingers became misaligned and she ended up hitting all the wrong keys.

One of the other students in Marlie's computer class had come to hate Ralph, or her version of Ralph, complaining that the tinny voice got on her nerves, particularly when it announced she had just done something other than what she wanted to. But Marlie liked Ralph. His voice, which, amusingly, carried a hint of a British accent, was strangely soothing. And she liked the way he was always patient, never emotional or judgmental. He did his job, and did it well for the most part, guiding her around, reading whatever appeared on the screen, and maintaining a distant but casual politeness. Several times, Marlie found herself talking back to him as if he were a real person.

Along with Ralph and the software that made him work, Roberta had also invested in an embosser so Marlie could print off Braille copies of her work. Of course, that had required more classes, wherein Marlie grudgingly learned the Braille system—grudgingly because accepting this new method of existence meant accepting her new condition and its limitations. As soon as she had appeased her mother by completing the classes, Marlie abandoned it all, withdrawing back into her shell and ignoring the computer completely. Now, she struggled to resurrect what she'd learned, hoping she hadn't lost the knowledge during her months of defiant indifference.

She took a few minutes to study the monitor screen, trying unsuccessfully to discern some detail among the multicolored patterns. Now that she had some sight back, she thought she might be able to identify the icons by their shape and color, maybe even use a mouse again, if the display could be enlarged somehow. But for now it all remained a blur—and a distracting blur at that—so she closed her eyes and let her fingers flutter over the keyboard, feeling for the bumps on the keys, positioning her hands in the appropriate spot, and searching her memory for the sequence of strokes that would start up the word-processing software. After several false starts, during which Ralph gently informed her of her mistakes, she finally succeeded.

She typed for over an hour, her fingers growing more confident with each stroke. She banged out a rough outline of the surgery story, listing the areas where further research was needed, formulating suggested camera shots, and detailing the overall flow of the piece, pausing periodically to let Ralph read back what she had written. When she was done, she felt around until she found the container that held her store of floppies, pulled one out, and stuck it into the appropriate drive. She copied the file onto the disk, transferred it to the embosser, and then printed off a Braille version of her work. When it was done, she gathered up the pages and set them aside, wanting to let them sit for a day or so before she read them again. After saving the file to the computer's hard drive as well, she finally bid Ralph farewell and turned off all the equipment.

She leaned back in the chair, a smile on her face.

After a few seconds, she reached for the phone and punched in Roberta's number. After the rude way Marlie had treated her this afternoon, she wanted to apologize. But when the machine answered, she hung up. This was something she wanted to do in person, not in a recorded message.

Feeling restless, she leaned back in her chair, her hands folded prayerlike in front of her, tapping her chin. Her gaze drifted to the light of her own glowance, and she raised her hands in front of her face, twisting and turning them as she marveled over the brilliant golden light emanating from her pores. Her attention shifted to the window, where a similar light blazed into the room, a product of the afternoon sun. She got up and walked over to the window, tilting her face to the sun's warmth, first closing her eyes, then opening them to the vibrant blue of the sky.

The day outside was warm and inviting, and her efforts on the computer had left her feeling bold and adventurous. It occurred to her that a walk might provide a pleasant way to expend some of her pent-up energy, but she hadn't been outside alone anywhere since the onset of her blindness. The very concept had always seemed too impossible, too dangerous. But she could see now, and while her vision was far from perfect, she thought it might be enough.

She made her way to the bedroom and changed into jeans, a blouse, and a pair of sneakers. As she headed for the front door, she was surprised by the galloping beat of her heart. It was silly, she knew, to attach such significance to something as mundane as a walk. Yet it felt momentous, as if opening the door to the outside might somehow open the door to her future.

She stepped out onto the porch and surveyed her surroundings. Off to the right, several hundred yards from the house, was a thick growth of woods. There was a fairly wide trail that meandered through it, and when she had first moved into the house she had once followed it for a hundred feet or so before turning back. To the left, on either side of the drive, was a smaller grove of trees that lined a strip of land between the house and the road. Realizing there was little sense, and possibly more danger than she wanted in the direction of the road, she took off for the woods.

The sun beat down on her face and shoulders, its warmth seeping deep into her bones. Though a light breeze rustled her hair and kept the sun's heat from becoming overpowering, the cool shade offered by the trees when she stepped onto the path still came as a welcome relief.

A canopy of leaves overhead dappled the sunlight along the path, creating a kaleidoscopic trail that was easy to follow. She stepped slowly and carefully, her eyes searching ahead for any variations in color or texture that might signal roots or rocks that could send her sprawling. Leaves crunched beneath her feet, while nearby birds and squirrels chirped and chattered their warning that a stranger was afoot. Above her, the wind soughed through the trees with a deep and pleasurable sigh, occasionally drifting down to settle like a lover's caress upon her skin—soft, gentle, and warm. With every breath she took she inhaled the smells of the woods: the earthy aroma of moss, the fragrant tang of pine, and the slightly acrid though not unpleasant scent of decaying leaves.

It occurred to her that she should have done this long ago, back when she could have seen all this beauty. Mother Nature had plenty of other gifts, however, with the feels, smells, and sounds of the woods all offering their own brand of pleasure. Marlie's other senses had become finely tuned over the past year, and now they served her well, filling in the details her eyes couldn't yet distinguish.

She had meandered for forty minutes or more when she heard a sound that made her pause. It was different from all the other noises, a sharp, high-pitched squeal like an animal in distress. It was there and gone, and for a second she wondered if she had really heard it at all. Closing her eyes, she cocked her head to one side and listened.

A moment later she heard another noise, different, but no less disturbing. It was a strange grunting sound that seemed oddly human.

She opened her eyes and squinted in the general direction it had come from, but all she could see was the green blur of trees and the lighter brown of the path, which disappeared around a curve a short distance away. Curious, she continued onward.

Beyond the curve, the path wended its way to the edge of the woods, abruptly giving way to an open field. The grunting sound continued and it was closer, louder now. She inched toward the perimeter of the trees and peered through the shrubbery to the clearing beyond. What she saw confused her.

There were two figures, one much larger than the other, and they appeared to be dancing, although their movements lacked the grace and fluidity of any dance Marlie had ever seen. She got the impression, mostly from their sizes and shapes, that one of the figures was a woman, the other a man. Her first thought was that she had happened upon lovers sharing a private tryst in the field, but she quickly tossed that idea aside. Something felt wrong here, like a puzzle piece that didn't quite fit even though it looked as if it should. A second later, it hit her.

The glowances.

The one surrounding the larger figure darkened as she watched, turning dense and black until it became a pendulous cloud of malignant weight that clung tightly to the man's shape. Its movement was slow but constant, like a covering swarm of bees or an oozing slime, making it seem as if it had a presence, a life of its own. And not a particularly pleasant one.

But even more disturbing was the woman. No longer standing, she had slumped to the ground, and her glowance had grown thin, almost transparent, like wisps of pale smoke. Rather than hugging her body, fingers of it dissipated into the air and were carried off with the wind.

She's dying.

The thought sprang, unbidden, into Marlie's mind. She briefly entertained the idea of hollering at the couple, or of stepping into the clearing to interrupt whatever was going on. But she hesitated, her conscience battling with her logic. On the one hand she felt obligated to do something. If the woman was in trouble, Marlie wanted to help her. Yet, if the man was up to no good, Marlie was hardly in a position to stop him. He had the distinct advantage of being able to see. If he killed the woman in the clearing, Marlie was sure he wouldn't hesitate to kill her as well.

Every instinct told her to stay quiet and hidden. And if her career as a journalist had taught her nothing else, it had taught her to trust her instincts. Had she done so a year ago, she might not be in the mess she was in now. Back then, the cost of her transgression had been the loss of her sight. This time, she might not be so lucky.

The woman lay perfectly still now, her glowance gone, the man crouched beside her.

Marlie weighed her options. Though there was a thick wall of shrubbery between her and the field, she felt open and exposed. If the man saw her standing here, she knew her chances of outrunning him were nil. She thought about trying to go back to the house to summon help but feared the man might hear her moving along the path. Instead, she slipped behind the trunk of a nearby tree and peered around its edge into the clearing. Her heart pounded inside her chest, and her leg began to tremble, doing the same herky-jerky thing it had done in Granger's office. An army of goose bumps marched along her skin and a shiver threatened, but she forced herself to hold perfectly still, barely breathing, barely blinking.

The man stood suddenly, and Marlie tensed, ready to bolt at the first indication he had seen her or was moving her way. By now his glowance had become a foul-looking mass, a black shroud of malevolence. The mere sight of it filled Marlie with an abhorrent disgust and frightened her to her very core. More than anything she wanted to turn away and run as fast as she could, but she stood riveted to the spot, watching with horrified fascination. She felt something tickle along the back of her hand, a tiny crawling sensation, and knew that some critter of the woods had found her out. She loathed bugs but resisted the urge to swat at the thing, fearful the commotion might give her away.

The man reached down, lifted the woman by the shoulders, and proceeded to drag her across the field. Though the clearing was mostly a shelf of hard slate, clusters of grass—some a foot or more high—had sprung up willy-nilly along the rocky terrain. As the man dragged the woman past several of these clumps, Marlie had to strain to keep her in sight. She kept searching for some sign of the woman's glowance, some indication she was still alive. But not a single shimmer of light emanated from her body.

The man waded into a dense expanse of grass surrounding a large boulder. There, he let go of the woman's body, and it disappeared completely from Marlie's view, obscured by the tall growth. He stood there a moment, gazing downward, then spun on his heel and headed back the way he had come. He moved with a hurried pace, traversing the field and disappearing into the grove of trees that bordered the other side.

Marlie remained where she was, watching the point where she had last seen him, wondering if he would return. A few minutes later she heard the sound of a car engine and the crunch of tires on gravel. The sound slowly receded, fading away into silence. And silent it was, she realized. The breeze that had been blowing had stilled, and even the critters in the woods behind her had fallen quiet.

With a grimace of disgust, she brushed at the crawling thing on her arm, which by now had moved from her wrist to her elbow. She finally let her gaze drift away from where the man had entered the woods and looked over toward the boulder. Slowly, she slid from behind the tree and, with one last glance toward the woods, climbed through the shrubbery in front of her, stepping into the clearing.

She set her sights on the boulder and began to work her way across the field. Carefully she skirted around the patches of grass, her progress slowed even more by the slippery, uneven surface of the rocky terrain. She was more than halfway to her goal when she heard a rustling in the trees to her right, near where the man had disappeared.

She froze, fear turning her blood to glacial ice.

Leaves crunched with the unmistakable sound of footsteps.

Panicked, Marlie looked back toward the woods she had just left, searching for the spot where she had entered the clearing. All she saw was a seemingly impenetrable wall of shrubbery that looked as though it was miles away.

The steps continued, growing louder, coming closer.

Chewing her lip in urgency, she looked toward the boulder. It was closer than the woods, and she thought if she crouched down low on the side farthest away from the woman, the grass and the rock would hide her.

She looked back at the woods, then again at the boulder, indecision stamped on her face.

More footsteps.

Marlie ran stumbling toward the boulder, all caution gone. She plunged into the moat of grass that grew up around it, the thick wiry stems grabbing at her legs like some multitentacled monster. With one hand she groped the top of the huge rock, found a small indentation, and anchored herself. With a little leap, she skirted around to its backside.

Her blurred vision took a split second to adjust, but it was a split second too long. By the time she realized what a horrible mistake she had made, her momentum was too great to stop. Her feet stepped into nothingness, the ground literally disappearing beneath her.

And she knew now why she could no longer see the woman.

chapter
13

In the space of a millisecond, Marlie processed the fact that what she had thought was a clearing was actually a plateau, the boulder the only thing separating it from a cliff. Her left hand, which had been resting on the boulder as an anchor an instant ago, became a claw desperately scrabbling along the rock's surface, the fingernails bending and ripping as they tried to penetrate stone. She twisted and writhed in an attempt to throw her body back toward the boulder and away from the drop, her free hand groping and grabbing at the tall grass. Her waist slammed into the cliff's edge with a force that ripped her breath away. The lower half of her body hung over the side, dangling in midair. The jolt of her landing made her lose her grip on the boulder and her hand slid off, leaving a line of bloody tracks in its wake. She felt herself start to slide over the edge and tightened her grasp on the grass with her right hand, the left one searching for a clump of its own. She found one and hung on with all her might. Her legs bicycled like crazy, her feet scraping along the cliff's face in search of a foothold.

One of her feet found a small outcropping of rock, barely large enough to hold her toes. The other found a tiny crack, and she wedged the side of her sneaker in as far as she could, barely half an inch of purchase. She held perfectly still, sprawled along the

vertical wall like some pathetic version of Spider-
man, her heart pounding so hard it actually made
her chest bounce against the dirt and stone.

And then part of the cliff gave way, chunks of it
raining down past her feet and knocking the one in
the crack loose. She yelped, and her hands tightened
on the grass as her body slid another few inches over
the side. She cast about frantically with the knocked-
loose foot until it again found its crack, and she
wedged the side of her shoe in.

She had no idea how big a drop lay beneath her,
but the brief glance she'd had before flinging herself
back toward the boulder had given her the impression of a vast open space. The wiry stems of the grass
were slicing into her hands like a garrote; her palms
were slick with blood and sweat. She was losing her
grip one centimeter at a time and feared if she didn't
do something soon, the ropy grass would slip
through her hands, plunging her to what she feared
was certain death on the ground below.

Carefully she shifted some of her weight to the
foot on the outcropping, her toes curling inside her
shoe as if they could grip the tiny ledge. It held, and
she shifted a little more, momentarily easing the
strain on her arms. Knowing she couldn't hold on
much longer, she squeezed her eyes closed, muttered
a quick prayer, and pushed against the outcropping
with her foot. She managed to throw first one elbow,
then the other onto the narrow ledge behind the
boulder. Summoning up the dregs of her energy, she
dragged herself up the rest of the way, rolling onto
the ledge and flopping onto her back.

She lay there feeling her body tremble and ache;

shocks of pain coursed through her. The adrenaline that had flooded her system during the fall now gave her a vicious case of the shakes, rattling her bones so hard she worried she might shudder herself back over the edge. With a grunt, she turned on her side toward the boulder and slithered her body along its bottom edge, through the grass, and into the open field.

Her eyes played over the clearing, hunting for some sign of the man but finding only the blur of nature's color. With a grunt of pain, she eased herself onto her knees and sat back on her haunches, her eyes still searching, half expecting the blackness to leap out at her at any moment.

She heard the footsteps again, still in the woods but closer than ever, crunching their way over mounds of dead leaves. Her head spun toward the sound.

A brown blur burst into the clearing, followed by another. With a great flurry of motion the blurs rose into the air, heading right in Marlie's direction. She ducked as they flew clumsily overhead, their wings making a loud flapping noise, their shadows racing across her huddled form. Seconds later, they disappeared over the cliff, and the cry of a wild turkey echoed up from the canyon below.

Turkeys! A bunch of goddamned turkeys.

Marlie flashed on a memory from her childhood, when she had been sitting on her father's lap listening to him tell a scary story. At the end of his tale, the scary thing coming through the woods toward the group of frightened kids turned out to be a wild turkey. Marlie had cried foul at that, but her father swore that wild turkeys sounded just like a man when they walked through the woods. Marlie hadn't believed him then. She did now.

She squeezed her eyes closed and dropped her head into her hands. Giddy with relief, she laughed, though it had a hard, brittle sound to it.

The woman.

"Oh, God." Moaning, she pushed herself up from the ground. Her side ached and throbbed, each breath a knife point in her ribs. The muscles in her legs quivered, liquid and weak. Both of her hands were trying to cramp, the fingers curling into claws, the torn fingertips on the left one throbbing like a toothache. She rubbed her palms together gently, hoping to get some circulation going, wincing at the pain and the sticky feel of half-dried blood.

She took a tentative step, unsure if her legs would continue to hold her, then another and another, moving back toward the woods she had come from. Her eyes sought out some sign of the path, some break in the wall of endless green. When she couldn't find it, she simply plunged through the first halfway decent opening she found.

The idyllic peace of the woods had vanished. Now the chitterings and chirpings seemed taunting and menacing. What had once been a gentle breeze was now a trickster's toy, stirring limbs and rustling leaves, making Marlie whip her head back and forth in fear the man had come back after all. Shrubs and vines snatched at her every step; thorns ripped at her jeans. A cloud of tiny insects whined around her head in search of an easy meal, and she batted them away, only to have them return in seemingly larger numbers.

She stumbled along for what seemed an eternity before it occurred to her that she might be lost, that she might wander and thrash about well into the night while hundreds of tiny eyes watched from the shadows.

Stay calm, she told herself. *Think. Reason. Keep a clear head.*

What if she was wandering in circles? Or moving in the wrong direction, away from the house instead of toward it? She started to cry and hated herself for it. Feeling vulnerable and helpless was something she had grown familiar with during the year of her blindness. But never, ever had she felt this naked and defenseless. The numerous aches and pains that plagued her body dimmed in comparison to the anguish of her despair.

She had crested a small incline and started down the other side when a large tree root rose up from the ground and snagged her foot. First she windmilled her arms for balance, then, when she knew it was hopeless, she flung her hands out to break her fall. She tumbled and slid for several yards, rolling over shrubs, crashing into roots, finally coming to a halt against a tree stump. Pain burst through her body like fireworks.

The tears came full force now—hard, racking sobs. She didn't try to stop them, didn't try to move, just gave them full release, letting them purge her anger and frustration. When she was spent, she sat up and looked around, totally at a loss as to what to do next. In front of her was a solid wall of trees and shrubs. Same thing behind her and to her right. But to her left, about ten feet away, was an opening and, beyond that, a lighter swath of land.

The path.

The sight of it recharged her batteries, and she clambered stiffly to her feet, taking a moment to brush away the sticks and moss clinging to her clothes and hair. Her mind cleared, her thinking suddenly straight and focused. She worked her way to the path, then stopped and raised her face to the sky, gazing through the overhead canopy of trees. The sun was to her right, low on the horizon. She knew the woods lay east and north of her house, so to get home, she needed to head west. Turning toward the sun, she hurried along the path.

Ten minutes later she broke into the clearing that held her house. Its shadowy shape rose up several hundred yards away, and she locked on the image like radar, storing it in her mind. Then she focused her eyes on the ground, determined not to fall victim to more obstacles. She moved ahead at a rapid but cautious pace, eager to get inside, eager to be safe, eager to find help.

Wait.

The image of her house as she had just seen it flashed through her mind, and she realized something . . . some *thing* about it was wrong.

A car.

That was it. She had seen the shape of a car parked in front of the house. Puzzled, she slowed her pace and raised her head, looking again.

The man was only a few feet away, and as he reached his arms out to her, Marlie screamed.

chapter 14

He grabbed her roughly by the arms. "Marlie! Jesus Christ, what's wrong?"

"William?" she said, her voice hoarse and weak. "My God, William." She slumped gratefully against him, wrapping her arms around his neck and clinging to him as if he were a life raft.

"Marlie? What the hell is going on? And what are you doing out here? When I couldn't find you in the house I was worried sick." He pried her away from him and gave her a head-to-toe perusal. "Christ, look at you. You're bleeding everywhere. Marlie, talk to me."

Her chest heaved with panic, each breath like a stab wound in her side. "There . . . there was a . . . an accident," she managed. "In the woods."

"An accident? In the woods? You were in the woods? Alone?"

Marlie nodded. Her throat felt raw.

"What the hell were you doing in the woods?"

"Walking," she wheezed with some irritation. "William, I saw something . . . someone . . . out there." She gestured back toward the clearing and winced as the movement made another set of fireworks go off in her ribs. "A man . . . and a woman. I think he killed her."

"What?" The question came out like a gunshot. "Who killed who? What the hell are you talking about?"

"We need to call the police. Now!" She ducked from beneath his hands and headed toward the house. Every step was agony, and the ankle that had caught in the tree root felt stiff and swollen. She knew she had to keep moving while she still could, but she didn't get far before William grabbed her. Not hard, but strong enough to halt her progress and trigger more lightning bolts of pain.

"Marlie, wait," he said. "Tell me what happened. Tell me what you saw."

"There's no time, William!" she snapped, shaking him loose. "There's a woman out there and she's either dead or injured. I need to get help." He let her go this time, following close on her heels to the house. She beelined for the kitchen and grabbed the phone, but when she tried to focus on the numbers, they were one big blur. She tried feeling for them instead, but the fingers on her left hand were torn and ragged, those on her right, numb. Frustrated, she handed the phone to William. "Call nine-one-one," she told him. "Tell them we need police and rescue out here now. Tell them someone may be dead."

William hesitated. "Marlie, tell me—"

"For God's sake, William! Just do it, dammit!"

An ambulance attendant had already wrapped Marlie's ankle, fitted her with a rib belt, and was cleaning the wounds on her hands when Carvelle arrived, storming through the front door with all the quiet and subtlety of a mad bull. Marlie heard him holler "Where is she?" at one of the myriad police officers milling about the house. A moment later he charged into the kitchen, halting a few feet from where Marlie sat at the kitchen table.

Marlie looked up at him and flinched when she saw his glowance. It was dark, as black in spots as the one she had seen surrounding the man in the field. But where the earlier one had been dense and solid, Carvelle's was gauzy and mottled, interspersed with gray. Nor was there the pendulous weight she had seen in the other one. Carvelle's glowance was spiked and turbulent, like the leading edge of a massive storm front. They were different, no doubt, but the similarities were strong enough to make Marlie shudder.

"What the hell happened here?" Carvelle asked of no one in particular.

Marlie stared at him, but offered no answer. She really didn't know what had happened. Though her house and the surrounding grounds were swarming with police, she had yet to hear what, if anything, they had found in the clearing.

For a while, she had entertained the hope that her interpretation of things was totally off the mark. Perhaps the woman wasn't dead after all, her body lying at the bottom of a cliff. But then the policemen around her grew secretive and somber, huddling in the corners and whispering among themselves. The officer who had been the first to arrive, and who had made some general inquiries before heading outside to investigate further, returned some twenty minutes later with a much more pointed list of questions. The air of breezy officiousness he'd displayed in the beginning had given way to grim seriousness. Marlie had answered him as best she could, until William stepped in and brought the questioning to a halt.

"Don't say anything more, Marlie," he said. Then he turned to the officer. "As her lawyer, I'm advising my client not to say anything more until I've had a chance to confer with her."

"You are not my lawyer, William," Marlie grumbled.

"She's a witness, not a suspect," the officer said with admirable patience.

"Yes, but we all know where such things can lead," William argued. "Give me some time to talk to her first."

"For God's sake, William!" Marlie snapped, aggravated by the pain that resulted from the paramedic's ministrations. "I don't need a lawyer. I didn't do anything. Now, get out of here and let me talk to Officer Gellar."

"Marlie, I'd advise you—"

"I said, get out."

He had stormed from the kitchen, obviously pissed, and Officer Gellar had resumed his questions, taking Marlie step by step through the sequence of events.

Now, with Carvelle's thundering arrival, Gellar steered the detective into the hallway just outside the kitchen and started filling him in on what he knew. He kept his voice low, no doubt thinking Marlie wouldn't be able to hear what he said.

She heard every word.

"We got us a homicide," Gellar said. "Woman,

mid-thirties. She's in a ravine about a mile from here on the other side of the woods. Her body was dropped over a cliff so it's pretty messed up, but from the marks on her neck, I'd say she was strangled."

"How does *she* figure in?" Carvelle asked, and though Marlie couldn't actually see him, in her mind she saw him toss his head in her general direction.

"She witnessed the whole thing."

"Witnessed?" Carvelle said, his voice askance. "But she can't—" He bit off the rest, but Marlie knew what would have followed. "What the hell was she doing out there?"

"Said she was taking a walk," Gellar explained. "Apparently she happened onto the scene either while the murder was in progress or just after it happened, before the guy ditched the body."

"How'd she get banged up? Did he attack her? Can she ID him? Can he ID her?" His questions shot out like machine-gun fire.

"No," Gellar said with a weighty sigh. "She's vision impaired, so she couldn't make out much detail and never got that close to either of them. Said she went to look for the woman after the man left, thinking she was lying in the weeds. Problem is, she didn't know the cliff was there. Apparently she went over the edge—that's how she got banged up— though she managed to keep from falling and pulled herself back up by grabbing onto a chunk of the weeping love grass that's growing out there. She's one lucky woman. That cliff is at least a fifty-foot drop. By all rights, she oughta be dead, too."

Marlie suppressed a shudder and squeezed her eyes shut.

"Was the man on foot?" Carvelle asked.

"He was while she saw him," Gellar answered. "Though she did say that after he disappeared into the woods she heard a car start up off in the distance and drive away. She said it made a crunching sound, like it was on gravel. There is an old gravel logging road out there. In fact, if you follow it around far enough, it will take you to the bottom of that cliff, although at the moment there's a dead tree across the road, blocking any access. I have some men out there now, looking for tire tracks. Unfortunately, the gravel doesn't make for the best imprint."

"Christ," Carvelle said. "What a friggin' mess." There was a moment of silence. "This guy didn't see her, did he?"

"She says no, though I don't know how she can be so sure with her vision as bad as it is. Then again, if he had seen her, I imagine she'd be dead too."

"What a friggin' mess," Carvelle said again.

"There's one other thing," Gellar said. "We have a tentative ID on the victim. Thought we recognized her just on visual, but she's pretty banged up so we weren't sure. However, we found a work ID in the pocket of the blazer she was wearing." He paused dramatically, and Marlie held her breath, her ears perked.

"Well?" Carvelle thundered, clearly impatient. "Who is it?"

"It's Veronica Cumberland," Gellar said.

Marlie gasped before she could catch herself.

The paramedic, thinking he had hurt her, muttered an apology.

"Better known as Ronni Cumberland," Gellar continued. "One of the head reporters over at WKAL, which just so happens to be where Ms. Kaplan here used to work."

chapter
15

Marlie found herself alone in the kitchen for the first time since she got back from the woods. The paramedic had left some time ago, and the continuous flow of police officers streaming through for a cup of coffee, the use of the phone, or a glass of water had ceased. A short while ago Carvelle had shooed the last of them out of the house and, at the moment, he was out there with them. William hadn't shown his face back in the kitchen since Marlie tossed him out, and she had no idea if he was even still around.

She knew from the deepening length of the shadows that the hour was growing late, though she didn't know the actual time and frankly, didn't much care. Her mind was too busy digesting the fact that the murdered woman she had seen was Ronni.

Time and again she replayed the scene in her mind, wondering what Ronni was doing out there in the first place, and who her murderer might have been. Ronni had been killed in what amounted to Marlie's backyard. Was that purely coincidence? Had Ronni been on her way to see her? Marlie shook her head. That made no sense. There was no reason she could think of that Ronni would come by, and even if there were a reason, why would she use an abandoned logging road that required a hike of a mile or more in order to reach the house? Hell,

Marlie hadn't even known that road existed until today and doubted it could be found on any area maps.

None of it made any sense. And the more she thought about it, the more frightened she became. She wrapped her arms tightly around herself, watching the shadows grow longer with each passing minute and wishing someone would turn on the lights. She thought about doing it herself, but the switch was across the room and she wasn't at all sure her bruised and battered body would get her there in one piece. Dammit, she wished Carvelle would come back inside, or that her mother were here. The darkness, combined with the utter stillness on the heels of the industrious noise of the past few hours, was both unnerving and suffocating.

She eyed the phone on the wall across the room and thought about calling Roberta. Sooner or later, her mother would have to know what happened. And night was rapidly approaching. Marlie didn't much like the idea of spending it alone in the house. Gritting her teeth, she pushed herself out of the chair, her body fighting her every inch of the way. It hurt like hell, but she shoved the pain aside as best she could, knowing she had to move around some or, at the rate her muscles were stiffening up, she'd be totally immobile in no time. She worked her way across the kitchen with the bowed and shuffling gait of a woman three times her age. First, she hit the light switch, banishing the shadows that lurked in the corners. Then she reached for the phone, but the bulky bandages on her hands made it nearly impossible to pick up the receiver. She fumbled it out of the holder, then promptly dropped it on the floor. "Dammit!"

"Need a hand?"

Marlie jumped at the sound of the voice and whirled around, eliciting enough pain from various parts of her body that she saw stars. "Carvelle!" she said, wincing. "You nearly scared the life out of me."

"Sorry." He eyed her a moment, then walked over and settled a hand on her shoulder. "Are you all right?" he asked gently.

Marlie nodded.

"The paramedic said you refused to go to the ER."

"I don't need a hospital. I'm sore as hell, but I'll live."

Carvelle sighed heavily, then bent over to pick up the phone. "Did you call someone?" he asked, placing it back in the cradle.

"Not yet. I was about to call my mother, to see if she could come over."

"She's already on her way."

Marlie's eyes grew wide with surprise. "She is? How?"

"I called her myself a few minutes ago on my car phone. I figured you would want her here."

"I see," Marlie said, grimacing as a vicious spasm coursed through her back.

"Dammit, you should see a doctor," Carvelle grumbled.

Marlie waited for the spasm to pass so she could speak. "I'm fine, Carvelle. Besides, my mother is a doctor."

"Fine. At least go sit down. You look like you're about to collapse any second." He wrapped an arm gently about her waist and helped her shuffle her way back to the table. He eased her into a chair, then grabbed another one, setting it down so its back was directly in front of her. He straddled it, resting his arms along the top and settling his chin on his hands. "Want to tell me what you were doing in the woods?" he asked.

Marlie scowled at him. "I was taking a walk, enjoying the sunshine," she said, the pain making her feel irritable. "Why is that so hard for anyone to comprehend?"

Carvelle shrugged. "It's not, but it is a little out of character. Let's forget *why* you were out there and move on to what happened." He paused, then said, "You know who it was, don't you?"

Marlie nodded.

"Did you know who it was when you first saw her?"

"No. I had no idea until I heard Gellar tell you out there in the hallway."

If Carvelle was surprised she had overheard their conversation, he didn't show it. "Any idea what she was doing out here?"

"None at all. When I saw her at the station this afternoon—"

"Whoa! Hold up," Carvelle said. He tipped his chair onto its back legs, leaning closer. "You saw Ronni this afternoon at the station? At WKAL?"

"Briefly, yes," Marlie answered, reliving the sting of humiliation that had marked her visit with Granger. "I was there for another reason, but I bumped into her and we exchanged a few words in the hallway."

"But you didn't make any arrangements to meet her out here for some reason?"

Marlie shook her head. "I didn't even know that clearing existed. I've walked more than a hundred feet or so into those woods before today. Even when . . . even before," she finished, her voice dropping.

"Did she say anything to you while you were talking that might shed some light on any of this?"

"Well, sort of," Marlie said, biting her lip when she realized she was going to have to cop to eavesdropping outside Ronni's office door. "It wasn't anything she said exactly, but rather what I heard. When she was on the phone. I was outside her office in the hallway," she explained with a tinge of embarrassment.

Carvelle's head thrust forward a few inches, like a curious turtle. "What? What did you hear?"

"Basically, it was a squeeze play. She was telling whoever was on the other end of the phone that she was about to expose them, or something about them. She was calling to offer the person a chance for rebuttal, to tell their side of the story."

"Is that normal procedure?"

Marlie shrugged. "Depends. If you truly have the goods on someone and you're absolutely sure your facts are right, there's nothing that says you have to let the person know. Most people do, however, sometimes out of courtesy, but more often because it spices up the story and can make for some pretty hot film clips. On the other hand, if the facts are a little murky, it's always safer to present both sides of the issue, and let anyone involved have a say. That way you avoid getting sued."

"Which do you think this was?"

"The former. Ronni was pretty confident on the phone, said she had plenty of proof. Though she has been known to bluff. We all do at times while we're still trying to get the facts. But judging from Ronni's past behavior, I'd wager she was looking for a reaction rather than being considerate. She wasn't the common-courtesy type, if you know what I mean."

Carvelle nodded. "Go on. What else did she say?"

"Well, she agreed to meet whoever it was, alone, without a camera crew or anything, to discuss things."

"Meet them when?"

Marlie screwed up her face, trying to remember Ronni's exact words. "I'm not sure. I don't think she said when, or if she did, I don't remember it."

"Damn."

"But . . . she did tell me later, when we were talking in the hallway, that she was on her way to meet someone, and if she didn't get going she'd be late. I'm not sure if she was going to meet the same person she was talking to on the phone, though I did get that impression."

"I don't suppose you have any idea who it was on the phone?" Carvelle asked, with a tone that suggested he already knew the answer.

"Sorry, no."

"No clue at all? Could you tell if it was a man or a woman? Think back. Was there anything she said or did that might give us a hint?"

Marlie closed her eyes, thinking back, trying to recall each word of Ronni's end of the conversation as it drifted out over the transom. Bits and pieces of it came back to her. *I intend to expose everything I know . . . I'm offering you the opportunity to present your side . . . I'll be happy to meet with you but understand, it's not going to change things . . . the public has a right to know . . . I don't see how you can possibly defend any of this . . . trust me, I have proof aplenty, and it's solid . . .*

Marlie was shaking her head, about to tell Carvelle there was nothing there, no clue. But then her memory went a step further, remembering the sounds she had heard once Ronni had hung up the phone. She sat bolt upright, the movement making her back scream with pain. "Of course!" she said, wincing. "The tape! Why didn't I think of that sooner?"

"What are you talking about?"

"Ronni would have taped the conversation. She taped them all. Everyone knew it. It's illegal as hell, but for some reason no one's ever called her on it."

Carvelle catapulted himself from the chair and hurried from the room. Marlie heard him open the front door and call to one of the officers. She couldn't make out what followed next, but it didn't matter; she was fairly certain Carvelle was dispatching someone to Ronni's office immediately to collect any tapes they could find there. Granger would stroke out.

A few minutes later he was back, again straddling the chair in front of her. "Sorry," he mumbled. "Let's move on to what happened out there in the field. Tell me everything you can remember, everything you heard, or saw."

Marlie did as he requested, beginning with her

decision to take a walk, her progress along the path, and the odd screech she had heard, followed by the grunting sounds. But when it came time to describe what she then saw in the clearing, she paused. Should she mention the glowances? She suspected Carvelle would lend them little credence, more interested in solid facts than some visual aberration. Admitting to them might even lessen her credibility as a witness in his mind. Yet she couldn't shake the feeling that they were somehow critical, particularly when it came to the pendulous black evil that had surrounded the man.

Misinterpreting her hesitation, Carvelle said, "Gellar told me about the cliff. I know how badly that must have shaken you up, but I need to know what happened out there, Marlie. Everything."

His mention of the cliff brought back all the horror of that moment, and Marlie shuddered. "It shook me up, all right," she admitted.

"You're damned lucky you didn't kill yourself," Carvelle said a bit gruffly. "What the hell were you thinking, walking around out there on your own like that?"

Marlie folded her arms over her chest, trying not to wince at the pain it caused. Her eyes shot sparks. "You know, I *am* a big girl, Carvelle. I'm quite capable of taking a simple walk by myself for Christ's sake. I'm not some helpless little cripple."

Carvelle burst into laughter, and Marlie stared at him, unsure if she should be amused, angry, or merely stunned.

"Sorry," he said, still chuckling. "It's just such a shock to hear that sort of feisty independence coming from you. I had heard you were capable of it, but I've never seen it before. It's rather refreshing."

Marlie scowled at him, part of her pleased that he was pleased, but the rest of her mightily miffed that he was so enjoying himself at her expense. "Don't play shrink on me, Carvelle. It doesn't suit you."

"Okay," he said, doing a lousy job of suppressing his mirth. "Sorry." He cleared his throat and shifted in the chair. "Let's start over, shall we? Tell me what you saw when you first came to the clearing."

Marlie let out a weighty exhalation and squeezed her eyes closed, taking a moment to summon up the scene. "I could tell there were two of them," she began. "And judging from their size and shape, I was fairly certain one was a man, the other a woman." She opened her eyes and looked at Carvelle, who was staring back at her intently. His glowance had turned to a rose-colored swirl, but as soon as she opened her eyes, it began a rapid fade to gray. She closed her eyes again, part of her mind returning to the scene in the clearing, the other part keenly aware of Carvelle's gaze upon her. "I hid behind a tree and watched them, trying to figure out what was going on. To be honest, I thought at first that I'd happened onto a couple of lovers rendezvousing in the boonies. But then I realized something wasn't . . . right. That the woman was in danger."

"Was she still alive at that point?"

Marlie sucked in her lower lip, then released it, raking her teeth over it as she did. She opened her eyes again, looking at Carvelle with a sad expression. "I don't know," she said. "She didn't seem to be moving, but I don't know if she was already dead or just unconscious." Her expression turned to one of agonized guilt, and she punched her thigh. "Damn! I should have done something, said something. Maybe I could have stopped it. Maybe Ronni would still be alive."

Carvelle reached over and settled a hand on her arm, his thumb idly stroking her skin. It occurred to Marlie that tonight was the first time in all the months she'd known him that he had actually touched her. "You did the right thing," he said. "Had you tried to interfere, chances are both you *and* Ronni would be dead."

She knew Carvelle was right, but still couldn't shake the feeling that she was somehow responsible.

"Tell me," Carvelle went on, his tone curious. "You obviously couldn't see these two people very clearly, yet you approached the clearing quietly and then hid behind a tree. What was it that made you wary of the whole scene in the first place? I mean, how did you know the woman . . . Ronni . . . wasn't just ill, or that these two weren't lovers?"

"Well, there was the sound, that odd grunting noise. It seemed . . . I don't know . . . wrong somehow." She paused a moment, thinking, then decided, *what the hell*. "And then there were the glowances," she said matter-of-factly. She chewed on her lip again, her eyes focused on Carvelle.

"The what?"

"Glowances. That's how I think of them." She went on to give him a brief explanation of her childhood night-light and how the term glowance had been created. "I suppose you could call them auras. They're clouds . . . coronas of light and color that emanate from everyone I see. They've been present ever since my surgery."

"Okay," Carvelle said slowly, thoughtfully. "So there were these . . . glowances around Ronni and the man in the clearing?"

Marlie nodded. "Normally, they appear as a light, a radiance that encircles a person. But in the case of this man, it was more like the dark, a heavy black void that clung to his body like a thick swarm of gnats." She paused and shuddered with the memory. "It had power, presence," she went on, her voice haunted. "I could feel it. It was like evil itself, manifested in the form of this shifting blackness."

Carvelle stared at her. "So, these glowances you see, they're different from one person to the next? What I mean is, could you identify someone from their glowance?"

Marlie knew where he was heading and almost hated to burst the bubble of hope she could hear in his voice. "They are somewhat different with each person," she said. "But they change all the time, both in size and color. I think . . ." She stopped and shook her head.

Carvelle leaned forward. "What? What do you think?"

Marlie shrugged. "I don't know. This is all conjecture on my part and maybe they're nothing more than a weird medical aberration. But they seem to be related to emotion or thought. For instance, if someone is happy they seem to have a large, radiant glowance. Usually gold or white. Love appears as pink. That kind of thing."

"I see," Carvelle said, nodding again. "So a person's glowance might be pink one minute and gold the next. Is that what you mean?"

"Basically, yes."

"Did Ronni have a glowance when you saw her out there?"

Marlie grimaced. "Sort of. I suppose that was another reason I felt something was wrong. Her glowance was thin and pale gray, like wisps of smoke. And it was fading, almost as if the wind was carrying it away. Soon it was gone altogether." Another wave of guilt hit her as she realized the presence of Ronni's glowance when she first saw her might have meant she was still alive.

There was a long stretch of silence, and Marlie sensed Carvelle had come to the same conclusion, assuming, of course, that he put any stock in all this glowance crap to begin with. Finally he said, "Okay, continue. What happened after Ronni's glowance disappeared?"

Marlie filled him in on the rest of her story, explaining how the man had dragged Ronni across the field and left her lying, or so Marlie had thought, in the tall grass. Wishing to avoid yet another lecture, she skimmed over her own travails at the cliff, and also left out the fear and desolation she had felt in the woods as she had stumbled about trying to find her way back to the house. Instead, she skipped to the part where she had finally exited the woods and run into William.

"William?" Carvelle said, his tone puzzled. "You mean he was already here when you came out of the woods? You didn't call him when you got to the house?"

"Call him? Hell no! Why on earth would I call William?"

"Then why was he here?"

The question carried an obvious undercurrent of suspicion, as did the tone of Carvelle's voice. Until now, Marlie hadn't given much thought to why William was there. She'd been so glad to see him—to see anyone—that the mystery of why he was there at all hadn't occurred to her. Now she wondered. Then she realized that today was Thursday and that William—as well as Kristen—was supposed to be in Florida for another week or so.

"I don't know," she told Carvelle. "With all the excitement going on, I never thought to ask him. Is he still here?"

"I don't think so." Carvelle rose from his chair and walked over to look out the window. "Your mother is here," he said, his voice distracted.

Roberta strode officiously into the kitchen, moving quickly to her daughter's side. "What on earth is going on?" she asked. She felt Marlie's forehead, her palm cool and comforting. From there she reached down and grabbed Marlie's arms, examining the bandages.

Marlie felt five years old again, home in bed with the flu. She gently pushed her mother's hands aside. "I'm fine, Mom," she said, her voice carrying a surprising level of conviction. "Thank you for coming."

"You don't look fine," Roberta said. "You're pale as a sheet, your face is all scratched up, and you obviously did something to your hands. Would someone please tell me what the hell is going on?" She spun around and confronted Carvelle. "On the phone you said there was a murder?"

"It was Ronni," Marlie answered. "Someone killed Ronni."

Roberta's silence communicated her shock. When she did finally speak, it was as if her thoughts were spinning too rapidly for her to grasp onto any one. "But . . . she . . . Where? How?"

"I'll let your daughter fill you in on the specifics," Carvelle said. He turned to leave. "I've got some things I need to do."

Left alone, Roberta stared at Marlie, hands on her hips, one foot tapping with impatience. Marlie felt like a child who had been unwittingly and unwillingly placed upon the parental witness stand. She wondered if Roberta would chastise her impulsive foolishness for wandering into the woods in the first place, as had both William and Carvelle.

As quickly as she could, Marlie recapped the events, though she neatly skirted over the part about the cliff. She knew there was a chance someone would tell Roberta about it later on, but for now Marlie wanted to bury that part of the story; she felt foolish enough as it was. But she underestimated Roberta's attention to detail.

"What happened to you? To your hands . . . and the rest of you."

"I, uh, stumbled . . . when I was running back through the woods," she said. "I scraped myself up a bit. No big deal," she added with a shrug of indifference. Throughout her story, Marlie had looked directly at her mother, studying the subtle changes in her glowance as it appeared to calm down parallel to Roberta's demeanor. Now, with this blatant lie, she felt compelled to look away and stared out the window instead.

Roberta said nothing for a while, but she studied her daughter with an intensity Marlie could feel, if not see. Finally she said, "You stay here. I'll be right back. I want to talk to Detective Carvelle a minute."

"Carvelle? Why?" Marlie asked weakly.

Roberta ignored the question. "Sit tight," she said. "I'll be right back."

As Roberta left the room, Marlie hung her head and sighed with frustration.

chapter 16

Marlie had a restless night, haunted by nightmares when she tried to sleep and myriad sounds when she lay awake. The various aches and pains that coursed through her body didn't help. Twice she got up and found her way to the bathroom to swallow down a couple of aspirin, a task that should have been simple but was damn near impossible due to the bulky bandages on her hands. Roberta had offered to stay, just as Marlie had hoped, and she was grateful for her mother's presence. Just knowing someone else was there, a few steps or a mere call away, was reassuring. But it didn't stop the frightening images that seemed determined to intrude upon her mind.

When morning finally arrived, she was more than happy to see an end to the night. Her head felt drugged and fuzzy from a lack of sleep, and the rest of her body felt as if it were on the verge of rigor mortis. The delicious smell of fresh-brewed coffee told Marlie her mother was already up, and after doing a few minor exercises to try to loosen her joints, she followed the hypnotic scent to the kitchen.

"Good morning," Roberta said, her voice hoarse and groggy. Marlie guessed that she, too, had spent a restless night.

Roberta poured a cup of the fragrant brew and

carried it over to the table. Then she steered Marlie to a chair, taking the one directly beside her. "Let me see your hands," she said, reaching for them. "These bandages should be changed and I want to see what's underneath here. Besides, you'll never be able to drink your coffee with all this gauze." She began unwinding one of the bandages, shaking her head. "I don't know what it is with these paramedics and their love of gauze. You'd think they own stock in the company."

Once she had the hand exposed, she said, "That's not so bad. I think a little antibiotic ointment and a supersized Band-Aid will do fine. Be right back." She rose from the chair and left the room, heading for the bathroom.

Marlie gazed down at her hand, which lay palm up on the table, the fingers gently curled. She slowly made a fist, giving her fingers a test flex, relieved it didn't hurt too badly. Then she opened her hand wide, extending and spreading her fingers apart. That hurt like hell, the slices in her palm feeling as if they were trying to rip apart all over again. Wincing, she relaxed the hand again and waited for the pulsing pain to subside. She studied her palm, trying to see the wounds, but all she could make out were angry red blurs. Then she noticed her own glowance. At the moment, it was pinkish in color, calm, not turbulent. But near her hand, the banding circle of light thinned. She turned her hand sideways. Above the wounds on her palms, her glowance was very thin, almost not there. Almost as if the glowance itself had been sliced along with her skin. Marlie remembered her mother's story about David, the med student, and his claim that illness or injury somehow affected a person's aura.

Roberta came back, carrying the tools of her trade. She redressed Marlie's hand, then started unwrapping the other one. Marlie gave a practice hoist of her coffee cup with the newly bandaged hand, found she could manage just fine, and sipped it gratefully as she watched Roberta continue her ministrations. Once the second hand was revealed, Marlie could see the same odd thinning of her glowance around her palm, near the cuts. It thinned near the fingertips of this hand as well, since it was the one she had mangled on the boulder.

"There, that's better," Roberta said when she was finished. She leaned back and gave Marlie a critical look. "Don't take this personally," she said, "but you look like hell."

Marlie smiled. "I imagine I do. I didn't get much sleep."

"Gee, I wonder why."

Marlie let her gaze drift toward the window. The day looked to be another beauty; the skies were clear and brilliantly blue, the sun golden in its warmth. She wished her heart could be so bright and cheery. Her eyes settled on the bright red blur of Roberta's car, then she noticed a second car parked behind it. A faint glow shone from within, and she realized someone was sitting inside. "Is someone here?" she asked.

"Carvelle. He was here all night."

"Why?"

"I think he's concerned. About your welfare." Roberta didn't explain further; she didn't have to. They both knew what she meant.

"Shouldn't we invite him inside?" Marlie suggested. "It's kind of rude to just leave him out there like that."

"I did," Roberta said simply. "He declined. Said someone is coming to relieve him shortly."

Marlie digested that bit of information. Obviously Carvelle thought there was more than a chance that the man in the clearing might somehow know about her. The idea made uneasiness stir in the pit of her stomach, and she was glad for Carvelle's watchful presence. She wished she'd known he was out there earlier. Maybe then she would have been able to sleep.

"What would you like for breakfast?" Roberta asked, getting up and pouring herself a cup of coffee.

Marlie shook her head and gestured with her mug. "Just this is fine. I'm not very hungry."

"You should eat something."

"Maybe later." Marlie expected an argument, was in fact taking in a breath in preparation for one, but it never came. Curious, she turned away from the window and looked at her mother. This morning, her glowance was thin and transparent, bearing a frightening resemblance to Ronni's just before her death.

"Something is on your mind," Marlie said.

Roberta cocked her head and smiled.

"Out with it," Marlie encouraged.

"How can you tell?" Roberta asked. "The auras?"

Marlie nodded.

"Carvelle told me about them, about what you saw out there. Though he said you called them something else."

"Glowances," Marlie said. And once more she told the story of how the term had come to be.

"I remember that night-light," Roberta said with a wistful smile. "Your father picked it out for you." She shook herself, as if shaking off the memory. "Anyway, whatever you call these things, Carvelle's not sure what to make of them. Frankly, neither am I. But we both agreed it might be more than coincidence that what you saw was such an appropriate representation of what was happening. And I think you have begun to see some significance in these things yourself."

Again, Marlie nodded.

"I spoke with Linda Bosher late yesterday afternoon," Roberta went on. "When I explained what was going on with you, she was very excited. Said she'd love to meet and talk with you."

"When?"

"We didn't set a time. I wanted to get with you first. But I could call her back, see if she can fit us in today."

Marlie mulled the idea over. "You think this woman is legit, right? I mean, I'm anxious to figure out how to interpret these things, if there is any interpretation to be had. But I *don't* want to waste my time on a bunch of hocus-pocus."

"I know her reputation in the medical community," Roberta explained. "She's well respected, and her methods, while perhaps a bit unorthodox, have had good results. Beyond that . . ." She shrugged.

Marlie supposed the most she had to lose was an hour or so out of her day. She made her decision. "Let's do it," she said.

*   *   *

The office of Dr. Linda Bosher was located in a small house in the historic section of town. Marlie expected the place to have the same creaky floors, crooked doors, and lingering musty smell of age that plagued most such places, including her own. But while the building may have shown its age structurally, Marlie was pleasantly surprised to find that the air inside the office had a clean, outdoorsy smell to it.

After checking in with the receptionist, Marlie and Roberta settled into comfy waiting-room chairs. It was late afternoon, and the sun streamed in through a curtained window off to their side, cutting a wide swath of dappled light down the middle of the room. Marlie stared at it, her thoughts running back to the previous day's walk in the woods, remembering how the sunlight had created a similar, though more distinct pattern along the path. It occurred to her what a godsend it was to see the sunlight at all when, just over a month ago, she had thought she'd never see any light again. Then, she thought of Ronni and realized she had much to be grateful for, not the least of which was her life.

Her thoughts then turned to Kristen, and she frowned as she remembered her latest fury with William. She had called him earlier today, determined to find out just why he had shown up at the house yesterday. He claimed he had been called back to town on urgent business and that he had stopped by to drop off a gift Kristen had bought in Florida. When no one answered the door, he assumed Marlie was out with Roberta. But then he saw Roberta—alone in her car—a half hour later. So he returned to the house and found the door unlocked and Marlie's purse inside. That was when he became concerned that something might have happened to her. His explanation was clipped and defensive, making Marlie wonder if Carvelle hadn't already questioned him on the same matter.

The thought of William prowling around inside her house when she wasn't there was annoying enough to Marlie, but it wasn't the main reason she was angry with him. That came about when he told her that Kristen had stayed behind in Florida, electing to extend her visit with her grandparents another week. Marlie suspected it was merely William's latest attempt at distancing her from her daughter.

A door opened, jerking Marlie's thoughts back to the here and now, and she looked up to see a tall, slender woman with light-colored hair step into the waiting room. Her glowance radiated warmth in a welcoming yellow-gold corona. She glanced toward Marlie and Roberta, then quickly closed the distance between them, one hand extended in greeting.

"Dr. Gallaway, I presume?" she said, offering the hand to Roberta first.

Roberta nodded, rose from her chair, and accepted the proffered hand, shaking it vigorously. "Please, call me Roberta," she said.

"Only if you'll call me Linda."

"Fair enough, Linda." Roberta released her hand and gestured toward Marlie. "And this is my daughter, Marlie Kaplan."

Marlie stood, but rather than accepting the

woman's handshake as her mother had, she held her hands out, palms up, displaying her bandages.

"Oh, my," Linda said. "I think perhaps we will forgo the formalities in your case." Her gaze shifted up toward Marlie's face. "Yes, I recognize you from TV," she said. "Though your hair is quite different from the last time I saw you. Much shorter. I like it."

"Thank you," Marlie said. "Just one of the many by-products of my recent surgery."

"Ah yes, the surgery. I understand from your mother that the procedure has created a rather interesting side benefit."

Marlie looked skeptical. "I'm not sure how much of a benefit it is," she said. "For the most part, it's been more of a nuisance than anything."

"Well, that may be because you don't understand it yet, or know how to work with it. I must say, I'm really excited about this. It's rare that I can find someone who has the ability to see auras at all, much less to the extent you apparently can. I think this will be an enlightening meeting for both of us. Pun intended," she added with a chuckle. She turned her attention back to Roberta. "Will you be joining us?" she asked.

Roberta hesitated, giving a quick glance toward Marlie. "Well, I hadn't intended to," she said, though there was an anticipatory note in her voice that belied the words. She waited a few seconds more, then added, "I more or less just came along for the ride. Marlie can't see well enough to drive yet."

Marlie heard the disappointment in her mother's voice and watched as her glowance shrank and faded to a pale blue.

Blue, for feeling blue.

She knew the polite thing to do would be to invite Roberta to join them. After all, she was taking time out of her own day to chauffeur Marlie here and back, and having to sit in the waiting room killing even more time certainly didn't help. But Marlie wanted to discuss things with Dr. Bosher—at least this first time—alone.

"I'll try to make it quick, Mother," she said. Then, she tossed a conciliatory bone, as much to assuage her own guilt as to ease her mother's hurt. "And thanks for bringing me here. You've always been there for me, and I want you to know how much I appreciate it." She reached out and gave her mother a big hug. "I don't know what I'd do without you," she said, giving her a final squeeze. When she stepped back she saw that Roberta's glowance had already started to widen, its color radiating in shades of pink and gold. Smiling, she turned to Dr. Bosher and said, "Shall we?"

Dr. Bosher wasted no time in getting to the heart of the matter, starting in as soon as she and Marlie were seated. "I think this is so fascinating," she said. "I've been interested in auras for years, studying the various manifestations and interpretations. It took me a while to be able to see them myself, though once I got the hang of it, it became fairly easy. But if what your mother tells me is true, you can see them with a vividness no normal person could possibly rival."

Marlie frowned, chewing one corner of her lip.

"Something is bothering you?" Dr. Bosher asked.

Marlie shrugged. "I'm not convinced that these things I'm seeing are auras."

"Okay. Fair enough. Whatever they are, can you see one around me right now?"

Marlie nodded.

"Describe it for me."

"Well . . . it's a warm circle of light, bright . . . sort of radiant. It's wide, extending out a good foot and a half or more from your body, and the edges of it are waffling, almost as if it's breathing. Other than that, it's fairly constant and solid."

"Solid?"

"It's not twirling or moving much within the light."

"Others you have seen are more turbulent?"

"Some, yes."

"Okay. Go on. What color is it?"

"It's mostly gold and white, although there are hints of other colors in spots. Very subtle."

"Fascinating," Dr. Bosher said. "What you're describing certainly sounds like an aura, and the characteristics you describe are key to modern-day interpretive theories. But before I get into that, I want to get a feel for what your general knowledge of auras is."

"That's easy," Marlie said with a laugh. "Virtually none. I'm not sure I believe they exist."

"Oh, but they do." Dr. Bosher rose from her chair, walked over to a bookcase, and after perusing the titles for a second, grabbed a book off the shelf. "Have you ever heard of Kirlian photography?" she said, settling back into her chair and flipping through the pages of the book.

Marlie shook her head.

"It's named after Semyon and Valentina Kirlian, a Russian husband-and-wife team who lived in a small town in the Ukraine back in the thirties. Semyon was a maintenance worker who looked after electrical equipment in the local hospital. One day, he was repairing a diathermy machine and tested it by placing his hand on one of the pads as he activated the equipment. He saw what appeared to be a spark pass between the pad and his hand and wondered if the light from that spark could be photographed. With the help of his wife, he set up an experiment with photographic plates and managed to photograph what he and his wife believed was his energy field. The images created looked like a colored halo or coronal discharge."

Marlie frowned. "Can't the image be explained by more common phenomena?"

"Certainly there are those who argue such," Linda admitted. "But their arguments can't explain the phantom effect."

"The phantom effect?"

"Ah, here it is," Linda said, creasing the book open with her palm. She ran a finger down the page and began to read. "Researchers at UCLA proved through a series of experiments that when the correct frequency and potential are used to photograph a leaf, part of which has been cut away, the missing section of the leaf continues to appear in the photo as if it is still there. When photographed with a movie camera, the phantom image can be seen to fade in and out of the picture for about eight seconds before it disappears altogether.

"Not surprisingly, controversy over the cause of the phantom effect has arisen, and some argue that it results from residue left by the leaf on the film emulsion or glass plate. But researchers negated that theory by cutting the leaf *before* it ever came into contact with the film and then photographing it. The phantom image still appeared."

Dr. Bosher closed the book, folded her hands atop it, and looked at Marlie. "You look skeptical," she observed.

Marlie smiled. "I suppose I am, a little," she said. "It's all very fascinating, Dr. Bosher, but I'm not sure how it relates to my own experience."

"Please, call me Linda. And as for how it relates to you, let me expand on this aura theory a little more. They are believed by many to be an indicator of a person's physical and emotional state of being. A sort of energy field that reflects the subtle life energies within the body. They can reflect our health, our character, our emotional state. They can even, some believe, show the presence of disease long before the first symptoms appear. A diseased part of the body often has little or no aura around it."

Marlie thought back to her hands earlier that morning, and her mother's story about David Albright.

"Those who study this field more or less agree on all of those things," Linda went on. "Where the disagreement comes about is in deciding just how the varying shapes, sizes, and colors of these auras should be interpreted. Part of the problem with subscribing to any one theory stems from the differences that may occur because of photographic techniques, or, for those who can see the aura with the naked eye, the frequent vagueness of the images. That's why I'm so interested in your observations. If what you are seeing are, in fact, auras and not some bizarre manifestation of the computer chip in your brain, then you can provide a level of insight into this that has never been achieved before. Unless, of course, you want to believe the hundreds of hucksters who *claim* they can see auras but are really nothing more than New Age con artists."

"Then you admit there are some shysters out there."

"Oh, absolutely. But the fact that a few try to make a profit off a phenomenon they may or may not be actually experiencing, or even believe in, doesn't mean the phenomenon itself isn't real. Look at people's belief in some sort of god. Or in extraterrestrial life. Thousands, millions believe in those things, and who's to say they do or don't have some reality. No one can prove they do exist, but no one can prove they don't, either. It's that basic unprovability that opens the door for those who are looking to make a fast buck."

Linda set aside the book in her lap and leaned forward again. "Tell me something, Marlie. You've been seeing these auras for some time now. It's human nature to try to explain what we see, to associate it somehow with what we know or understand. Haven't you developed some sort of sense about these things? Haven't you begun to interpret them in your own way?"

Marlie thought a moment. "I suppose I have," she said. "What you said about one's emotional state. That's the connection I've made. The colors, the vibrancy of these lights seem to be reflective of the person's emotions." She paused, gazed off across the room, and smiled to herself. "You know, I used to think that interpreting what someone else was feeling was a product of analyzing their body language and facial expressions. Those are certainly the cues I used during my years as a reporter. But I've come to realize it's more than that." She looked at Linda. "Have you ever simply sensed that someone was upset? Or angry? Even though there were no outward signs to support that?"

"I have. I think we all have at some point. It's what some people refer to as vibes."

"Exactly! With the loss of my sight, I quickly realized that I could still sense a person's mood even though the usual visual cues weren't there. Of course, there are other hints, like tone of voice. But it's more than that. It's the vibe, as you call it. That's what these lights seem to be to me. Vibes."

"Well, if auras are a form of energy, as many believe, it wouldn't be a huge leap to think that this energy can somehow be felt by others," Linda said.

"I suppose not," Marlie said thoughtfully. "Though for me, it's a combination of seeing *and* feeling. I see what the light looks like, but I can also *feel* the emotional energy of the person I'm looking at."

"Tell me how you've reconciled the visual with what you sense."

Marlie leaned back in her chair and stared at the

ceiling. "Well, for starters I think that warmth, affection, and love manifest themselves in shades of pink. Hurt seems to appear—"

"Wait," Linda said.

Marlie lowered her head and looked at the woman with a curious expression.

"You're the skeptic here. So let me tell you how the modern theory I subscribe to interprets the colors, and you tell me if that jibes with your own experiences."

Marlie shrugged. "Okay."

"To start with, your interpretation of pink is right on the money. Hurt, the one you started to describe next, generally appears as shades of blue, often mixed with pink. Intellectual activity, or thought, generally appears as yellow or gold. Worry or concern is also yellowish in color. Happiness is gold to white. Anger appears as a dark or vivid shade, most often red which, oddly enough, is also the color of passion. Sort of in line with that old adage that there's a thin line between love and hate. Fear generally drains an aura of its color, making it appear gauzy or transparent." Linda paused, took a breath, and said, "How am I doing so far?"

Marlie gave her a grudging smile. "Not bad," she admitted.

"The general appearance of the aura changes with these emotions as well," Linda went on. "The happier or lighter the emotion, the more expanded and vibrant an aura is. Happiness is usually a very wide aura that seems to leap from a person's body, particularly the head and shoulders. Angry emotions tend to make an aura appear tight, drawn in, shut down. As does fear. The turbulence you mentioned earlier often matches the turbulence of the emotion being felt. The faster moving the aura is, the more turmoil the person is generally feeling. So while both thought and worry may appear as yellow, worry will produce a more active, more turbulent aura."

"What about hate?" Marlie asked. "What does hate look like?"

Linda cocked her head to one side and leaned back in her chair. "Hate?" she echoed. "True hate as opposed to anger?"

Marlie nodded.

"Black. As black as the heart of the person feeling it at the time. It's usually heavier, thicker than other auras. Intense anger can turn an aura black if it's strong enough, though more often it shows up as brown or green. And anger generally causes a turbulent, spiky type of aura, lacking the density of true hatred."

Marlie sat quietly, saying nothing, her mind recalling the chilling feeling she experienced in the clearing the day before.

"Have you seen an aura like this?" Linda asked.

Marlie sighed. "I've seen one worse than that," she said. "I think what I saw was pure evil."

chapter

17

It was Monday evening, and Marlie stood before the mirror in her bedroom, studying her reflection. In less than an hour she was accompanying Roberta to a political fund-raising dinner. It would be her first time out for a social event since the onset of her blindness. She was excited—and terrified.

Roberta, who had been volunteering with the Virginia Medical Society's political action committee ever since she retired, frequently attended such events. The numerous cocktail parties, golf outings, dinners, and the like gave her opportunities to meet with state lawmakers and lobby for the medical society's interests. Later, when the General Assembly was in session, it would make her efforts as a lobbyist that much simpler, since she had already laid down the groundwork. After four years of the work, Roberta now knew most of the state's legislators on a first-name basis. To her, the dinner was old hat.

To Marlie, it was rapidly becoming a terrifying prospect, and she was beginning to wonder what foolish impulse had made her decide to go along. She supposed boredom had been a factor to some degree. The same predictable routines she had found comfort in for the past year now made her restless and edgy. After being cooped up in the house all weekend, she was desperate to get out. The only thing that had provided an occasional break from the tedium was the ongoing news reports about Ronni's murder. It had remained the top story on all TV and radio newscasts, as well as a front-page item in the local newspaper, which Roberta read to Marlie each morning. Much to her relief, Marlie's name was never mentioned in conjunction with the crime, and while the proximity of the murder site to her house might have been problematic, as yet no one had made the connection.

Carvelle and his cronies had provided their watchdog duties all weekend with someone parked in an unmarked car in front of the house. But this morning Carvelle had announced the guards would cease after the current shift. Since it seemed that Marlie's involvement was known to no one other than the police, the on-site use of man-hours could no longer be justified. Plus, the forensics team had finished their investigation of the murder site and everyone was pulling out, leaving the area accessible to both the press and the general public. Should an overly curious reporter happen onto Marlie's property and notice the unmarked police car parked outside, he or she might make the connection that Marlie was somehow involved, a situation that could have terrifying ramifications.

Marlie had spent hours during the weekend mulling over Ronni's murder, trying to find some clue, some fact she might have overlooked. Twice she had spoken to Carvelle, hoping to glean new information, but all he had to offer were some details from the autopsy report, which revealed that Ronni had been strangled and was dead before she was tossed over the cliff, although the bruises left behind on her neck were, according to Carvelle, "atypical."

As for the tapes in Ronni's office, Carvelle said there were hundreds of them, each one containing several conversations. Though Ronni had preceded each taped conversation with a date, time, and the name of the person she was talking to, none of the tapes were labeled. Thus, Carvelle was forced to sit and listen to each tape from beginning to end, a task that proved to be both time-consuming and frustrating. Marlie had offered to help—she figured it would at least give her something to do each day—but Carvelle declined.

The more Marlie thought about Ronni's murder, the more it roused the investigator in her. It was the very type of sensational story she would have jumped on a year ago. She was itching to get back to work, she realized, and thought about talking with one of the other stations. This time, she wouldn't repeat the mistake she'd made with Granger. Before she asked anyone to hire her, she would arm herself with enough story ideas and work-ups to show she still had the talent and know-how, even if she was limited in some areas. Thinking about everything she needed to do was, at times, overwhelming, but she knew that somehow, some way, she would find herself a job. That was the only way she could ever hope to get Kristen back into her life.

It was primarily this determination that led to her decision to attend the dinner with Roberta. Marlie knew that many of the community's movers and shakers would be there, people with the type of power and contacts that could benefit her once she returned to work, or even help her find work. But the true clincher had been the person the dinner was being held for: Senator Richard Waring.

She had no idea if Waring was still interested in letting her do the interview, or if he might have already assigned it to someone else. But if there was any chance at all that she might still be in the running, she wanted to pursue it. Her initial distaste with Garrity's request and the rationale behind her as the choice had been a gut reaction. Now, she was more than ready to set her pride aside in exchange for an opportunity she knew would greatly enhance her chances for employment. She'd spent a lot of time during the past few days rationalizing it in her mind. There wasn't much she could do about her handicap, so she figured she might as well take advantage of any doors it might open for her. And if that meant serving as a political stepping-stone for Richard Waring's future gubernatorial campaign, then so be it.

It all seemed so logical when she thought about it, but as time for the dinner drew close, the reality of what she was about to do made her more anxious with each passing hour. She knew getting any time alone with Waring during the evening would be difficult, maybe even impossible. But worse than the prospect of not snagging Waring was her fear that she would somehow make a fool of herself or embarrass Roberta. To make matters worse, she was well aware that other journalists from a variety of media were likely to be in attendance. It was critical that she prove to them, and herself, that she was capable, able-bodied, and still able to think on her feet. One false move and the rumors would circulate through the entire journalistic community with record speed, dooming any chance she might have of being hired. The pressure she felt was enormous.

She dressed carefully and thoughtfully for the event, accepting Roberta's proffered help with her hair and makeup. For her dress she chose an above-the-knee, strapped, ivory silk number that came with a gold-embroidered bolero jacket. It also had a pair of matching gloves, and while Marlie thought they might be a bit too formal, she decided wearing them would be better than showing her bandaged and battered hands. The silk of the dress was deliciously cool and slinky against her skin, making her feel sexy and attractive. Though she couldn't see much more than a vague outline of herself in the mirror, she knew from when she had worn the dress in the past that it looked good on her, and while she was certainly not above using her feminine wiles to get ahead if she needed to, it was more the level of confidence the dress gave her that made her choose it. After much debate, she finally opted to finish off her ensemble with a pair of spiked gold heels, a decision she wasn't sure was wise. It had been over a year since she had worn heels of any sort, and these were higher, narrower than the utilitarian pumps she had worn during her working days. Heels like these would have been risky had she been able to see where she was going. Now, they gave a whole new meaning to the term "walking on the edge."

After several tottering practice runs in her bed-room, Marlie carefully worked her way to the living room, stepping slowly as she tried to accustom herself to the shoes. With each step her confidence grew a little more, and by the time she rounded the corner to the living room, her head was held high, her step far bolder than it had been just moments ago.

Someone—a man, judging from the size and shape—stood in the middle of the room. Marlie stopped short, one foot wobbling precariously on its skinny heel, her mind flashing back for a second to the woods on the day of Ronni's murder. But rather than the evil blackness, the glowance around this man was calm, complacent, and goldish pink in color. An instant later she recognized him, not from the way he looked but rather from the way he smelled.

"Hello," Carvelle said.

Marlie smiled at him. "You gave me a start for a second there," she said, one hand resting against her breast to still her racing heart.

"Sorry. Roberta saw me pull up and waved me inside. I think she's in her room."

"Oh."

An awkward silence followed as the two of them stood at opposite ends of the room staring at one another. Carvelle's glowance rapidly lost its warm color, turning into a smoky gray shroud that clung close to his body. Marlie thought back to her discussion with Dr. Bosher. This nearly transparent gray, she recalled, was symbolic of fear. Was Carvelle afraid of something?

"You going somewhere?" he asked.

Marlie nodded. "I'm going with my mother to a political dinner. A fund-raiser. I thought it would be nice to get out of the house for a while. The walls are starting to close in on me."

Another silence followed, and Marlie found herself growing irritated with the palpable tension that filled the room. Ever since the surgery, she had sensed something different about Carvelle, a shift in the paradigm of their friendship. It had first become apparent during his visit to the house after her discharge from the hospital. When he had questioned her the other night about Ronni's murder, he had seemed friendly and concerned. Yet as soon as Roberta arrived, he had taken his leave without so much as a good-bye, parking himself in the car all night and refusing to come into the house. Over the weekend he had stopped by several times to check on the guards posted outside and to provide Marlie and Roberta with updates on the investigation. But his behavior each time had been strictly formal and businesslike, as if merely being in Marlie's presence made him uncomfortable.

It was obvious to her that the easy camaraderie that had once defined their relationship had disappeared. She missed it, and the fact that she could neither explain nor understand it only increased her frustration. While she had no reason to believe her relationship with Carvelle was anything other than friendship, she couldn't deny an occasional thought—however subconscious—that it might someday be more. Now, she was beginning to wonder if she had manufactured the whole thing in her head. Perhaps the only motive behind Carvelle's visits over the past year had been a professional one. Or maybe she'd been fooling herself, too stupid to realize Carvelle felt sorry for her, just like everyone else. That would explain his recent withdrawal. Now that she had some sight back, his duties to the poor little blind girl could end.

The more she thought about it, the angrier she felt. Fueled by her insecurities about the coming evening, the flames of her ire flared.

Roberta walked into the room, breaking the stony silence. "Marlie," she said. "You look wonderful!" She turned toward Carvelle. "Doesn't she look wonderful?"

His only answer came in the form of a grunt, and Marlie felt the pain of his indifference tug painfully at her heart. She was hurting, but she'd be damned if she'd let it show. She thrust her chin at him, narrowed her eyes, and moved a few steps closer.

"Why so quiet, Carvelle?" she simpered. "Don't I look okay? Is something wrong? Don't you like the dress?" It was the same aggressive, rapid-fire sort of questioning that had made her journalistic interviews so successful. She pinned him with her eyes, hoping the intensity of her gaze was more focused than her actual sight.

"You look fine," Carvelle mumbled. His response couldn't have been more blasé.

"Fine?" Roberta echoed, the barest hint of a nervous titter in her voice. "You look better than fine, Marlie. You look stunning."

Marlie and Carvelle continued staring at one another, the tension between them thick and heavy. Marlie wished like hell she could make out his expression.

Roberta walked over and pulled gently on Marlie's arm. "We should be going," she said.

Marlie didn't move.

"We'll be late," Roberta tried, her voice a little sterner.

Marlie held her ground, waiting to see which of them would give in first. It was Carvelle who finally broke away by turning his head, raising his hand to his mouth, and coughing.

Marlie felt a rush of victory, but it was fleeting. Carvelle's odd behavior pained her enough that emerging triumphant in this particular battle of the wills gave her little satisfaction. Suddenly feeling as if she wanted to cry, she shifted her gaze to her mother and said, "I guess we best get moving. After you." Without looking back at Carvelle, she added, "Detective, I'm sure you can find your way out."

Roberta hurried from the room, apparently as eager to escape as Marlie was. Marlie followed, the vision of Carvelle, standing in the middle of the living room with that tight gauzy glowance wrapped around him like a shawl, stuck in her mind. Roberta opened the front door and stepped outside. Marlie was about to follow when she paused, curious as to whether or not Carvelle's glowance had changed in the few seconds it had taken her to walk to the door. She glanced over her shoulder for one last look at him and was startled half out of her wits to find him so close on her heels that he nearly ran into her when she stopped. His presence there rattled her. She hadn't heard him, smelled him, or sensed him in any way.

"For God's sake!" she gasped. "What are you doing sneaking up on me like that?"

"Sneaking up on you?" Carvelle repeated irritably. "What the hell are you talking about? I was merely following you out."

"Following me? Why?" Marlie shot back, knowing she was goading him but unable to stop herself. "I thought the watchdog patrol was over."

"In case you've forgotten," Carvelle said tightly, "I don't live here. Since the two of you are leaving, I thought it might be prudent if I did as well."

The filmy gray glowance was gone now, replaced by dark turbulent shades of red, green, and black. He pushed his way past her and stomped out to his car, muttering something under his breath.

Roberta ran after him, yelling for him to wait. He stopped beside his car where the two of them exchanged a few words that Marlie, despite her best efforts, was unable to hear. A minute or so later, he climbed into his car and started the engine, revving it along with his anger. The wheels spun up a cloud of dirt and dust as he maneuvered the vehicle in a fast three-point turn and disappeared down the driveway.

Roberta slowly walked back toward Marlie, stopping near her own car. "Are you coming?" she asked, the irritation in her voice apparent, though Marlie wasn't sure just who it was she was irritated with.

Marlie frowned, pulled the front door closed, and walked sullenly toward the car. The meager bit of self-confidence she had managed to drum up earlier was gone now, destroyed by the events of the past few minutes. Though the temperature outside was a moderate seventy degrees, the silk in her dress felt like ice all of a sudden. Wrapping her arms about herself to try and get warm, she wiped all thoughts of Carvelle from her mind and focused instead on keeping her balance as her heels wobbled precariously over the uneven ground.

They were almost at their destination before Marlie realized that she had no idea why Carvelle had shown up at the house in the first place.

chapter 18

The dinner party was being held in one of the nicer hotels in town. Tables had been set up in a giant U shape near the front of one of the ballrooms. A string quartet played in one corner, and their soothing melodies combined with the golden glow of a huge chandelier to lend the room a warm ambiance. More than fifty people were already there when Roberta and Marlie arrived, mingling about the room and talking in hushed tones punctuated by an occasional laugh.

Marlie had battled her nerves the entire length of the drive, still worried about her ability to pull off this first social event and still rattled by the frustrating exchange she'd had with Carvelle. Following Roberta through the hotel, her anxiety had risen in waves, finally reaching tidal proportions as they stepped through the doors of the ballroom.

"Wait," she said, grabbing Roberta's arm and pulling her back. "I'm not ready yet."

"Ready? Ready for what?"

"Ready for this." Marlie nodded toward the people milling about inside.

"Don't be silly," Roberta said. "No one here bites, at least not that I know of. You'll do fine. Just be yourself and mingle. It's like riding a bicycle. Pedal a bit and it will all come back to you." She gave Marlie a reassuring pat on the arm, then turned and walked away.

Marlie stood just inside the door and watched with mounting terror as her mother's shape melted into a nearby group of people, becoming indistinguishable from the mass. She was struck by a childish urge to run after her or, worse yet, to simply stand where she was and yell for her.

She took a few tentative steps deeper into the room, her heels picking up the faint tremors in her legs. Patting a nervous hand against her thigh, she scanned the throng, hoping to find someone else who stood alone, figuring a one-on-one would help ease her into the swing of things. But everyone was clumped together, their glowances blending and mixing in disorienting clouds of pink, gold, yellow, and blue.

Someone entered the room behind her, and after murmuring an apology, she stepped aside to let them by. She felt conspicuous all of a sudden, standing by the door, alone and nervous, an obvious fish out of water. She became convinced that all eyes were on her, watching, judging, and that people were whispering among themselves.

She zeroed in on a nearby group of people and moved toward them slowly, her eyes struggling to make out any detail among the blur of colors. The closer she got, the more annoying the glowances became, a gigantic cloud of mixing and mingling colors that obscured all else. There had to be someone here she knew. Over the years she had met several of her mother's colleagues; she desperately wanted to find one of them now. She tried to focus on voices, searching for one that might be recognizable, but they all swirled together in a loud murmur of sound, the perpetual humming of social bees.

A tiny piece of her confidence leaked away with every halting step she took, and she began to think this whole thing was a huge mistake. She should have started off more slowly instead of throwing herself into a situation that was too big to handle. Her chest felt tight and constricted, as if the air had grown too thin to breathe. The temperature seemed to rise several degrees, sending trickles of sweat weaving down her side. All those mingling glowances were like dozens of miniature suns, each one radiating an incredible amount of heat and burning all the oxygen from the room. Her heart pounded with the force of a hurricane surf, making the colorful coronas pulsate and shift like some giant living creature. A swarm of tiny twinkling lights flashed before her eyes as the walls of the room began to close in.

Oh, God. I think I'm going to pass out.

She had to get out of this room. If she fainted here in front of all these people she would make a total fool of herself. Sucking in a huge gulp of air, she turned back toward the door.

And froze.

Yet another assemblage—some twenty people or so—had gathered near the door. Like all the other groups, a mist of colors swirled and eddied around them, mixing and mingling until the shapes of the people who owned them became almost invisible. But near the center, one stood out clearly from the rest. It was black and pendulous, hanging as heavy as death itself and weighted with the distinctive mark of evil.

Marlie knew it in an instant.

The blood in her veins turned cold as ice, and the hair on her arms rose to attention. Her eyes roved over the myriad shapes in the group, trying to determine which one the horrifying blackness belonged to, but there were too many people, too many glowances obscuring her vision. Suddenly certain that the owner of that dark cloud was as focused on her as she was on him, she backed up a step or two. The mass of humanity behind her, which had seemed so onerous a moment before, now became a sanctuary. Slowly, she turned away from the entrance and faced the main part of the room.

Several groups of people were congregated nearby. She searched each one frantically for some sign of Roberta, hoping to distinguish her mother's glowance from all the rest. When that failed, she made an arbitrary choice and hurried toward the closest cluster of people, which was about ten feet away. She slowed as she approached the group's perimeter, giving one last glance over her shoulder toward the door.

The gathering by the entrance had dispersed like the first break on a pool table. Singles and couples spread out in all directions; several more people were coming through the door. Marlie searched everybody she saw, her head whipping back and forth, but the darkness was nowhere to be seen. It had simply disappeared.

Or had it?

Voices closed in behind her, the crowd swelling to the point that she was nearly a part of it now, and a new panic seized her. Her head craned around, scanning the glowances nearby, certain the black cloud had managed to join the mingling throng inside the room.

Nothing. It wasn't there. She searched the entire room, but all she could see were golds and pinks and blues radiating from every corner.

She wondered if she had imagined the whole thing. Maybe, in her panicked state, her mind had only imagined the black cloud. She gave her head a shake to loosen the grip of whatever insanity might be lurking there, and then another thought struck her. What if she hadn't imagined it? What if the black cloud *had* been there, still *was* there, and she couldn't see it now only because it had changed? She had seen how quickly they could alter their appearance—a matter of seconds in many cases. The owner of that black horror could be anyone in the room.

The group in front of her was about ten people strong and an arm's reach away. She backed up a step, anxious to keep a safe distance between herself and everyone else. Panic settled its stranglehold on her once again, and her only thought was of escape. Get out of the ballroom. Head for the foyer or the main lobby of the hotel. Once there, she thought, she could find someone—a hotel worker, or another guest—to hunt Roberta down and bring her outside.

She spun around, set her eyes on the door, and headed for it at a rapid clip. Halfway there, another thought struck her. Maybe the reason she could no longer see the black cloud in here was because it was out there . . . in the foyer . . . waiting for her.

She spun again, back toward the main part of

the room. The movement was a little too fast, too panicked, and she felt her foot give way as the slender heel of her shoe lost its anchor. The foot went one way, her shoe the other. She flailed her arms wildly to keep from falling.

"Whoa!" said a male voice. An iron hand gripped her arm. "Careful there."

Marlie stabilized herself and glanced up at her rescuer, relieved to see he was surrounded by a glowance that waffled with an enthusiastic golden-white color. He was tall and slender, his head topped by a mass of dark hair.

"Thank you," she said, feeling the flush of embarrassment flow up her neck like hot lead.

The man released his hold on her arm and said, "I don't know how you women do it. Those heels ought to be outlawed."

The voice struck a familiar chord, and Marlie struggled to place it. She squinted to get a better look at him, but his face remained a blur. Something about his hands drew her eyes there, and she was surprised to note that his glowance, which flared broad and bright around the rest of his body, thinned along his arms, eventually fading away altogether just above his wrists.

"It's a pleasure to run into you, Ms. Kaplan," he said with a chuckle. "Although I didn't expect to mean that quite so literally."

So he knew her. As someone who always prided herself on her ability to recall names and faces—or in this case, voices—Marlie was embarrassed by her inability to recognize him in turn. "I'm sorry," she said, smiling apologetically. "Your voice is familiar, but I'm afraid I can't see your face very clearly. I'm . . . a bit visually impaired."

"Well, I confess, I didn't recognize you immediately either. Your hair is different, much shorter." He paused a second, giving her an up-and-down perusal. "That, and the fact that your apparel this evening, while quite stunning, isn't what I'm used to seeing you in."

Marlie flashed him a puzzled smile. She definitely knew that voice. His identity hovered just beyond the boundaries of her memory. And something about his hands . . . the missing glowance . . .

"Please, forgive my rudeness." He reached over and took her hand, giving it a firm but gentle shake and continuing to hold on long after the official "shake" was over. Even though she was wearing gloves, Marlie could feel the twisted and uneven surface of his palm through the material, the result of severe scarring. It hit her like a flash who he was, just as he said, "I'm Richard Waring."

Marlie's eyebrows shot up at the revelation. "Richard Waring?" she echoed. "*Senator* Richard Waring?"

"I'm afraid so. Are you disappointed, a Democrat, or both?"

Marlie laughed, gave herself a mental slap for taking so long to recognize his voice, and tried to gather her wits. "None of the above. Just a little surprised to meet you. Actually, I was hoping to have a chance to speak with you this evening, but I never thought it would be this easy."

"Really?" he said. "Why?"

"Why was I hoping to speak with you, or why did I think it wouldn't be easy?"

"The former," he said with a chuckle. "I can guess at the latter." He glanced around the room, and Marlie took advantage of the moment to do the same. Still no sign of the black cloud. "You best hurry," Waring said. "I don't get these moments often."

"It's about the interview you wanted me to do," Marlie said. "Garrity called me several weeks ago and asked if I would be interested."

"Ah, yes. I understand you declined."

"I did," Marlie said with a nod, "but I would like the chance to reconsider. That is, if you haven't already gone with someone else."

"We've spoken to some others, although we have yet to make a decision." He cocked his head at her. "May I ask why you've changed your mind, Ms. Kaplan?"

Marlie considered her answer carefully. A dozen different platitudes, comments about her admiration for Waring or her support of his political efforts danced through her mind. But in the end she opted for the truth, something she thought Waring would respect. Not that she didn't admire the man or his work.

"I want to return to work, Senator Waring. But at this point my visual handicap seems to be too great an obstacle. The station turned me down when I asked to come back. Frankly, an exclusive with you might be just the ticket I need to get my foot in the door."

"Are you saying the station has refused to take you back because of your sight limitations?"

Waring's voice had a hint of righteous indignation in it, and Marlie saw her chance. Fighting employment discrimination of the physically handicapped was one of Waring's favorite causes. If she played her cards right, she just might be able to use that fact to her advantage.

"Unfortunately, yes. Although the station manager, Joe Granger, was smart enough not to admit that was the reason. He blamed it on budget cuts, but I happen to know the budget came through intact." Marlie sighed. She was laying it on thick, and she knew it. "All I asked for was a chance to prove myself, to show I can still do the job," she said wistfully. "Which is why I am asking you to reconsider me for your interview. Though you need to understand that I'm basically freelancing at this point. Without a station affiliation, there is no guarantee the interview will even air."

"I see," Waring said thoughtfully. "Is that why you turned down Garrity's request initially?"

"Partially, though I must admit I was a bit put off by his admission that the main reason you wanted me to conduct the interview was for the PR value my condition provided."

"Pardon me?"

"You know, your support of both women's issues and those of the handicapped. What better way to communicate that than by using someone who fits both those categories in your interview. I would make the perfect campaign poster child."

"Ms. Kaplan, I'm sorry if Garrity—"

"No need to apologize, Senator. I understand the logic behind the decision and to be honest, at this point my moral indignation has taken a backseat to my desire to return to work."

"But you don't understand," Waring said. "Garrity's implication that I wanted you as a showcase for my platform is totally off the mark. I asked him to contact you because I know and like your work. You're honest, forthright, and your reputation within your own profession is stellar. Probably the only negative thing I've ever heard about you is that you have a tendency to be a bit reckless at times, taking risks others might not. Personally, I admire risk takers. Your ability or inability to see has nothing to do with your job integrity and skills, Ms. Kaplan. Your handicap didn't play into my decision at all. In fact, I heard your handicap had been, uh, resolved with some sort of newfangled surgical procedure."

"Not resolved exactly," Marlie told him. "I'm still limited, though at least I can see something now."

"Look," Waring said, "I apologize for any leaps Garrity might have taken on my behalf. He tends to be a bit, shall we say . . . overzealous when it comes to some of his PR duties. I asked him to contact you because I admire and respect your work. No other reason. As I'm sure you know, a personal interview of any sort is not something I look forward to. However, I've come to realize it is something of a necessary evil at this point in my career. If I must do it, I would prefer it be with someone I feel I can trust. And you, Ms. Kaplan, fit that bill."

"Thank you. I appreciate your faith in my abilities, Senator."

A woman sidled up to Waring, slipping her hand around his arm. "Senator! So good to see you!" she murmured seductively. "Will you be long here? Because I have someone you simply must meet. Do you remember me telling you about Mr. Hollander?"

Waring smiled at the woman. "Hello, Marjorie. Do you know Marlie Kaplan?"

As the woman gave Marlie the once-over, her glowance took on hints of an ugly greenish brown color. "No, I'm afraid I don't," the woman simpered. "Should I?"

Marlie smiled. She knew exactly the type of woman Marjorie was. Filthy rich, probably divorced or widowed, and hoping she could buy herself an attractive rising politician for a future husband. Judging from Waring's own glowance, Marjorie was going to be disappointed.

"Ms. Kaplan is one of the best TV reporters in the area," Waring said. "In fact, I'm giving her an exclusive interview."

"Really?" Marjorie said, failing to hide either the skepticism or the jealousy in her tone. "That's nice."

Marlie was speechless, unsure she had heard him correctly and not knowing if she could believe him if she had.

Waring sighed and glanced around the room. "Well, as much as I've enjoyed our little chat, Ms. Kaplan, I guess I should go and schmooze with some of the other guests. That is my main reason for being here, after all. Thank you for your time, and I will be in touch."

He disappeared into the crowd on Marjorie's clinging arm. Marlie stood stunned, staring after him, afraid to believe.

chapter
19

It was as if the brief exchange with Waring gave Marlie the official stamp of approval. Within minutes of his departure the crowd swelled toward her, taking her into the fold. Introductions were offered and hands were shaken, enough so that her own began to throb. At first she was wary, wondering if one of them might be the owner of the mysterious black glowance. For a good fifteen minutes she kept glancing toward the door, expecting to see it there, watching and waiting for her. But eventually her struggle to keep track of who was who, matching names with voices since all the faces were a blur, became a full-time job, and she pushed all thoughts of the darkness to the back of her mind. Even if its owner was here, she realized she was in the safest place possible, surrounded by hundreds of people. Her earlier panic had been silly, and she was glad she had managed to get it under control before she made a complete fool of herself. She still wasn't convinced the whole thing wasn't some aberration of her own, manifested out of her fear and anxiety.

Many of the people she met knew her, either from her stint on WKAL or through Roberta. Everyone was polite, if a bit solicitous. Inevitably the story of her past came up, and at first she felt uncomfortable talking about the explosion, her blindness, and the surgery. But after the fifth iteration or so, with most people reacting with little more than polite curiosity, it became comfortably routine. Marlie was surprised to discover that a few folks even regarded her as some sort of heroine, simply for having survived that awful night. If anyone felt otherwise, they hid it well.

Forty minutes after her arrival, Marlie found she was relaxed and actually enjoying herself. She was no longer searching the crowd for some sign of her mother, and the mysterious black cloud was all but forgotten. Then, an all too familiar voice whispered in her ear.

"God, you look incredibly beautiful." Though the words themselves were flattering, their source robbed Marlie of any pleasure she might have felt.

"William," she said, turning to look at him, her displeasure apparent in her tone. "What are you doing here?"

William slapped a hand over his chest and gave her a wounded look. "Hell, Marlie. If I didn't know better, I'd think you weren't glad to see me."

Marlie glanced around to see if anyone was close enough to overhear their conversation. Seeing several people nearby, she grabbed William's arm and dragged him off to a more isolated spot.

"Whoa," William said with something that sounded disturbingly like a giggle. "Trying to get me off to yourself?"

Marlie released his arm and got up close to his face. Her nose wrinkled as she caught a strong whiff of alcohol on his breath. "You're drunk," she said with disgust.

William laughed. "I might be," he slurred. "But hey, so what if I am?"

"What are you doing here, William?"

"I was invited. "What are *you* doing here?" He took a staggering step back, and his head moved up and down as he scoped her out. "You really do look fantastic by the way," he added. "I was watching you earlier, right after you first arrived. You were a sight to behold."

Marlie opened her mouth, prepared to come back with some scathing remark, when someone grabbed her elbow for the second time that evening. This time, it was Roberta.

"Marlie? Is everything all right?" she asked with forced politeness.

"Why wouldn't everything be all right, Roberta?" William slurred, clipping her name so that it came out "Berta." He draped a possessive arm over Marlie's shoulder. "I'm simply having a chat with my wife." Marlie ducked from beneath his arm, and he tottered, nearly losing his balance.

"Ex-wife," Roberta shot back, emphasizing the "ex." She then cupped Marlie's elbow and steered her away. "I believe it's time to be seated for dinner. Shall we?"

As they walked away, Marlie heard William mutter "Bitch" under his breath and wondered if it was directed at her or her mother.

"I should have known he'd be here," Roberta said once they were settled at the table. "I'm sorry."

"It's not your fault, Mom. Besides, it's not as if I can avoid him forever."

"Well, other than that, are you enjoying yourself?"

"I am," Marlie admitted, almost surprised to realize it was true. "It was a bit scary at first, but once I got acclimated, things rolled right along." She debated mentioning the black cloud, then decided against it, still wondering if she hadn't imagined the whole thing.

"I noticed you seemed to be mingling okay," Roberta said, giving Marlie a soft nudge in the ribs with her elbow. "You even managed to snag time with Senator Waring. What were you talking about?"

"Just chitchat," Marlie said. She was reluctant to mention their discussion about the interview. Though she had clearly heard Waring declare to that Marjorie woman that he was giving Marlie an exclusive, she knew things were far from official. She didn't want to make a fool of herself by getting excited over something that might never happen.

"That's not what he said," Roberta said knowingly. "I chatted with him briefly myself, hoping to discuss the assisted-suicide bill that will be coming up this session, but all he wanted to talk about was you."

"Me?"

"Yes, you. He said he remembers you from when you were at WKAL and is quite impressed with your work."

"He just said that because you're my mother."

"I don't think so. His praise seemed pretty genuine to me."

Marlie tried to keep her face complacent, though on the inside her heart was leaping.

"He also said something about you doing an

interview with him? An exclusive, I believe he said."

That made two declarations. Marlie leaned closer to her mother and talked in a half whisper. "He did say he intended to give me an exclusive, although he said it to someone else, not to me. Do you think he means it?"

"It certainly sounded that way to me."

At last, Marlie allowed herself to believe, if only for the moment. Closing her eyes, she smiled with excited anticipation. "This could be just what I need, Mom. If I can go to Granger with an exclusive Waring interview in hand, don't you think he'll reconsider his refusal to hire me back?"

"He'd be a fool not to. And if he is that stupid, there are other stations I'm sure would be happy to take you on." She reached over and gave Marlie a brief one-armed hug, then withdrew as a waiter leaned in between them to set down their shrimp cocktails. "I think you're on your way, my dear," Roberta said when the waiter had moved on. She picked up her already loaded shrimp fork, dipped it into the rich red sauce, and held it aloft in front of Marlie. "Now, let's see if the food we get tonight is worth the five hundred bucks the medical society doled out for each plate."

The dinner was good, and Marlie found herself chatting throughout most of the meal with the gentleman seated on her left. He was a young physician—an internist—who had only been in practice a few years. His conversation was witty, his persona charming. When Marlie realized he was flirting with her, her self-confidence rose considerably.

As soon as everyone had finished eating, one of

the attendees stepped up to the podium and proceeded to introduce Waring. Waring himself was
greeted with thunderous applause and the light of a
thousand camera flashes. Marlie was fascinated by
the reaction it had on his glowance, making it pulse
with a vibrant golden glow that emanated warmth,
light, and charm. Pockets of color appeared in it, a
kaleidoscope of undulating shades that both
soothed and excited. Marlie couldn't help but wonder if this hypnotic cloud of energy had something
to do with Waring's current level of popularity.
Seeing it made her feel warm and happy and confident somehow. It seemed to have a life of its own, an
undeniable force she could almost feel. If it had this
effect on her, might it not affect others the same
way, even if they couldn't see it?

As Marlie listened to Waring talk, she found herself as enchanted with his rhetoric as she was with
his glowance. *He's definitely smooth,* she thought.
*Bright, captivating, intelligent, handsome . . . the perfect
mix.* That got her to wondering about his personal
life. Was he seeing someone? Back when she was
working at the station, there had been constant
rumors as to whom Waring might be dating and a
seemingly endless supply of interested and attractive
young women trailing him wherever he went. But
none of the chief suspects had stayed chief very
long. In fact, the apparent dearth of any significant
relationships with the opposite sex had even triggered a brief flurry of suspicion that the senator
might be gay. Thanks to her self-imposed isolation
over the past year, Marlie realized she was totally in
the dark as to the man's current status. Hell, for all

she knew, he might be married by now.

With a sigh, she thought about all the work she had to do to prepare herself for the interview. Prior to the warehouse explosion, she had begun building a file on Waring in hopes of getting just the sort of interview it now seemed was hers. A copy of the file was at home in her office—a fortunate stroke of luck, she realized. She had learned early on in her career that news happened when it wanted to, not when she was in the office. After several callouts at odd hours, where she found herself wishing she had the information contained in her work files, she had started copying all current files and storing them in her office at home. Having the information at her fingertips had proven to be extremely valuable on several occasions.

She wondered what had happened to her files at the station. Several of them were outdated by now and had probably been archived, but some had been long-term projects. She had no doubt that Ronni, or someone, had gone through them, but whether or not they had been maintained was anyone's guess.

As she watched and listened to Waring speak, she tried to recall as much of his file as she could, culling out those facts pertinent to the story she was already building in her mind. He was the CEO of one of Virginia's largest banks, having worked his way up over the years from his initial job as a teller. Adopted as a child, the identity of his birth parents remained unknown, and as far as anyone knew, Waring had never tried to find them. To all appearances, his adoptive parents had been loving and nurturing, Waring's relationship to them extremely close. It was that very devotion that had touched the hearts of many in Waring's community six years ago when his parents were killed in a fiery car crash. The tragedy was made even greater by the fact that Waring had also been in the car, barely escaping with his life only to then watch his parents burn to death. It was during his efforts to save his parents' lives that he had sustained the terrible burns that now scarred his hands.

The trauma of watching his parents burn to death, combined with the physical trauma of the accident itself, had led to a long program of mental and physical rehabilitation. It was months before he was able to resume his duties at the bank, as a head injury incurred in the accident had robbed him of much of his memory, chewing big holes in the past decade or so and forcing him to relearn many of the basics of his career, his friends, and his life.

A lesser man might have given up. Waring not only fought his way back, he did it with dignity, humor, and finesse, allowing adversity to mold rather than defeat him. His triumphs reflected much about his personal strength and determination; they also established him as something of an icon to the common man, many of whom had struggles of their own to overcome.

Another rumbling of applause reverberated through the room, marking the end of Waring's speech. Marlie shook off her musings and focused in on Waring as he left the podium. Within seconds, half the room had risen from their seats, merging together near the stage steps where Waring was now descending. The crowd quickly flowed around him, like some giant amoeba enveloping its prey. But even buried within a perimeter that was a dozen bodies deep, Waring was easy to spot. His glowance leaped from his head and shoulders in a hugely expanded corona that seemed bright enough to light up half of Washington. Marlie watched, transfixed by the radiance of that warm light, her mind already formulating the story she would do on the man she felt certain would be Virginia's next governor.

chapter
20

After arriving home so late the evening before and staying up to review the night's events with Roberta, Marlie was more than annoyed when the phone woke her from a sound sleep the next morning. She fumbled on the nightstand, found her watch, and flipped open the face. Her fingers told her it was a few minutes before eight, and she groaned, rolled over in the bed, and pulled the pillow over her head. On the tenth ring, she gave up, irritably threw the pillow aside, and snatched the offending device off the bedside table. "Hello," she grumbled.

"You don't sound very friendly."

Marlie's eyes shot open. "Granger?"

"I take it I woke you."

"You did," she said combing her fingers through her hair and wondering why the hell he was calling her at all, much less at this hour. "I was out kind of late last night."

"So I heard."

"Huh?"

"I mean I heard you were at the medical society fund-raiser last night."

"Heard from who?"

"Senator Waring. He called me himself, just a few minutes ago."

"He did?" Marlie's heart flip-flopped. "Um, yes.

I did speak with Waring briefly last night."

"Seems you did more than just speak to the man. I don't know what you did or said, but you obviously made one hell of an impression. He informed me he's willing to give the station an exclusive interview, a *personal* interview, but only if you are the one doing it."

The beginnings of a smile crept into the corners of Marlie's mouth. This was far more than she could have hoped for. "We did discuss an interview," Marlie said. "Although not in the context of any specific station."

"Yes, yes. He wants you, that much was clear. But surely you wouldn't take this to some other station, Marlie."

"What options do I have, Granger? You've already made it clear you don't want me back at WKAL."

"Yes, well . . ." Granger coughed, then cleared his throat.

Marlie's smile broadened, and she reached behind her head to plump up the pillow, settling herself in and getting comfortable. She was going to enjoy this.

"Listen, Marlie. About the other day when you came to the office . . . I . . . well . . ."

She knew he was struggling, and also knew he was hoping she would jump in and make this easier for him. Much as she liked Granger, she wasn't about to let this moment go without squeezing every ounce of satisfaction she could from it. She remained silent.

Granger drew in a deep breath, then muttered

something unintelligible. Marlie continued to wait. It didn't take long.

"What I'm trying to say, Marlie, is that perhaps my judgment was hasty. I should have been more willing to consider what you were proposing, to give you a chance. You were one of my top reporters, and your skills can benefit the station regardless of any limitations this . . . uh . . . situation has imposed on you. And frankly, I'm in a bit of a bind staffing-wise, what with losing Ronni and all. . . ." His voice trailed off into another awkward silence.

"I see," Marlie said. And she did. She wasn't good enough to work for Granger last week, but now, with the loss of one of the station's top reporters and a newsbreaking interview hinging on her presence, he was suddenly having a change of heart. She wasn't fooled by his capitulation, and the still painful memory of her humiliating visit to the station left her feeling a bit vindictive.

"I don't know, Granger," she said. "I've been giving some serious thought to approaching one of the other stations. Somewhere where my abilities as a journalist weigh more heavily than my physical limitations."

Granger muttered again. "Look, Marlie. If you want me to admit I'm an asshole, I'll do it."

Marlie said nothing, her smile widening when she heard Granger's weighty sigh of resignation.

"Okay, I'm an asshole. There. Are you happy?"

"No, but you're getting there."

"Goddammit, Marlie! What do you want from me? Tell me and it's yours."

Marlie could almost see Granger squirming on

the other end of the phone. She was torn between wanting to savor this moment of victory and feeling the tiniest bit guilty over torturing someone who had basically been a good boss and, in some regards, a good friend as well. Still, this was an opportunity she couldn't ignore.

"Okay, Granger. Here are my terms. I want the same title and position, same salary and benefits I had before my accident."

"Consider it done."

"I want my old office back."

"Hmm. The police have had it sealed off, so I'll have to check with them to see when we can go back in there, but as soon as we can, it's yours."

"I'll need an assistant, someone who can read files, do some research, help me with transportation and such. If you have an intern or a student, that would be perfect."

"No problem. It just so happens we have an intern who recently started. We were going to assign her to work with Ronni. Consider her yours."

"Great. I'll also need some special equipment installed on my computer, a voice synthesizer with the accompanying software, and a Braille embosser for printing. You can contact the Virginia Association of Workers for the Blind and they'll give you all the specifics."

Granger grunted, and Marlie took that as an assent.

"I also want free rein on the editing of this piece. My word is final on what gets cut and what stays in."

"Now, Marlie, you know I—"

"Otherwise, I go over to Channel Seven and take the senator with me."

"Shit." Silence followed but Marlie held firm, letting Granger work it out for himself. "Fine. You win. Anything else?" He sounded beaten and tired, and Marlie's guilt swelled a little.

"A contract. Six months. If at the end of that time you don't feel I can perform my job, don't renew it."

"I can live with that."

"Then I think we have a deal."

"Great," Granger said, though his tone belied his words. "I'll have personnel draw up the contract today. How soon can you start?"

Marlie thought about that. She knew she would need a few days to reacclimate herself to the station and figure out how to work around her limitations before she actually began working with Waring. There was little point in waiting. It wasn't as if her calendar was already full. "I'll come by tomorrow to sign the contract and do whatever else I need to do to get settled," she said. "I'm anxious to get started on this."

"Fine. See you tomorrow then."

If Granger was pleased with her decision, his grudging tone certainly masked it well. Still, it wasn't enough to dampen Marlie's spirits. She hung up the phone and flung back the covers, climbing out of bed with more enthusiasm than she had felt in months—years even. She was pulling on her robe, happily anticipating sharing her good news with her mother, when she heard the doorbell ring. "Busy morning," she muttered as she made her way to the door, wondering what this remarkable day held in store for her next.

Carvelle. Marlie recognized him immediately, not so much by his shape and size, although she'd become accustomed to them by now, but by his smell. Carvelle never wore cologne or aftershave, but he had a distinctive fragrance about him—wonderfully fresh and clean, like newly laundered sheets. The memory of last night's awkward exchange was still fresh in her mind, but at the moment she was flying too high to dwell on it. She decided to let bygones be bygones.

"Good morning," she greeted cheerfully.

"You're mighty happy," Carvelle grumbled.

"I am, indeed," Marlie said, ignoring his dismal tone. "Won't you come in?" She raised her nose to the air, sniffed, then said, "I don't think Mom is up yet, or if she is, she hasn't had time to start the coffee. Want to help me get some brewing?"

Carvelle shrugged, then said, "Sure." He stepped inside and eased the door closed. Marlie led the way to the kitchen, where she grabbed the coffeepot from its burner and handed it to him. "Here, fill this with water."

Carvelle did as instructed while Marlie busied herself with measuring the appropriate amount of coffee into the filter and placing it in the basket. When all was ready, she flipped the coffeemaker on, then turned to face Carvelle, who had taken a seat at the kitchen table. She studied him a moment, then asked, "What's wrong?"

"What makes you think something's wrong?"

Marlie shrugged. "You're too quiet for one thing. And I can sense there's something on your mind." This was a little less than the whole truth.

She did sense something was bothering him, but it was more from the fact that his glowance had a tight, worried look to it than anything else.

"I have some news," he said slowly. "About Ronni."

The somber tone of his voice sent a shiver racing down Marlie's spine with the speed and feathery touch of a millipede. She walked over and took the chair catty-corner to him. Carvelle turned his own chair sideways, leaning forward, elbows on his knees, hands folded in front of him.

"You found the tape, didn't you?" she said.

Carvelle scoffed and shook his head. "Those tapes. Christ! That's all I've done for the past four days is listen to those friggin' tapes. You certainly were right about one thing. That woman never took a shit without taping it." He reared back suddenly and looked at Marlie. "Sorry," he mumbled.

Marlie smiled. "Don't worry. I've heard worse, and besides, I think I've grown used to your little colloquialisms by now. So, did you find *the* tape?"

"Not exactly. The good news is that I've finally finished listening to all of the tapes we found, and they make it relatively easy to reconstruct Ronni's dealings with the people she encountered in her work."

"And the bad news?"

"The bad news is that we found no tape with a date and time that coincides with when you were at the station. Closest we found was one from earlier that morning, around ten o'clock. The other bad news is that, judging from some of the conversations I listened to, the list of people with a motive for killing Ronni Cumberland is longer than my arm."

"Ronni wasn't known for her gentle and easygoing personality."

"The woman was an out-and-out bitch, if you ask me. She certainly had a knack for pissing people off."

"I know," Marlie said with a deprecating smile. "I've been on the receiving end a few times myself."

"Bottom line is, there's no tape for this conversation you said you overheard. You're sure you weren't there earlier in the day?"

"Positive. I went to the beauty salon first, and the appointment there wasn't until ten. I know I was there at least an hour, probably longer."

"Then maybe she didn't record this conversation you heard."

Marlie frowned, thinking back. "No, I'm sure she recorded it, Carvelle. I heard her turn the recorder off and take the tape out."

"I'm inclined to agree with you. Given the extent of her collection, I can't believe she didn't record this one conversation. Hell, she even recorded phone calls to her mother. But if that tape is there, I haven't found it."

"What about phone records? Is there any way to trace the call?"

"To a point. The station has a PBX system, and a rather antiquated one at that. All calls come in through the main line and are then transferred. We can get records of all the calls that came into the station, but where they went from there is anybody's guess. There were over fifty calls that came in around the time you said you were there."

"Anything significant in those?"

"I don't know. We haven't finished processing all the information yet. But I did find something of interest on one of the tapes," he said.

"Which was?"

"The last taped conversation we have from the day in question was with someone you know."

"Who?"

"William."

Marlie reared her head back in surprise. "William? What business did Ronni have with William?"

"Well, their conversation on the tape dealt with someone William defended a couple of years ago, on a robbery charge." Carvelle's voice had softened noticeably, but rather than having the comforting effect Marlie suspected he intended, she found herself bracing for the blow she sensed was coming. Her suspicion grew even stronger when Carvelle reached over and laid a reassuring hand atop her own. She snatched it back, sandwiching both hands between her knees.

"So what?" she said. "Just because Ronni had a conversation with William about someone he defended in the past doesn't mean anything. I did a story myself once on one of William's clients. He's a defense attorney. His work and clients are bound to be newsworthy from time to time."

"True," Carvelle said slowly. "But William's clientele tends to be a bit higher class than this guy."

"He does pro bono work on occasion."

Carvelle let that point go and moved on. "During his conversation with Ronni, she said she wanted to meet with him, to discuss things further.

He agreed, saying he would call her back that same day to set the time and place."

He hesitated, giving Marlie time to absorb what he was saying. He knew she had when the blood drained out of her face, leaving her wide-eyed and pale.

"And there's something else," Carvelle said, grimacing as if his words were causing him physical pain. "I ran the name of this client of William's through the national database and came up with a hit. Several, in fact. The guy was a drifter and a petty thief for the most part. He also had several aliases. But I did find a recent picture of him where, interestingly enough, he had a chip in one of his front teeth."

"So?"

"So, the skull of the shooter we found in that meat warehouse where you had your, uh, incident, also had a chip in his front tooth. On a whim, I sent out the dental films to several of the places where this guy had been and, bingo—we got us a match."

Marlie stared at him slack-jawed, the implications spinning through her mind.

Carvelle sucked in a deep breath, then blew it out fast and hard. "Apparently," he said, "your ex-husband once defended the same guy who tried to kill you that night in the warehouse."

chapter 21

Marlie's gaze dropped to the floor and she shook her head, first slowly, then more vigorously. "No," she mumbled. Then again, "No." She looked at Carvelle, her expression imploring. "Are you telling me you think William had something to do with that gunman in the warehouse? You can't seriously believe that."

Carvelle sighed heavily. "Am I sure? No. But look at the facts, Marlie. You've told me before that one of the biggest issues between you and William was your work. He didn't like it, thought you took too many risks, thought you were neglecting him and your daughter. Was it a big enough issue for him to try to scare you by staging this thing at that meat-packing plant, never intending to actually hurt you? I don't know, but it seems possible. Did his anger and resentment over the divorce run deep enough that he perhaps *did* want to hurt you? I don't know that either."

Marlie opened her mouth to object, but Carvelle held up his hand. "I know, I know. It's all supposition at this point. But it's not so far-fetched as to be impossible. And I can't ignore the fact that William spoke with Ronni on the day she died and said he would call back later. Or that he has a prior connection to the man who shot at you in that warehouse."

Carvelle paused. Marlie sat quiet and stunned,

trying to digest the enormity of what he was suggesting.

"Finally," Carvelle went on, his voice softer than before, "I can't ignore the significance of *where* Ronni was murdered, almost as if it were a message."

Marlie shoved her chair back, stood up, and walked over to the coffeepot. She busied herself for several minutes, fixing two cups of coffee, her mind churning while Carvelle watched her. She remembered wondering herself if Ronni's murder and its proximity to the house were somehow significant. And then she thought about William and how much he loathed the place. She was dumping two spoonfuls of sugar into Carvelle's cup when she stopped, whirled around, and faced him with a look of frightened dawning.

"William was there. The other day, with Ronni. When I came out of the woods . . ."

Carvelle slowly nodded. Marlie turned back to the mugs on the counter and stirred Carvelle's coffee vigorously, the spoon clanking loudly against the ceramic. It wasn't until Carvelle startled her by reaching out and stilling her hand that she realized how distracted she was. She hadn't heard him come up behind her, hadn't sensed him at all. Again.

"Let me have that," Carvelle said softly, easing the spoon from her hand. He set it on the counter, grabbed Marlie by the shoulders, and turned her toward him. "Look, this is all speculation at this point. It may turn out to be nothing."

"You don't think so, though, do you?" Marlie asked, staring up at him, tears welling in her eyes. "Christ, he has my daughter." She ducked from beneath Carvelle's hands and began to pace out a small strip of the kitchen floor. "You don't think he'd hurt her, do you?" Then, before he could answer, "My God. Kristen! I've got to get her out of there."

"Marlie—"

"No. NO!" she said, shaking her head and slamming the air with her fist to punctuate her denial. She stepped up her pace. "I don't believe it. William has his problems—*we* have our problems—but he wouldn't go that far."

Carvelle watched her with a pained expression, the muscles in his jaw twitching wildly. At one point he reached out to stop her mad pacing, but he was a hairsbreadth too slow. His hand met only air and, after a moment, he let it fall back to his side, his eyes continuing to follow her tortuous route.

"William wouldn't do that," Marlie muttered, more to herself than anyone else. She was wringing her hands together as she wore out a strip of linoleum. "He wouldn't do that." She stopped suddenly, frozen to the spot, remembering last night and the black cloud. William had been there. Could the black cloud have been him?

"William wouldn't do what?" came a voice from across the room.

Marlie and Carvelle both spun around. Roberta stood just inside the doorway, wearing a knee-length nightgown and a ratty old terry-cloth robe. Her hair was mussed, her face still bore the mark of a pillow crease, and her voice was raspy. She eyed the two of them curiously, her gaze moving from Marlie to Carvelle and back again.

"What's going on? What wouldn't William do?" she repeated.

Marlie glanced around, spied the chair she had been sitting in before, and promptly made her way toward it. She collapsed into the seat, propping her elbows on the table and burying her face in her hands.

Carvelle watched her a moment, a pained expression on his face. He walked up behind her, his hand extended as if he were about to caress the back of her head. At the last instant, his hand fell to his side and he turned to face Roberta. "I think you better sit down," he said.

By the time Carvelle had filled Roberta in, Marlie was somewhat composed, but distracted. Her eyes gazed out the kitchen window, staring at nothing in particular.

"So this is mostly speculation at this point," Roberta said to Carvelle. "Though admittedly there are an awful lot of things here to chalk up to mere coincidence."

Carvelle nodded.

Roberta sighed and joined her daughter in staring out the window. "Well, as you probably know, I'm no fan of William's. But I have to agree with Marlie on this. Much as I despise the man for things he's done in the past, I don't think he's capable of murder."

"I hope you're right," Carvelle said. "For your granddaughter's sake."

His words made Roberta pale, and Marlie swung her head around to give Carvelle a terrified look. "Why are you so quick to assume the worst about him?" she asked. "Is there something more you're not telling us?"

"No. Why are you so quick to defend him?" Carvelle growled back.

"Because he's my husband, or was. You don't live with a man, share his bed and his life for sixteen years, without getting to know him."

Carvelle flinched, as if he'd been slapped.

"And he's the father of my child. Do you seriously think he'd hurt Kristen?"

Carvelle chewed the inside of his cheek a second before he answered. "You tell me," he said. "You're the one who was married to him."

Marlie gaped at him. "What the hell is that supposed to mean?" she snapped, her eyes narrowing.

Carvelle shrugged. "Just what I said."

Marlie felt an inexplicable surge of anger and once again shoved her chair back and began to pace. "Jesus Christ, Carvelle," she huffed. "What's with you lately? Can't you give a straightforward answer? You're always so damned introspective and quiet. Mr. Never-say-anything. Mr. Noncommittal."

"I'm sorry. I take it I hit a nerve?"

He didn't sound sorry at all, and while she wasn't sure, she suspected he was taunting her. Her anger peaked, and she stomped over to where he was sitting. After a second's worth of groping, which only fueled the flames of her fury higher, she braced her hands on the arms of the chair and bent down, her face inches from his own. She had the satisfaction of seeing his glowance collapse around him like heated shrink-wrap.

"I don't know what the hell your problem is lately," she seethed. "And frankly I don't care. This is my daughter's life we're talking about, dammit. Put your personal insecurities and idiosyncrasies aside for once and quit beating around the bush. Do you think he's involved or not?"

She expected Carvelle to back away, but he held his ground, staring back at her. Though she couldn't make out the expression on his face, his glowance started shifting with the rapidity of a tornado—darkening, thickening, compacting itself into a swirling mass of thunder and electricity Marlie swore she could feel.

"Fine," he hissed from between clenched teeth. "You want my opinion, I'll give it to you. I think William's a control freak and an asshole. I think the type of mental and emotional abuse he has inflicted on you over the years is cruel, sneaky, and heartless. He's a manipulative, exploitive, self-serving son of a bitch. And that's based solely on what I know of him through you, and I'm sure there's plenty you haven't told me about."

Shocked by the fury of his words, Marlie backed off a bit. Carvelle immediately lunged forward, taking up the space, becoming the hunter rather than the hunted. "Furthermore," he went on, "I can't believe you let him have your daughter in the first place. If you hadn't been so busy moping around and feeling sorry for yourself, he never would have been able to pull that off."

This time, Marlie was the one who flinched. If

Carvelle had meant to sting her with his words, he'd certainly succeeded. "How the hell would you know?" she shot back. "You weren't there."

"Oh, but I was," Carvelle said smugly. "Maybe not in the actual courtroom, but I listened to you whine on about it long enough to have a pretty good idea of what happened."

"Whine? You think I was whining? Oh, this is just grand!" She pushed herself away from him and started pacing again.

"I think you like being pitied," Carvelle shot back. "Maybe if you play the poor-old-me role long enough, William will take you back."

Marlie whirled on him, furious. From behind her, Roberta pleaded, "Please you two, can't we—"

Marlie didn't give her a chance to finish. She looked at Carvelle. "You're just jealous," she sneered, wagging a finger at him.

"You mean like your drunkard of a husband was last night?" Carvelle shot back.

Marlie opened her mouth for another come-back, then froze as the implication of Carvelle's words hit her. She snapped her mouth closed and stared at him, her eyes narrowed. "How do you know about last night?"

"He was there," Roberta said quietly.

Marlie looked over at her mother, then back at Carvelle. "You were there? Why?"

"To watch over you," Roberta said.

"Quiet, Mother. I want to hear Carvelle's answer."

Carvelle stared at her a moment, then both his body and his glowance deflated like an untied balloon. "I don't need this shit," he mumbled. With that, he rose from his chair and strode from the room.

When Marlie heard the front door slam, she whirled on Roberta. "Why was he there? I thought they had called off the guard."

"They did, but I think it was more of a budgetary decision than anything. Paul is still concerned."

"Concerned about what? That the murderer saw me? He didn't."

"Well, there's always the possibility that the killer might have found out about you since then. Or that the murder occurring where it did has some significance."

Marlie shook her head. It didn't make any sense. There was absolutely no reason to think Ronni's killer had any idea she had seen him. So why was Carvelle following her? Watching her? Was he really that concerned about William's possible involvement in all this? Or was it something else? The words "police corruption" echoed through her mind. And she remembered the black glowance at the dinner last night.

"Where?" Marlie asked Roberta. "Where was Carvelle last night?"

"What do you mean?"

"Was he in the room?"

Roberta shrugged. "I saw him a couple of times, but always by the door. Why? What difference does it make where he was?"

Marlie chewed one side of her thumb, her brow furrowed in thought. "Maybe none," she said. "Or maybe it makes all the difference in the world."

chapter

22

As soon as Carvelle left, Marlie snatched up the phone and called William's parents in Florida. His mother, Rachel, answered, her tone politely strained as soon as she knew who was calling. This air of barely contained civility was nothing new; the woman had behaved that way from the first day Marlie met her. Rachel's dislike stemmed from her belief that Marlie had stolen her son away from her and was nowhere near good enough for him. The fact that Rachel was a lifelong housewife who would never have considered working outside the home didn't help Marlie's cause any. Their relationship most likely would have deteriorated altogether long ago had it not been for Kristen's buffering influence.

William's father, on the other hand, was a sweet, good-humored man who had taken Marlie in as if she were one of his own. Marlie adored him and thought he was the most patient man to ever walk the earth, given his tolerance of Rachel's continuous harping and haranguing. David and Rachel Kaplan were the most mismatched couple Marlie had ever met, and the secret of their nearly fifty years of marriage evaded her to this day.

At first, Marlie feared Rachel wasn't going to let her talk with Kristen. "She's still in bed," Rachel said with a haughtiness that brought her stony visage firmly to Marlie's mind.

"Could you please wake her?" Marlie asked, trying to keep her voice civil. Losing her temper or acting panicked would do little for her cause at this point. "It's important that I speak with her."

Rachel didn't answer right away, and the picture of her face in Marlie's mind turned angrily stubborn. But then she said, "Hold on," and dropped the phone with a clatter that Marlie suspected was intentional. Several minutes later, a groggy-sounding Kristen came to the phone.

"Hi, Mom."

"Hi, honey. How's everything going down there?"

"Pretty good," she said with sleepy enthusiasm. She yawned loudly. "I met this girl, Stephanie. She's visiting her grandparents too, and they live just a few houses down the road. Anyway, Steph knows a lot of other kids around here, so it's pretty cool."

"That's great. When do you think you'll be coming home?"

"Dad said this weekend," Kristen answered with obvious disappointment. "I kinda wish I could stay next week, too, because Steph and her grandparents are going to the beach for a few days and they invited me along. They go there every year for the Fourth of July and Steph says they have the best fireworks. You can lay in the sand and watch them over the ocean. And after that they have this big party right on the beach, with bonfires and a real band and everything."

"That sounds like fun," Marlie said, an idea burgeoning in her mind. "Heck, I'd enjoy doing something like that myself. Why don't you ask your father if you can stay on until next week?"

"I already did, but he said no."

"Want me to talk to him?" While she wasn't wild about the prospect of Kristen being under Rachel's dour influence any longer than she had to be, she figured that, at least down there, she would be safe. Rachel might be an opinionated and cold-hearted old woman, but Marlie trusted her with Kristen's welfare.

Kristen didn't answer right away, and Marlie wasn't sure if it was because she was excited about the prospect, still too sleepy to grasp what was being said, or surprised that Marlie would even suggest the possibility. Finally, she said, "Do you think he'd let me?"

"I don't know, but I'll ask him if you want."

"But if I stay here next week too, by the time I come back I'll be leaving for the Poconos with Brittany. That means I won't have any time to visit with you."

"Well, honey, you know how much I look forward to our time together, but I also want you to enjoy yourself and your summer vacation. These kinds of opportunities don't come up often, so you best take advantage of them when you can. There will be other chances for us to get together. If staying down there is what you really want to do, that's okay with me."

"Really?"

"Really," Marlie said with a laugh. "I swear."

"I love you, Mom."

A piece of Marlie's heart melted even though she knew the declaration had been bought. "I love you, too, honey. I'll talk to your father and get back to you, okay?"

"Okay. Thanks!"

Marlie hung up the phone and breathed a sigh of relief. Knowing Kristen was safely tucked away in Florida, far from William, made her feel better.

"She wants to stay on?" Roberta asked from where she was still sitting at the table, nursing her cup of coffee.

Marlie nodded. "At least that will buy me some time," she said. "If William agrees to let her stay, by the time she comes home she'll be packing her bags again for two weeks in the Poconos with Brittany and her family."

This time, it was Roberta who nodded. "You know, maybe you should talk with Stuart Larsen," she said thoughtfully, referring to the lawyer who had represented Marlie in the divorce and custody hearings. "Tell him what's going on and see what he says."

"I will." Marlie snapped her fingers. "By the way, that reminds me! You'll never guess who called earlier this morning." She proceeded to fill Roberta in on her conversation with Granger and his offer of her old job back.

"Marlie, that is stupendous!" Roberta hopped up from her chair and walked across the room to give her daughter a big hug. "I am so proud of you," she said, letting go and beaming, both literally and figuratively. "Now I *know* you need to talk to Larsen. With the way things are going, you just might have a chance with the custody situation."

"Maybe," Marlie said, scarcely daring to hope.

"I'll call him this morning. But first I want to talk to William and make sure he's willing to let Kristen stay in Florida."

"Knowing William, he'll say no, simply because you suggested it."

Marlie considered that a moment. "Hm, you're probably right." Suddenly, she smiled and gave her mother a smug look. "I guess I'll just have to let him think it's his idea."

"And just how are you going to do that?"

"Watch," Marlie said. "And learn from the master."

She dialed the number for William's office while Roberta resumed her place at the table. After several minutes on hold, during which Marlie feared William would be unavailable or unwilling to talk to her, she was finally put through.

"Hello, William," she said, her tone only mildly caustic. "How's your hangover?"

"What do you want, Marlie?" he growled, ignoring her question.

"Aw, feeling a bit grumpy after your little drinking binge last night, eh?" she asked with saccharine sweetness.

"Get to the point, Marlie. I'm busy."

"I just wanted to let you know that, as of tomorrow, I will once again be an employee of WKAL. Full-time, with a six-month contract."

"I'm happy for you," William grumbled in a tone that was anything but. "As usual, your priorities are all screwed up."

"Not this time, William. The way I see it, having a job, a contract, and partial sight back makes me a candidate for mother of the year. So prepare yourself, because I intend to drag your ass back into court and get my daughter back."

William scoffed, then groaned, as if the action had caused him pain. Marlie smiled. Judging from the condition he had been in at the dinner last night, pain this morning was highly likely.

"Which reminds me," Marlie went on. "I want Kristen to spend this coming weekend with me, to compensate for the one I missed."

William was silent, and Marlie could almost smell the burning rubber as the wheels in his head spun frantically. She pushed a little harder. "I spoke to her this morning, so I know she's coming home this weekend."

"Well, not exactly," William jumped in. "I did tell her that, but she really wants to stay on there another week. She's made some friends down there and they've invited her to go to the beach with them. I told her no initially, but I've since reconsidered. I just haven't had a chance to tell her yet."

Marlie smiled and gave her mother a thumbs-up. "Dammit, William!" she said into the phone, summoning up her best tone of indignation. "This shit is going to stop. You can't keep me away from my daughter."

"I'm not," William retorted. "You're managing to do that all by yourself. You know, I would have thought you'd learned by now, but obviously you haven't. If you continue to put your job ahead of Kristen and me, you'll have to learn to accept the consequences."

"That's not fair, William, and you know it. In

order to prove I can take care of Kristen, I need to show I have some level of independence and responsibility. Getting my old job back will do that. Not to mention that I'm going to need the money. But you're determined to punish me every time I try to better myself."

"You seem to be forgetting that it was your job that got you into this mess in the first place, Marlie." He sighed and muttered something unintelligible under his breath. "You just don't get it," he said. "I'll see you in court."

He hung up, and with a smug grin of satisfaction, Marlie did the same. She turned toward her mother. "Okay, that's taken care of," she said. "Next call is to Larsen. And then I wonder if I might impose upon you to drive me out to do some shopping for some new clothes. I don't want to show up for work tomorrow looking like a ragamuffin."

"Be happy to." Roberta got up and shuffled over to the sink, setting her coffee cup on the drainboard. "I'll be ready as soon as I get a shower." She headed out of the kitchen, then paused in the doorway, turning back toward Marlie. "By the way, I just want you to know that this scheming manipulative side of you comes from your father, not me."

Marlie smiled and muttered, "Yeah, right."

chapter 23

"They look fine to me," Roberta said, sitting in her car outside WKAL and scanning the two copies of the contract Marlie had carried out to her. "All the provisions you mentioned are included, and I don't see any funny language here that might be suspect. Both copies are the same. I'll read the whole thing aloud to you if you like."

Marlie shook her head. "That won't be necessary," she said. "I trust your judgment. I'll scan my copy into the computer later and let Ralph read it back to me."

"Ralph?"

Marlie laughed. "That's what I named the voice in my synthesizer."

"You gave it a name? I thought you hated that thing."

"I do . . . or rather, I did. Actually, I never hated the synthesizer, just what it represented. But that was no reason to take it out on Ralph. He does his job and he's a nice enough guy. Kind of cute, too," she teased.

Roberta chuckled.

Marlie took the contracts in hand, then leaned over and gave her mother a quick kiss on the cheek. "Thanks for bringing me down here."

"No problem," Roberta said, starting up the engine. "When do you want me to pick you up?"

"Five-thirty? Or I can call you."

Roberta shook her head. "I've got a lot of errands to run today and won't get back to the house at all. But if you give me a time, I'll be here."

"Okay, five-thirty it is. I don't want to overdo it my first day back anyway, so a set time to quit will be good."

"Okay. See you then."

Granger was being appropriately contrite, though unusually quiet this morning. When Marlie had first come into his office, he had been perfunctory and businesslike, reiterating the specifics of the deal they had struck over the phone and then handing her the contracts. He had been more than accommodating, informing Marlie that the modifications to her computer would be installed by the end of the week and that the police investigations unit had released Ronni's office for use just that morning, so Marlie could move in and make herself at home. The intern he had promised, a twenty-three-year-old named Damaris Dedulonus—whom Marlie vaguely remembered being introduced to on her last visit to the station—was ready and waiting, eager to work and excited about the prospects. It was everything Marlie had hoped for and then some.

Now, as she entered his office for the second time, she was determined not to let Granger's odd reticence get to her. She plopped both copies of the contract down on the desk.

"Everything looks fine," she told him. "Do you have a pen?"

Granger handed her one, and Marlie flipped to the back page of the first contract, carefully positioning the pen beside the bright red arrow tag that pointed to the signature line. Her hand shook; it had been more than a year since she'd written her signature—or anything for that matter—and she hoped Granger wouldn't notice. The first signature rendered, she repeated the process on the second contract, relieved to note that her hand was a little less tentative the second time around. When she was done, she handed both the pen and the contracts to Granger, who promptly applied his own signatures. He set the pen aside and handed her one of the copies. He then gave her the keys to Ronni's office.

"Thanks," she said.

"Have Cindy call Damaris and send her to your office. And welcome back," he added almost as an afterthought, his attention already focused on some papers he held in his hand.

Realizing she'd been dismissed, Marlie took her leave, stopping at Cindy's desk.

"So how does it feel to be officially back?" Cindy asked.

"Good. I'm anxious to get to it. Granger told me to ask you to hunt down this intern, Damaris, and have her come to my office."

"Will do," Cindy said. "But first, I want you to come up to the newsroom with me and meet some of the folks who have come on board since you left."

"Maybe later?" Marlie posed. The idea of meeting some of the others, particularly those who knew her from before, made her nervous. She still harbored fears that some of them held her responsible for Chris's death.

Cindy shook her head. "Nope, now," she said, pushing away from her desk and heading for the door. "I have to drop off some stuff there anyway." She took off down the hallway, leaving no room for further debate. Resigned, Marlie reluctantly followed along.

Cindy summoned the elevator, and Marlie decided to take advantage of the wait. "So, what's the scuttlebutt here at the station on Ronni's murder?" she asked.

"Everyone is a little spooked," Cindy said. "And also a little curious, wondering if it was some hot story that got Ronni killed." The elevator announced its arrival with a melodic chime, and the two women stepped inside. Cindy hit the button for the fourth floor. "The cops haven't said much," she went on as the doors slid closed, "but the fact that they confiscated all those tapes of hers would lead one to suspect it had something to do with work. They wanted to take all of Ronni's files, too, but Granger put a stop to that. He let them copy whatever they wanted, including the files on her computer, but the originals stayed here."

The elevator chimed again as they reached their destination, and Cindy grew quiet as the door slid open.

"Surprise!"

A chorus of voices rose up from a sea of glowances. Marlie blinked, her mouth hanging open in shock, her mind taking several seconds to assimilate what was going on.

"Well, go on," Cindy said with a shove at the small of Marlie's back. "It's your welcome-back party. Get out there and be welcomed."

A huge banner was strung up above the cubicles, and written across it, in letters so large Marlie could actually read them, were the words WELCOME BACK, MARLIE! It damned near made her cry, whether from the emotion of the moment or her unexpected ability to actually *read* something, she wasn't sure. She stepped out of the elevator and the crowd immediately enveloped her. Hands clapped her shoulders and shook her hands while voices, both familiar and not, greeted her effusively. Introductions took place, and old friendships were renewed. Before she knew it, she was touring the newsroom and the adjacent studio with several people she had known for years, reminiscing about old times.

An hour later, feeling jubilant and relaxed, she thanked everyone and, after a good ten minutes' worth of good-byes, finally climbed back into the elevator and headed for her office. Never in her wildest dreams had she expected such a reception. Over the past year, her mother had told her countless times that no one felt ill will toward her over Chris's death, that she was just as much a victim as he was. Now, for the first time, Marlie actually let herself believe it was true.

Back on the second floor, she climbed out of the elevator and moved along the hallway to the door of her office. After fumbling with her key in the lock, she finally managed to open the door, stepped inside, and flipped on the lights. It took her eyes a moment to adjust to this sudden onslaught, but eventually she was able to make out the desk, topped with the computer and phone, two filing cabinets, and a credenza. She flashed back to the day of Ronni's murder, remembering how she had asked Ronni if she could have her old office back if Granger agreed to let her work. The irony was bitter.

Footsteps echoed behind her, and Marlie turned to see the figure of a tall, slender woman with dark hair standing in the doorway. She was encircled by a narrow but bright glowance that waffled gently. "Damaris?" Marlie asked.

"Yes, hello!" The young woman stepped forth, hand extended, and gave Marlie a handshake hearty enough to nearly loosen her shoulder from its socket. "I'm sorry I missed your little welcome-back reception," she said. "I was doing some research in the library."

"Really?" Marlie said. "On what?"

"Well, on you, actually. Ms. Kaplan, I can't tell you how excited I am about working with you. I've followed your career for several years. In fact, you've always been something of an idol to me."

Marlie shot her an amused and skeptical look. "Really?"

"Really. And I'm not just saying that to brown-nose." She made a couple of grudging sideways nods. "Okay, I've been known to brownnose before, when I have to. But I'm not now, I swear."

Marlie suspected that the narrow outline of the young woman's glowance reflected the nervousness she was obviously feeling.

"I've studied your style very closely," Damaris continued, somewhat breathless. "I love the way you can present both sides of an issue in a seemingly fair, neutral manner, yet still manage to communicate your personal views. It's very subtle. And it works so well because of the way you come across, that neighborly, best-friend kind of thing. I like the fact that you aren't afraid to take on a story, no matter how controversial it may be. Plus, you always seem to go that extra mile, digging up facts that others miss. You aren't afraid to take risks, and I admire that."

Damaris was the second person in recent days to see risk-taking as an admirable suit rather than a foolish one. Senator Waring had been the other. Marlie was impressed and a little amazed. For the past year, she had been convinced that people viewed her as reckless and thoughtless for this very behavior.

"That's very flattering, Damaris," Marlie said. "Thank you."

"My pleasure, Ms. Kaplan. Besides, it's all true."

"Look, if we're going to be working together as closely as I think we are, there are a couple of rules we need to agree upon," Marlie said.

"Okay." Such young enthusiasm. Marlie was a bit envious.

"First off, you will call me Marlie. None of this Ms. Kaplan stuff. Secondly, this hero-worship stuff is all very nice, but it can't get in the way of us doing our jobs. One of the most important aspects of succeeding in this business is having good instincts and learning to trust them. So if you ever disagree with me, I want you to speak up. If you ever get a feeling about someone or something, tell me. If you have an idea, share it. I'll always be willing to listen. On the other hand, you need to be careful about maintaining your objectivity when reporting any facts or research you dig up. You are serving as my eyes in essence, and it's important that you not color my perspective, at least initially. Save the impressions for later. Does that make sense?"

"Absolutely."

"And finally," Marlie went on, "everything you see, everything we discuss, everything you hear in this office must remain absolutely confidential. You are never to discuss our work with anyone outside the station at all, and no one within unless I say so first. Understood?"

"Understood."

"Good. Let's get started."

After hunting down an extra chair for Damaris, they began by turning on the computer and going through some of the files. Fairly certain that Ronni's death had something to do with a story she was working on at the time, Marlie was anxious to peruse the files to see if anything leaped out at her.

There were a number of directories, each one containing notes, comments, memos, and outlines for various stories, none of which seemed particularly sensational, certainly not worth killing someone over. One of the files had to do with the story on Marlie's surgery, and she was curious to see what Ronni had pulled together on it so far. Rather than having Damaris read it to her now, Marlie had her run down the hall and borrow a floppy from Cindy, since there were none to be found in Ronni's office (no doubt these had been confiscated by the police as well), and then copy the file. Later, Marlie would take it home, load it onto her own computer, and have Ralph read it to her.

Having struck out on the computer, Marlie had Damaris move to the drawers in the desk. Though the desk had a lock, apparently the police had been unable to find a key because the upper edge of the center drawer had been gouged and splintered from someone's efforts to pry it open. The drawers were all empty except for a smattering of office supplies in the middle drawer and a single, empty plastic container of the type that held microcassette tapes in the right upper drawer. Marlie knew this had to have been the drawer where Ronni stored her vast supply, but she made no mention of the tapes to Damaris, not knowing if her enthusiastic assistant was aware of Ronni's controversial habit and not wanting to suggest that such a thing might be acceptable.

Marlie suspected any files that had once been in the desk drawers were now among those stacked haphazardly atop the credenza. After perusing the file cabinets and discovering that they, too, had been culled, with some of the files returned in no apparent order and others heaped onto the piles, Marlie knew it would be a while before they could hope to get things organized. Beneath the stacks, inside the cabinet of the credenza, was a smattering of videotapes, which, like the files, were in no apparent order. The police had been thorough, Marlie realized. Unable to think of any other way to do it, Marlie sat down with Damaris and they started going through the files one at a time. Damaris skimmed each one, giving Marlie a synopsis of its contents, and Marlie then decided whether they would keep it out for a closer look or file it away in one of the drawers.

Around one o'clock, tired and a little frustrated at finding nothing of interest, Marlie suggested to Damaris that they break for lunch. Damaris drove them to a nearby restaurant, where Marlie fully intended to find out as much as she could about her new assistant—sort of a practice run at brushing up on her interviewing skills. But as they were heading back to the station an hour later, Marlie realized it was she who had done most of the talking, responding to Damaris's never-ending questions about her past, the station, the warehouse explosion, and so on.

Throughout the afternoon, they continued to wade through the files. Not surprisingly, they came across one on Senator Waring, which, after having Damaris read several pages of the notes, Marlie realized was her own file from a year ago, though Ronni had apparently added to it. Wondering if Ronni had been working on anything with Waring recently, Marlie had Damaris do another quick run-through of the list of files on the computer to see if any of them sounded like they might be related. But the file names all seemed to be fairly indicative of their content, and none sounded as if they had anything to do with Waring. Marlie had Damaris set the hard file aside so they could come back to it later.

By five o'clock, they had gone through the stuff on the credenza and most of the drawers in the file cabinets. Both women were tired and dusty, and the desk now boasted a small stack of files Marlie had designated for a closer look at some future date, including the one on her eye surgery and the one on Senator Waring. While they had run across several files involving relatively controversial matters or people, Marlie didn't see any that hadn't already aired or that contained the sort of revelations one might be motivated to kill over. Disappointed, she sent Damaris home for the day and went down to the lobby to wait for her mother to pick her up.

On the ride home, Marlie excitedly filled her mother in on the day's events, from Granger's odd reticence and the welcome-back party to her frustration at finding little in the way of suggestive stories among Ronni's files. After jabbering on for a good fifteen minutes, Marlie realized her mother was quieter than usual and that her glowance had a worried, pensive look to it.

"So that was my day," she concluded. "How was yours? Did you get all your errands done?"

Roberta shook her head and sighed. "No, though I managed to knock off a few and even got to have lunch with a friend."

"Well, that must have been nice."

"Uh-huh," Roberta said, obviously distracted.

Now Marlie was certain there was something on her mother's mind. Since her subtle fishing expedition wasn't getting anywhere, she decided to be more direct. "What's up?" she asked.

"What do you mean?"

"There's something on your mind, something you're not telling me. What is it?"

Roberta smiled. "You know, that aura ability of yours could get to be really annoying."

"You're stalling, Mother. Spit it out. Is something wrong?"

"No, there's nothing wrong." She paused a moment and sighed. "But there is something I've been meaning to tell you. I was going to mention it last week but with everything that's happened . . ."

"Yes?" Marlie said, feeling the muscles in her neck and shoulders tense. What terrible news was going to hit her now?

"I've met someone. Another doctor."

Marlie didn't get it at first, but then she saw her mother's glowance take on hints of vibrant red near its center. It dawned on her then, and she breathed a sigh of relief. "When you say someone, you mean like a significant someone? A boyfriend?"

"I'm a little old to be having anything called a boyfriend," she said. "How about male companion?"

Marlie laughed and shook her head. "Okay, male companion it is. Now give me all the specifics, like his name, how you met, what he does, what he looks like . . . I want it all."

Roberta shot her a look. "Nosy thing, aren't you?"

"I'm a reporter, remember?"

"Okay, his name is Joe Carter and he's a pathologist. For the past month he's been doing some research for the medical society on some legislation we're working on and that's how I met him."

"He's handsome, of course?"

"Very," Roberta said with a sigh. "He has the most beautiful head of snow white hair I've ever seen, blue eyes, long legs, and the most incredible hands."

Marlie's eyebrows shot up. "Mother!"

"Not that way!" Roberta said laughing. "I mean he has incredible-*looking* hands. His fingers are long and slender and his nails are perfectly manicured. Nicely shaped."

"Nicely shaped," Marlie echoed. "We're still talking about his hands here, right?"

"Well . . . ," Roberta said suggestively.

"Say no more." She gave her mother a wicked smile. "So have you two dated?"

"Dated? No. Not unless meeting for a cup of coffee to discuss legislation counts. But he has asked."

"Great! So when are you going?"

Roberta shrugged. "I don't know. With all that's been happening lately, I haven't felt as if I could really agree to anything just yet."

Marlie felt an instant surge of guilt. Here she had been so wrapped up in her own needs, she hadn't given much thought to the sacrifices her mother might be making on her behalf. "Is that why you were hesitant to tell me about him?" she asked. "Because you thought I would feel as if you were abandoning me?"

"No," Roberta said quickly. "It's not that. I was afraid you might feel I was cheating on your father somehow, or something like that."

"Criminy, Mom. Dad's been dead for over ten years. I loved him and miss him, but I certainly never expected you to spend the rest of your life pining away for him. You're a young, vivacious woman. I'm thrilled you've found someone."

"Really?"

"Yes, really. And furthermore, I think you should go home as soon as you drop me off and call him up and tell him you're ready for that date."

"But you shouldn't be left alone after—"

"Mother, I'm fine. You know as well as I do how boring it's been around here lately. If something was going to happen it would have by now. Hell, even the cops have pulled out. If you don't count Carvelle and his overzealous paranoia, there isn't anyone who thinks I'm in any danger at this point. Besides, I have some work I want to do tonight on the computer, pulling together some notes for my interview with Senator Waring. You've been wonderful to stick by me through all this, but enough is enough. Go home. Get a life."

"But—"

"No buts about it. This discussion is concluded."

"You always were a stubborn child."

"Gee, I wonder who I get *that* from?"

chapter 24

Though tired when she left the station, Marlie felt invigorated and energized by the time she got home, bolstered by the fact that she had survived her first day back at work without any major catastrophes and delighted over Roberta's revelation about her burgeoning love life. She fixed a salad and some soup for dinner and settled down in front of the television to listen to both the local and national evening news while she ate. Following the news was a habit she had once indulged with ritual faithfulness, as keeping her finger on the pulse of current events was key to her job. But over the past year she had lost interest in the goings-on of the outside world, too wrapped up in her own personal hell to care much. Now, that would have to change.

When the news was over, she put in a call to Kristen, relieved that David answered the phone instead of Rachel. She and David exchanged a few pleasantries, and Marlie could just imagine the look of stern disapproval on Rachel's face as she listened in. When Kristen finally got on the phone, she was bubbly and excited as she filled her mother in on the latest highlights of her social life, which Marlie found wistfully simple and uncomplicated. Then it was Marlie's turn, and she shared the events that had led up to her return to work, as well as the uneventful success of her first day back on the job. Kristen seemed genuinely impressed and excited about all that had happened, even going so far as to say, "I'm proud of you, Mom." It was just what Marlie's fragile confidence needed.

An hour later, when she finally hung up with Kristen, Marlie was eager to get to work on the Waring interview. There was much to be done. First, she had to find the copy of the Waring file she kept in her office here at home. She cursed herself for not having had the forethought to ask Roberta to come in and pull the file for her. While Marlie knew its approximate location, she wouldn't be able to read the labels on the many files she had in that same drawer. That meant going through the hit-and-miss process of pulling sheets from various files, scanning them, and then letting Ralph read them back to her until she found the right one. The good news was that she had kept her files in alphabetical order, and the one on Waring, filed under *W,* would be close to the back. Once she found it, she would have to scan the entire file into the computer, save it, and print out a new copy on the embosser.

With hours of work ahead of her, she decided to first change out of her work clothes into something more comfortable. She started off for her bedroom but paused as she approached the door to her office, a frown creasing her face. Ever since her homecoming from the hospital, she had left the lamp in her office ablaze, allowing her to glimpse the trophies whenever she passed by the room. Now, however, the room was dark, the lightbulb apparently having reached the end of its life.

Heading back the way she had come, she went to the closet in the kitchen where the spare lightbulbs were kept and carried one back to the office. Feeling her way toward the lamp, she unscrewed the old bulb, replacing it with the new one. As she screwed it past the last few threads, her eyes squinted in anticipation of the coming onslaught of light. But nothing happened. Puzzled, she loosened the bulb, then tightened it again to be sure it was properly seated. Still nothing. She removed the bulb altogether and held it to her ear, giving it a gentle shake. It was quiet, no tinkling rattle from a broken filament. Thinking it might be faulty, she went out to the living room and took a bulb she knew was working from another lamp. But even when she screwed this one in, the room remained in darkness. That meant it was probably the wiring, and she made a mental note to call an electrician in the morning. She had stalled long enough on getting the place rewired.

In the meantime, she supposed she could still work on the computer even without the light. That was, after all, what it was set up for. As she considered this option, her eyes drifted over toward the desk, and her brow furrowed in puzzlement. There, beneath the dust cover on the computer, a green light glowed, looking ghostly through the milky white plastic. She walked over and pulled the cover off. The computer sat quiet and lifeless, the monitor screen a darkened face. But along the front of the CPU, a tiny green beacon shone where there should have been only darkness. Puzzled, Marlie reached over, found the monitor's power button and hit it. It sprang to life, revealing an already booted-up screen.

She stared at it, trying to understand. Then she remembered how she had come in here and worked on the computer last week, on the day of Ronni's murder. Somehow, she must have forgotten to turn the CPU off when she was through.

As long as the computer was already on, she figured she might as well go ahead and work in the semidarkness. Lecturing herself on her forgetfulness, she left the office and headed down the hallway to change her clothes. But when she reached the entrance to her bedroom she stopped, perplexed yet again. Where she was expecting an open doorway, she found, instead, a solid white wall. As if she didn't quite trust the message her eyes were sending to her brain, she reached out and ran her hand over the smooth cold surface.

What the hell was this? She never, ever closed the door to her bedroom, or any of the other doors in the house for that matter. The only exception was the door in the kitchen that led to the cellar, and the occasional closing of the bathroom door when it was in use. Open doorways had been critical to maneuvering around when she was blind, and both she and Roberta had made a habit of leaving them that way.

She thought back to that morning, wondering if some bizarre distraction of thought might have made her close the bedroom door. No, she was sure she hadn't. Maybe the house was haunted after all, she thought with a nervous laugh. Or . . .

An idea began to dawn, one that made her skin crawl. She turned around and went back to the office. Standing in the doorway, she felt along the wall until she found the switch that controlled the outlet the lamp was plugged into. She flipped it up, and the previously dead lamp sprang to life, bathing the room in light.

For several long seconds, she didn't breathe. She looked over at the computer again, wondering now if she had really been forgetful, or if . . .

Her eyes crawled toward the bookcase against the far wall where the trophies gleamed with their brilliant shine. Sucking in a deep breath, she closed her eyes and traveled back in time to the months before her surgery. Feeling along with her hands, she carefully worked her way across the room, her mind counting and measuring each step, a flicker of a smile gracing her lips when she felt the edge of the bookcase exactly when she expected to. With movements practiced over many months and many repetitions, she reached up and felt along the books on the shelf just above her waist. When her fingers found the spine of the fattest one, a weighty tome nearly three inches thick, her hand moved straight up to the shelf above where she knew the first of the trophies should be.

All she felt was empty air. Her heart began to race.

Resisting the urge to open her eyes, she moved her hand a smidgen to the left, then to the right, then further to the left, until she finally felt the cold hardness of the trophy. She slid the statue along the shelf to its proper spot, then moved her hand straight up from there, feeling the plastic covers of the videotapes on the next shelf. Her fingers lightly followed them to the end, where she placed her thumb on the edge of the last one and then stretched her hand to the right. Normally, her pinkie would have brushed up against the second of the trophies. Tonight it found nothing.

This time her eyes did open, and they widened with frightened dawning. Had someone been in her house? And if so, why? The light, the computer, the bedroom door, the out-of-place trophies. All suggested that someone had been here, prowling through her things. Why? Robbery?

She shook her head. If someone wanted to rob the place, they would have taken the TV or the stereo, both of which were still in the living room. Or the computer or any of the other equipment here in her office. Things had been touched, but nothing seemed to be missing.

If robbery wasn't the motive, what was? Did this have anything to do with Ronni's murder? Her heart pounded inside her rib cage like some terrified animal trying to escape. She tried to force herself to remain calm, but the hairs along the back of her neck rose to attention and she whirled around, suddenly certain someone was standing behind her.

The room was empty, at least of any human forms. No glowances. She breathed a heavy sigh of relief.

The thought of someone going through her things left her feeling violated and vulnerable. Her face screwed up in disgust, and she hugged herself, wondering if whoever had been here had gone through the whole house, handling her most personal possessions—her clothes, her shoes, her *underwear*. That made her think of the closed bedroom door, and a new idea sprang to mind, one that made her heart pound even harder. What if someone was still here? Hiding in the bedroom?

Slowly, quietly, she tiptoed across the hall, her eyes fixed on the bedroom door. She set her ear against the cold wood and listened. If anyone was in there, she couldn't hear so much as a breath. Glancing downward, she noticed a narrow ribbon of light that marked a small gap between the bottom of the door and the floor. Silently, she dropped to her knees, placing her cheek against the floor and peeking through the gap with one eye. Other than a small portion along the wall to the right of the door, she could see the entire room. The lamp beside her bed was on, its light casting a golden glow around the bed. Those corners of the room she could see were dark and shadowed; there was no other light, no glowances anywhere in the room.

Satisfied the room was empty, she stood and opened the door. After checking the closet to be sure no one was hiding there, she spent several minutes examining items in the bedroom to determine if anything was out of place. If it was, she couldn't find it. From there, she moved to the end of the hall and the bedroom that Roberta used when she stayed here. Everything there looked fine, though Marlie had to admit she spent so little time in the room she doubted she could tell if anything had been moved.

If someone had been in the house, how had they gotten in? She hurried to the front door, unlocked and opened it, and checked along the frame, feeling for any evidence it might have been jimmied. Everything was intact. She closed it, threw the dead bolt, then quickly went to the utility room off the kitchen and did the same examination on the back door. Everything there was intact as well. She then made rounds of the rest of the house, checking all the windows to be sure they were locked and secure and even going so far as to peek in all the closets and inside the shower to be sure the house was devoid of any unwanted visitors. That done, she headed for the kitchen, where she poured herself a small glass of wine and settled in at the kitchen table to think.

She spared a glance toward the phone and briefly entertained the idea of calling the police, but she had no idea what she would say to them. All she had was supposition and guesswork, a gut feeling. What did she have to offer in the way of definitive evidence? As far as she could tell, nothing was missing, and there was no real proof anyone had been in the house.

The thing with the computer was easily explained, as she could have left it on last week after she finished working. Though at one time it was probably second nature for her to turn it off, it had been a long while since she had so much as touched the thing, and with all that had happened at the station earlier that day, her emotional state hadn't been at its best. Had she been rattled enough to have overlooked turning off the computer? Possibly. And what about the trophies? Maybe she was wrong about those. Maybe the last time she cleaned she had been a little too careless replacing them on the shelves. Come to think of it, when was the last time she dusted in there? She couldn't remember. Maybe Roberta had seen the buildup and decided to do it herself, leaving the trophies just off their marks.

Then there was the light. That one bothered her a little more because she was certain it had blazed away without interruption since that first night home from the hospital. Still, it wasn't totally inconceivable that in her excited and distracted state of mind this morning, she had inadvertently flipped the light off. And closed the bedroom door.

She shook her head and took another sip of wine. A bit too much coincidence. No matter how hard she tried to justify all these minor alterations, she couldn't quite convince herself they meant nothing.

She wrapped her arms around herself and gave the room a wary once-over, wishing like hell that Carvelle and his cronies were still maintaining their guard post out front. Then it struck her how ironic it was that this should happen so soon after the guard detail had been discontinued. The only people who knew about the guards were the cops themselves, she, and Roberta.

Police corruption.

The words sprang into her mind, and she could still hear the muffled voice that had uttered them over the phone little more than a year ago. Was it possible the police were somehow involved in Ronni's murder? Ronni had taken over both Marlie's office and her files. What if she had decided to look into the investigation Marlie had barely started a year ago, an investigation that had come to a screeching halt on that fateful night at the meat plant? Come to think of it, where was the police corruption file? She and Damaris hadn't run across it today in the office. Marlie doubted Ronni would have archived it, given the sensational subject matter. Granted, there wasn't much in the file, but Ronni would have kept it for future reference, maybe even added to it.

What if Ronni had been talking to someone on the police force during that overheard phone conversation? That might explain why no tape of that particular conversation had been found—or had it? What if Carvelle found a tape that implicated his own force? Would he hide it?

Her mind was running in circles, her thoughts flying out in all directions. She chugalugged the last of the wine and carried the empty glass to the sink, where she washed it out. As she turned to set it in the dish rack, something caught her eye off in the corner. When she realized what she was seeing, the wine glass slipped from her hand and fell into the sink, shattering into dozens of tiny pieces.

There, beneath the door that led to the cellar, was a narrow ribbon of light, just like the one she had seen beneath her bedroom door. The cellar light was on.

Don't panic. Think.

She forced her breathing to slow and stared at the tiny swath of light, her mind spinning. Had Roberta gone down there for something, forgetting to turn the light off when she was through? Keeping her eyes on the basement door, she backed up to the phone, groped for it, and punched in her mother's number. When the machine answered, she hung up, her eyes still watching the door, half expecting someone to come bursting through it at any moment. She tried to imagine what possible reason Roberta might have had for going down there, but came up empty. They kept nothing of importance down there; the dirt floors and ever-present dampness made it ill suited for storing anything. Then she remembered her conversation with her mother in the car on the way home. Roberta hadn't been back to the house all day.

Moving back toward the sink, Marlie slid open a drawer and took out the biggest carving knife she could find. The sheer weight of it made her feel a little less vulnerable, but her heart still quaked with terror and her palm felt sweaty along the knife's wooden handle. She would have to go down there, she realized, and the idea made her shudder. The dank tunnels that ran beneath the house had never been one of her favorite places, fascinating though their history may have been. Now, with every nerve in her body on edge, they posed even less of an invitation. And considering their labyrinthine layout, someone could hide down there for a long time without being found. She debated simply blocking the door with a chair, making it impossible for anyone within to get out, but knew that would only postpone the inevitable. Sooner or later, she, or someone, would have to go down there and look. She again thought of calling the police, but now she wasn't at all sure they could be trusted.

Resigned, she slowly approached the door. She twisted the knob with one hand while holding the knife at the ready with the other. The hinges, old and rusted like nearly everything else in the house, groaned as she pulled the door open. A single bulb hung overhead, highlighting the stairwell in stark relief. Every muscle in her body flinched with tension for the split second it took her to realize no one was there. Her shoulders sagged with relief, but it was short-lived. The overhead light barely penetrated beyond the stairs, and a frightening vista of long shadows and darkened corners waited below.

Thinking back to her explorations when she had first moved into the house, she remembered needing a flashlight to negotiate the farthest corners of the cellar and the tunnels themselves, which had no light source of their own. Ground-level windows were at either end of the basement, but they were scratched and dirty, letting through little in the way of light during the day. Now that darkness was fully settled, they would be useless. She searched her mind, trying to recall where she had kept the flashlight, an item she'd had little use for during the past year. But looking for it would mean turning her back on the doorway, something she was loathe to do at this point. She didn't think anyone was in the basement, but she was *sure* no one was in the house. Leaving the cellar door unguarded at this point would eliminate that one bit of surety.

Besides, she thought with some irony, who was better equipped for negotiating in the dark than she? Given the total blindness she'd lived with for the past year, moving around in the darkness might actually give her an advantage. And if, perchance, someone was down there, their glowance would give them away. She didn't want to go down there at all, but she knew she would never be able to sleep in the house until she convinced herself she was safe and alone.

Her mind made up, she reached along the wall, felt around for the light switch, and flipped it, plunging all but the upper few steps into darkness. Sucking in a deep breath to lock in her resolve, she used her free hand as a guide along the railing and carefully worked her way down the steps.

When she reached the bottom, she took a moment to collect herself and recall the layout of the basement in her mind. She quickly scanned the area to her left, and finding no signs of any glowances, she turned to her right. Nothing there either, but she knew the entrance to the tunnels lay in that direction. She took a few more steps forward until her free hand brushed against the far wall; then, with one last longing glance toward the top of the stairs and the meager rectangle of light from the kitchen, she turned to her right and moved off into the darkness.

The wall beneath her palm was cold and damp, its surface threaded with thick sheets of cobwebs. Suppressing a shudder, she moved slowly and carefully, feeling about with her foot first before committing to each step. The floor consisted of nothing but hard-packed dirt that muffled all noise. Other than the hard raspy sound of her breathing, the basement was as still as death itself.

Some ten steps into her trek, her hand knocked up against a wooden surface that jutted out from the wall at a right angle, and she knew she had reached the cabinet that marked the entrance to the tunnels. Sturdily built and hinged on the inside, the cabinet was a masterfully designed piece of camouflage. A latch, inside below one of the shelves, released a mechanism that allowed the whole thing to swing away from the wall, revealing the tunnels beyond. Marlie remembered her amazement when she had first seen it, an innocuous-looking structure that offered nary a clue as to its true function. She had marveled at the ingenuity and craftsmanship that had gone into its creation. The entire structure was both quaint and mysterious in its design, and Marlie had recognized its potential almost immediately. When she first entertained the idea of doing a story on the Civil War and the Underground Railroad, the one thing she knew she wanted to film was the slow and rather ominous opening of the cabinet, adding in just the right lighting and sound effects to lend an eerie element to the overall mood. Even more telling would be the closing of the cabinet once they were on the other side.

Now, she thought it ironic that she was about to become the victim of her own sensationalism. Feeling along the front of the cabinet, she opened the doors, then searched beneath the shelves until she found the mechanism. It, like the wall, was shrouded in spiderwebs, and as soon as she released the catch, she snatched her hand back and quickly wiped it on her hip. Needing both hands to grab the cabinet and pull it open, she tucked the knife in her armpit. Grabbing the edge of one of the shelves, she pulled.

The cabinet swung away from the wall with a loud creak of protest, the ancient hinges worn and rusted with age. Marlie wrinkled her nose as the smell of dank earth, eerily reminiscent of a newly dug grave, spilled out into the basement. Once again grabbing her knife, she stepped around the edge of the cabinet and looked behind it, relieved to see no break in the never-ending blackness. No glowances. The temperature within the tunnel was several degrees cooler than that of the cellar, and a chill rapidly filled the air, making Marlie shiver.

Thinking back to her brief exploration of the tunnels over a year ago, her memory filled in what her eyes couldn't see. A little over a yard in width, the main passageway curved around for some fifty feet or so before it branched off into three other tunnels. She recalled how the ceiling, which was high enough to allow someone to stand erect near the entrance, sloped downward in spots farther in, so one had to stoop in order to pass through. And as if the tunnels weren't dark enough on their own, the ceiling had been black as night, its surface covered with a thin coating of soot. Marlie guessed it had come from burning torches used in past eras as a light source.

During her first, and only, foray into the labyrinthine passages, she had followed the right-most tunnel, encountering yet another branching a little farther in. Again taking the right, she had continued past several more intersections, always keeping to the right, until she reached a dead end. Backtracking, she realized it would be foolish to explore any deeper until she had some way of marking her trail; otherwise she might get hopelessly lost. Reluctantly, she had returned to the entrance, intending to try again in the near future. Fate, however, had intervened.

The same sense of intrigue and mystery she had felt then seized her now. Her fear that someone might be lurking within dissipated, and she stepped over the threshold, lightly tracing over the uneven surface of the wall with her left hand. The mixture of clay, dirt, and rock felt clammy and cold beneath her touch, and she remembered feeling a smidgen of claustrophobia the first time she had been here. Now, unable to see the narrow confines of the walls around her, she felt more at ease.

Using her left hand along the wall as a guide and waving the knife in front of her like some bizarre antenna, she made her way along the first length of the tunnel. The blackness here was total, as dark and empty as the whole world had been during the year of her blindness. Yet rather than terrifying her, it felt oddly comfortable. She suspected part of that stemmed from knowing this blackness was only temporary. Rather than feeling like the prison it had been before, it was more like a brief visit with an old friend.

Eventually her hand felt the wall angle sharply to the left, and she knew she had reached the first intersection. She paused and chewed her lip with indecision. This had become something of an adventure for her now, and the urge to move ahead and explore the left side of the tunnel was great. Just a little ways, she finally decided.

She took another step, and her foot collided painfully against a hard unyielding object, upsetting her balance. Fearing she was about to fall, she flung her right hand out to stabilize herself. The opposite wall was much closer than she expected, and her wrist slammed against its hard surface, knocking the knife from her hand. Cursing, she now remembered the one detail about the tunnels she had forgotten. Like the rest of the basement, the floor of the tunnel near the entrance was hard-packed dirt, but deeper in it became mixed with rocks that jutted up willy-nilly from just below the surface.

When the throbbing in her toes subsided, she crouched down and felt along the ground for the knife, her hand following a back-and-forth search pattern between the walls, moving an increment ahead with each pass. After searching as far as she could reach in front of her, she pivoted in her squatting position to look behind her. A little off balance, she braced herself with one hand against the wall. Her fingers found a crack where they touched, and they idly played over it while her other hand swept the floor in search of the knife. It was several fruitless sweeps later before her mind registered the fact that there was something odd about the crack beneath her hand. It was smooth and straight along its edges, too deliberate to be anything but man-made. About an inch tall as well as wide, it formed the shape of a sharply pointed *V*. Giving it her full attention, she explored in more detail and realized it wasn't a *V* after all, but an *M*, cut into the stone about a foot above the floor. Her first thought was that someone had cut their initials into the wall, and she searched the surrounding area to see if any other letters had been carved nearby. Nothing. The *M* stood alone. Maybe the person who had done it had time for only one initial.

Deciding to abandon her search for the knife,

which she no longer felt the need for anyway, she stood and rubbed her hands together to dust the dirt off. Her near stumble had shown her the foolishness of this exploration in the dark. She would come back another time when she was better prepared. Once again extending her hand, she located the wall to use as her guide. Her mind was idly processing the thought that she needed to turn right to get back to the main passage when it hit her that the *M* might be something other than someone's initial.

Could it be? She felt a trill of excitement at the thought. Reaching with her left arm, she groped about until her hand found the far wall, then she felt along that until she felt the angle marking the center tunnel. Floating her left hand over the wall and stepping more carefully this time, she made her way down its length until she came to a sharp angle, indicating a turn. She reached across to the right side and felt an angle there as well. She had reached another branch.

Moving back to the left side, she crouched down and started feeling along the wall, her fingers playing lightly over the surface. She found it in about the same place as the other had been, only this time the letter was an *R*.

R for right, L for left, M for middle.

A bolt of excitement coursed through her body, and she quickly stood and moved back to the tunnel on the right, prepared to travel its length to the next intersection. But then her inner alarm jangled and she paused. What if she was wrong? Sure, it seemed logical now, but all she had to go on was two letters. And who knew what they really stood for. If she was wrong and ventured any deeper into the tunnels, she might not be able to find her way back. Besides, the fact that the exit had never been found made her suspicious it no longer existed. It wouldn't be surprising to discover that someone had sealed it off. The commonsense thing to do was return to the house and come back another time, when she could mark her progress and test her theory at the same time. Still, the temptation was great. She stood there for several minutes, arguing with herself, knowing in the end there was only one thing she could do. That awful night in the meat warehouse had taught her to always trust her instincts, and instinct told her to turn around. With a little sigh of frustration, that's what she finally did.

By the time she was back in the kitchen, the intrigue of the tunnels had been replaced by her knowledge that someone had been in the house. It dawned on her that if the tunnels beneath the house did still lead to the outside at some point, the reverse was true as well. She dragged a chair over to the cellar door and wedged it beneath the knob, adding a call to a locksmith to her mental checklist for tomorrow. Then she dug another knife out of the drawer.

It was a while before she felt comfortable enough to go to bed, and then she couldn't sleep. The hours dragged by as her mind continued its endless circling, trying to make sense of all that had happened, trying to sort out the facts in a way that seemed logical. When she did finally sleep, her kitchen knife tucked safely beneath her pillow, she tossed and turned, tormented by dreams in which dark clouds of thundering evil loomed in the corners of every room, seeped up through the floorboards from the cellar below, and hovered outside the house, just beyond the windows, searching for a way to get in.

chapter
25

When Roberta came by the following morning to drive Marlie to work, she was all aglow. As Marlie suspected, the cause of this transformation was Roberta's first official date with Joe Carter, which had taken the form of dinner and a movie.

"I know it's silly," Roberta said. "Probably a midlife crisis or something, but I suddenly feel twenty years younger. I loved your father more than anything, but after being together so long, I had forgotten what the first blush of love can feel like."

"Are you saying you're in love with him, Mom?" Marlie asked, grinning widely.

Roberta shrugged and giggled like a schoolgirl. "I think I might be," she said. "The way he looked at me at dinner—oh!" She snapped her fingers. "That reminds me. Guess who we saw at dinner?"

Marlie shrugged. "I have no idea."

"William. And he wasn't alone. He had some blond woman with him, and judging from the goo-goo eyes they were making at one another, I'd say it was more than a business acquaintance."

Marlie felt a puzzling and inexplicable stab of jealousy. She shook it off, angry with herself. "Did you speak to him?" she asked.

"No, but I know he saw us. You know, Marlie, if he has someone new in his life, it's even more important that you start doing something soon about your custody situation."

Marlie frowned, feeling a mighty surge of irritation. Damn William! She wouldn't put it past him to go off and marry some bimbo on the spur of the moment just to strengthen his position as the custodial parent. There wasn't much he wouldn't stoop to—

Then it hit her. Of course! William! That's who had been in her house. It all made sense to her now. She had put him on notice that she was preparing to resurrect the battle for custody. She knew he would stop at nothing to make sure she failed, including snooping around her house and going through her computer files looking for anything he might be able to use against her. Getting in would have been easy enough. He had been to the house plenty of times, including that day when she was in the woods. She wouldn't put it past him to have "borrowed" one of the spare keys hanging in the kitchen so he could get a copy made. Not only that, Kristen had a key.

She almost laughed with relief. Last night she had been so paranoid, imagining all sorts of things when the truth was staring her right in the face the whole time. Then, as quickly as it had come on, her relief vanished as she recalled Carvelle's revelations about William's involvement with Ronni. Obviously there was no hard evidence tying him to the murder at this point or he would have been arrested. Yet Carvelle had seemed pretty sure of himself.

Marlie shook her head. She had lived with William for some sixteen years and thought she knew him pretty well. He was sneaky, conniving, controlling, manipulative . . . but a murderer? She simply couldn't see it. But she *could* see William staging that whole scene at the warehouse, teasing her with a phone call that hinted at police corruption and then hiring that hapless drifter he once defended to fire some random shots. He might have seen it as a lesson to her, hoping it might scare her into quitting her job. The resultant explosion was an accident no one could have foreseen, but it did result in a death. If William had been responsible, how far would he go to keep it a secret?

She added an alarm company to the growing list of people she would call today. Not only would it give her a greater sense of security, it would keep William from making any future unauthorized visits.

"Did you hear me?" Roberta asked.

Marlie shook off her thoughts and focused on her mother. "Sorry, Mom. I sort of drifted there. What were you saying?"

"I said you need to keep close contact with Stuart Larsen on this custody thing. If you give William an inch he'll steal the proverbial mile. Don't trust him for a minute."

Marlie nodded, giving her mother a weak smile. "I won't," she said.

Damaris was waiting when Marlie arrived at the office, and they spent an hour over coffee discussing the stories Marlie wanted to work on, including the Waring interview, the prospective piece on the underground tunnels (which fascinated Damaris), and the one on Marlie's eye surgery. After tossing around some ideas, Marlie put in a call to Senator Waring's office to firm up the details of the interview. Garrity answered the phone and informed her that the senator was out but expected to return momentarily, at which time he would get back to her.

The phone rang a few minutes later, and Marlie answered, hoping it was Garrity calling back. But it was William.

"What the hell do you think you're doing?" He hollered so loudly Marlie flinched and pulled the phone away from her ear. From the corner of her eye she saw Damaris's head shoot up and knew she had heard it too. She clamped the phone back to her ear and immediately regretted it as William continued his thundering tirade.

"If you think you can win Kristen back by siccing the cops on me, I swear I'll have your ass in court so fast you won't know what hit you. And when I'm done, you'll be carrying your head out in your hands."

Damaris grabbed several files off the credenza and began looking through them in earnest.

"I have no idea what you're talking about, William," Marlie said in the sweetest voice she could muster.

"Bullshit! You sicced that goddamned detective friend of yours on me, didn't you? He's been all over me for the past two days, asking a bunch of questions, implying that I'm somehow connected to Ronni's murder. There's no reason in hell for them to even look twice at me unless you told him something, Marlie."

"On the contrary, William. Any conclusions Detective Carvelle may have arrived at, he did so on his own. I had nothing to do with it."

"You lying bitch!" Marlie heard a loud bang on the other end of the phone, as if he had punched or slammed something. "Let me tell you something," he seethed with a tight, visceral voice. "For someone who thinks she wants to be some sort of ace reporter, you sure don't do your homework. Before you go trusting anything your friend Carvelle tells you, you might want to look into his past and the death of his partner. See what sort of people you're associating with."

"What are you talking about?"

"Find out for yourself, Miss Bigshot. I've got better things to do. I'll see your ass in court."

He slammed the phone down, making her flinch yet again, and after a quick, sideways glance at Damaris, Marlie hung up as well. Damaris continued to look as if she were totally engrossed in whatever file she was currently rifling through, but from the way her glowance swirled with excited flashing colors, Marlie guessed the young woman had overheard most of the conversation. Either that, or she'd run across one hell of an interesting file.

"Damaris?"

"What?" The word came out a little too quickly and with the faintest tinge of guilt, confirming Marlie's suspicion.

"I've got some stuff I need you to do."

Damaris set aside the file in her lap and twisted toward Marlie. "Okay," she said.

"Take the file on Senator Waring, go through it,

and list out any information it contains. Then write me up as much of a biography as you can from it, noting what holes you think need to be filled. Focus on personal stuff—his childhood, education, the family tragedy, his struggles to overcome his physical and emotional trauma—that sort of thing. Then hit up the newspaper and gab-rag archives and see what scuttlebutt you can dig up about who he's dated over the past year or so and what sort of social life he leads."

Damaris had already dug the file out of the pile on the desk and was doing a quick flip-through. "Got it," she said. "How soon do you need it?"

"Yesterday?" Marlie said with an apologetic smile.

"I'll get right on it."

"Are you familiar with the media library upstairs?" Marlie asked.

"I am. In fact, I spent much of my first week in there. It's pretty impressive."

Damaris wasn't the first person to say that. Housed on the top floor of the station, WKAL's library was one of the best to be found anywhere and the envy of many other stations.

"Good," Marlie said with a smile. "Dig up anything you can, no matter how mundane it may seem to be at the time."

"Will do."

As soon as Damaris was gone, Marlie leaned back in her chair and closed her eyes. William's outburst had upset her more than she realized. Now she was even more convinced it had been him in her house yesterday, and the knowledge both frightened and angered her. The reason for her anger was obvious. The fright stemmed from a sudden level of doubt about William and what he was capable of. If Carvelle was sniffing around him that hard, he must have some pretty strong suspicions.

Her mind shifted to Carvelle and William's allusion that something might be amiss. Was William merely striking out blindly in anger, or did he really know something about Carvelle?

Marlie pushed out of her chair and headed down the hall to Cindy's office. After exchanging the perfunctory morning greetings, she said, "Cindy, I need to ask a favor of you."

"Shoot."

"Do you still have that friend who works in personnel down at the police station?"

"Rosie? Yeah, she's still there."

"Is she still an incurable gossipmonger?"

Cindy laughed. "She loves to tell tales, no doubt about that. Loose lips she has, but she isn't totally without caution. There are some things she doesn't tell me. I think it depends on what I'm asking for, and why, and whether or not she feels the source can be traced back to her. What is it you want to know?"

"I want to find out as much as I can about Detective Paul Carvelle."

"You mean that guy who's been snooping around Ronni's office the past few days?"

"One and the same. I want to know where he came from—I think he's relatively new to the area—and if there were any problems where he worked before. Also, I heard that his partner, whose name I don't know, was killed in the line of duty sometime back. I'd like to know the specifics."

Cindy shook her head. "I can probably get the work history for you, especially if I tell her we're looking at doing some sort of profile on him. But I don't know about the partner's death. An investigation like that isn't something that would be available to someone like Rosie."

"Surely there must be some internal gossip that floats around when someone on the force is killed."

"True, but gossip isn't necessarily fact, remember."

"I'll settle for the gossip right now. Besides, one thing I've learned in this business is that there's usually a fair amount of truth behind most gossip. The trick is to sort out the facts from the embellishments and supposition."

Cindy shrugged. "It's worth a shot, I suppose." She glanced at her watch. "We haven't done lunch in a while. I'll call her now and see if she's free today."

"Thanks, Cindy. Let me know what you find out."

Marlie returned to her office wearing a thoughtful frown. She picked up the phone, and unable to remember the extension for the media library, she dialed the switchboard and asked to be connected. When Damaris answered, Marlie asked her if she was alone.

"I am," Damaris said. "There was someone in here when I first came up, but she's gone now."

"Good. Listen, while you're searching through the archives, see what you can dig up on the name

Paul Carvelle, or Detective Carvelle. I'll take whatever you can find, but I'm particularly interested in anything related to an incident that occurred a little over a year ago when his partner was killed in the line of duty."

"I remember hearing something about that," Damaris said. "I think it was some sort of drug bust that went wrong."

"Don't restrict your search to our area. He hasn't been on the local force all that long but I don't know where he worked before he came here. See if you can find out."

"Gotcha."

"Damaris?"

"Yeah?"

"Keep this strictly to yourself. If anyone else comes into the library while you're there, work on something else."

"I understand." With that, she hung up.

Marlie did the same, smiling at the melodrama she had heard in Damaris's voice. It called to mind the thrill of anticipation she herself had felt with some of the cloak-and-dagger stuff, especially back when she first started at the station. In many ways, Damaris reminded her of herself at that age. And surprisingly—surprising because in the past, Marlie had studiously avoided taking on any of the interns, seeing them as more of a nuisance than anything—she was looking forward to mentoring Damaris, showing her the ropes and teaching her the ins and outs of the trade, as well as some of its secrets. Perhaps by doing so, she could relive some of her own youthful exuberance.

Shaking off her reminiscences, Marlie picked up the phone and arranged to have a locksmith come by on Saturday. Next she called a home security systems company, but quickly learned that before she could install any sort of alarm, she would have to upgrade the wiring throughout the house. She suspected the cost of that was going to be prohibitive, at least until she had a paycheck or two under her belt. She was about to call to see if someone would give her a rough estimate when the phone rang.

"Marlie Kaplan."

"Good day, Ms. Kaplan."

Marlie was surprised. She had been expecting Garrity to call her back to set up her interview with Waring, but it was the senator himself on the line. "Senator. How are you?"

"Fine, thank you. And you?"

"Doing well. Thank you for asking."

"So how does it feel to be back at work?"

Marlie thought about that for a moment. "It feels a little scary, actually," she said. "But in a wonderful way. Thank you for helping to expedite the process. I'm grateful."

"No reason to be. I was only hurrying the inevitable. Talent like yours can be ignored for just so long."

"Ah, there's a taste of that elegant rhetoric that has served your political career so well."

Waring chuckled. "And in return, there's a taste of that refreshing honesty that has served *your* career so well. At least we've both learned to capitalize on our strengths."

"Touché," Marlie said with a laugh. "So, when

would you like to pair your rhetoric with my refreshing honesty in the form of an interview?"

"Well, soon. But first I have a few requests of you."

"Okay," Marlie said slowly, a sinking feeling in her gut. Was he about to make this interview near impossible by imposing a bunch of restrictions or off-limit topics? If so, she would be in a bit of a fix. Her entire return to work hinged on this one interview. If it turned out to be mediocre at best, she could pretty much kiss any meaningful future work good-bye. "You can ask," she added, feeling a mixture of panic and pique stir in her gut. "But I'm not promising I'll agree."

"Fair enough," Waring said. "My first request is that the interview not be one of those tabloid-flavored exposés on my personal life. I understand you will want to mention certain aspects of it, but I would prefer the main focus of this interview be on my political track record, future plans, and positions."

Marlie frowned. "Obviously your political leanings will play a major role in this, Senator Waring, but—"

"Please, call me Richard. I've never been a big fan of formality."

Marlie pursed her lips, a bit irritated with his interruption. "All right. As I was saying, your political life has already been covered fairly thoroughly in the media. What people want now is the more personal stuff."

Waring sighed. "I realize there is some interest in my life outside the political arena, although I'll be damned if I can understand why. Still, I think that can be downplayed. Or at least doled out piecemeal. I would prefer this interview focus on the issues I represent, not my lifestyle."

"Forgive me, Sen—Richard," Marlie interrupted. "But focusing primarily on your political agenda does nothing to distinguish you from dozens of other politicians, some of whom may be your future opponents. You need something that will set you apart from the crowd, make you stick in people's minds, make them think of you as a heroic and noble person."

"Heroic and noble?" Waring scoffed. "That's a bit of a reach."

"Not really. Not when you look at what you've had to overcome to get to where you are now. People in today's society hate the rich and privileged. What they go for are the hard-luck stories, where people triumph over adversity and manage to beat the odds. That, Senator Waring, is the true American Dream these days. And you are perfect for the leading role."

"I have to admit, this all makes me rather uncomfortable," Waring said hesitantly.

"Well, if it makes you uncomfortable enough, don't do the interview. But if you agree—and I think you do—that the time has come for you to put your face and your life out for public inspection as a means of furthering your political goals, then you might as well make the most of it. You don't have to like the power of the media, but you need to recognize its existence and use it to your advantage." Marlie paused and held her breath. She was taking a huge gamble here, she knew. But all her years in this business of dealing with people had taught her to read them fairly well, even over the phone. Besides, she had little to lose. If Waring didn't give her the freedom to do this interview the way she wanted, her future chances for employment might quickly end up circling the drain.

"It's that cursed persistence and tenacity of yours that makes you such a good reporter," Waring said with a chuckle. Marlie breathed a sigh of relief, sensing she had won. "It's one of the things I like best about your style, but I have to admit it also makes me a bit wary. Why do I get the feeling I'm throwing myself to the sharks?"

"You think I'm a shark?"

Again he chuckled. "No, no. If I did, I'd cancel this interview right now."

"Then are we agreed that a strong personal slant on this piece is called for?"

Waring let out a weary sigh. "Okay, I'll tell you what. I'll agree to do it your way if you'll consider doing me a favor."

"What kind of favor?"

"As I said, I'm not terribly comfortable about this whole idea in the first place, and I'm also not big on formality. Given those two facts, I would ask you to consider making this process a little easier for me by doing things under . . . shall we say . . . less than typical circumstances."

"Meaning?"

"Meaning, I would like you to have dinner with me one night this week."

"Dinner?" Marlie was confused. "You mean you

want me to film the interview over a dinner?"

"Not exactly . . . uh . . . what I mean is, yes, I would like to begin the interview process over dinner, but just you and me, at least initially."

Marlie frowned. "I'm not sure I understand. This *is* a TV interview and—"

"I realize that, Ms. Kaplan. May I call you Marlie?"

The sudden change of subject threw Marlie off balance. "Uh, sure," she stammered.

"Let me be more succinct, Marlie," Waring went on. "I'm asking you to have dinner with me. A social dinner, not a professional one, although we can certainly discuss some of the details of the interview while we eat, if that's what you want."

Marlie was at a loss for words. After a long and rather strained silence, she said, "Are you asking me out on a date?"

Waring laughed. "Yes, I suppose I am."

"I see."

"You don't seem overjoyed at my invitation. Is that because it violates your journalistic integrity, or just your personal taste?"

Marlie laughed. "Well, it does raise some questions as to my objectivity," she pointed out. "And if you're doing this simply to flatter me or sway my opinions in your favor so the piece will shed you in a better light, it's unnecessary. I've been a big supporter of yours for a long time."

"I trust your judgment on the piece, Marlie," Waring said. "That's why I requested you in the first place. I just thought the dinner might be a nice way to get to know one another a little better and lend a more casual tone to this whole thing."

"I understand. And I'm not totally averse to the idea of dinner. But I don't want anyone to misconstrue my motivations for doing this story. That runs the risk of negating the good it's intended to do you."

"Well, no one needs to know about the dinner, do they?"

"Given your current popularity with the media, the odds are pretty good that someone will notice us together and come to their own conclusions, right or wrong."

Waring cleared his throat. "Well, um, I actually had something in mind that would eliminate that problem."

"And that would be?"

"That we dine at my house."

Marlie's eyes grew wide with both surprise and excitement. Getting that intimate of a peek into Waring's life was more than she could have hoped for, particularly given his reluctance to do the interview in the first place. Seeing where he lived, *how* he lived, would give her great insight into the man. She wondered how big his place was, how it was furnished. Did he have pets? Was his lifestyle ostentatious or simple? Dozens of possible scenarios filled her mind, then abruptly vanished as she realized that the intimate details of his house would be little more than a blur to her with her limited eyesight. Insecurity reared its ugly head, but Marlie forced it back down, determined to figure out a way to do this. In the meantime, she couldn't let the opportunity pass her by.

"Interesting idea," she said.

"Tell you what," Waring said. "The invitation to dinner still stands, but forget any suggestion I might have made that it is anything but a professional get-together. We can discuss the interview and outline the piece while we eat. Will that make you feel better about keeping your personal and professional lives separate?"

"It would."

"Good! But I warn you, once this piece is done, I may suggest more dinners."

"Fair enough."

"Great! That's settled then. Now, how about when?"

"My schedule is pretty open," Marlie said. "You choose."

"Well, at the risk of sounding pushy, how about tonight? I suggest that only because I have engagements every other night this week, which will put us into next week sometime before I have another opportunity."

Marlie bit her lip, feeling a ball of panic rise in her throat. Was she prepared enough to do it that soon? She wondered how much information Damaris would be able to glean by day's end. Still, she didn't want to have to wait until next week to get started. And Granger would be impressed with how quickly she was moving. "Tonight will be fine," Marlie told him. "What time?"

"How about seven? May I pick you up, since I'm assuming you are unable to drive yet?"

"Seven will be fine, and I appreciate the offer of a ride. That's very kind of you. But before I agree you should know that I live a fair way out in the country off Holliman Road. It's a good forty-five-minute drive from town."

Waring assured her it would be no problem, then asked for directions, which Marlie struggled to provide. It had been some time since she'd seen the route with her own eyes, much less driven it, and the details had grown fuzzy in her mind. She admitted as much and gave him her home phone number so he could call in the event he got lost.

When she hung up, Marlie leaned back in her chair and smiled. What an unexpected turn of events! She was flattered by Waring's interest in her, and not totally uninterested herself. But she would need to be careful to keep things on a professional level, at least in the beginning, in order not to compromise the piece. Still, this interesting twist in their relationship certainly couldn't hurt. Even the smallest hint of intimacy was likely to make the man open up to her and reveal things he might not otherwise. Who knew where it might eventually lead?

chapter
26

It was late afternoon when Damaris finally returned to the office with the results of her research. Beginning with the information on Waring, she removed a thick sheaf of pages from the file and proceeded to read from them.

"Richard Davenport Waring, age forty-two, single, six feet one inch tall, weight approximately one-eighty-five. Hair is dark brown, eyes hazel. His father was a construction worker, his mother a secretary. Waring himself is the CEO at Virginia Federal Bank with an estimated net worth of somewhere between one and three million dollars."

Marlie whistled. Waring's phenomenal success was a story in itself—from humble beginnings to millionaire status. But she knew his current wealth could actually play against him. In today's society, a line was often drawn between the haves and the have-nots. The key would be to mention it but not dwell on it, focusing on the journey rather than the destination.

Damaris continued. "He was first elected to the state Senate five years ago in a landslide victory over the incumbent. He has sought reelection twice since then, winning both times by significant margins. He is a fearful deliberator, both eloquent and tenacious. He does his homework and rarely loses a debate against an opponent. During his five years in office, his political agenda has been that of a fairly liberal Republican, with—"

"I'm pretty familiar with his political agenda already," Marlie interrupted. "What were you able to dig up on his personal life?"

"Plenty. You know of course that he was adopted."

Marlie nodded. "I thought about trying to locate his birth parents once, but never got around to doing it. Besides, digging up someone's adoption records isn't easy."

"Apparently Ms. Cumberland tried."

"Really? How do you know? Is there something in the file?" Marlie leaned forward with renewed interest.

"There's a ton of stuff in this file, including some things that shouldn't be."

"Such as?"

"Such as medical records. I don't know how she got her hands on them, but there are several of them here, everything from his treatment after the accident six years ago to stuff from his childhood."

"Ronni was nothing if not determined," Marlie said sourly. "What else is in there?"

"News clips, names, phone numbers, some biographical data on both him and his parents."

"What about the adoption? What did she have in there regarding that?"

"Nothing specific, exactly. But I ran across a list of crossed-out names and phone numbers that Ms. Cumberland had written down on a scrap of paper. It didn't look particularly significant at first and I was about to skip past it when one of the names caught my eye: Nancy Rougemeyer."

Damaris paused, and Marlie gave her a shrug and a shake of her head to indicate the name meant nothing to her.

"It's an unusual name," Damaris went on, "and one I happen to know. You see, I'm adopted, and when I turned twenty-one I contacted the agency that handled the adoption to inquire about my birth parents. I was assigned a confidential intermediary, someone who will open the records, get in touch with the parties involved, and initiate contact if all are in agreement. The name of my intermediary was Nancy Rougemeyer.

"Seeing that name in the file got me to wondering if it was the same woman. And if it was, whether or not the other names listed on that paper were also people related to adoption agencies. So I called the numbers listed next to the names. Every one of them is an adoption agency in the northern Virginia area."

"So Ronni tried to track down Waring's adoption records," Marlie mused. She felt a tiny trill of excitement as she thought about what a great addition this could be for her profile. It smacked a bit of talk-show hype, but it would make for compelling footage nonetheless.

"It looks that way," Damaris said.

"I take it she didn't find them."

"There's nothing else in the file, if that's what you mean," Damaris said. "But there is one interesting thing about that list of names. All but one of them had a phone number listed beside it, and all but that one were crossed out, as if they were being eliminated from the list. Actually, the sole name left doesn't look as if it's part of the list. It's written off to the side, sort of like an afterthought."

"Any ideas on who it is or what it means?"

Damaris shrugged. "Not really. I called several adoption agencies in the area, but no one recognized the name. Nor is it listed with information."

"Did you talk to these other names she had listed, the ones that were affiliated with adoption agencies?"

Damaris shook her head. "I doubt Ms. Cumberland got anywhere with the adoption agencies. It's hard enough for people who are part of the adoption triad to get any information, much less an outsider."

"Plus," Marlie pointed out, "we don't know if the agency involved was even in this area, or if an agency was involved at all. It might have been a private adoption."

"There are some other avenues we can try," Damaris said. "An inquiry to the local Department of Health or a search of one of the many registries. There are several registries on-line, as well as a number of standard ones. The problem is, we would be asking about a relatively public figure and that might rouse some unwanted curiosity. Even if we did get some information, it would only be non-identifying stuff, things like the age and occupation of the birth parents, or if you're really lucky sometimes even something as vital as a birth date. But that still leaves an awful lot of hunting and guesswork to be done. Trust me, I know."

"You've been hunting for your birth parents?"

Damaris nodded. Her glowance, Marlie noticed, had narrowed, taking on dark shades of blue and lavender.

"Any luck?"

"Just a lot of false hope and dead ends."

"I'm sorry."

Damaris gave a halfhearted shrug and wrapped her arms around herself. "So, have any ideas on what to do with this one name that's left on the list?"

Marlie thought about it. "What is the name?"

Damaris shuffled through the file on her lap and found the piece of paper. "Dennis Lomax," she read.

"Dennis Lomax?" Marlie sat up straighter, a look of surprise on her face.

"Yeah. You know him?"

"I certainly do," Marlie said. "Assuming it's the same one. And knowing Ronni . . ." She let the sentence hang, turning suddenly and looking at the desk. "Did you run across an address or personal phone book in here anywhere? Or even a Rolodex?" she asked.

"No," Damaris said. "That's odd, isn't it? I hadn't realized it before."

"The cops probably took it," Marlie decided. She picked up the phone and dialed in the number for long-distance information, entering the area code for Richmond. She then asked the operator for the Bureau of Vital Statistics at the Department of Health. After taking a moment to commit the number to memory, she dialed.

"Dennis Lomax, please," she said to the woman who answered.

"I'm sorry, but Dennis is out of the office at the moment. May I take a message or would you like his voice-mail?"

"Voice-mail, please." Marlie waited while the woman switched her over, then listened to Dennis's brief, "I'm not here now so leave a message at the tone."

"Dennis. This is Marlie. Please give me a call at your earliest convenience. It's rather important. Call me either at work or at home." She left both numbers, then hung up.

"So who is this guy?" Damaris asked.

"Dennis is an old friend of mine from school. For the past six years he's been working on a special project compiling a computer database of everyone who ever lived in Virginia by pulling together information from birth, death, tax and Social Security records, marriage and divorce records, you name it. He also happens to be a rather talented hacker, although he would prefer that most people not know that and will deny it with his dying breath. He has access to several federal databases as well, and has tracked down some folks for me before."

"He can do that?" Damaris asked.

"If you mean is he capable, then yes. Very. If you mean is he allowed to, well, that's a bit murkier," Marlie admitted. "Dennis has done some favors for me because we used to be . . . very good friends."

"Friends?" Damaris repeated, suspicion tingeing her voice.

Marlie smiled. Damaris had good instincts. "Okay, maybe a little more than friends."

"Is he still burning a torch for you?"

Marlie laughed. "Yes, I suppose he is."

"How long has it been since the two of you were . . . well, you know."

"A long time." Marlie gazed off, her mind traveling back in time. "It was back when we both first started college. Let's see, that was about twenty years ago."

"Wow. And he's still pining away after all this time?"

"I wouldn't call it pining," Marlie said with a laugh. "Besides, as long as Dennis has his computers, he's happy. They were his first and, at times, his only love. That's one of the reasons we broke up. I didn't take too well to coming in second behind a piece of machinery. Anyway, when he calls back, I can find out if Ronni contacted him about Waring. In the meantime, tell me what else you have. Anything on the accident?"

Damaris shuffled some papers, then began reading again. "In essence, they lost control on a wet road, hit a guardrail, bounced off that, and hit a tree. Waring, who was riding in the backseat, was able to get himself out of the car. His parents, however, were pinned in the front seat and Waring was trying to get them out when the whole thing caught fire. Another car happened along at this point, and witnesses said that if it hadn't been for bystanders who held him back, Waring would have burned to death along with his parents. As it was, he suffered burns on his hands and arms before someone pulled him away from the car."

"My God," Marlie muttered. "Can you imagine what he went through? The pain he had to have suffered, both physically and mentally . . ." She paused, squeezing her eyes closed as the horrifying image of Chris in his final moments leaped into her mind.

"It had to have been awful," Damaris agreed. "And there's a cruelly ironic twist to the story. In addition to the burns and his other injuries, Waring sustained a nasty concussion. Along with a severe, and certainly understandable, case of depression, he also experienced extensive long-term memory loss, whether from the head trauma, the psychological trauma, or both, no one really knows. And while the memory loss left gaping holes in his past, leaving him unable to identify close friends and family and robbing him of most of his adult life, the one thing he could remember with torturous clarity was every horrifying detail of the accident."

Marlie grimaced, wondering what sort of hell it must be to have your only memories consist of the most painful moment in your life. She understood all too well what it was like to be stuck in a continuous replay of life's horrors, thanks to her own recurring nightmare. But at least she had the rest of her past intact, with plenty of good memories to balance out the bad.

Damaris continued her story, and though Marlie had heard most of it before, she listened intently, Damaris's retelling of the events seeming to bring them to life. "It was several months after the accident before Waring returned to work, and when he did, he had to reacquaint himself with many aspects of his job as well as most of the people he worked with. That reacquaintance process worked both ways it seems, as Waring returned to work a changed man. In addition to losing over twenty pounds, he apparently experienced something of a personality change as well, a change for the better according to most. Whereas before he was rather reserved and businesslike, after the accident he was gregarious and outgoing. And while he might have had to relearn many of the details of his job, everyone seems to agree he was a quick study. Some surmised that parts of his memory returned, though no one really knows and Waring has never said one way or the other. Whatever happened, it certainly didn't hurt his career any. Despite the fact that he was known for his ultraconservative investment decisions—enough so that he earned the nickname Wary Waring—when he returned after the accident, he delved into some pretty risky stuff, making some daring investments that paid off handsomely both for himself and many of his bank's clients. Consequently, by the time he decided to run for the Senate a year after the accident, he had a bevy of wealthy, influential, and very pleased customers firmly on his side. Between that and the big chunk of the public's heart he stole with the story of his parents' death, his predecessor never stood a chance. And the rest, as they say, is history."

"Fascinating," Marlie said, both her tone and her expression distracted. In her mind, she was realizing how crucial it could be to again play on that public sentiment by resurrecting the horrors Waring had managed to survive. Yet she also knew that dredging up those memories would likely cause him terrible anguish, maybe even piss him off enough that he would change his mind about the interview.

She would have to play that card very carefully, feeling her way along, looking for the right moment, the right opportunity. The last thing she wanted was to destroy the rather unique relationship they seemed to be building, which she suspected might prove to be as interesting to her personally as it was professionally.

"What about his love life?" Marlie asked Damaris. "Find anything on that?"

"Nothing long term. Apparently he had a woman he was pretty tight with at the time of the accident, a Suzanne Farrington. Rumor had it they were thinking marriage even, but they broke up just a month after the accident. Since then, there have been a few one-time-type dates, but nothing serious."

Marlie furrowed her brow in thought. "See if you can track down this Suzanne Farrington and talk to her. Maybe she has some insight into the accident that we can't find in the published sources."

Damaris nodded, scribbling something on a piece of paper. "Well," she said. "that's pretty much it on Senator Waring. Do you want what I found on Detective Paul Carvelle?"

At the mention of his name, Marlie felt her heart grow heavier. For a while, her excitement over the pending Waring interview had allowed her to forget all about William's innuendos. Now, with one simple sentence, Damaris had brought it all back. And judging from the tone of her voice, she had found something significant. A big part of Marlie didn't want to hear it, but the other part won out.

"Okay, tell me."

"Well, he joined the local police force about a year and a half ago," Damaris began. "He came here from Canton, Ohio, where he worked on their force for fifteen years. He has a degree in computer programming, and his first promotion to detective was in the computer crimes division, where he investigated cyber stalkers, hackers, on-line con artists and sex offenders. Then, after the death of his wife, he asked for and received a transfer to homicide where he—"

"Wife?" Marlie interrupted. "Carvelle had a wife?"

"He did. Lisa Manning Carvelle. She died—was murdered actually—almost seven years ago. She was six months pregnant at the time."

"Murdered? My God! How?"

"She was one of three employees shot during a bank robbery. One of the other employees also died, the third was injured, but recuperated."

Marlie couldn't have been more stunned. Carvelle had had a wife? A pregnant wife? Why hadn't he ever mentioned the fact?

"Anyway, as I was saying, he was transferred to homicide, where he worked for five years, and then he relocated here, taking a position with the local department, also in homicide. He had only been here a few months when his partner, whose name was Michael Phillips by the way, was killed. Apparently Carvelle and Phillips responded to a call about a murder at a crack house. A drug deal gone bad kind of thing. They showed up, and after they'd been on the scene for half an hour or so, someone discovered several junked-up dealers hiding inside a false closet. A rather panicked and chaotic shoot-out followed, and when it was all over, the junkies were dead, as was Phillips. When Internal Affairs investigated—"

"Wait, wait," Marlie said, holding up her hand and frowning. "I don't understand. Phillips's death was certainly tragic, and perhaps indicative of an error in judgment on the part of the patrol cops who were first on the scene, but I don't understand why IA got involved."

"Two reasons. Turns out Phillips was doing some undercover work for IA, sniffing out some rumors about bad cops who were on the take. According to IA, he was closing in on several of the prime suspects, told them he knew who they were but had no solid proof yet. He didn't give IA any names."

"Which perhaps makes his death a little too coincidental," Marlie mused.

"Exactly. But that's not the only reason IA got involved. It seems Phillips was killed by a bullet from Paul Carvelle's gun."

"What?" Marlie fairly shouted the word.

"Well, there was a lot of gunfire going on in the house, and it was dark. Several other cops were injured by gunshots from the druggies. One of the patrolmen who was there said it was like being inside a fun house, with terror coming at you from every corner. The cops were caught completely by surprise and their efforts weren't very well coordinated. According to Carvelle's testimony, he saw one of the drug dealers pop around a corner and fire at him, then duck back behind the wall. Carvelle moved in and, just as he reached the corner of the wall, someone stepped out. Carvelle pulled the trigger on reflex. Unfortunately, it was Phillips rather than the druggie."

Marlie looked away, trying to absorb everything Damaris was telling her. She couldn't believe Carvelle had never so much as hinted at any of this in the many times they had talked over the past year. She glanced back up at Damaris. "I assume Carvelle was exonerated," she said. "Given that he's still working."

"I guess IA bought his story, though he did serve several months of probation time. One thing that worked in his favor was the testimony of the other cops who were there, and the fact that another officer was hit by a police bullet, although he was fortunate enough to only be grazed. But word has it they're still not convinced the whole thing was an accident and that Carvelle is still being closely watched."

"How on earth did you manage to dig all this up?" Marlie asked, amazed. "I can't believe you found all of this in the newspaper and video archives."

"A lot of it was there. But I tapped into an inside source for most of the IA stuff."

"What inside source?" Marlie asked, the question framed in skepticism.

"Well, my roommate, Christine, has been dating one of the cops on the force for the past six months."

"I'll be damned," Marlie mumbled. She looked at Damaris with newfound admiration. "You've done some excellent work on this. I appreciate your initiative and thoroughness."

"Thank you." Damaris's glowance gleamed brightly beneath the praise. "I'm having fun with it. I was afraid I was going to be stuck doing scut work, you know, getting coffee for some superstar reporter or working as an errand girl. That's what most of my friends are doing with their internships."

"Well, I'm glad you're enjoying it. And I'm also glad you're here to help me. I wouldn't be able to do this on my own, and frankly I wasn't crazy about the idea of having to work with someone. I've always been more of a solo act. But I think we're going to work well together. You have all the right instincts and, more importantly, the hunger."

"Hunger?"

"For the story. If you don't have the hunger, the drive to dig a little deeper or search a little harder, you won't get anywhere in this business. You've got to be aggressive, actively pursue the facts and work the system. Develop sources and contacts. Otherwise you'll be stuck forever doing those field reports on the county fair, informing the world about whose pig won the blue ribbon."

Damaris laughed. "Yeah, one of my classmates got the pig patrol," she said. "Thank you for keeping me out of the mud, so to speak."

"You're more than welcome," Marlie said with a smile. "And don't get too cocky. You've been lucky this time, in that you already had a good contact in place. It won't always be that easy. Finding and maintaining those kinds of contacts is key to your future success. It's hard work. You have to nurture them, stay in touch even when you don't need them. And whatever you do, don't ever betray them. Never give up your sources unless they agree to it. Integrity is key."

"Understood."

"Good," Marlie said with an approving nod. Then she assumed an expression of exaggerated sternness. "Now, get back to work before we both end up judging cow pies."

Damaris responded with a snappy salute, a "Yes, sir!" and a glowance that flared with the bright golden light of a thousand suns.

chapter 27

Roberta's enthusiasm as she helped Marlie prepare for her dinner with Senator Waring was greater than Marlie's own. Grateful to see her mother so happy, Marlie sat before the mirror in her bedroom and tolerated Roberta's seemingly endless fussing over her hair and makeup. Her own mind, however, was paying no attention to the blurred image in the mirror. Instead it was exploring the two trains of thought that had occupied most of her day, crazily switching tracks back and forth. The first was how she could maneuver Waring into talking about the tragic period of his life without angering or upsetting him to the point that he cut off the interview entirely. The second had to do with Damaris's startling revelations about Carvelle. Given Waring's imminent arrival, Marlie was trying to stay focused on the upcoming interview, but the situation with Carvelle kept pushing its way to the forefront of her thoughts.

If she had any doubts about the veracity of Damaris's thirdhand information on Carvelle, they were eliminated when Cindy reported back on her luncheon discussion with Rosie, who had essentially verified Damaris's story. Questions had been racing through Marlie's mind ever since, questions whose answers she wasn't sure she wanted to know, though that reticence wasn't enough to keep her from digging. Part of Marlie's need to know sprang out of her confusion about Carvelle's current behavior and motives, but another part of it came from her burning curiosity about Carvelle's wife and their marriage.

Given Damaris's disturbing revelations about Carvelle, Marlie was rethinking the warehouse incident. She couldn't help but wonder if Carvelle's assignment as the chief investigator of the incident was merely a coincidence, or if the hints of police corruption that had led her there in the first place were somehow tied to the hints of corruption that seemed to shadow Carvelle. If there was a connection, it might explain his persistence in pursuing the case when most other investigators would have set it aside long ago. Was he afraid she could somehow connect him to that night?

The more Marlie thought about it, the more she began to see recent events in a new light. First there was the fact that Carvelle claimed he couldn't find a tape that corresponded with the phone conversation Marlie had overheard in Ronni's office. Could that conversation have been with Carvelle himself? And if so, didn't it make sense that he would conveniently claim that a tape of said conversation never existed?

Then there was the political dinner where Marlie had seen what appeared to be the same black glowance she'd seen in the clearing. While she couldn't identify the owner of that terrifying blackness, the fact that she had seen it near the entrance to the banquet room, where Roberta had seen Carvelle standing as he supposedly served his watchdog duty, was telling.

Finally, there was that whole thing with someone searching her house less than forty-eight hours after the police watch had been called off. Maybe it hadn't been William after all. The timing *was* awfully coincidental, almost as if it were an indication of inside knowledge.

The only thing Marlie couldn't figure out was why? What interest would Carvelle have had with her in the first place? Marlie didn't even know him at the time of the warehouse incident, and certainly had no cause to suspect him of any involvement in police corruption schemes.

Unless . . .

Unless Carvelle got wind of Marlie's anonymous caller somehow and headed him off at the warehouse. Marlie had always assumed that the body found in the warehouse that night had been that of the shooter. Was it possible the man had been dead before she and Chris ever got there, and it was someone else who fired those fateful shots? Someone who managed to escape the subsequent conflagration?

When she had received the call that led her to the warehouse that night, she had gotten the distinct impression the caller was a cop himself, even though the man had never come right out and said so. Yet Carvelle had said the man whose body they found was a petty criminal and a drifter. How would someone like that have any inside knowledge about police corruption? Carvelle knew from listening to the tapes that William had called Ronni on the day she was murdered. And according to Damaris, Carvelle had worked in a computer crimes division on the Ohio police force. How hard would it be for someone with Carvelle's computer knowledge to "create" an identity for the unknown victim, an identity that he knew, after listening to the tapes, would implicate someone who had called Ronni on the day of her death and also obscure the dead man's real identity?

Yet, if the man who died in the warehouse had been a cop, wouldn't there have been an intense investigation when one of the members of the force suddenly turned up missing? Unless there was some other plausible theory to explain away his absence. Marlie made a mental note to have Damaris look back and see if any cops quit the force just prior to the warehouse incident.

The doorbell rang and Marlie was more than glad to tuck her mental musings aside. This constant circular thinking—suspecting William one minute and Carvelle the next—was making her crazy. But the melodic sound of the chime was a Pavlov-type trigger for a whole new set of anxieties. She instantly switched her thoughts to the coming evening and Waring. While she had insisted their dinner be conducted on a professional level, the knowledge of Waring's apparent interest in her on a more-than-professional basis made her nervous. Not that the idea was an unpleasant one—far from it. But Marlie hadn't dated anyone in twenty years. When she and William split up, she had been too busy and too emotionally cross-wired to even consider dating. And of course, dating hadn't been high on her list of priorities following the warehouse accident.

Not that anyone had asked.

"Well, aren't you going to answer the door?" Roberta asked, giving Marlie a little nudge.

"Would you get it, Mom? I need a minute."

Roberta eyed her daughter worriedly. "Everything all right?"

"Everything's fine, Mother. I'm just a little nervous is all. I want another few seconds to collect myself. I'll be right there. In the meantime, here's your chance to discuss that physician assisted suicide bill you never got to talk about at the dinner."

Marlie listened, mentally tracking her mother's footsteps to the front door, hearing the sound of the latch being thrown, followed by Waring's hearty greeting. "Dr. Gallaway! Good to see you again."

"Likewise, Senator Waring. Please come in. Marlie will be ready in just a moment."

Marlie turned and gazed at herself in the mirror, something she had done frequently over the past hour, although now she was really seeing herself for the first time. Her hair was growing quickly, and the short curls tousled around her head in a loose cap. Her dress was black, elegant but simple according to Roberta. And while the top boasted a high neckline and three-quarter-length sleeves that would otherwise be modest, everything above her bustline was done in sheer black lace. It was sexy without being blatantly so. Or at least that was what she hoped. She cocked her head and studied her own glowance, which was turbulent in conjunction with her thoughts, spotted with pools of deep purples and blues on a narrow band of pale yellow. It gave the overall effect of being bruised, not unlike her psyche.

Before heading out to meet Waring, she ventured across the hall to her office and dug around until she found her spare handheld recorder in a drawer of the desk. Checking to be sure it had a tape in it, she dropped it into her purse, fortified herself with a sigh, and headed out to the main part of the house.

She found them in the living room. Roberta was giggling like a schoolgirl over some comment Waring had made, and Marlie could see her mother's blush in the rosy shade of her glowance. Waring's, on the other hand, shone with the same brilliant, warming radiance she had seen at the fundraising dinner, the sheer light of it brightening the room.

"Wow," Waring said as Marlie stepped into the room. "You look stunning."

"Thank you," she said, feeling her face and ears grow hot. "But my mother really deserves all the credit. She's the one who put me together."

Waring let out a warmhearted laugh. "Ah, yes," he said, giving Roberta an approving glance. "In more ways than one, I venture. Good looks obviously run in the family."

"My, my," Roberta said, fanning herself with her hand. "No wonder you're so successful as a politician. Do you exercise such flattering hyperbole on your opponents, as well?"

Waring laughed again, more boisterous this time. "Only when I have no other recourse," he said. He turned back to Marlie. "I love your house, and your mother was just filling me in on some of its history. She said you have tunnels in the basement that date back to the Civil War?"

Marlie nodded. "Actually, I suspect they're older than that even." She briefly filled him in on the Civil War aspects of the tunnels' history. "They are quite fascinating, something of an engineering marvel, considering their extent and structure and when they were built. And of course, there is their historical significance, as well."

"Fascinating," Waring said. "I take it you've explored them then?"

"Some," Marlie said vaguely. She considered mentioning her foray last night, but thought better of it. Then she remembered the kitchen chair that was propped beneath the basement door and flushed with embarrassment. She wondered if Roberta had noticed it. If she had, she hadn't mentioned it. Of course, lately Roberta chalked a lot of things up to what she undoubtedly thought of as Marlie's eccentricities.

"Well, I've always been fascinated with that period of history," Waring said. "If you decide on any future explorations, I'd love to come along."

His comment gave Marlie a sudden flash of an idea—conducting part of Waring's interview within the tunnels, tying his own political platform of aiding minorities to the emancipation platform of the Civil War. It had potential, and she tucked it away until she could give it more thought.

"In the meantime," Waring went on, "I don't know about you, but I'm starving. Are you ready?"

"I am," Marlie said. She gave her mother a quick buss on the cheek and turned to head for the door. Waring reached out and took her hand, gently guiding it to the crook of his elbow. Marlie wrapped her fingers around his arm, keenly aware of how the hard muscle beneath his sleeve contrasted with the silky softness of the material in his jacket.

"Don't forget to be back by midnight," Roberta said after them. Then to Waring, "She's most unattractive as a pumpkin."

Waring roared. Coming from anyone else it might have sounded false and forced, but Waring made it seem genuine. Just one more aspect of his mystical charm. "I see the sharp wit is an inherited trait as well," he said. "Don't worry, Dr. Gallaway. We'll be back before midnight and I promise to take good care of your daughter and behave like a gentleman."

Marlie bristled slightly at Waring's mention of taking care of her but let it go, realizing he likely only meant it figuratively. As for behaving like a gentleman, the man oozed a sensuality that left Marlie in doubt whether or not good behavior was what she really wanted.

From what few details Marlie could make out, Waring's car appeared to be a nondescript, older-model sedan. *Fitting,* she thought, making the first of her mental notes. *As informal and unpretentious as its owner.* As Waring settled her into the front seat, she caught the faintest whiff of a men's cologne—a lingering remnant—mixed with a tinge of pipe tobacco.

"Do you smoke a pipe?" she asked as Waring turned the car around and headed down the driveway. From the corner of her eye, she saw his head pivot sharply toward her in surprise.

"Now, how in the hell did you know that? I never do it in public."

"Ah, but you do it in the car at times, don't you? I can smell it."

"Amazing. You must have one heck of a nose. I do smoke in the car on occasion, but only rarely. And the last time was quite a while ago. I hope the smell isn't offensive."

"Not at all," Marlie assured him. "It's very subtle, and pleasant. I'm not sure the average person would even notice it. But my sense of smell has become very keen over the past year or so, ever since I lost my sight." She paused a moment, a wistful expression on her face. "My father used to smoke a pipe from time to time. Brings back memories."

"Is your father deceased?"

Marlie nodded. "He died nearly ten years ago. Brain tumor."

"I'm sorry."

"Thanks. I still miss him, although time does seem to soften the pangs." She realized this turn in their conversation gave her the perfect opening. She hesitated only a fraction of a second, concerned that it might be a mistake to bring the topic up so soon, but loathe to let the opportunity slip away. "I suppose it will take more than mere time to ease the pangs for you," she said softly.

He said nothing for a long time, and Marlie's heart skipped a beat. But then he said, "Time helps some, though I'm not sure I'll ever be able to totally wipe away the horror of that night. And, of course, I have this as a permanent reminder," he added, holding up one of his scarred hands.

"You loved your parents very much," she said, more of a question than a statement.

"They were good people. Simple people. They taught me everything they knew, supported me in whatever I wanted to do, and loved me unfailingly, as if I were their own. I've heard other adopted children talk about how they feel something missing in their lives because they don't know who their biological parents were. But probably my parents' greatest legacy is the fact that they left me emotionally and mentally fulfilled to the point that I never felt the need or the desire to seek out my birth parents."

"What about now?" Marlie posed. "With your adoptive parents gone, you are essentially alone in the world. Doesn't that make you even the least bit curious about your other family?"

"I'm not alone," Waring said. "I have distant relatives—aunts, uncles and cousins. And I've never believed that family is defined by any sort of blood connection, but rather an emotional one. The woman who gave birth to me was little more than a conduit for my entry into the world. Any emotional ties that might have existed were obviously not strong enough. So what purpose would it serve to look for something that doesn't exist?"

Marlie looked over at him, fascinated by the sudden change in his glowance. It swirled with passionate reds, dark and intense. "You're angry with her, aren't you?" she asked.

"With who? My birth mother?" He seemed to contemplate the suggestion. "No, I wouldn't call it anger. More of an indifference."

"You assume she gave you up out of some lack of emotional attachment or commitment. But isn't it possible that her life circumstances were such that she had no choice? Might not her decision have been an unselfish one, designed to assure you of the best possible life as opposed to fulfilling her own emotional needs?"

"I don't know. And I suppose I never will," he said flippantly. "So tell me, given that keen nose of yours, maybe you can tell what we're having for dinner, since I cooked most of it before coming to get you."

Clearly, he was done discussing the matter of his birth mother. Marlie was disappointed and considered pushing the issue, but instinct told her to let it go for now. Maybe an opportunity would arise later to bring it up again. Something that emotional was better dealt with in bits and pieces anyway. So she laughed, sniffed the air, and said, "Nope, no hint of dinner. But I'm impressed that you cooked."

"Impressed? Why?"

She shrugged. "Oh, I don't know. Busy politician. Bachelor. I suppose I assumed you either ate out most of the time or had someone who cooked for you."

"Well, you're right on one count. I do eat out quite often, but rarely by choice. It's mostly business dinners. Whenever I can, I prefer to eat at home and fix my own meals. I dare say I'm a pretty decent cook, though you'll have to be the judge of that tonight."

"Well then, I should probably warn you that my sense of taste has become heightened along with my sense of smell."

He glanced over at her with a grimacing smile. "Uh-oh," he said, the warmth of his glowance belying the words. "Promise you'll be gentle with me, okay?"

chapter 28

"Well, this is it," Waring said, guiding Marlie through the front door of his house. "It's not much, and certainly doesn't boast anything as exotic as underground tunnels, but I call it home. Would you like a quick tour?"

"I'd love one," Marlie said, gazing about the room before her and trying to determine as much detail as she could in the blurred shapes and shadows. From what she could make out, Waring's house was much like the man: laid back and practical, but with a touch of refinement. Though his home was part of a fairly well-to-do private community with spacious grounds and a guarded entrance, it was smaller, less ostentatious than those of his neighbors, at least on the outside. Inside, however, Marlie got the distinct impression of ambient luxury as her feet sank into soft, plush carpet and her eyes took in the subdued tones and warm glow created by the recessed lighting overhead. The overall feel of the place bore a striking resemblance to the feel Marlie got from Waring himself, or at least from his glowance.

Straight ahead was the living room, its ceiling high and vaulted, a huge stone fireplace taking up most of the wall to the right. The far wall had floor-to-ceiling windows that looked out onto a two-tiered deck and the deepening shadows of dusk beyond.

Waring explained that off to the right, behind the fireplace wall, was a bedroom he used as an office, and a guest bath. To their left was a wrought-iron staircase that spiraled up toward a loft and what Marlie presumed were more bedrooms.

Waring steered her to the left side of the living room and up a couple of steps that led to the kitchen. Beyond the kitchen was the dining room, which struck Marlie as incongruous with the rest of the house. The furnishings she had seen thus far were soft and rounded, arranged to create the illusion of cozy spaciousness, the overall color scheme one of muted pastels. The kitchen gleamed from the warm glow of burnished oak cabinets, copper pots that hung from a rack suspended from the ceiling, and a glossy hardwood floor. But by comparison to the rest of the house, the dining room was stark and cold. At its center was a huge squared-off table surrounded by twelve large clunky chairs, and along the left wall was a tall and imposing sideboard, all of them built from the same heavy dark wood. The carpet and walls were white, harshly reflecting the light from a huge chandelier that hovered over the table like some alien spacecraft. Despite the mammoth area occupied by the table, the room had a peculiar empty feel to it.

"You have a lovely home," Marlie commented, turning away from the uninviting dining room and facing the kitchen.

"Thank you. Personally, I wouldn't mind something a bit smaller, but I do have an image to uphold. And I like the neighborhood. It's quiet, the neighbors are friendly without being intrusive, and the houses are spaced far enough apart to give you some privacy."

Marlie noticed a glass table with four chairs in the far corner of the kitchen. A Tiffany-style lamp hung from above, casting a warm jeweled light across the ceiling. Two places were set at the table; at its center was a candle surrounded by a wreath of fresh cut flowers.

Seeing the direction of Marlie's gaze, Waring said, "I hope you don't mind eating out here. I could have set us up in the dining room, but frankly, I hate that room. I do have certain social obligations as a part of my job, and I suppose the dining room works well enough for those. But tonight I wanted something a bit more relaxed and informal." He turned and gazed into the dining room. "That room always seems so formal, so . . ." He struggled for the word.

"Cold? Stark? Rigid? Ceremonial?" Marlie suggested.

Waring laughed. "You don't mince words, do you?"

"It's not in my job description. I love your kitchen. Eating out here will be fine." She raised her nose and sniffed the air appreciatively. "And judging from the smell, I hope it will be soon."

Waring sat her at the table with a glass of wine while he put the finishing touches on their meal. Twenty minutes later, they were indulging themselves in stuffed chicken breasts, boiled red potatoes, and fresh asparagus with hollandaise sauce. Their dinner conversation was light and Waring carried most of it, prattling on about such topics as the weather, current affairs, and the local political cli-

mate. For her own part, Marlie mainly listened, con-
centrating on her meal, grateful she could now see
well enough to eat without the use of her fingers to
find and guide her food onto her fork. She thought
about dragging out her tape recorder but felt it
would be too rude to do so while they were eating.
But as soon as their plates were empty and Waring
went to clear them, Marlie asked him if she could
tape the rest of their talk. After a disconsolate sigh,
Waring agreed.

Despite his obvious dislike of the tape recorder,
Waring continued to chat away as he replaced their
dinner plates with bowls of strawberry shortcake
made with homemade cake and real whipped cream.
Marlie marveled at how domestic he was for a long-
term bachelor and at how comfortable she felt in his
presence. While part of her mind listened to him,
commenting whenever it was required, another part
was already formulating her report, figuring out how
to incorporate the observations she had made this
evening into the more personal part of Waring's profile. Showing his warmth, his personality and
charm, would be crucial to the piece. The question
was how best to do that. Conveying feeling through
the medium of TV could be challenging at best,
impossible at worst.

If only I could televise that glowance, she thought,
for its golden radiance—brighter and more intense
than any others she had seen—seemed to embody
the feeling of comfort and confidence Waring
instilled in her. The combined effects of the wine
and the meal left her feeling sleepy, content, and
somewhat entranced. Thus, she was caught unaware

when Waring's conversation suddenly took a more personal turn.

"You have a daughter, do you not?" he asked.

Marlie shook off her reverie, the surprise showing on her face. "I do. How did you know that?"

He smiled cryptically. "You journalists aren't the only ones with sources, you know. I believe Kristen is her name?"

Mention of Kristen reminded her of William, Carvelle, and her suspicions about them both. "It is," Marlie said, her concern reflected clearly in her tone. Waring didn't miss it.

"I'm sorry," he said with a frown. "Have I upset you? I didn't mean to. It's just that Garrity dug up some old tapes of your earlier work and I was reviewing them recently. You made mention of your daughter in one of the reports, and I thought I'd ask . . ." His voice trailed off and he shrugged. "I'm sorry."

"You have nothing to be sorry for," Marlie said, dismissing his apology with a halfhearted wave of her hand. "I'm the one who should apologize. It's just that . . . well . . . the topic of my daughter is a difficult one right now."

Waring leaned across the table and laid a reassuring hand over hers. "Problems?" he asked.

"Sort of," Marlie said vaguely. She chewed the side of her lip, as much to keep herself from giving in to a sudden urge to cry as to hold her tongue tight.

Waring's hand squeezed her arm, his touch managing somehow to be both firm and gently soothing. While she was aware of the scarring along his hand, Marlie found it not at all repulsive. His glowance radiated a quiet warmth from his upper arms to his head, seeming to reach across the table to her and seep through her skin, warming the blood in her veins, as were the three glasses of wine she'd had with dinner.

"I'm willing to listen, if you want to talk about it," he said, his voice soft. "Though I'll certainly understand if you prefer not to."

Marlie gazed longingly at the reassuring comfort of Waring's glowance a few moments longer, debating, knowing that unburdening herself would be an immense relief, but recalling her own insistence that this evening remain on a professional level, not a personal one. The battle waging within herself was short, but intense. In the end, she caved in.

For the next half hour she filled Waring in on her history with William, Ronni's murder and the fact that she witnessed it but couldn't identify the killer, and Carvelle's suspicions about William's possible motive and connection. After a moment's debate, she even shared her thoughts about Carvelle and his possible connection to the rumored corruption in the local force. She left out the part about her eavesdropping and Ronni's tapes, figuring that copping to her coworker's unethical habits might scare Waring off, particularly if he or Garrity had ever spoken with Ronni themselves. She also refrained from telling him about the glowances. While she certainly gave them more credence now than she had initially, she was all too aware of how bizarre it might sound to someone else.

Waring listened with rapt attention and made no comment until she got onto the subject of

Carvelle. At the mention of police corruption, he interrupted her.

"Before you go any further, there is something I want to tell you. But first you have to promise me that this is strictly off the record. This is not information you can use in any way, shape, or form until it is all resolved. When it is, I will see to it that you get first, if not exclusive coverage of the story."

Puzzled and curious as hell, Marlie agreed. Waring reached over and turned off the tape recorder, which Marlie had forgotten was even on. She grimaced when she realized she had just taped herself unloading her life's story to Waring.

"A couple of years ago," Waring began, "one of my employees at the bank came to me with a report of some rather suspicious dealings on the part of one of our customers. Not that having customers who indulge in slightly shady dealings isn't a part of the business. But this particular employee, whose brother happened to be a local police officer, knew this customer and his reputation for drug dealing and money laundering. Generally, banks don't get involved in their clients' business. A reputation for discretion is crucial to our success. But in this case, the employee unfortunately mentioned what he had observed to his brother and the police approached us. The reason for their interest went deeper than this particular customer's drug connection. There was reason to suspect that part of his business dealings involved cops who were on the take, willing to sell their silence and look the other way."

Marlie listened, both enthralled and upset. She was almost relieved to have her suspicions of police corruption verified, but that was offset by her concerns about Carvelle, which were growing stronger by the minute.

"Because of my position in the legislature and my stance against crime," Waring went on, "I was infuriated to think our local police might be crooked. So I approached the police commissioner and demanded an investigation into the allegations. If we had dirty cops on the force, I wanted them gone and prosecuted to the fullest extent of the law. But I think I underestimated the power of the brotherhood. Somehow, word got out that an investigation was going on and things started to tighten up. The one cop we felt fairly certain we could trust—the brother of my employee—was killed a short while later, supposedly in the line of duty, although the circumstances were highly suspect."

Marlie felt her blood grow cold. "That wouldn't have been Michael Phillips, would it?" she asked, bracing herself for the answer she knew was coming.

"It was," Waring said. "And he was killed by a bullet from his partner's gun, who was—"

"Paul Carvelle," Marlie finished for him. Waring nodded, and Marlie felt the wonderful dinner she had just eaten start to curdle in her stomach. They both sat in silent contemplation a while, Waring with his chin propped in the palm of his hand, Marlie wringing the life out of her napkin.

Finally, Marlie said, "This investigation, is it still ongoing?"

"Very much so. I've helped Commissioner Gaines to organize a task force to look into the allegations and make some serious headway in cleaning up our force. It's all very hush-hush at this point. Only a few key officials are even aware of the investigation. The idea that our local police force may be peppered with criminals is not something we want the public to know, at least not until we've managed to resolve the situation."

"Understood," Marlie said. Despite the sickening feeling growing inside her, a small part of her brain realized what a groundbreaking story this would be when it finally did come out. And she would have first dibs at it. The thought made her heart beat even faster.

"I get regular reports from Commissioner Gaines on the progress of the investigation, which I'm sorry to say has been minimal to this point. I would caution you to take great care, Marlie. There is nothing more dangerous than a dirty cop in my opinion. If they get wind of the fact that you know any of this, your life could well be in danger."

"Do you think they are connected with Ronni's murder somehow?" Marlie asked, explaining to Waring about the file she had started sometime back on the subject of police corruption—a file that Ronni would have had, but was now nowhere to be found.

"I don't know," Waring said. "I'm not sure if the commissioner has even considered the angle, but I'll mention it to him the next time I see him. I suppose if Ronni was investigating the force and found something on one of the cops, it's not too far-fetched to think that one of them might have killed her to avoid exposure." He paused, reached across the table, and gave Marlie's arm a squeeze, his hand lingering for a long second before he pulled it back. "I'm worried for you, Marlie," he said.

"Thanks for your concern. But I'll be fine," she said without conviction.

Waring shook his head. "This whole situation worries me. Who the hell can you trust? If the cops *are* involved with Ronni's murder, they know you were a witness. And if they get any hint at all that you can identify the killer . . ."

Marlie opened her mouth to assure him that she couldn't identify the killer and that furthermore, the cops knew that. But then she remembered her discussion with Carvelle about the glowances, and how the black one surrounding the murderer had radiated a distinctive malevolence unlike any other she had seen. If Carvelle was the murderer—

She shook off the thought. No matter how hard she tried, she couldn't imagine Carvelle doing such a thing. Yet she also knew her judgment might not be at its best right now, tainted by her personal interest in him. Yes, some things about him didn't add up, some secrets he had kept from her. But murder? She just couldn't believe it. She'd stake her life on it.

Which, she realized with a frisson of panic, was exactly what she was doing.

True to his word, Waring pulled up in front of Marlie's house just before midnight and escorted her to the front door. Marlie was grateful for his guidance; nighttime was particularly bad for her, as the shadows seemed to mix and mingle as one, making

the negotiation of stairs and such even more treacherous than usual. On the porch, he paused and gestured toward Roberta's sporty little red car, still
parked in the drive.

"I see your mother is waiting up for you," he
said, making Marlie feel like an adolescent who had
just returned home from her first official date.

Marlie smiled apologetically. "I guess some
habits are hard to break."

"You should be flattered."

"Flattered?"

"That you have a parent who cares enough
about your welfare. Not everyone is so fortunate."

Marlie thought his observation odd, and perhaps a bit out of character. She wondered again if he
didn't harbor some sort of resentment toward the
woman who had given him up at birth.

The truth was, Roberta's continued presence at
the house had less to do with concern than curiosity.
Joe Carter was out of town for a few days, and with
nothing else to do, Roberta had insisted on staying
at the house until Marlie's return, anxious for a
report on how the evening had gone. Marlie had
agreed, but not before soliciting a promise from
Roberta to keep the house tightly locked.

Despite this precaution, which Marlie considered merely prudent, she had managed to convince
herself that nothing was likely to happen, at least
not now. After much thought on the situation earlier today, she had decided that whoever had been in
the house wasn't likely to return soon. She still
believed William was the most likely culprit,
although her suspicions about Carvelle had clouded

that conviction some. Whoever it was, if they were after something in particular, they either found it or determined it didn't exist. If they planned to return for another search, they would likely wait for some time to pass before making another attempt. She also realized that if *she* was what the person was after, there had been opportunity aplenty. If someone had wanted her dead, she would be.

It was just as well that her concerns were somewhat allayed, for her worst fears had been realized when she finally got an estimate on replacing the wiring in the house. Though she had made very good money prior to the accident and had stashed away a healthy savings account, the only income she had had for the past year was her workers' compensation payments, which had taken six months to be approved. Consequently, her savings had dwindled to almost nothing. The money it would cost to fix the ancient wiring was more than what she had left. So with a certain level of resignation, she realized that this project, as well as the alarm system, would have to wait. There was some security in knowing all the locks would be changed when the locksmith came by on Saturday. At least that way, if it was William who had broken in and he had a key, it would no longer work.

As if in complement to her thoughts on the wiring, the light on the porch flickered several times, then went out, plunging Marlie and the senator into darkness. It spooked her, and she quickly turned and fumbled with her key until she found the lock. She opened the door and held it, letting the interior light wash out onto the porch. Waring took it as his cue.

"Well," he said, shuffling his feet like an awkward-feeling schoolboy, "I best be on my way. But I want you to promise me you'll be careful, and that you'll call me if there is anything more you find out, or anything I can do for you."

"I will," she agreed.

"Good. I'm sorry we got so sidetracked this evening. I'm afraid we didn't get much done toward your interview."

"That was as much my fault as anyone's," Marlie said. "And I really don't mind. It felt good to unload."

"In that case, I'm glad I could be of service. And in all honesty, I'm rather pleased we got sidetracked, because now I have an excuse to invite you for another dinner."

Marlie considered his offer. While the intimacy afforded by dinner at his place had been ideal for establishing a level of comfort that made it easier to discuss more personal things, it also created its own brand of distractions. At some point, she would have to bring in a cameraman and make the interview more formalized. But for now, she thought, another dinner wouldn't hurt. It would give her a chance to build on their relationship and create a bond of trust between them that would make the final interview run more smoothly. Besides, she wouldn't mind another evening alone with the man.

"You name the time and place," she told him.

"How about Monday evening? Around seven? I'm supposed to attend some stuffy dinner in support of one of my colleagues that night, but I would love a legitimate excuse to beg off."

"Monday works for me."

"Shall I pick you up again?"

"Actually," Marlie said thoughtfully, "how about having dinner here and letting me cook this time?"

"Was my cooking that bad?"

Marlie laughed. "Not at all. In fact, it was superb and I fear you may find my own culinary talents to be seriously lacking in comparison. I can promise you edible, but not gourmet."

"Edible works for me. I'm actually a man of simple tastes. In fact, if you promise not to tell anyone, I have a secret to share with you."

"Shoot."

"Off the record, right?"

Marlie nodded, amused and a little perplexed.

Waring leaned in a little closer and she caught a whiff of the same cologne she had smelled in the car. It had a pleasantly subtle woodsy scent. "My all-time favorite food in the world is meat loaf," he said, his voice so low it was almost a whisper.

Marlie reared back and looked at him, a wide grin on her face. "That's it? That's your big secret?"

Waring shrugged. "It is. Garrity tells me it's something best kept under wraps, that the future governor of the commonwealth should have tastes a bit less, uh, pedestrian."

"Well, I'll let you in on a little secret of my own," Marlie said. She mimicked Waring's own behavior by leaning in closer to him before she spoke. "Garrity is a jerk."

Waring let out a low chuckle. "He is something of a know-it-all," he admitted. "If it wasn't for the fact that he's right ninety-nine percent of the time, I'd toss him out the door. But frankly, he's really good at all the stuff I don't understand or want to deal with. Like this PR crap and figuring out how to present oneself to the public. I hate it. It seems too manipulative and phony to me. Kind of like this interview we're doing. But I recognize the necessity of playing by the rules, and Garrity knows those rules better than anyone. Besides, I've known him since we were kids. He's been around so long, he's like a permanent fixture."

A question popped into Marlie's mind but disappeared just as quickly, the mesmerizing light of Waring's glowance and the soothing tones of his voice seeming to muddle her thoughts all of a sudden. Instead, she wondered if Waring would finally let go of his gentlemanly behavior and try to kiss her good-night. Even more confusing was the realization that she hoped he would.

Her wish was only partially granted.

"I best be going," he said, and he gently grasped her hand, kissing the back of it. The softness of his lips was a sharp contrast to the scarred ridges of his hand. "Good night, Marlie."

A moment later, she was watching the fading glow of his taillights as they disappeared around the bend in the driveway.

chapter 29

The next morning, Damaris was settled between several stacks of paperwork on the office floor by the time Marlie arrived. She greeted Marlie with a cheery "Good morning!", a cup of coffee, and a blueberry muffin.

"Boy, you sure know how to kiss up," Marlie teased.

"Can't help it," Damaris said, settling into her chair beside the credenza with her own coffee in hand. "I'm deathly allergic to both cow pies and pork."

Marlie laughed.

"So how did your dinner with Senator Waring go?"

"It went well," Marlie said, "although I didn't get as much as I'd hoped. We're getting together again Monday night at my place and, hopefully, we'll be able to move forward with the actual interview after that. In fact, if you would leave the file on him here with me today, I want to scan it into the computer later. My computer adaptations are supposed to be installed sometime this morning."

"That's great," Damaris said, handing Waring's file to Marlie. "Did you let on that we're digging into his adoption?"

Marlie shook her head vehemently, almost choking on a mouthful of coffee. "No!" she said once she managed to swallow the hot liquid. "Absolutely not.

I'm not sure he's going to be at all pleased by the fact. I suspect he harbors some resentment toward his birth mother, though he won't admit it."

"But you're still going to look into it, aren't you?"

"Absolutely."

"Good. By the way, I spent some time last night reviewing the file to see if there were any other tidbits that might give us a clue as to his birth parents."

"Find anything?"

"Actually, I did find one thing in the medical records that might be helpful. Twice in his past, Waring was typed for blood transfusions. The first time occurred when he was only eight and apparently fell off a roof he'd climbed onto to get a baseball. He ruptured his spleen and had emergency surgery at a nearby hospital to have it removed. During surgery, he received two units of blood. The second occasion, of course, was the night of the car accident, though no transfusion actually occurred. But that's not important. What is important is his blood type: AB-negative, which happens to be very rare. Less than one percent of the population in fact. If we assume Waring was born somewhere in the northern Virginia area, which is likely given when his adoption occurred and the fact that his adoptive parents lived here at the time, then we might be able to track down his birth by pulling records for the day he was born and determining each baby's blood type. Chances are there were only a handful, if that many, that were AB-negative."

"That's a great idea, Damaris."

"Thanks, but it's hardly foolproof. Blood types,

particularly the baby's, aren't necessarily a normal part of the birth record, but in this case we may get lucky. If Waring's birth mother's blood type was A, B, or O, her baby would have suffered from what's called an ABO incompatibility, which is caused when the mother's blood develops antibodies against her infant's."

"I'm not sure I understand. You mean like the problem a baby can have if the mother has Rh negative blood and the baby is Rh positive?"

"Similar, but ABO incompatibility generally isn't as severe. The baby would have a higher than normal bilirubin from all the hemolyzed blood cells, but it's easily treatable and recovery is usually complete. The point is, if the problem did occur, it, along with the blood types of both the mother and the infant, would be part of the medical record. Of course, the tricky part will be getting copies of any medical records. They aren't public documents. I'd like to know how Ms. Cumberland got ahold of the ones she did on Waring."

"My mother might be able to help with that," Marlie suggested. "She's a pediatrician, retired, but fairly well known in the area. With her credentials, maybe she could get area hospitals to pull records from around that time."

"Hm . . . that might work," Damaris said, excitement edging into her voice. "Particularly if she told them she was doing a study to try and link some sort of adult disorder with ABO incompatibility in infancy. That would narrow the field considerably."

"How do you know all this medical stuff, Damaris?"

"My sister is a nurse who works in a newborn nursery. I used to help her study back when she was in nursing school."

"Is she adopted too?"

Damaris shook her head. "No, my parents had her naturally, but there were complications and my mother had to have a hysterectomy. So they decided to adopt me. Mom and Dad both came from big families and the thought of raising an only child was inconceivable to them."

Marlie couldn't help but note how easily Damaris referred to her adoptive parents as Mom and Dad. "Your parents sound like wonderful people," she said.

"They are."

"How do they feel about your search for your birth parents?"

Damaris shrugged. "They've been supportive, though I know it can't be easy for them. My sister, on the other hand, has been a big help, really rallying to my cause. I think she thinks it's romantic or something. She's dating this lawyer and she's even bullied him into helping me track down some records," she said with a laugh. Then she snapped her fingers. "Speaking of the law, Detective Carvelle called for you right before you came in. He wants you to call him back. I've got the number if you need it."

"Did he say what he wanted?"

"Nope. Sorry."

Marlie frowned, wondering why Carvelle was calling and trying to decide if she should call him back or stall until she could gather more information.

"Damaris, I wonder if you might do me a favor?"

"Sure."

"See if you can talk to your roommate's boyfriend again and ask him what he knows about the warehouse explosion I was involved in last year. See if he knows anything about how Carvelle got assigned to investigate it, and what information there is on the body that was found inside. Also, find out if he knows anything about any cops who may have resigned or disappeared from the force around that time."

"Disappeared?"

"Yeah, as in quit without notice, or perhaps even someone who might have been let go or who moved away suddenly. Anything that seems at all odd or suspicious."

"Okay. I think he's coming over tonight. I'll try to talk to him then."

Marlie had a troubling thought. "Damaris? How well do you know this boyfriend of your roommate's?"

Damaris shrugged. "Fairly well. He seems like a decent guy. Christine has been seeing him for six months and they're getting pretty serious. Why?"

"I don't know. I'm just a little concerned about what's going on down there at the station. I'm fairly certain there are some crooked cops involved and I don't want you or Christine to put yourselves in jeopardy. And I don't know who, if anyone, can be trusted. So just be careful, okay?"

"I will, but I really think—"

A knock on the door stopped Damaris in mid-sentence. Marlie glanced toward the opaque window and caught a glimpse of a shadowy figure just before Damaris stepped in front of the door, blocking her view.

A second later, Marlie heard the deep rumble of Carvelle's voice. "I'm looking for Marlie Kaplan."

"Well, you've come to the right place," Damaris said cheerfully, and she stepped aside, waving her arm in a "come on in" gesture.

Carvelle ignored the invitation and stayed where he was. "Hello, Marlie," he said.

His voice sounded edgy and tentative, a perfect match for Marlie's own feelings. She hadn't expected him to show up and wasn't sure she was ready to talk to him yet. Between the sour note that had marked the end of their last get-together and all the discoveries she had made about him since, her feelings for this man had become very muddled and torn. Judging from the tone of his voice and the way he ignored Damaris's invitation, she guessed he was feeling a bit wary of her as well. Then a horrible thought occurred to her, and her eyes shot up to the transom window above the door. It was open several inches, just as it had been on the day of Ronni's murder. How long had Carvelle been standing out there before he knocked? Was it possible he overheard what she and Damaris were discussing?

The idea made her wince inwardly, though she concentrated on keeping her face complacent. "I was just about to call you," she said in what she hoped was a calm voice. "Damaris, have you met Detective Carvelle?"

Damaris, bless her, stepped right up and extended her hand. "It's a pleasure to meet you," she said. "I've seen you here before, but I don't believe we've officially met. I'm Damaris Dedulonus, Ms. Kaplan's assistant."

Marlie was impressed with Damaris's aplomb. The young woman was well aware of Marlie's investigation into Carvelle and of the suspicious items they had uncovered in his past. Yet there was nary a hint of restraint as she greeted him.

Carvelle shook her hand, mumbled back a greeting, and then politely participated as Damaris indulged in a few social pleasantries. Marlie was grateful for the extended exchange as Damaris was once again blocking Carvelle from her view. She used the momentary reprieve to gather her wits.

Damaris finally turned back toward the credenza, where she scooped up a pile of folders. "Well, I'll leave the two of you here to talk." She moved toward the door, then stopped, as Carvelle was blocking her way. Forced to move away from the sanctuary of the doorway, Carvelle either had to step back into the hallway or come into the office. He opted for the latter, doing an awkward little dance number with Damaris before she managed to get past him. He stood in the middle of the room, looking awkward and uncomfortable, his eyes aimed toward the files still stacked on the credenza. Marlie prayed the one on him was among those Damaris was taking with her.

As if the young woman had read her mind, Damaris said, "I've got the files on *all* those stories we were working on yesterday and I'll see if I can't finish them up today. I'll be in the newsroom if you need anything."

Marlie decided then and there that Damaris Dedulonus was a gift from God. "Thanks, Damaris. Call me if you run across any problems."

"Will do." Damaris then briefly turned her attention to Carvelle before exiting the office. "It was a pleasure to meet you, Detective."

"Likewise." Carvelle made a tip-of-the-hat gesture, even though he wasn't wearing one.

As soon as Damaris was gone, Marlie turned her plastic smile to Carvelle and said, "So what brings you here?"

"I tried to call you at home last night, but your mother said you were out."

"I was."

"May I ask where and with whom?"

Marlie's eyebrows shot up. "May I ask why you want to know?"

"Just curious," Carvelle said, moving closer to Marlie's desk. "It goes with the job."

Marlie realized he was trying to read the files on her desk and, as subtly as she could, she reached over to pick up the one on Waring, intending to turn it facedown so Carvelle wouldn't be able to read the name. Unfortunately, her aim was a tad bit off and instead of picking it up, she knocked the entire file off the desk. The many pages contained inside slid out, scattering themselves all over the floor.

"Dammit!" Marlie muttered, dropping to her knees and trying to scrape the pages together.

"Let me give you a hand," Carvelle said, bending down to help.

"I don't need your help," Marlie tossed back caustically. To her dismay, Carvelle completely ignored her objection and gathered up a small stack of papers. It was several moments later when she realized he had stopped helping and was reading instead. She made a snatch for the pages he held in his hand, but to her embarrassment, she missed. "Dammit, Carvelle. Give those to me."

He handed the pages over and said, "It looks like you've got quite a file on Senator Waring here."

"I'm interviewing him for a story, a personal profile. Okay?" she said with no small amount of exasperation.

"I'd say it's personal," Carvelle observed. "You've got medical records in there. How the hell did you get your hands on those?"

"I didn't," Marlie said, stuffing the rounded-up pages back inside the folder and tossing the file onto the desk. "Ronni had them. That's her file. Don't tell me you didn't go through it when you and your men ripped apart the office."

"We have a copy of it, I'm sure, but I haven't gone through every single file. Only those that seemed current. It's rather unethical to use his medical records, don't you think?"

"Who said I'm using them?" Marlie snapped back. She rose to her feet and sank back in her chair. "I'm not investigating his health," she said defensively. "I'm simply using the records to reconstruct events that occurred around the time of the accident that killed his parents."

"I see," Carvelle said, nodding thoughtfully. He stood and took the chair Damaris had been in a short while ago. He leaned forward, elbows on his knees, his hands folded prayerlike in front of him.

"So tell me," he said. "Do you have private dinners with all of the people you do personal profiles on?"

Marlie stared at him, the implications of his question slow to dawn. "How do you know that?"

"Your mother told me when I called. Although she called it a date, rather than an interview."

"It was a preliminary meeting, to outline the specifics of the interview and what we'll broadcast," Marlie said, her anger growing as she realized his earlier questions had merely been a front. He had known all along where she was last night. "Though what business that is of yours is beyond me. I didn't realize checking up on my social life or my professional ethics fell within the purview of the police department," she said with acidic sarcasm.

"It doesn't."

"Then why the hell are you here?"

Carvelle sighed heavily, leaning back in his chair and gripping both of the armrests. "Actually, I came by to give you an update. I finally got back the information on all the calls that came into the station on the day of Ronni's murder around the time you said you were here."

"And?"

"One of them was traced to the office where William has his practice."

"Shit." Marlie stared at the floor—at Carvelle's feet actually—her anger swiftly replaced by a sinking feeling of doom. "You've confronted William with this?" she asked, raising her gaze to Carvelle's. His glowance was quiet, subdued, and nearly colorless.

Carvelle nodded grimly. "I've talked to him, yes."

"And what does he say?"

"That Ronni called him to ask about this guy he'd defended several years before, wanting to know if William could tell her where she could find him. William then told her he was tied up at the moment and would have to look up the guy's file and get back to her, but that he wasn't keen on giving out information on one of his clients unless he knew the reason why. Ronni refused to tell him over the phone but offered to meet him somewhere and discuss it. William said he would get back to her. That all occurred during the first phone call, and the tape we found from earlier in the day verifies that."

"And now you have proof that he did call her back?"

"Well, we have proof he called the station. That's all we can trace. Once the call comes into the main switchboard, there's no way of tracking where it goes from there. But since he admits to calling Ronni the second time, it's kind of a moot point. He claims he called her back to arrange a meeting with her for the following day."

"But we have no way of knowing if that's true," Marlie surmised.

"No," Carvelle admitted. "The only way we can know for sure is if we find a tape of the conversation, yet there doesn't seem to be one. I find it hard to believe Ronni didn't tape the call, given how obsessive she was about all the others, but I've been through every tape we found in this office and there's nothing during that time frame."

"Maybe she had other tapes at home? Or in her purse?"

"We found her purse in the trunk of her car, which was parked in a restaurant lot about five miles from the logging road. Apparently, whoever killed her met her at the restaurant and they rode out to the murder site together. Ronni's car was locked and we found the keys near her body at the base of the cliff, so I don't think anything in the car was touched. There were no tapes in her purse, though we did find some in her car and more in her apartment. But I've listened to every one of them and none fit the bill."

Carvelle's reference to anything being touched made Marlie think of something else. "Did you find any fingerprints anywhere near the scene?" she asked.

Carvelle shook his head. "He must have been wearing gloves."

Marlie frowned. The one thing she and Carvelle did agree on was that Ronni would have taped the call. Why wasn't it among the others? It made no sense at all. Unless it *had* been there and perhaps had other calls recorded on it besides William's, like one from Carvelle or another cop, for instance?

"There is also the fact that William has no real alibi for the time of Ronni's murder," Carvelle went on, totally unaware of Marlie's suspicions. "He left the office just before noon and didn't return for the rest of the day. He says he drove out to your place, found you weren't home, and figured you were out with Roberta. Then later he saw Roberta driving alone. So he went back to your place and that's when you met up with him."

"That jibes with what he told me at the time.

Did you ask him why he came out to my place?" she asked, suddenly remembering William's claim that he'd come by to drop off a gift Kristen had bought for her—a gift Marlie had yet to see.

"I did. He told me it was none of my business."

Marlie let out a humorless laugh. "That sounds like William, all right."

"I have to tell you, he was pretty defensive the whole time I was talking to him."

Knowing William, Marlie suspected offensive was closer to the mark. "Are you going to arrest him?"

Carvelle shook his head. "We don't have any real proof. All the evidence is circumstantial at best, and even that's not very strong. Frankly, I'm a bit bothered by how readily he admits to being in the vicinity of the murder. As a defense attorney, he has to know how bad that looks. Then again, I'm sure he also knows how foolish it would be to lie about it when you can place him at the scene around the time of the murder. We may not have any hard evidence at this point, but I have to tell you, Marlie, what we do have is pretty damning. And you are one of the key components."

Marlie caught his innuendo immediately. Carvelle was implying her own safety might be in jeopardy if in fact William was guilty and thought she could somehow finger him. Then again, Carvelle might just be fishing around, trying to see if she could recall any more details from that fateful day, something that might point the finger somewhere else.

The phone rang then, and it was Debbie Kincer

announcing that the man from Workers for the Blind was here to install the synthesizer and software on her computer. Marlie told her to send him up, then turned back to Carvelle.

"I've got an appointment," she said dismissively. "You need to leave."

"But I'm not finished talking with you," Carvelle said irritably, as if that were the only deciding factor on when their conversation would end.

"Well, I *am* finished talking with you," Marlie snipped.

"No, you're not."

Marlie gaped at him with disbelief. "Yes, Carvelle, I am. And frankly, after the way things went the last time we talked, I don't know why I bothered to let you in here." She knew she was goading him but didn't care. He had cast the first stone—perhaps unwittingly, perhaps not—the motivation mattered little to her at this point. She knew she had scored her own hit when his glowance took on an angry red hue.

Look," Carvelle said, his voice tight. "I apologize for the way I behaved the other day. I was angry and I spoke without thinking."

"Well, maybe the next time you decide to tromp all over someone you'll give it some thought first," Marlie said with acerbic sweetness. She pushed herself out of the chair and headed for the door, intending to open it in preparation for the man coming up from the lobby, and as an invitation for Carvelle to leave. But Carvelle sprang from his own chair and grabbed her arm, halting her progress.

"Dammit, Marlie! Listen to me."

"Get your hands off me," she seethed, shaking him loose. She marched imperiously toward the door and flung it open. "I think I've listened to you quite enough. You can leave now." Her eyes narrowed in anger. Her own glowance flared with the same tones as Carvelle's, so that she was now literally seeing red.

Carvelle rolled his head and muttered "Jesus Christ" under his breath. Then suddenly he was in her face, his nose just inches away from hers. "I'm sorry if I offended your tender sensibilities the other day," he said, sounding not sorry at all, "but it's not my fault you aren't willing to face the facts."

"I'm facing the facts," Marlie said, holding her ground.

"No, I don't think you are. Think, Marlie. If William is involved with this because of some long-standing jealousy he has over you, you're really playing with fire by cavorting with someone like Senator Waring. If William gets wind of it, it's bound to set him off."

"*Cavorting?*" Marlie seethed. She was furious now. She nodded toward the hallway and said, "Get out."

"Hey," Carvelle said, holding his hands up in supplication. "I'm just being honest, calling it as I see it."

Marlie's eyebrows shot halfway to her hairline. "Honest?" she said, her voice turning shrill. "You want to talk about honest? All right, let's do that, Carvelle. Tell me why you never once mentioned the fact that you had a wife, a *pregnant* wife, no less. Or that she was murdered. Or that you were investigated as a result of your partner's death because it was a bullet from *your* gun that killed him. You want to talk honest, Carvelle? Then answer those questions for me!"

Carvelle stared at her, his glowance now tight and withdrawn. "How do you know all that?" he asked with frightening calm.

"Never mind how, just answer the questions."

A ding signaled the arrival of the elevator, and Marlie looked down the hallway. A man stepped off the elevator, looked both ways, then headed toward her. He carried several packages in his arms. "Miss Kaplan?" he said when he was only a few feet away.

Marlie nodded.

"I'm Joe Wijtman, from Workers for the Blind."

"Yes, I've been expecting you. Please come in." Marlie waved him through the door, giving Carvelle one last dismissive glance. "We'll continue this discussion later," she said to him in a low voice.

At first she thought Carvelle was going to refuse to leave, but then he stormed past her into the hallway, heading for the stairwell. Marlie watched him go, expecting a sense of relief, but feeling only a strange emptiness instead.

chapter 30

After spending nearly two hours with Mr. Wijtman going over the equipment and software he was installing, Marlie spent the rest of the day playing with her new setup. One of the treats in store for her was a dictation-software program that allowed her to speak into a headset and have her words appear as type on the screen. It also allowed her to issue verbal commands for most of the mouse functions, eliminating many of the cumbersome keystroke combinations she'd had to use before. Ralph was included too, of course, but it was a newer, improved Ralph, one that Mr. Wijtman said had the ability to read Web pages, giving Marlie access to the Internet.

After a quick but enjoyable lunch with Cindy, Marlie checked her messages and discovered that Dennis Lomax had returned her call. Unfortunately, by the time she called him back he was again out of the office, and she was forced to leave another message. Eager to start developing her story on Waring, she spent the afternoon scanning the many pages of his file into the computer, then dictated some of her own observations from their dinner the night before. When she was through, she copied the information onto a disk and dropped it into her purse, planning to load it onto the computer at home so she could work on it over the weekend.

When Roberta arrived to drive her home at the end of the day, Marlie knew something was up as soon as she saw the bright opalescent gleam of her mother's glowance. The something turned out to be a conference Roberta wanted to attend, one that started on Sunday and ended on Tuesday, meaning she would be out of town and unable to drive Marlie back and forth to work for a few days. Even as Marlie assured her it would be no problem—she was sure Damaris wouldn't mind playing chauffeur for a day or two—she found herself wondering at her mother's enthusiasm for the trip. Revelation came when Roberta revealed that Joe Carter would also be attending.

Marlie was delighted to see her mother so happy and full of life, and it was mainly for that reason she decided not to bring her up to date on the latest news about William. Besides, if Roberta knew about Carvelle's latest suspicions, she might cancel her trip out of concern for Marlie's safety. And the last thing Marlie wanted to do was have her mother put her own life on hold for a single minute longer. As she stood on the front porch waving at Roberta's fading taillights, Marlie was seized by an odd sense of melancholy. Her mother was moving on, she realized, leaving Marlie behind to fend for herself. It was as it should be, and while she felt capable and determined to succeed, she was nevertheless saddened by this inevitable change in their relationship.

After fixing herself dinner, Marlie went into her office and fired up the computer. She took the tape recorder (which still held the tape from last night's dinner), the tape of Waring notes she had dictated in the office the other day, and the floppy disk of

Waring's scanned file from her purse. She started by loading Waring's file onto her hard drive, planning to let Ralph read it to her. No doubt the whole thing was in total disarray after the spill this morning, and she might need to do some cutting and pasting in order to get it in some semblance of order.

It proved to be an arduous task. This afternoon she had scanned well over fifty pages of material, and as she feared, it was a veritable potpourri of jumbled facts. Realizing she could spend hours simply listening to Ralph read back a lot of stuff she already knew, she decided to try to skip through the pages and go straight to any information there was from the night of the accident. She was still hoping to find a way to broach the subject without getting Waring too upset and wanted to be up to speed on all the details. After opening up the search window, she took a minute to think of a keyword that would take her directly to those portions of the file. She finally decided on the word "accident."

As soon as Ralph announced a find, Marlie had him read and knew she had hit pay dirt when his atonal voice said, "accident with possible blunt trauma to the upper torso and—" Marlie paused Ralph, moved back a bit in the document, and let him read again.

"Thirty-four-year-old Caucasian male brought to the ER [Ralph read ER as one word so it sounded like a cockney version of "her"] following a single-car motor-vehicle accident. Patient presents with possible blunt trauma to the upper torso, and exposure to fire with moderate to severe thermal damage to the distal portions of the upper extremities. Preliminary exam revealed a patient in acute distress, alert but somewhat disoriented. Lower extremities intact with no sign of fracture or severe injury, though there is some mild bruising. Both upper extremities exhibit second- and third-degree burns from fingers to elbow, with gross tissue loss near the tips of the phalanges. Patient hypotensive and tachycardic upon arrival, respirations mildly labored. Patient's primary complaints were of moderate to severe pain in the area from his elbows to his wrists in conjunction with his thermal injuries, an aching sensation in his chest, and severe headache. Multiple contusions were apparent on the upper torso and face as well as a large hematoma above the right eye, which was swollen and ecchymotic.

"Patient was exhibiting mild confusion upon arrival, aware he was in a hospital but unsure of the date or the city he was currently in. He was able to recall details of the accident. Patient was stabilized with Ringer's Lactate and sent for chest and abdominal films to rule out smoke inhalation and blunt trauma. Following that, his disorientation seemed worse and he was subsequently sent for a skull series and CT scan to rule out cranial fracture or hemorrhage. All films were normal and the patient was admitted to the burn unit pending skin grafts to his hands. Neuro consult ordered and neuro status to be closely monitored."

Marlie paused Ralph, taking a moment to digest what she had heard so far. Obviously, Waring was in severe shock when he arrived, but while he was certainly banged up and suffering from rather severe burns to his hands and arms, his injuries were not immediately life-threatening. His confusion at this point could have been attributable to shock, head trauma, psychological trauma, or any combination of these. Curious about the actual extent of his head injury, Marlie started Ralph up again and heard him read off a laundry list of items that were apparently part of Waring's ER orders, including saline dressings to his burns, X rays of his abdomen, chest, and head, a type and cross match for two units of blood, and the neuro consult.

Ralph announced another page and began reading a newspaper article on some of Waring's political exploits. Marlie stopped him and initiated the search again. This time she got the police report of the accident and listened, fascinated, as Ralph reiterated the facts Damaris had given Marlie earlier.

When that was finished, Ralph announced a new page and began reading what was obviously the results of Waring's X rays from the night of the accident. "Both A and P and lateral chest views normal with no signs of disease or injury. Cardiac shadow within normal limits. Impression: normal chest. Flat plate of the abdomen following possible blunt trauma reveals normal bowel and gas pattern with no evidence of free air or blood. Liver and spleen appear intact with no evidence of bleeding or shifting. There is—"

The phone rang, and Marlie paused Ralph in midsentence to answer it.

"Hello?"

"Hello, Marlie. It's Dennis."

"Dennis! I'm so glad you finally caught up with me."

"Sorry it took me so long, but I was out of town for a couple of days. Just got back today." Then, in a lower, sexier voice, Dennis said, "My but it's nice to hear your voice again."

Marlie smiled, and a flood of memories filled her mind. They were good memories, for despite the way their relationship turned out, she and Dennis had truly liked one another and had enjoyed their time together. She still felt a great deal of affection for him. They were simply meant to be friends rather than lovers. "It's good to hear your voice, too," she told him. "It's been a while."

"It has at that. I thought perhaps you had forgotten me."

"Forget you, Dennis? Never."

"How are you?"

"Doing fine. You?"

"Could be better, could be worse. You know how it goes." He paused a moment, then said, "How are you really doing, Marlie? I know about the accident last year. I was going to come and see you, but when I called your mother, she said she thought it would be better if I didn't. She said you weren't accepting any visitors."

"That's true. I wasn't. I was in something of a funk."

"Understandable, considering. Your mom told me about your eyesight. I'm really sorry, Marlie."

"Actually, I have my sight back, or at least some of it."

"Really? You mean the injury was only a temporary thing? I got the impression from your mother that it was permanent."

"We thought it was." She then proceeded to tell him about the surgery, knowing that in Dennis's mind, having a computer chip implanted in one's brain would be something akin to sainthood. As she suspected, he was suitably impressed.

"That would explain why you left me a number for the station. I have to confess, I was surprised. I had heard you'd left your job after the accident."

"I did, but I'm back now."

"That's great, Marlie. I know how much your job meant to you. I'll bet you were a real hellion when you found yourself cooped up in the house, unable to work."

"Something like that," Marlie admitted coyly.

"So let me guess. Your call to me is either prompted by a sudden attack of remorse over your failure to keep in touch and the fact that you dumped me so unceremoniously all those years ago, or you need something. I would venture to say it's the latter?"

Marlie laughed. As a stereotypical computer geek who spent endless hours isolated from the rest of humanity, and whose best friend was a collection of wires, phone lines, and microchips, tact was not one of Dennis's strong suits. "Busted," she said. "You know me too well, Dennis."

"Obviously I never knew you well enough or you wouldn't have dumped me for that creepy lawyer guy."

"You know as well as I do that we never would have worked out, Dennis."

"Yeah, but neither did he."

"Touché."

"So lay it on me, darling. Whatcha need?"

"Actually, I'm calling because I found your name in a file that belonged to one of my fellow reporters."

"Oh, yeah. That Cumberland bitch."

Marlie was a bit taken aback. It was unlike Dennis to be so vituperative.

Apparently sensing Marlie's shock, Dennis quickly added, "Sorry, but the woman was a bit too abrasive, manipulative, and demanding for my tastes, though it's pretty awful what happened to her. I heard about it on the news. They catch the guy yet?"

"No," Marlie said, an image of William leaping into her mind. She shook it off, unable or unwilling to deal with it at the moment.

"That's a shame. Anyway, this Cumberland woman calls me up a few weeks ago and asks me to help her in tracking down the birth mother of this Senator Waring guy. She tried to tell me she was doing this at your request and that you were the one who had given her my name and number, but I knew better than to believe that."

"I don't know how she got wind of my connection with you, Dennis, though it may have been that she found something in one of my old files. After the accident, she inherited all my stuff, including my old office. I assure you I never mentioned you or any of the things you've done for me to her or anyone else." She winced then, remembering that she had done just that with Damaris.

"Don't worry about it," Dennis said. "I trust you. I did get to know you that well, at least."

"Thanks, Dennis. So I take it you didn't help Ronni out?"

"Hell no. I led her on for a while and let her give me all the stuff she had so far. But she ticked me off with that lie about doing it at your request. Plus, this guy she was looking into isn't your average Joe Schmoe. He's a fairly public person. I have to be careful about stuff like that."

"So you never followed up on any of it?"

"I didn't say that."

For several long seconds, Marlie didn't breathe as she absorbed the significance of Dennis's last words. Finally she said, "Then you did follow it up?"

"Sure did. I confess, she had my curiosity piqued. Plus, it was something of a challenge."

Marlie's heart sped up to a trot, and she felt almost giddy when she imagined what an impact her story about Waring would have if she was actually able to uncover his birth origins. The viewing audience would go nuts if they had a chance to witness the reuniting of Waring with his long-lost birth mother.

"What did you find?" Marlie asked with breathless anticipation.

"I found plenty. There were a half dozen adoptees born in Virginia on the same day as Waring, and I was able to track most of them. None of those led to Waring or his adopted parents. However, I did uncover one birth that I couldn't trace at all once the babies left the hospital."

"You mean baby?"

"Nope, babies. Plural. They were twins. Hold on a minute and let me get the file." Dennis dropped the phone with a clatter while Marlie digested this latest revelation. A minute or two later, Dennis was back on the phone. "Here it is. Twin boys, born in Warren County, Virginia, at St. Gertrude's hospital. The mother was one Martha Springer, the father, Robert Colbert. The babies' names on the birth certificates were Jonathan and James. But after their discharge from the hospital, all traces of them disappear. No death certificates, no Social Security numbers, nothing. Obviously, their names were changed, though if they were adopted, it wasn't through any agency I can find. Might have been a private thing."

Marlie's heart went from a trot to a canter. "What about the parents?"

"Both dead. The father was killed before the babies were born, actually. Died in a car accident. The mother died about fifteen years later, apparently the victim of a drug overdose. Her employment records in the state are virtually nonexistent, so either she moved away or she never worked. Judging from the way she died, and the fact that it occurred in the same county where the twins were born, I'd guess the latter."

"Is there any way to trace the babies, or identify them if you tracked them down?"

"Footprint, maybe. Or if there are any blood samples still on file from their birth, we could do DNA testing."

Marlie thought a moment, chewing on her lip. "Dennis, do you know what the blood type on these babies was?"

"Blood type? No. Why?"

"Waring's blood type is AB-negative and I understand that's relatively rare." She then explained the potential incompatibility problem that Damaris had told her about earlier.

"Hmm, I see where you're going with this, but I don't know, Marlie. I'd have to get my hands on the hospital records and that may not be easy. Warren County was pretty rural back then, and the hospital was small. Unless someone has taken the time to go back and computerize all their old files, those records are probably buried in some dusty storeroom somewhere."

"Can you try, Dennis? This means a lot to me."

Dennis let out a put-upon sigh that Marlie remembered well, even after all these years. "Okay. But you're going to owe me big for this one," he said.

"Name it."

"Dinner. Just you and me. For old time's sake."

"You're on."

chapter
31

As soon as she hung up the phone, Marlie remembered that she had intended to ask her mother about checking on area hospital records in search of AB-negative babies born on Waring's birthday. Now, Dennis had made the task that much easier by pinpointing a particular hospital to start with. If she came up empty with St. Gertrude's, she would have to figure out where to go from there.

Marlie dialed her mother's number, then quickly hung up when a man answered, assuming she had dialed wrong. But when she called a second time, taking care to make sure she hit the right keys, a man answered again. Irritated, Marlie blurted out, "Who is this?"

"This is Joe Carter. Who is this?" His tone was jovial, the question teasing. Marlie's eyes widened with the revelation and she felt a sudden pang of jealousy. The emotion confused her and left her stuttering.

"Uh, this is, uh . . . um . . . is Roberta there?"

Joe Carter laughed and set the phone down. "You must be psychic, Bert," Marlie heard him say. "I don't know how you knew this would be for you, but you were right."

Marlie heard him chuckle at his lame joke and grimaced, anticipating Roberta's swift and scathing chastisement. Her mother had always hated the nickname Bert, and had threatened bodily harm or worse to anyone who dared use it. But then, Marlie heard her mother's comeback: "Being psychic is just one of my many talents, Joe. I'll tell you about some of the others later."

Marlie's eyebrows shot up in surprise. The tone of her mother's voice was one she hardly expected and barely recognized: soft, mellow . . . could it be . . . flirtatious? She felt as if she had just stepped into the *Twilight Zone*, but before she had a chance to give the situation any more thought, Roberta picked up the phone and said, "Hello?"

"Mom? It's Marlie."

"Hi, honey. What's up? Is everything okay?"

"Everything is fine," Marlie said, feeling just the opposite. When Roberta had first told her about Joe Carter, Marlie's excitement had been genuine. But the image of their relationship in her mind had been far more platonic, far less involved than this. It was as if someone had just zapped her with a stun gun. She felt weak, paralyzed, immobile. Shaking it off as best she could, she said, "I was just calling to ask you for a favor." Marlie then explained what she wanted Roberta to do and why. When she was through, she waited, listening to a foreboding silence on the other end of the phone.

Finally, Roberta said, "I can't do that, Marlie. Not only would it be a violation of my professional ethics, but it's a terrible invasion of Senator Waring's privacy."

"But it's the only clue I have, Mom. Can you imagine how exciting it would be if this did turn out to be Waring and he has a brother—a twin brother, no less—that he doesn't even know exists?"

"Does he know you're doing this?"

"No," Marlie admitted. "But if it does pan out, I intend to tell him. I wouldn't air anything about it without his permission."

"This could prove to be a huge embarrassment to him, Marlie."

"It could also prove to be a turning point in his campaign for governor. Just think how much the public will eat up a story like that. Long-lost brothers reunited."

"I'm sorry. I can't . . . I won't help you."

Anger flared in Marlie like a burning book of matches. Though some distant part of her mind knew the thought was irrational, she wanted to blame her mother's refusal on Joe Carter. *Bert,* she thought snidely. Where the hell did this guy get off calling her mother Bert?

"Fine," Marlie said, fighting back a sudden threat of tears. Though she had tried to mask her hurt and anger, she knew both were blatantly obvious in the inflection of that one word. The awareness only made her feel worse. "Thanks anyway," she said quickly, while she still had a voice. "Sorry I bothered you. Good night, Mom."

"Good night, Marlie."

Roberta's ready capitulation, her failure to try to talk things out, was like the slamming of a door to Marlie. On one side of that door was their old relationship, the one they had shared for the past year. On the other side was this new one, the one Marlie knew in her heart was better for both of them, but which tore at her nonetheless. Determined not to cry like the child she now felt she was, she gently replaced the phone and distracted herself by going back to work on the Waring file.

Marlie slept fitfully Friday night, plagued by dreams of being deserted in the middle of desolate, lonely landscapes where she hollered for hours without so much as a whisper of wind for an answer. She wandered aimlessly in these nightmarish worlds for what seemed an eternity, but the landscape never changed, stretching itself out in that rubberized, nonphysical way that only happened in dreams. The nightmare repeated itself over and over again, each setting more barren and isolated than the one before. During the last two iterations, Marlie had realized she was naked.

She didn't need a psychiatrist to explain the dreams. She knew it was her mind's way of expressing her feelings of abandonment, vulnerability, and trepidation about the future. But understanding the psychology made the dreams no less frightening, or her sleep any less fitful. Consequently, she awoke Saturday morning feeling tired and edgy, a graininess to her eyes and a lassitude in her limbs.

The first thing she did after having two extrastrong cups of coffee was call the station and ask one of the weekend people to dig up Damaris's phone number. After committing the number to memory, she placed the call, half expecting to get a machine or no answer at all. A young woman

Damaris's age was likely to be out doing something fun and exciting on a beautiful summer Saturday. But to her surprise and delight, Damaris was at home.

After asking for a ride to and from work on Monday and Tuesday, which Damaris was more than happy to provide, Marlie then filled her in on the conversation with Dennis. As Marlie expected, Damaris's excitement was at least as great, if not greater, than her own.

"Listen," Damaris said. "I've been doing some cruising on the Internet here at home, hitting up some adoption sites and search databases to see if I could find anything. I'll post a few queries about this woman we think might be Waring's birth mother and then I'll head into the office and do a search on her to see what I can dig up."

"You don't need to spend your Saturday cooped up in the library," Marlie said, though she was admittedly impressed by Damaris's interest and drive.

"I don't mind," Damaris said. "Besides, this whole puzzle has me intrigued and until I get some answers, I'm not going to be able to focus on anything else anyway."

Marlie smiled. Damaris had the hunger, all right. "I'd offer to come in and help you, but I have an appointment today," she explained, remembering the locksmith.

"No problem. I kind of like working alone anyway."

Marlie shook her head in amazement and wondered if it was possible to be reincarnated while you were still alive. Damaris was so much like her, it was uncanny. "Did you have a chance to talk to your roommate's boyfriend?" she asked.

"I did, but he didn't come up with anything. He said he would ask around though."

Marlie winced. "I'm not sure that's a good idea, Damaris. I'd rather not let on that we're looking into this and, as I said before, I'm not sure who we can trust."

"Well, I may be wrong, but I've known Allen for six months now and I think he's okay. Christine is no dummy. She wouldn't be dating him this long if she thought he was a bit off. And anyway, he doesn't really know what it is I'm after, other than the information about Carvelle, and even with that he's not sure what angle I'm coming from. Though I have to tell you, despite everything that happened, Allen really likes Paul Carvelle and speaks pretty highly of him. I don't know what Carvelle's reputation is among the other guys at the station, but Allen thinks he's a good cop who got caught in a bad situation. Apparently, that whole incident with his partner's shooting shook Carvelle up pretty bad. Allen said Carvelle was ready to quit the force after that, but his captain talked him into staying on. So apparently someone else thought he was worth salvaging."

As Marlie digested this latest information, her doorbell rang. "I have to run," she told Damaris. "My appointment is here. Good luck with your research and call me if you hit on anything."

"I will. Talk to you later."

The locksmith, whose voice Marlie recognized

from their phone conversation, was a short, portly fellow with a relaxed-looking glowance that spun in a lazy pinwheel of opalescent color. After she explained what she wanted, he went right to work, but a few minutes later he called her to the front door.

"I assume you're changing these for security purposes," he said, pointing to the old locks on the door.

Marlie nodded.

"Well, I know you said you only want to replace what you have, but I'd like to suggest you consider an upgrade."

Marlie eyed him dubiously.

He quickly rose to her challenge. "Watch this," he said, and in less than ninety seconds he had picked both the knob lock and the dead bolt. "These here locks are easy pickings," he said wryly. "Now, this lock"—he reached into a bag and pulled out a box—"is much more reliable. It has—"

Marlie raised her hand to halt his sales pitch. "Okay. Let's skip the preliminaries and get to the meat of the matter. How much?"

He told her.

"Fine," Marlie said. "Just do it."

He went merrily about his work, whistling away as he changed the locks on both the front and back doors. When he was through, Marlie then asked him to install a dead bolt on the kitchen side of the cellar door.

Her request was met with several seconds of puzzled silence while the locksmith eyed the chair that was still propped beneath the door. Then he said,

"These are good locks, lady, but they're intended to keep people out, not lock them in."

Marlie stared at him a moment, debating whether or not she should explain her rationale for the lock. No doubt the guy thought she was either some paranoid eccentric or a total whacko who intended to lock someone up in the cellar, keeping them captive down there for years on end. But frankly, her restless sleep the night before had left her feeling irritable and impatient, and she didn't really care what he thought of her.

"Just do it," she told him.

He shrugged. "Okay" he said. "It's your house."

This time, he didn't whistle.

chapter
32

As Saturday stretched into Sunday with no word from Damaris, Marlie assumed her assistant had yet to uncover anything significant and refrained from trying to track her down. But she found herself growing more agitated and restless with each passing hour and couldn't quite shake the feeling that something big was lurking out there, something career-making. Not just *a* story but *the* story. It was a feeling she remembered well, a tauntingly vague certainty that her big break was just around the next corner. Back in her heyday, she had referred to it as her edge. Roberta had called it tenacity and persistence, Cindy, a burning curiosity. William, on the other hand, had declared it a form of insanity. Whatever it was, it had its grip firmly on her now, and being cooped up in the house was making her crazy. She felt she should be out there in the trenches with Damaris, turning up the next rock to see what hid beneath. She was therefore delighted when Dennis called her back Sunday evening, though his first words were not encouraging.

"I tried to find some way to dig up those hospital files on the twins like we discussed. But as I feared, the records from back then are stored somewhere off site. They do have copies on microfiche, but without some sort of proper authorization, no one is going to give me anything. Short of breaking into the place, I have no way of getting my hands on them. I even made a few phone calls to see if anyone knows someone who works at St. Gertrude's, but struck out there as well."

Marlie then informed him of Roberta's refusal to help her get ahold of the records. "I guess I'm back to square one," she said dismally.

"Not necessarily," Dennis said, his voice suggestively teasing. "Have I ever let you down before?"

Marlie felt her pulse quicken. "Are you saying you found something?"

"I did. But I have some good news and some bad news. Which do you want first?"

"The good news," Marlie said without hesitation. She was more than ready to hear something good for a change.

"Well, I got to thinking about this whole blood thing you mentioned, with the type being so rare and the potential for incompatibility problems, and wondered if the regional blood bank might have any records that could help. So I hacked into their computer system, which has files dating clear back to the Second World War, and struck gold. It seems there was a request put in to hold several units of AB-negative blood for twin newborns who were being cared for at St. Gertrude's. Their date of birth corresponds with that of the twins I told you about earlier."

"Then the twins you found *were* AB negative," Marlie said, her excitement growing.

"And that's not all. I did a search for all the records they had for AB-negative blood types. Lo and behold, I found two units that were shipped for transfusion into one Richard Waring back when he was eight years old."

"Yeah, I know about that."

"How?"

"I have a copy of his medical record from the incident," Marlie explained. "But just because Waring's blood type matches that of the babies, doesn't mean he was one of them."

"Not in and of itself, but there are a whole bunch of other factors the blood bank types for besides the basic ABO type and Rh factor. Those subtypes tend to be fairly unique to each individual. And those on Waring matched with those of the twin babies perfectly. While it's not impossible to find a perfect match in an unrelated person, it's highly unlikely. In addition, I found another record from five years later of a type and cross match done on a thirteen-year-old boy who was treated for a bruised kidney and hematuria. The date of birth listed on the kid's record was the same as Waring's, and every one of this kid's subtypes matched Waring's perfectly. So I did a trace back on the kid's name and guess what?"

Marlie didn't answer. She was holding her breath.

"I couldn't find any trace of a birth certificate for this kid, nor could I find any birth certificates with the name of the woman who was listed as his mother, other than her own."

"My God," Marlie said. "Do you think this kid was Waring's twin brother?"

"Makes sense to me. All the clues fit, though it's hardly definitive proof. Still, I figured it would give you a place to start looking."

"Dennis, you are truly amazing," Marlie said.

"Aren't I though?" he came back with no trace of modesty. "You want the name of the kid and his mother?"

"Of course I do. But wait, let me switch to the phone in my office so I can type this in on the computer. I don't want to risk my memory on this one." She set the phone down and hurried back to her office, picking up the extension on her desk. The computer was already on, the word-processing software already up. Marlie hit the proper keystrokes to create a new document, then told Dennis she was ready.

"The mother's name was Carla Denver, the kid's name, who would be the same age as Waring is now of course, was Sam Denver. No mention of a father. There's no address listed on the record, but the hospital the kid was treated in was Memorial in Arlington, not far from where you are."

"Denver?" Marlie repeated the name even as her fingers were typing it into the computer.

"Just like the city," Dennis said.

Marlie frowned. Something about the name seemed familiar to her, but after several seconds of searching through her memory she shrugged. Maybe it was Denver the city that struck a familiar chord, though she couldn't think of any situation recently where Denver or Colorado had come up in discussion.

"I don't suppose you've had a chance to search for anything more current on either of them," Marlie asked.

"Actually, I have," Dennis said. "But that's

where the bad news comes in. I found an employment record on Carla Denver for the two years following the date on that blood-bank record. She worked as a waitress in a restaurant called Denario's, also in Arlington. But after that, I can't find any trace of her. For all intents and purposes, she simply disappeared off the face of the earth."

"And the son?"

"Same thing with him. There's nothing on either of them after 1973."

"Nothing at all?"

"Nope. No employment records, no death certificates, nothing."

Marlie frowned.

"Is Waring going to be happy about this if it turns out he's one of the twins?" Dennis asked.

"I don't know, Dennis. Though I suppose I'm going to find out." Then, another thought occurred to her. "Dennis, I wonder if I could impose on you for one more thing."

"Name it."

Marlie told him what she was after, and Dennis agreed to see what he could find.

"Thanks, Dennis. As I said before, I owe you one."

"Just don't forget our dinner date."

"I won't. I promise."

And with thoughts of dinner on her mind, Marlie hung up and went out to the kitchen to begin preparing the lasagna she wanted to make for her dinner with Waring tomorrow night.

chapter
33

Monday dawned rainy and overcast, a heavy pall of gloom settling over most of northern Virginia. Something about rainy mornings always left Marlie feeling sleepier than normal, and today had been no exception. She had turned her alarm off and gone back to sleep, waking a half hour later in a panic. She still wasn't ready when Damaris arrived to pick her up, so she invited her assistant in for a quick cup of coffee, filling her in on Dennis's latest findings as she finished her morning routine.

As it turned out, Damaris had her own news, which she told Marlie during their drive to the station. "I tracked down Suzanne Farrington, the woman Waring was dating at the time of the accident? I called her last night."

"Did you get anything interesting out of her?"

"Not much. She's married now and has two kids. Apparently, her breakup with Waring was not on friendly terms. He essentially dumped her and I think she's still bitter over it. She echoed some of the other reports we found that said Waring underwent something of a personality change after the accident. She said it really changed him, changed his whole outlook on life."

"I would imagine so," Marlie said. "Something that traumatic is bound to affect the way you look at things. It had to have been one of the most significant moments in Waring's life. That's why I want to focus on it for part of the interview. That accident had a lot to do with making Waring the man he is today."

"Has he talked about it much?"

Marlie shook her head. "Not yet," she said with renewed determination.

When they reached the station, Damaris headed for the resource library to see what she could dig up on the Denver family while Marlie settled in at her desk to copy the revised Waring file she had worked on all weekend onto the computer. Next, Marlie started reviewing and editing her notes, refining her outline for the piece. But after a while she found herself staring at the screen's blur of light, tapping her fingers with restless agitation, her focus gone. The same edginess that had plagued her all weekend was still with her. After checking the time on her watch, she picked up the phone and called the library to see what progress, if any, Damaris might have made.

"Good timing," Damaris said. "I was just about to call you with an update. I checked on that restaurant where Carla Denver worked in the early seventies, but it's long gone. Closed down about fifteen years ago and now there's a shopping center where the restaurant used to be."

"Figures," Marlie grumbled.

"But," Damaris added hopefully, "I did a search of the Arlington phone books from that same time period and found several Denvers listed. No Carlas, but there were two that had the first initial C and one of those disappeared from the listings about the same time Carla and Sam Denver disappeared. I thought I might drive out to the neighborhood where that listing lived and ask around to see if anyone remembers a Carla Denver and her son Sam."

"That's kind of a long shot," Marlie said with a frown. "It's been over twenty-five years. The chances of finding someone still living in the neighborhood who was there back then, much less who remembers their neighbors from that time, are pretty slim."

"Granted," said Damaris. "But I don't know what else to do. Unless you have a better idea."

"What about checking the crisscross to see who lives on that street today? Then look up those names in the old directories and see if you can find a match."

"That's a great idea," Damaris said excitedly.

"Let me know if you find anything."

Five minutes later, Damaris called Marlie back. "I got one!" she said, her voice excited. "I found a Bessie Pettigrew in the crisscross and thought her name sounded kind of oldish, so I looked her up in the seventies directories and there she was."

"Did you call her?"

"Yeah, but she hung up on me. I don't think she hears too well. I thought I might drive out there and try to do a face-to-face with her, see if I have better luck."

"It's worth a shot," Marlie agreed.

"What about lunch?" Damaris asked. "It's only eleven-thirty, but I know you don't have any transportation to go anywhere. Do you want to eat now?"

"No, don't worry about lunch. I can always get Cindy or someone to drive me if I need to, but I was

thinking of doing the vending machine today anyway and eating at my desk."

"Are you sure?" Damaris asked.

"Quite. I need to do some final work on my outline for the Waring interview before my dinner with
him tonight."

"Okay then. I'll check back with you sometime
this afternoon and let you know how it's going."

Marlie was munching on a ham-and-cheese sandwich that tasted an awful lot like the cardboard it
came in when Carvelle called her. Whether it was
her overall mood or the acrimony that had pervaded
their last meeting, Marlie was filled with a sense of
foreboding as soon as she heard his voice. The
oppressive gloom outside her office window didn't
help. Huge thunderheads had rolled in, effectively
eliminating all traces of sunshine.

After a greeting that was cold, perfunctory, and,
Marlie thought, a bit cautious, Carvelle said, "I have
some news on Ronni's case that you should know."

"Why do I get the feeling it isn't good news?"

Carvelle neither verified nor negated her suspicion; he simply started in. "We had an anonymous
tip over the phone this weekend from a guy who
claims someone on the street tried to sell him a gold
bracelet. The guy said it was a great price and he was
all set to buy the thing when he recognized it. Said
he remembered seeing it on Ronni Cumberland during her newscasts. He knew it was the same one
when he saw the unique twisted shape, which he

described as being like two serpents intertwined. Sure enough, when we played back some of Ronni's old videotapes, there was the bracelet, always on her right arm."

"I'm familiar with it," Marlie said. "I believe it was a gift from her mother. As far as I can recall, she always wore it."

"You're right, it was a gift from her mother. And it wasn't on her body when we found her, nor did it turn up anywhere among her other possessions. Frankly, until this guy called us this weekend, we weren't even aware it was missing. At first we thought the guy might be one of those loonies looking for his moment in the spotlight, but then he told us about an inscription that was engraved on the inside of this bracelet. When I checked with Ronni's mother, she verified it."

"Can this guy identify the person who tried to sell him the bracelet?"

"Can and did. Said he recognized *him* from TV as well." Carvelle paused, and Marlie heard him suck in a deep breath. "Marlie, he identified William."

Marlie gasped. "Is he sure? Maybe he just thinks it was William."

"He was sure. Described William to a T and even mentioned one or two trials William has been involved with that earned him some airtime. It was enough to convince a judge to issue a search warrant for William's house and office. Want to guess what we found?"

Marlie felt a wave of nausea pass over her.

"It was in one of his desk drawers at home."

"Oh, God," Marlie moaned.

"I'm truly sorry, Marlie," Carvelle said. "I know you don't want to believe William is capable of something like this, but I think the evidence at this point is too compelling to ignore."

It certainly was. And maybe a little too convenient, Marlie thought. Something about all this made no sense. William had a lot of undesirable traits, but stupidity wasn't one of them. If he had killed Ronni, Marlie couldn't imagine him taking the bracelet, much less keeping it in his desk drawer, or trying to sell it on the street.

"Who received the anonymous call?" she asked Carvelle.

"I did."

"And you have no idea who it was?"

"No."

"Who searched William's house?"

"Well, three of us were there, but I was the one who found the bracelet. Why?"

Marlie ignored the question and fired back with one of her own. "What did William have to say about it?"

"Nothing. Haven't found him yet. We've issued a warrant for his arrest, but he apparently left his office not ten minutes before we arrived and didn't tell anyone where he was going or when he would be back. He's not at home and when the firm had him paged and tried his car phone, there was no response."

"Do you think he knew you were coming?"

"Can't know for sure," Carvelle said. "Though it certainly looks that way. Those lawyers can be a tight-knit group. I wouldn't be surprised to find that someone tipped him off."

Especially if that someone suspected William was being set up, Marlie thought.

"You haven't heard from him, have you, Marlie?"

"No," Marlie said a bit crossly. "Don't you think I'd tell you if I had?"

"I'm not sure," Carvelle said. Then, in a more wounded tone, "Besides, I know I'm not high on your list of favorite people these days."

Marlie said nothing.

"I'm concerned about you, Marlie. About your safety," Carvelle said carefully. "William knows you saw him that day and even if he believes you can't identify him, just the fact that you were there is likely to make him nervous. If he thinks you are somehow to blame for all this he may come after you."

"Come after me?" Marlie said weakly. Though she was still struggling to find some other answer to all of this, Carvelle's words struck fear into her heart. What if William *was* guilty? If he knew the cops had decided to arrest him, he might attribute the action to something Marlie had told them. It was clear from his prior conversations with her that he laid the blame of Carvelle's investigations firmly at Marlie's feet. This might be enough to push him over the edge.

"We have no way of knowing what he'll do at this point, Marlie," Carvelle said, echoing her own thoughts. "He may well be desperate."

"I . . . I don't think he'll hurt me," Marlie said with little conviction.

"Sure enough to stake your life on it?"

For some reason, his challenge irritated her. Maybe it was the fact that he was robbing her of the last few fragments of her hard-held denial. When she didn't answer him right away, Carvelle took advantage of the silence.

"I don't think you should be alone while he's still out there," he said. "I was thinking perhaps it would be better if you stayed somewhere else tonight, someplace in town where he wouldn't know to find you, like a hotel. I'll help you find one."

Marlie was shaking her head long before she could verbalize her refusal. She wasn't about to sacrifice her dinner with Waring.

Carvelle cleared his throat. "We can have dinner somewhere first. I'd . . . um . . . I'd like to have a chance to talk to you, to explain some things."

The reference to his deception only served to seal Marlie's decision. "I'm not going anywhere," she told him. "Besides, I won't be alone tonight. Senator Waring will be with me." While Waring was only coming for dinner, Marlie knew she had implied that he might be staying longer. She made no effort to clarify, letting Carvelle make of it what he wanted. His lengthy silence told her the ruse had had the desired effect.

"Fine. Do what you want," he said tersely. "But I'd be careful if I were you, Marlie." The words carried an ominous tone.

"Your warning has been noted," she shot back. "Good day, Detective."

chapter 34

Marlie continued her work on the Waring interview, finalizing her thoughts and trying to leave herself enough flexibility to address the adoption issue if Damaris had anything to report when she returned. As she worked, she was vaguely aware of the ever-growing tempest outside. The rain had started an hour or so ago, beginning as a light sprinkle but quickly becoming a downpour. The clouds had become so dark and heavy that it looked like dusk outside rather than midafternoon. Bright flashes of lightning pierced the distant horizon, and the low rumble of thunder rolled in on waves that seemed to crest a little higher with each entreaty. The muffled timpani of raindrops on the window grew steadily louder, until it banged away like thousands of pellets being flung at the glass.

It was nearly five o'clock when the storm reached its peak. Sheets of rain lashed against the window while thunder rattled the walls. Streaks of lightning fractured the sky. Marlie was standing at the window watching the maelstrom when the phone rang.

"Marlie? It's Damaris." Her voice sounded tinny, distant, as if she were calling from a long, long distance away. The line crackled with the static of Mother Nature's fury.

"Damaris, are you okay? I was beginning to worry."

"I'm okay, but my car isn't doing so hot. The damned thing just up and died. Stranded me in the middle of nowhere. The tow truck just got here. In fact, I'm calling you from a phone in the truck. I'm sorry, Marlie, but it doesn't look like I'm going to be able to drive you home as we planned. I don't even—"

The static took over, drowning out Damaris's voice for several seconds. Then Marlie heard a faint "—you hear me?"

"I can hear you now, but I lost you for a bit," Marlie yelled back.

"This storm is something!" Damaris said. "I haven't seen one this bad in years. Anyway, as I was saying, judging from the expression on this tow truck driver's face, I kind of doubt they'll have my car fixed anytime soon, so you should probably try to make other plans for in the morning as well."

"No problem," Marlie said. "I'm sure I can find someone else to take me home tonight and to pick me up in the morning. If all else fails, I can call a taxi. So don't worry about me. Are you okay?"

"I'm fine. Just a little annoyed. Though I suppose I should be grateful this beast of a car has lasted this long. Sorry to let you down like this, but I have some news that might make up for it."

It took a second for the words to sink in. "Mrs. Pettigrew?" Marlie said, scarcely daring to believe it.

"Sure enough," Damaris said, obviously pleased with herself. "She's a sweet old lady who must be at least in her nineties. She's half deaf, so it made for an

interesting discussion, but despite the hearing problem Bessie's as sharp as any twenty-year- old I know.
She hit on the name Carla Denver right away. She
remembered her because—"

Once more a loud crackling ripped Damaris's
voice away. Marlie waited for it to clear, periodically
calling out to Damaris, but to no avail. Eventually,
the line went dead. "Damn!" Marlie said, slamming
the phone down. Of all the times for the phone to
fail. She sat tapping her fingers with irritation, trying
to think of a way to get Damaris back when the
phone rang again. Quickly, Marlie snatched it up.
"Damaris?"

There was a long pause before a man's voice
answered. "Marlie?"

"Senator Waring," Marlie said, recognizing the
voice.

"You know, if you keep greeting me with such
apparent disappointment in your voice, I'm going to
develop a complex. And I thought we agreed you
would call me Richard."

"Sorry, Richard," Marlie said. "You caught me
off guard. I was expecting a call from my assistant.
We just got cut off by the storm and I thought you
were her calling back."

Not to be intimidated by anything as mundane
as a direct connection as opposed to a cellular one,
the lightning made its presence known on this line
as well, though certainly with less fury. A constant
muted crackle punctuated every word.

"The storm's a doozy, isn't it?" Waring observed.

"That it is," Marlie agreed. "Listen, I'm glad you
called because I was just about to call you." She

explained about her lack of a ride because of Damaris's car problems and suggested that she might be late for their dinner engagement as a result. She offered to either meet him at a later time or to reschedule the dinner altogether. Waring, however, had another idea.

"Why don't I just come by the station and pick you up?" he suggested.

A blinding white flash of lightning struck not far from the station, its accompanying thunder rolling over the building so hard one of the pictures on Marlie's office wall fell to the floor. Suddenly, the prospect of riding home with a tall, strong, capable man seemed like a pretty good idea. "If it's no problem, I would appreciate it," she said, reaching over and turning off the computer and its various peripherals. She then bent down and unplugged the power strip from the wall socket.

"No problem at all. I'll be finished here in about half an hour and then head your way. If the traffic isn't too bad, I should be there around six." Another bolt of lightning struck with a tremendous bang, and through her window Marlie saw sparks flash on the not-too-distant horizon. An earth-shattering tembler of thunder rode in piggyback, rattling the building a second time. "Then again," Waring said ominously, "if that's any indication of what's to come, don't be surprised if I'm a little late. I can help you prepare dinner once we get to your place, or if you prefer, we can grab something on the way."

"Actually, most of the dinner is already fixed. I just need to pop it in the oven for a bit, chop up some salad, and we'll be ready to go."

"Good. Then I'll see you at six or thereabouts."

"I'll be waiting in the lobby." Marlie hung up the phone, relieved not to be holding it any longer in the midst of the storm. Though she knew such a thing was rare, she had heard reports about people who were electrocuted while talking on the phone in the middle of a lightning storm.

The wind outside had picked up, and now it teased and taunted its way around the building, howling like some ghostly apparition bent on haunting the earthbound. Yet another huge dagger of blinding light split the sky and struck the earth, followed by a clap of thunder comparable to a sonic boom. Generally, Marlie loved electrical storms, but she had to confess that the sheer fury of this one made her nervous. This was the type of storm that occasionally spawned tornadoes, or dumped enough of a deluge to create flash floods that could sweep cars, trees, and lives away in a matter of seconds.

She felt the face of her watch, realized it was only a few minutes past five and still nearly an hour before Waring would get here—assuming of course, that his journey was unhampered by both the traffic and the weather. On a good day, the roadways in and around the DC area were almost always jammed up; the area was notorious for its horrific traffic problems. Given the current state of the weather, Marlie was pretty certain tonight's rush hour would be snarled into creeping clumps.

A horribly loud noise, not unlike machine-gun fire, suddenly filled the room. Marlie spun toward the window, both puzzled and frightened until she realized what it was. Hailstones, some the size of golf balls, were battering the window by the thousands. The lights in the office flickered off, then on. Despite the sticky humid heat that normally prevailed this time of year, the temperature in the room seemed to have dropped to arctic levels within the past few minutes.

The noise from the hailstones grew so loud, Marlie covered her ears with her hands. Any minute, she expected to see the window in her office shatter and have the wind and hail charge into the room and pummel her.

Then just as quickly as it began, the noise stopped, replaced by a far gentler patter of rain. The lights in the office flickered again, then went out. This time, they stayed out. With the black clouds that hovered low in the sky, little light penetrated into the room. It was as if night had fallen with the speed of a boulder.

Marlie hugged herself and rose out of her chair slowly, barely able to make out the faint gray rectangle that marked her window. She waited, knowing the building had a backup generator that would kick in any second. From somewhere in the bowels of the building she heard a loud thump, followed by a series of clangs, bangs, and other mechanical sounds. Moments later a rush of warm air charged through the heating vent that was built high up on the wall by Marlie's desk. As the air passed through the grate, Marlie heard another noise, much fainter than any of the others, so faint, in fact, that someone without her finely tuned hearing probably wouldn't have noticed it. It was an oddly hollow scraping sound that lasted only a second or two, but it instantly triggered something in Marlie's brain. In a flash she was back in time, to the day of Ronni's murder when she had stood outside the office door listening to Ronni pace inside. She had heard a noise then that had that same hollow ring to it. It had been more of a clatter than a scrape, but the cavernous echo was unmistakably the same.

The idea hit her as hard and fast as the lightning had struck beyond her window. Her heart began to race, and a little chill of excitement coursed through her body.

The lights in the office finally came back on, and Marlie stared at the heating vent. Slowly, she made her way over to it, standing on tiptoe and running her fingers over the louvers in the grate. The space between them was a little wider than her fingertip, plenty of room. Straining to stand a little taller, she tried to get her eyes level with the first slat, but the grate was too high. She turned and quickly surveyed the furniture in the office. Her chair swiveled and had a wheeled base—too dangerous. The desk and credenza were too heavy to move. But Damaris's chair was perfect—four legs, no wheels, no swivel. She shoved her own chair aside and dragged the other one over, positioning it beneath the vent. Carefully climbing onto the seat, she steadied herself with her hands against the wall and stuck her face up to the grate.

Behind the louvers was a long tunnel lined with something metallic. The light from the office behind her did little to illuminate the vent's interior; the louvers were angled the wrong way for that. But what little did manage to eke its way in reflected brightly off the walls. Down on the floor of the vent, just inside the grate, Marlie thought she saw a darker shape, a flaw in that metallic expanse of silver-white. Pulling back, Marlie groped around the perimeter of the grate with one hand, feeling the four screws in each corner that held it in place. She climbed down off the chair and yanked open the middle drawer of her desk. There, she felt around among the contents until she recognized the shape of the knifelike letter opener. She grabbed it, shoved the drawer closed with her hip, and once again mounted the chair.

With one finger, she found the slot of the screw anchoring the lower right corner of the grate, then guided the end of the letter opener into it. Gripping the handle as tightly as she could, she leaned her weight against it and tried to turn it counterclockwise. At first, nothing happened; the screws were tightly sealed in place not only with their threads but by a coat of paint as well. After taking a breath, she tried again. This time the letter opener slipped out of the notch and she nearly fell off the chair. Cursing, she continued her efforts until she finally realized she had stripped the head of the screw.

She took a few seconds to rest and think. Then she used the letter opener to gouge and scrape at the paint that surrounded the remaining three screws. When that was done, she tackled the one in the upper right corner and, after several grunting attempts, it finally loosened. Exhilarated with her success, she attacked the screw in the upper left corner, which gave way with little effort. But the one on the bottom left proved to be as stubborn as its counterpart on the right. By the time she managed to get it loose, she was sweating and the muscles in her arms and hands were aching. She tossed the screw aside, then applied the letter opener to the edge of the grate near the final, stripped screw, trying to pry the entire thing away from the wall. It gave a millimeter at a time until the whole thing suddenly popped free, once again almost making her topple from the chair. The grate fell to the floor with a loud clatter, followed by several chunks of wall plaster. Tossing the letter opener onto the desk, Marlie reached into the vent and felt along its floor. Her hand found something square and flat—a computer floppy disk—and beside it, another object.

A microcassette tape.

35

Marlie climbed down off the chair and stood a moment in the middle of her office staring at the items she held in her hand. Rain still pattered against the window, but she could barely hear it above the roar of blood in her ears. Her heart pounded with fearful excitement. The phone rang, and the shrill sound made her jump.

Waring.

In her determination to get inside the heat vent she had forgotten he was coming to pick her up. She answered the phone and told the evening receptionist she would be right down. Then she hung up and tried to decide what to do next. It dawned on her that if this was the tape everyone had been looking for, then perhaps her suspicions about Carvelle had been wrong. She debated calling him to tell him she had found it but decided to wait and play it for herself first, to see if it was indeed the tape they were looking for. But her tape recorder was at home, still sitting next to the computer from when she'd used it over the weekend. She thought about popping the disk into the computer to see what it contained, but the machine was turned off and unplugged. And Waring was waiting for her. There was no time.

She shoved the tape and the disk into her

purse, flipped off the lights and locked the door, then headed downstairs to meet Waring.

He was waiting at the front desk, chatting with the evening receptionist. Despite the gloomy weather, he seemed to be in a good mood. His glowance radiated warmly, and he chatted throughout most of the drive, filling her in on his day and the latest political scuttlebutt. Though the weather had created several traffic jams as well as some areas of flooding, the brunt of the storm had been centered over the city, and things improved considerably once they hit the more rural roads. They made the usual forty-five-minute drive in just over an hour and were less than half a mile from the house before Waring grew silent, giving Marlie a sidelong glance.

"You seem awfully quiet this evening," he said. "Bad day?"

Marlie shook her head. "No, not really. The storm just has me spooked."

Throughout the ride home she had been debating whether or not it would be appropriate to tell Waring about the tape. Uppermost in her mind was her concern that it would provide the final nail in William's coffin. The idea of contributing to William's demise created a storm of emotion within her that nearly matched the turbulence of the one that had been raging outside a short while ago.

Despite her misgivings about its contents, she was anxious to listen to the tape. She was keenly aware of its presence inside her purse, sitting there like some ticking time bomb, just waiting for her to detonate it. She doubted she would have any chance to listen to it in privacy while Waring was at the house, yet she was loathe to have to wait until he left.

She was still undecided when they arrived at the house. She set her purse with its ominous contents on the small table in the foyer while she hung up Waring's raincoat. "Would you like a drink?" she asked him, thinking it might help if she could just get her mind off the subject.

"I'd love one. What have you got?"

Marlie laughed. "To be honest, I'm not sure. But if you'll follow me out to the kitchen I'll show you where the liquor is and you can help yourself while I get dinner started. I don't know about you, but I'm hungry."

"I'm more than hungry," Waring said rubbing his stomach. "I'm ravenous. If there's anything I can do to help expedite the meal, please put me to work."

"I do need to chop up some stuff for a salad, and frankly, my sight limitations make it a slow process. So if you'd like to help with that, I'll be happy to let you. But I'm afraid our eating time will be determined by the baking of the lasagna. Sorry, but we have at least forty-five minutes before we eat, although I'm sure I have something here we can snack on in the meantime."

Marlie led him out to the kitchen and showed him where the liquor was stored in the pantry. Waring sorted through the bottles and came up with some scotch and soda. He fixed drinks for both of them while Marlie turned on the oven and tossed in the pan of lasagna she had prepared the night before. She then retrieved all the salad makings from the crisper drawer in the refrigerator and set herself and Waring at the table with a cutting board, strainer, and the appropriate cutlery.

"So," Waring said once they had begun. "Any news regarding Ronni's murder?"

Marlie was so startled by his mention of the very topic that was uppermost in her thoughts, she dropped the paring knife she was using. She gave him a weak smile and said, "You must have been reading my mind."

"Then there is news," Waring said, setting his own knife aside. He folded his arms along the edge of the table and leaned forward. "Tell me," he said softly. "Does it involve your husband?"

Marlie sighed and frowned. "It does," she said dismally. She then filled him in on Carvelle's story about Ronni's bracelet and William's subsequent disappearance.

"I'm sorry," Waring said quietly. He reached over and laid his scarred palm atop her hand. "This must be very difficult for you."

Marlie nodded, fighting a sudden urge to cry. "There's more," she said quietly, succumbing to the seduction of his kind concern. "Something I didn't tell you about before. Ronni had a habit of recording all of her phone conversations. It was something many of us knew about, and while we didn't approve, no one ever did anything to stop her." She then told Waring about her presence outside Ronni's office door the day of the murder and the phone conversation she had overheard. "I was fairly certain Ronni recorded that conversation," she went on. "But no one was ever able to find a tape among the hundreds she had that corresponded to that particular time and phone call. The police traced all the calls that came in, but they all go through the main switchboard and there's no way to track them from there. But they do know William was one of the people who called the station during the time period in question."

Waring's color, along with his glowance, had paled considerably as he listened. "My God!" he said, shaking his head. "I had no idea you were going through all of that." He paused, then added, "I must confess I'm a little shocked to hear that Ms. Cumberland recorded phone calls. She's always had something of a reputation for less than professional behavior, but I had no idea it ran that deep."

"There's no denying what she did was wrong," Marlie admitted. "But in this particular instance it may be providential. That tape could provide incontrovertible evidence as to who killed her." Marlie sighed, pulled back from his touch, and folded her arms over her chest in a vain effort to comfort herself. "Unfortunately," she said, her voice despondent, "I'm afraid that person is my ex-husband."

"But you can't be sure of that without the tape, can you? Granted, the thing with the bracelet is pretty damning, but William is a defense lawyer and I would imagine he could find a way around that."

Marlie chewed her lip and stared at him for several long moments before making her decision.

"I found the tape," she said flatly. "Or at least I think I have." She then related the tale of her adventure with the heating vent.

"Do you know what's on them yet?" Waring asked, his voice barely above a whisper.

Marlie shook her head. "No, the computer in the office was unplugged and my tape recorder was here at the house. I didn't want to keep you waiting any longer, so I stuck them in my purse and brought them home with me."

"Have you told the police about this?" Waring asked. "That stuff is evidence, is it not? Perhaps you should turn it over to them right away."

"I thought about that," Marlie admitted. "But I want to be sure it's the right tape first. And," she added with a sigh, "I guess I need to hear William's conversation for myself before I turn it in."

Waring nodded his understanding. Outside, the wind howled, battering the ancient frame of the house so that the walls creaked and groaned like some arthritic elder. A deep rumble of thunder echoed off in the distance, and Marlie glanced toward the kitchen window as the rain's volume picked up, pelting against the glass like a huge swarm of insects trying to get in.

"Sounds as if we haven't seen the last of the storm," she said, rising from her chair and heading for the pantry, where she dug up several candles. Carrying them over to the table, she set them out in the center and, using the box of matches she kept over the stove, lit two of them. "The wiring in this old place isn't very reliable," she explained to Waring. "We may be eating by candlelight."

"Sounds romantic," Waring said. Any other time, Marlie might have thrilled at those words, but at the moment, they seemed wholly inappropriate and ill-timed. Seeming to sense his gaffe, Waring shifted nervously in his chair, glanced toward the stove, and asked, "How much longer before the lasagna is ready?"

"Marlie flipped open the face of her watch and felt the dial. "About twenty-five minutes," she said.

"Plenty of time to listen to that tape."

chapter 36

Marlie went down the hall to her office to get the tape recorder. From there, she went to the foyer to get the tape from her purse. A flash of lightning brightened the night sky, casting the foyer in bas-relief. Several moments later, a loud peal of thunder sounded, closer than the last one. As Marlie's fingers closed around the tape, she felt the disk as well. But she decided to let it wait. With the storm closing in, it wouldn't be wise to try to run the computer. She could peruse the disk later; the tape was the key item for now.

She settled in at the kitchen table and popped the tape into the recorder. Neither of them said a word, but Waring let forth a sigh as weighty as her own. The room crackled with tension. Bracing herself, Marlie felt the buttons on the side of the tape recorder and hit the one for play, only to hear the hiss of an empty tape. She stopped it, hit the rewind button, and let it go until it reached the beginning. Then she hit play a second time.

There were a few seconds of leader tape, then Ronni's voice stating, *"Thursday, June sixteenth, eleven-fourteen A.M., Mike Lieber."* Following that was a five-minute conversation between Ronni and this Mike Lieber, who apparently was someone she dated on occasion. Their talk denigrated into some sexy repartee at one point, making Marlie blush. Nervous, she fidgeted with her watch and checked the time. The lasagna still had ten minutes to go.

Marlie was relieved when the conversation with Lieber ended, but her anxiety level quickly stepped up a notch when she heard Ronni's voice announce the next recording. *"Thursday, June sixteenth, eleven-thirty-five A.M., William Kaplan."* As if a special-effects team were in place to add to the drama of the moment, a brilliant flash of lightning lit up the room so that, for a second, it looked like an overdeveloped snapshot. A wall-shaking explosion of thunder followed close on its heels. Feeling a rush of panic, Marlie's thumb found the stop button on the recorder and pushed it. The lights in the kitchen flickered, went out, then came back on.

Marlie held the recorder in a tight, sweaty grip, preparing herself for what was to come.

The phone rang.

Normally, with an interview under way, especially with someone as important as Waring, Marlie would have ignored the call. But now, it provided the perfect means for stalling the inevitable. Still clutching the recorder in her hand, she rose from her chair and made her way to the phone, tossing a quick "Excuse me" over her shoulder to Waring.

"Hello?" she said, surprised that her voice sounded so weak and shaky.

"Marlie?" It was Damaris. "I see you managed to get home okay."

"I did. How's the car?"

"Terminal. I left it at the garage and had my roommate pick me up and bring me back here to the station."

"The station? Why didn't you go home?"

"Because I needed to follow up on something. I was trying to tell you about it earlier when I called you from the tow truck, but we got cut off before I had a chance to finish. It's about what I found out from Mrs. Pettigrew."

Shit! Here was Damaris ready to fill her in on the latest about Waring's possible twin brother and Waring was sitting not ten feet away at her kitchen table! "Can this wait until morning?" Marlie asked. "I'm in the middle of something important at the moment."

Damaris's sixth sense was working again, thank goodness. "He's there, isn't he? That's right! You were scheduled to have dinner with him tonight."

"That's right," Marlie said, giving Waring a smile and holding up one finger on the hand that held the recorder to indicate she wouldn't be long. He was watching her but was keeping himself busy cutting up the rest of the salad. Marlie chastised herself. This was the ultimate in unprofessional behavior. Invite a big-name candidate over for dinner and then ignore him while he prepares the meal. She should fire herself for this one.

"This is perfect," Damaris said. "Because you're not going to believe what I found out."

Marlie was torn between her curiosity and her unwillingness to leave Waring hanging while Damaris filled her in. In the end, the reporter in her won out. "Okay, shoot," she said.

"Bessie remembered Sam and Carla Denver very well. She said the boy was quiet and withdrawn, sort of frail looking, and that his mother had a severe drinking problem. Sam, she said, always seemed to have a passel of bruises on him. Several times, Bessie heard Carla screaming at the boy and beating him, and heard his own cries begging her to stop."

Marlie listened with a growing sense of horror. She focused on keeping her face complacent, so she wouldn't reveal her feelings or the content of Damaris's information to Waring, who was still watching her from his chair as he sliced tomatoes. The phone crackled in her ear as Mother Nature let loose with another volley from the heavens. The wind threw a sheet of rain at the kitchen window.

"Anyway," Damaris continued, "Bessie felt sorry for young Sam and tried to befriend him, inviting him over for cookies and milk and giving him a chance to talk. After a while, he opened up a little and Bessie found out there was a father in the picture as well, who apparently had been even more abusive than Carla. But one night, not long before Carla moved herself and Sam into Bessie's neighborhood, the husband apparently just disappeared. During the two years or so that Sam and Carla lived there, Bessie tried to find out more about the father, but she says that's all Sam would tell her.

"Then, one night about a month or so before Carla and Sam moved away, Bessie found Carla wandering the streets out front, drunk and disoriented. She brought her inside and gave her some coffee to try to sober her up. She said Carla was a real mess, crying and rambling on about her husband, Ed, and how the ghosts had finally gotten him. Bessie believes Carla was merely delusional, but she was intrigued by her story nonetheless. Carla started talking about the house she, Ed, and Sam had lived in right before she and Sam moved to the current neighborhood. Carla insisted the house was haunted. Said it was an old place, dating back to the Civil War, and that it had these tunnels beneath it that the slaves used to use."

Marlie felt a chill run down her spine, and she turned her back to Waring, no longer sure of her ability to keep a straight face.

"Sound familiar?" Damaris asked.

"It does," Marlie said carefully, her mind whirling crazily as she tried to piece this puzzle together. She quickly thought of a way to word her next question without giving Waring any clues as to what she was discussing. "Did she happen to know the exact address?"

"No box number or anything," Damaris said. "But she did say it was on Whitepine Road, about thirty-five miles outside of town."

Marlie's shoulders slumped with relief, and she turned back toward Waring. The garlic smell of the lasagna hit her, reminding her to check the time. She did, and realizing the cooking time was done, she made hand signals to Waring, asking him to take it out of the oven. As he approached the stove, Marlie kept the earpiece of the phone tight against her head, both to make sure Damaris's voice couldn't be heard beyond the confines of her own ear and to enable herself to hear better above the growing cacophony of the storm.

"I thought sure you were going to say something else," Marlie said. And though some distant part of her memory told her otherwise, she added, "I've never heard of Whitepine Road."

The kitchen window lit up with a flash of white light and thunder rolled over the house. Waring, who had just pulled the pan of lasagna from the oven, dropped it with a loud clatter on top of the stove. Marlie looked over at him and mouthed the words "Are you okay?" assuming he had burned his hands. He didn't answer her, and Marlie noted his glowance was shrunken and thin, nothing more than varying shades of gray. She wondered if he was frightened of the storm, which was now howling overhead with the shrillness of a banshee.

"Oh, but you have heard of Whitepine Road," Damaris said through the phone. "At least indirectly. That's why I wanted to come back here to the station. I couldn't believe there was more than one house with those slave tunnels beneath it in the area. Sure enough, while the road you live on was referred to by a simple route number for most of this century, there were several years, during the sixties and early seventies, when it was noted as Whitepine Road on the maps. Then it was changed to Holliman Road back in 1975 in honor of a farmer who saved the lives of a dozen kids who were injured in a school-bus accident the year before."

Of course! Now Marlie remembered why the name Denver had sounded so familiar to her when Dennis first mentioned it. Back when she had done her research on the history of her house, she had uncovered the fact that a family named Denver had lived there for some thirteen years, beginning in the late fifties. And now that she thought about it, she vaguely remembered seeing the name Whitepine Road on one of the earlier maps.

Another brilliant streak of lightning briefly turned the night into day, and a loud explosion rattled the windows. The accompanying thunder followed almost instantaneously, triggering a set of vibrations that threatened to shake the house loose from its very moorings. The lights went out, plunging the kitchen into undulating candlelit shadows. A roar of static came over the phone, then all sound ceased as the instrument went dead.

Over by the stove, Waring said, "I'm not sure it's wise for you to be talking on the phone in the middle of this." His voice was raised so he could be heard over the storm as it pummeled the house.

"It went dead anyway," Marlie said, replacing the phone in its cradle. She became aware of the tape recorder still clutched in her hand and held it out in front of her, staring at it.

"Want to wait until we eat before you listen to that?" Waring asked her.

Marlie didn't know what to do. Her mind was still reeling from the shock of discovering that Waring's adopted sibling, assuming that's who Sam Denver was, had once lived right here in this very house. Obviously, she needed to do a lot more groundwork before she broached the whole adoption issue with Waring. Hitting him now with a bunch of jumbled, half-baked facts might turn him off to the whole subject for good. And there was still the matter of the tape.

She shook her head. "The lasagna should set for ten minutes or so anyway. Let's get this over with."

She walked over to the table and set the recorder on it. Settling back in her chair, she waited for Waring to take his, then hit the play button.

The conversation kicked in midway through a sentence, and Ronni's voice could faintly be heard above the rage of the storm. Marlie reached over and cranked the volume up.

. . . interested in finding out more about him, Ronni's voice said. *It's critical to a story I'm working on.*

William's voice came next, and Marlie tensed, waiting to hear what he would say.

I'm willing to discuss this with you, though I can't promise I'll give you what you want. There is the matter of client confidentiality.

Fine, Ronni said. *All I'm asking is that you hear me out. When can we meet?*

I'm leaving the office for lunch in about half an hour. Want to meet me somewhere?

Marlie's heart sank. There it was. Proof, in William's own words, that he had arranged to meet Ronni on the day of her death rather than the following day, as he had told Carvelle. She felt sick, and the garlicky aroma of the lasagna suddenly seemed cloying, sending a wave of nausea through her. She looked up and met Waring's steady gaze, his image blurring as tears welled in her eyes. Embarrassed for him to see this display of emotion in her, she turned away, gazing out the window instead.

Her heart leaped into her throat as she saw a cloud of shimmering red through the rain that slaked down the glass. At first, she thought it was a fire, set off by a lightning strike. But then she realized the red had a distinctively human shape to it and knew it wasn't flames she was seeing, but a glowance.

Someone was standing just outside the window.

William's final meeting arrangements with Ronni were drowned out as Marlie let out a terrified shriek. She leaped from her chair, backing away from the window and glancing toward Waring with a terrified look. "There's someone outside the window," she said.

Waring looked, then rose out of his chair to move closer. "I don't see anyone," he said, his face almost pressed against the glass.

William bid Ronni good-bye on the tape, and several seconds of hissing silence followed.

Marlie stared at the window, the image of that flaming red figure burned so vividly in her mind that for a moment she wasn't sure if it was still there or not. But as Waring had indicated, she now saw nothing. She raked her hand through her hair, her face screwed up in confusion.

Ronni's voice came back on the tape. *Thursday, June sixteenth, eleven-fifty-two A.M.*

"I saw someone there," Marlie said to Waring. "I'm—"

A loud bang echoed down the hallway from the direction of the main foyer. The shriek of the storm surged into the house, the sound of its fury suddenly amplified tenfold. Marlie's blood froze as she realized that bang had been the sound of the front door being flung open against the wall. The wind that raged outside found its way through the portal and into the house, reaching down the hallway with its cold damp fingers and blasting into the kitchen, drowning out the sound of Ronni's voice on the tape and ripping Marlie's last words away. The candles on the table guttered beneath the wind's fury, waging a brief and hopeless battle for survival before they were snuffed out. Total darkness settled over the kitchen like a heavy blanket.

"Maaaaaaarlieeeeeee!"

Though the shrieking yell blended in with that of the wind almost perfectly, Marlie still recognized it as William's voice, and the realization drove a cold spike of terror through her heart.

chapter

37

Dammit! Marlie thought. Why hadn't she remembered Carvelle's warning and thought to lock the front door once she and Waring were inside?

For a few seconds the wind eased and the rain outside lightened as the storm gathered its strength for the next onslaught, allowing Marlie to once again hear Ronni's voice on the tape.

. . . for returning my call so quickly. I'm sure you'll be very interested in what . . .

Another flash of lightning lit up the outside sky, creating a strobe effect in the kitchen and leaving Marlie more blind in its wake than the darkness had. She turned and squinted in the direction of the entrance to the kitchen, looking for the fiery red mark of William's glowance but seeing nothing but blackness. The wind howled with renewed force, driving rain through the open door and into the foyer, flinging handfuls of the stuff at the windows and walls, hammering it into the roof. Somewhere in that rapid-fire timpani, her heart was doing its own share of pounding, blending in with the fury of the storm.

More lightning, and Marlie gasped as she caught a fleeting glimpse of two figures by the kitchen table. Panicked, she turned to grope for the phone, then remembered it was dead. She heard a loud grunt followed by a crash. Her gaze swept the darkness searching for glowances, but her eyes were still struggling to recover from the blinding flashes of lightning. Something smashed painfully into her shin and she yelped, jumping back a few feet. She reached down and felt one of the kitchen chairs lying on its side. Once again the kitchen was lit up in a fiery display, and she saw the two figures were now by the doorway, locked in a struggling embrace.

Slowly, she backed up until she hit the counter, then felt her way along it toward the far end of the kitchen. She hissed with pain when her hand touched the stove, still hot from the lasagna. Turning around, she gingerly groped its surface and that of the surrounding countertop, searching for anything she could use as a weapon.

Outside, the storm quieted, as if it had been suddenly robbed of its strength.

. . . intend to expose everything I know . . .

Marlie realized the tape was still playing. A chill raced down her spine as she recognized Ronni's words as the same ones she had heard outside the office on the day of her murder. Her mind raced. Who was Ronni talking to? Was it William again? That made no sense. She had already arranged to meet him. Why would she call him back?

I would like a chance to discuss this with you first, a male voice said from the tape. *There are certain things you may not be aware of.*

Marlie listened to the voice with a growing sense of disbelief. She recognized it instantly, and the pieces of the puzzle began to fall into place.

And I think you may have made some incorrect assumptions. Before you decide to—

Marlie heard a click, and the voice ended abruptly. Outside, the worst of the storm had passed as quickly as it had come on, and the room had grown strangely quiet, with only the hiss of a much gentler rain falling upon the window. In the silence, Marlie heard a heavy *clunk* as the tape player was dropped back onto the table. Her eyes, given a reprieve from the blinding flashes of light, could now make out two vague shapes in the room. One lay on the floor near the entrance to the kitchen, its glowance gauzy and narrow. Wisps of it drifted into the air, floating off on the occasional gusts of a now much milder wind that still wove its way down the hall. The sight of that dissipating glowance struck panic in Marlie, as she remembered all too well the last time she had seen one like it, and what it had meant.

But the second glowance, which stood not far from the first, frightened her even more. Even though its color nearly matched the darkness, its heavy malevolent mass was still distinguishable. She knew now whom that glowance belonged to, and wondered how she could have not known it before. It all made sense. Waring's glowance had always been so distinctly different from all the rest, with its overpowering glow and manipulative charm.

"Marlie?"

The sound of his voice, so calm and controlled, was chilling.

She thought fast. For the moment, she had a slight advantage in that she was less hampered by the darkness than he was. As quietly as she could, she inched her way toward the cellar door, keeping her eyes riveted to that murderous cloud of darkness the entire time.

"Marlie, where are you?"

He said it like a patient parent chastising his child. She wasn't about to answer him, knowing that any sound would give her away. He moved then, slowly feeling his way over to the table, and Marlie suddenly remembered the candles and the box of matches she had left sitting there. If he managed to find them and light them, he'd be on her in a minute. She moved a little more quickly, trying to stay quiet, reaching the door to the cellar at the same time Waring reached the table.

She grabbed the doorknob and turned it slowly, praying it wouldn't squeak and give away her position. It turned quietly, and she gave the door a gentle tug. Nothing happened. Then, she remembered the lock. Cursing to herself, she reached up, felt the key, and slowly turned it in the lock. The dead bolt slid back with a tiny *thunk*. Waring's head snapped up, and Marlie knew he had heard the noise. She gave the door a yank, less cautious this time, and nearly cried with relief when it opened. Her hand groped for the railing, and she headed down the stairs at a reckless pace. From the kitchen above, she heard Waring chuckle, a decidedly maniacal and unpleasant sound that made the hair on her arms and neck rise to attention.

She reached the basement floor without incident and flung herself toward the wall ahead. Sparing a quick glance back up the stairs, she saw a brief flare of light that then settled into an ambient glow. Waring had found the matches and candles. A renewed sense of panic hit her, and she scurried along the wall toward the cabinet that marked the entrance to the tunnels. When she reached it, she flung the front doors aside and reached in with a trembling hand in search of the lever that would release the catch.

She grabbed a shelf with both hands and pulled with all her might, wincing as the hinges creaked and groaned. She looked back toward the stairs, saw that Waring had yet to descend, and hurried into the tunnel, pulling the door closed so he wouldn't be able to find her.

Running her left hand along the wall the way she had on her last venture down here, she quickly moved deeper into the tunnel until she reached the first intersection. There, she waved her hand out in front of her like an antenna and stepped ahead until she reached the center tunnel. Then she continued along its length a little more slowly, not wanting to repeat the fall she had taken during her last excursion. Not five steps along its length she froze, her eyes wide with terror. From behind her, the familiar creak of the cabinet's hinges echoed down the tunnel.

Waring had found her! How the hell did he know? Had he seen her run in here? She was sure she'd managed to get inside the tunnel and close the cabinet before he'd reached the stairs. So how had he known?

It came to her then. Sam Denver had lived in this house. Sam Denver was Waring's twin brother. Richard Waring was really Sam Denver.

"Marlie?" His voice echoed through the tunnel, reverberating off the rock walls. The sound of it catapulted her down the tunnel to the next junction, where she knelt quickly to feel for the next carving. She prayed her interpretation of the carvings was correct or else she might end up wandering down here forever, caught in an endless maze of dirt, rock, and darkness.

"Marlie, you can't hide from me. I know these tunnels like the back of my hand."

Marlie plunged headlong down the right-hand tunnel, ducking when she felt her hair brush against the ceiling. A few feet later the ceiling rose back up enough for her to again stand upright. She picked up her speed, then paid for her heedless flight when she stubbed her toe on a rock jutting up from the ground. She windmilled her arms in an effort to keep her balance, but fell anyway, landing on her side, another sharp-edged rock catching her in her hip. Gritting her teeth against the pain, she scrambled to her feet, repositioned her hand along the left wall, and continued.

"My parents, or rather the animals who called themselves my parents, used to lock me up down here for punishment, you know," Waring went on, his voice sounding even closer. "I had lots of time to explore in here. Did you know there's a code? But of course you do. You were exploring these tunnels yourself back when you first moved in, weren't you?"

Marlie reached another intersection, squatted and felt along the wall for the carving, found an *L*. She scurried off as fast as she dared, a little more cautious since her tumble. The tunnel ran on a downhill incline now. Her hip burned with pain, and a sticky wetness ran down her leg.

"I couldn't let you do that, Marlie. You might have discovered my secret. It's a good thing I ran into your husband that day a year or so ago. He wasn't too thrilled about this place, you know. He bitched for fifteen minutes straight about all the time and money you were wasting on this house and your grandiose idea of exploring these tunnels. As soon as I heard that, I knew I had to do something to stop you."

Marlie tried to tune him out; the sound of his voice only made her feel more panicky. Another intersection. An *R*. She moved into the right-hand tunnel.

Waring laughed, and the crazed tone of it made Marlie whimper with terror. Her foot collided with another rock, sending an electric jolt of pain up her leg, but she managed to stay upright and keep moving. Another intersection, and an *M*. She headed off down the center tunnel, the incline growing even steeper. With every step she took, the distinctive odor of the underground passage grew stronger. It was a nasty dank smell—a mix of earth, mold, and decay.

"I knew you wouldn't be able to resist that hint about police corruption," Waring said. He was still close, keeping pace with her easily. Marlie prayed this endless maze would end sometime soon. She felt her only hope for escape was to find an exit and reach open land. If there was an exit.

"Things didn't turn out quite the way I had

planned for you, Marlie, although I must admit it was mighty considerate of that filthy little grunt I hired to shoot you to take care of himself that way. Saved me the trouble of having to do it. Nice of him, don't you think? Of course it turned your camera friend there into a crispy critter too, didn't it?"

Marlie's heart crawled into her throat as the implication of Waring's words hit her. He had been responsible for that whole mess at the warehouse, for Chris's death and her blindness. The whole thing had been a setup, designed to lure her in and kill her, simply to . . . To what? To keep her from exploring these tunnels? But why? Waring had said something about his secret. What did that mean? Surely the mere existence of these tunnels wasn't worth killing someone over.

"Have you figured it all out yet, Miss Star Reporter?" Waring yelled in a mocking tone. "Surely you're at least as good as that bitch Cumberland, and she managed to work it out on her own. She may have been a bit unprofessional, but you have to admit she was one smart cookie."

He was taunting her now. He was following the trail marked out by the carvings, assuming she knew of them and was going that way too. But, he wasn't sure, she realized. That's why he was trying to goad her, hoping she would say something so he could verify her location. She reached yet another junction and took a precious moment to pause. Her chest was heaving from fright and sheer physical exertion. Kneeling down, she felt for the carving and found another *M*. She chewed her lip in indecision, all too aware of Waring's proximity. At the far end of the tunnel she had just come down, she saw the faint glimmer of candlelight. Every second counted. *Instinct.* She had learned to always go with her instinct.

She crossed over and headed down the right-hand tunnel.

"Yep, she was smart all right. Just like my brother. Of course, he wasn't just smart, he was lucky, too. Dear old Mom sold him to the good parents. I was the one that got thrown to the wolves."

Sold. Waring had said his brother was sold to the good parents. That explained why there was no trace of an adoption anywhere.

The ground beneath Marlie's feet had leveled some, but the terrain was much more treacherous, studded with rocks everywhere she stepped. A few feet more and she ran into a dead end. Quickly, she moved over to the other side of the tunnel, her hand finding the wall's surface, and turned back to face the way she had come. She stopped, listening for Waring, to see if he had followed her or taken the center tunnel. If he took the middle road, she could double back and return to the house.

She took a few tentative steps forward and something snagged at her feet, something loose and long that tangled between her legs and wrapped around her ankle. She stopped and reached down to pull it away, frowning when her fingers felt cloth. Then her fingers felt . . . *fingers!* Before she could stop herself, Marlie let out a yelp. She scrambled away from the horrible thing that held her leg, kicking her foot out to shake it loose. Her other foot hit on one of the many rocks jutting up from the earth and again she lost her balance, toppling over backward. She hit the floor hard and her head came down on the edge of a rock, slamming the side of her skull. She saw stars.

Then the stars blinked out and she saw nothing at all.

chapter
38

The first thing Marlie became aware of was pain—sharp, shooting pain that zapped down her leg, throbbed in her hip, and coursed through her head. At first she had no idea where she was but then she moaned, and the odd echo she heard brought her memory back into sharp focus. Her eyes flew open.

Waring squatted just a few feet away, the candle he had carried with him resting near his feet. In one hand, he held something long and narrow, which glistened brightly along its lower half, reflecting the light from the candle—a knife, Marlie realized. Waring saw the direction of her gaze and waved the weapon in front of him.

"This is yours, I take it?" he asked. "I found it back there near one of the intersections. Kind of you to leave it for me."

Marlie squeezed her eyes closed in dismay as she remembered her last foray down here and how she had dropped the knife and left it behind. Now, the weapon she had once wielded for her own protection was likely to become the instrument of her demise.

She opened her eyes again and glared at Waring. His glowance hung around him like a death pall, black as the night, undulating and pulsing with evil. Wincing, Marlie slowly pushed herself to a sitting position, pain momentarily snatching her breath away. When she did breathe again, she had the odd sensation of being able to smell the evil that clung to Waring, a stench of rot and decay, like death itself. Then she looked around and realized it wasn't Waring's glowance she smelled but the lingering odor of decomposition from the skeletal remains that were heaped up beside her. The flesh was long gone, leaving only the bones and the clothing, but the smell hung in the air, trapped within this dead-end leg of the tunnel, steeped into the walls. She clamped a hand over her mouth and tried not to gag.

Waring chuckled. "Marlie, meet my brother, Richard," he said with an air of pleasant insanity. He gestured toward the other skeletons with the knife. "And my mother, Carla, and my father, Ed."

Marlie stared at him in horrified disbelief. Waring—no, *Denver,* she realized—was totally, completely, and dangerously mad. The full ramifications of what he had done were just now beginning to dawn on her. "The car accident. That's when you killed him, wasn't it?" she said.

Waring bestowed the smile of a proud parent on her. "I knew you were smarter than that Cumberland woman," he said. There was a brightness to his eyes that was unnatural and unnerving. "Although, technically, you're incorrect. I killed Richard before the accident. It was imperative, you see, that his body never be found, so it wouldn't have done to have him involved in the car accident. I must confess, my brother put up one hell of a fight. It was quite impressive. And helpful, too. Thanks to him, I had all the necessary bangs and bruises to make it appear as if I had also been in the accident. From there, it was easy.

"I whacked both of Richard's parents, rendering them unconscious, then put them in the car and drove out to that spot where the road curves. I stopped, positioned them in the front seat, weighted the gas pedal with a cinderblock, and let her rip." He chuckled, the gleam in his eyes growing even brighter for a moment. "I'll bet that sucker was doing at least forty when it hit. But, as luck would have it, the impact wasn't enough to kill them. I had intended to burn the car all along, but I honestly thought they'd be dead by the time I did it. They came to just as the flames were really taking hold. The driver's side door was dented enough that it wouldn't open, but I thought at one point they might actually get out on the passenger side."

He shook his head then and sighed. "Rotten bit of luck with that car coming by when it did. I picked that road particularly because it's so seldom traveled. It could have been worse, though. At least I'd had time to toss the cinderblock over the side of the road and start the fire before anyone came along." He thought a moment and chuckled softly to himself. "That idiot who pulled me off the car thought I was trying to save them when in reality I was trying to keep them from getting out of the car." He shrugged. "It all worked out in the end. And the burns I suffered took care of the problem of the fingerprints."

"The fingerprints?" Marlie said, confused.

"Yep, the fingerprints," Waring said, nodding slowly. "That was the one snafu. Even identical twins have subtle differences in their fingerprints. Besides, my fingers were already scarred from climbing up through the shaft that marks the other end of the tunnels in here. Given his position at the bank, I was fairly certain Richard had his fingerprints on record somewhere. If they ever fingerprinted me, I had to have some way of explaining why they didn't match. I hadn't really figured out how I was going to handle it, but as luck would have it, fate intervened." He held his scarred hands in front of his face and twisted them back and forth in the candlelight.

"Hell of a price to pay, though. It hurt like a son of a bitch."

"Then . . . the accident . . . you staged that whole thing, just to kill off your brother's adoptive parents?"

"Brilliant, wasn't it?" he said smugly.

Marlie turned and looked at the skeletons, her face distorted with disgust. "Why?" she asked. "You've killed all these innocent people. And for what?"

"Innocent?" he scoffed. "Hardly. Do you have any idea what it's like to spend your childhood with a couple of drunken, abusive parents, Marlie? Parents who beat you for every imagined transgression? Beat you hard enough that you end up in the hospital with broken bones, massive bruises, and even a damaged kidney?"

Marlie remembered the blood-transfusion record Dennis had found for thirteen-year-old Sam Denver, who'd had a bruised kidney and blood in his urine. She grimaced.

"And if they weren't beating the hell out of me,

they tossed me down here in these tunnels, locked away for days on end with only a few bits of food thrown in every now and then. Can you imagine what that was like, Marlie? Living down here in this endless darkness?"

"I know what it's like to live in darkness. Thanks to you."

Waring laughed. "Yes, a delicious bit of irony, that. My original intent, of course, was to simply kill you. It was the perfect setup: an ambitious, risk-taking young journalist who wanders into an aban-doned meat plant after receiving an anonymous tip. They never would have figured it out. In fact, they never did, did they? Once you were dead, I intended to cave in parts of the tunnel near the house to assure no one else would get curious and try to explore. But as it turned out, your punishment was much better than death. Instead, you got to sample a taste of what my life was like. And of course, I then decided to leave the tunnels the way they were so I could keep an eye on you."

He paused and cocked his head as he looked at her. "You look very innocent when you sleep, Marlie. Did you know that?"

Marlie's eyes grew wide with shock. "You spied on me? You came into my house and spied on me?"

"Sure," Waring said with a shrug. "Why not? It wasn't like you were going to see me," he taunted cruelly.

"It was you who broke into my house," she said, realization dawning. "You got in through the tun-nels."

"I needed to know if you were onto me," he said.

"It was a little too coincidental seeing you at that political dinner and then finding out you'd had a sudden change of heart about my interview."

"Then why did you have Garrity ask me to do the interview in the first place?"

"As soon as I heard you had that surgery and some sight back, I worried that you might want to start delving into the tunnels again. If you did, I wanted to know, so I figured it was better to keep close tabs on you. Of course, there was the simple fact that I really did need the publicity to push along my gubernatorial plans. And frankly, I figured you were safe. With your limitations, I didn't think there was much risk of you stumbling onto the truth if you did do the interview."

Marlie had thought nothing could sting as much as the revelation that Waring wanted her to do the interview strictly for her token appearance as a handicapped woman. He had just proven her wrong. "I uncovered a lot more than you may realize," she shot back. "Including who your birth mother was."

He didn't seem at all surprised at that, and Marlie was struck with another revelation.

"You killed her, too, didn't you?"

"Yeah, but there was little challenge in that one. I knew she had sold us; Ed and Carla were quick to remind me of that whenever they felt the need to point out how unworthy I was. All those years when I was growing up, I vowed that someday I would find the bitch who gave me away and make her pay for what she did to me. I was fifteen when Carla finally told me my mother's name during one of her drinking binges. Carla didn't know it, but it was my need to discover that one bit of knowledge that kept her alive after I killed old Ed there," he said, gesturing with his head toward the pile of bodies.

"As soon as Carla told me what I needed to know, there was no reason to keep her around anymore. So I killed her and went off on my own. Took me all of about two months to hunt my mother down." He let out a derisive snort. "She was no better than Carla. Just another addict. She was half dead already when I found her. It didn't take much to give her an overdose and make it look like she had done herself in accidentally."

Marlie shuddered as she realized Waring—no, Denver—had committed his first murder when he was barely an adolescent. "But why kill your brother?" she asked him. "He never did anything to you. He was as much a victim as you were."

Waring shook his head slowly, giving her a disappointed look. "Marlie, really. How can you think that? My dear brother had everything. He had no idea how lucky he was, what he had. While he was enjoying the fruits of a normal childhood and two parents who loved and nurtured him, I was struggling each day simply to survive. Richard took what he had for granted, never realizing just how fortunate he was. He had a family who loved him, money, respect, and a career. And everyone liked him, even our birth mother. When she told me about him just before I killed her, she positively glowed with pride. You see, she had kept track of him, but never bothered with me. Richard always got all the breaks.

"At first, I wanted nothing to do with him. But eventually I got curious and tracked him down. For years I followed his life, watching while he kept snatching the golden rings and I kept scrabbling in the dirt just to make a living. I finally grew tired of it and decided it was my turn to enjoy the good life."

While he talked, Marlie noticed his glowance gradually shifting from the heavy and malignant blackness it had possessed earlier to a lighter, less threatening shade. She took that as a sign that his mood, at least for the moment, had become more benign.

"It took years of careful planning. Unlike you, Marlie, I take the time to think things through before I act. By then, I had established a new identity for myself with the help of some friends I made on the street. Richard was already making his career in banking, so I got myself a job as a teller in a bank in Ohio. But that didn't work out quite as well as I'd hoped. Handling all that cash every day and seeing how the better half lived made me impatient. So I planned a robbery. It should have been easy; after all, I had the advantage of inside information. But one of the tellers recognized me and I was forced to kill her. By the way, you know her husband I believe. Paul Carvelle?"

Marlie gasped in shock.

Waring chuckled. "Yeah, that was basically my response when he showed up here on the local force several years later. I figured he'd managed to track me here somehow, though I was fairly certain he didn't know who I was. When I heard about that little problem he had with shooting his partner, I figured I could keep him in rein easily enough by creating a cloud of suspicion around him regarding the police corruption thing, which, by the way, is legitimate. I confess, it gave me a scare when he was assigned to investigate the warehouse explosion involving you; I thought he was onto me then. But I quickly realized he was blindly shooting in the dark. He's just a dumb dick like all the rest of them."

Marlie gave him a look of disgust. "You can't seriously think you can continue to get away with this," she said.

Waring shrugged. "Why not? I've gotten away with it for the past six years. As for Ronni Cumberland, your husband has been a big help to me there. The police are certain he's the murderer. As soon as you told me William was a suspect, I knew what I had to do. Now, the police have their culprit and no one is the wiser. Except for you, of course. But that problem will be taken care of momentarily."

He sighed and looked about the interior of the tunnel. "I suppose I will have to finally arrange that cave-in," he said wistfully. "Having you disappear is likely to arouse too much curiosity."

He looked at her then. "And I must confess, killing you will be such a waste. I really liked you, Marlie. You're an attractive, bright woman. It's a shame you had to find that damned tape. I was hoping you and I could have a more . . . permanent relationship. The excitement and romance of a pending marriage would have added a lot of oomph to my gubernatorial campaign. And frankly, as Garrity so wisely pointed out to me, having one of the area's top reporters for a wife would have made my PR problems so much easier to handle."

Garrity. Waring's mention of the name made Marlie flash back to that night of their first dinner, when Waring had said something to her on the porch about knowing Garrity since childhood. She vaguely remembered how a fleeting thought had passed through her mind and realized she had almost figured it out then. She knew from the information she had profiled on Waring from a year ago that Garrity was from out of state somewhere. And he had that faint New England twang. Yet Waring had spent his entire life right here in the area.

"Does Garrity know the truth about you?" she asked.

"Know? Hell, he helped me mastermind the whole thing. It was a stroke of luck running into him when I did. We were both young at the time, but we knew even then that we were kindred spirits. Garrity has certain talents that have proven to be useful. He was the one who broke into William's house and planted the bracelet."

Marlie gaped at him, incredulous. "God, you're a cold bastard."

"Which is why I have succeeded in politics when my brother never would have," he said. "Sometimes holding political office means making difficult decisions that are based on logic rather than emotion. Like now."

His glowance began to shift wildly, resuming the frightening malevolence Marlie knew all too well. She scrambled for something to say, to keep him talking, trying to stall him until . . . until what? Sooner or later, it was going to come down to a one-on-one struggle for survival. She needed time, time to think.

"Tell me something," she said, amazed her voice sounded as calm as it did. She shifted her position some, as if to make herself more comfortable, but in the process she positioned her feet beneath her so she could more easily rise to a standing position should she need to try for a quick getaway. "How did Ronni figure you out?"

Waring sighed heavily and didn't answer right away, as if he were debating whether or not to do so. Finally he said, "Admittedly, there is a flaw. It seems my brother had his spleen removed when he was younger. I did not. That Cumberland bitch picked up on the fact that mine is still there from a copy of my medical record when I was treated following the car accident. I tried to tell her it was an error, but she insisted on seeing my scar to prove I had, in fact, had the surgery. I knew then that she wouldn't give up and that I would have to kill her."

Marlie gave herself a mental kick. She vaguely remembered Ralph reading back the ER record to her, and a note about the abdominal organs, including the spleen, all being intact. Yet Damaris had clearly told her about the earlier splenectomy. She should have caught it.

"She was easier than I thought," Waring mused. "I arranged to meet her in a restaurant parking lot and she got into my car to talk to me. It didn't take me long to realize that while she was aware of my true identity and suspected that I had killed my brother and his parents, a lot of her knowledge was just supposition. The dumb bitch was bluffing. She was sniffing up the right tree, but still wasn't sure what she'd hunted down. Though I knew with time that she would.

"I don't think she believed I would be bold enough to do anything to her there in a public parking lot. She was wrong. I knocked her out, drove out here intending to kill her and bring her into the tunnel with the rest of my collection, but then I discovered I couldn't get to the shaft because a tree had fallen down across the road, blocking the way. She was starting to come around by then, but was still confused and out of it enough for me to get her out to that field. I figured if I killed her there I could dump her body over the cliff, then come back later and get past the tree on foot to drag her body into the tunnel. But the police got there first, thanks to you."

"I saw you," Marlie said. "I saw you kill her."

"Yeah, you gave me quite the start when you told me you'd witnessed the murder, though I relaxed once I realized you truly didn't know who it was you had seen."

Waring's glowance had lightened some as he talked about Ronni, but now it resumed its malevolence. Marlie tensed. "They'll find you, you know," she said, desperate to keep him talking. "If Ronni could do it, someone else will eventually figure it out as well."

"I'll deal with that when the time comes," Waring said with casual indifference. He rose to his feet, and Marlie's heart clutched within her chest. She reached behind her, feeling around among the bones that lay there, searching for something, anything she could use as a weapon. Swallowing down her disgust, she wrapped her fingers around a shaft of bone, wondering with some bizarre, distant part of her mind whose it was and what part of them she had.

Waring began to move toward her, the knife held in his hand. "I intend to make this as quick and painless as possible for you, Marlie," he said. "I meant it when I said I liked you. I really don't want to see you suffer any more than is necessary."

She looked around frantically for some avenue of escape, but the only way out was past Waring. There was no way she'd ever get by him. Unless . . .

Mustering every spare ounce of strength she had, she flung herself forward along the ground, reaching out with the bone she gripped in her hand and swinging it against the candle. It fell over, hot molten wax flowing over the flame and drowning it out. They were plunged into an abyss of total darkness. Quickly, Marlie rolled on her side toward the wall and searched for some sign of Waring's glowance. Her heart sank when she realized that the awful, reeking blackness of it made him virtually invisible in the dark.

"That was stupid, Marlie," Waring said angrily.

Marlie zeroed in on his voice and knew he stood a few feet to her right. She considered making a run for it and trying to get past him. But then she realized he was almost as adept in this darkness as she was and her chances of getting away from him would be slim. She believed him when he said he knew the tunnels like the back of his hand. As quietly as she could, she rose to her feet but stayed crouched down, frantic and frightened, not knowing what to do next.

And then she saw it. The merest hint of shimmering, vibrant, angry red.

She lunged toward it with all her might, close to the ground so she wouldn't accidentally impale herself on the knife, her shoulder smashing into his knees. The momentum behind her lunge made him stagger back, lose his balance, and fall to the floor. The knife was knocked from his hand, making a loud clatter as the metal of the blade struck one of the stones in the earth. Marlie came down on top of his legs and quickly scrambled off, trying to scoot past him down the tunnel.

His hand grabbed her ankle, dropping her to the ground. She kicked at him and tried to wriggle loose, but he hung on with the tenacity of a pit bull. She could feel the ridges of his scars biting into her skin. Doubling her efforts, she kicked even harder with her free foot, but his recovery was quicker than she had anticipated, and before she was fully up, he was on her. One arm wrapped around her waist, the other snaked around her neck as he pulled her back hard against his chest. He staggered to his feet, letting go of her waist and using both hands to tighten the grip on her neck. Marlie felt her feet leave the floor. Her hands clawed at the vise around her neck, her feet kicking frantically at the air. Her head began to pound, feeling as if it would explode; her mouth gaped open as she struggled to get air past the strangling band of his arm. An explosion of colored stars burst all around her and she knew she was about to pass out.

Then, several feet in front of her, she saw a glow of light—not the radiant corona of a glowance, but a bright tunnel of white light—warm, welcoming, beckoning. As her vision narrowed, her mind focused on that light and sought it out as her destiny. She tried to lift her arm and reach for it, but she had no strength left anymore. The light grew brighter, warmer, offering peaceful release. It was the last thing she saw before the darkness settled on her once again.

Voices. Everywhere, voices. She vaguely remembered the beckoning tunnel of light and assumed she was hearing the voices of the dead. There was warmth against her cheek and the pleasant lull of a soothing, comforting whisper near her ear, calling her name.

She realized her eyes were closed and opened them, prepared to see heaven. What she saw instead was the pile of bones in the tunnel.

"Marlie?"

Again that soft whisper. Warmth against her cheek, rising and falling. Breathing. Something stroked her hair. She raised her eyes and saw the shape of a face, its perimeter radiating a warm, pink glow.

"Are you all right?" the face asked, and she knew then it was Carvelle.

She pushed herself away from him and sat up, then instantly regretted the action. The warmth of his chest where her head had lain moments ago had felt so wonderful, so secure, that she wanted to lay back against him. He reached up and gently tilted her chin, looking at her neck.

"Can you speak?" he asked her.

She didn't know. Her throat felt raw and thick. She let out a little cough, then said, "I think so." It came out little more than a whisper, but intelligible.

She looked around her then and saw other people hovering nearby, each one carrying a flashlight. The darkened shape of someone lay prostrate on the ground a few feet away, totally absent of any glowance, the knife glistening in an outstretched hand.

"That's Waring," Carvelle explained. "He came at me with the knife and I had to shoot him."

Marlie shook her head. "He's not Waring," she said, struggling to make herself heard. "He's—"

"His twin. I know."

Marlie's surprise was apparent in her expression.

"Damaris figured it out," he explained. "She had a feeling something wasn't quite right when she found out Waring's twin had once lived in your house. When she got cut off from you on the phone, she went down to your office and started going through that file you had on Waring. She hit on the fact that he supposedly had his spleen removed when he was eight, yet had a perfectly good one several years ago when he was seen in the ER following the car accident. Just to be sure it wasn't an oversight or an error, she tracked down the ER doctor who had examined Waring and asked him about it. As luck would have it, the guy remembered Waring and the incident well. The horror of the situation made it stick in his mind. Anyway, he swore Waring had no scars when he examined him. That got Damaris worried and she called me."

Carvelle looked down at the ground and shook his head. "I should have figured it out sooner," he said dismally. "I should have made the connection about Waring's hands. Remember me telling you that the strangulation marks we found on Ronni's neck were atypical?"

Marlie nodded.

"Well, manual strangulation typically leaves bruising in specific spots and in the shape of the fingertips. But while the bruises we found on Ronni's neck were where we expected them to be, the appearance of the bruises was odd. They were narrower and less even than what we normally see. And then there were these ridges, suggesting an uneven surface and uneven pressure. I thought then that is was the result of some sort of glove the killer was wearing, which was borne out by the lack of fingerprints anywhere. But as soon as Damaris told me what she had found it all suddenly clicked into place. The ridges on those bruises were from the scars on Waring's hands.

"Anyway, as soon as I talked to Damaris I tried to call you but your phone was dead, so I drove out here and found the front door wide open and William passed out on the kitchen floor."

"William!" Marlie croaked. "Is he—"

"I think he'll be okay. He got knocked around pretty hard, and I think he's got one hell of a concussion and a few broken ribs, but the paramedics say he'll survive."

Marlie squeezed her eyes closed with relief. Despite all the antagonism between her and William, she had once loved the man. Plus, he was Kristen's father. Much as she hated him at times, she didn't want him dead.

Carvelle reached into his shirt pocket and pulled out a microcassette tape. "I found this in the tape player on your kitchen table. Where on earth did you find it? Was it inside that heating vent in your office? I saw where someone had taken it off the wall."

Marlie nodded.

"What made you look there? I never would have thought of it."

"I heard it," Marlie said, grimacing with the pain it triggered in her throat. She knew that was hardly enough of an explanation, but Carvelle, bless him, didn't ask for anything more. "There's a computer disk, too. In my purse," she croaked.

"Well, it's pretty obvious from listening to this tape that Ronni had the goods on Waring," he said. "Though I confess that when I first heard William's conversation, agreeing to meet Ronni later that day, I thought we had finally nailed him. But there's another conversation after the one with Waring, where Ronni called William back and changed the time of their meeting to the following day. I think William was confused about the calls and forgot that he had actually arranged to meet Ronni that same day before she called him back to change it."

Wincing as she prepared to speak again, Marlie said, "Waring planted Ronni's bracelet in William's house."

"I know. We heard him tell you that. Sound travels amazingly well down here." He paused, looking down at the ground with an embarrassed expression. "That's why William was here. He was certain you had planted the bracelet in his house, supposedly to further your custody cause by framing him for Ronni's murder. He was pretty pissed."

Marlie nodded, remembering the sharp, shrill way William had yelled out her name. After hearing that, she had been convinced he was capable of murder and just as certain she was about to become his next victim.

"I'm sorry I was so hard on William," Carvelle said. "But the evidence was just getting to be too much. It was him who steered us toward the tunnels, by the way," he added. "Though even then catching up to you was damned near impossible. What a maze. If it hadn't been for our ability to hear you and Waring talking, I don't know how we would have found you."

"The light," Marlie croaked.

"What?"

"The light," she repeated. "I saw the glow from your flashlight at the end of the tunnel and I thought it was . . . *the* light. You know, the one people have reported seeing when they're clinically dead." She shuddered then, and wished for the warmth of Carvelle's body against her own again. "I thought I was dead."

Carvelle reached over and stroked her cheek with the back of his hand. It was an exquisitely gentle and touching gesture. "So did I. Christ, you scared me to death," he said, his voice thick with emotion. "I thought I was too late. When I saw you slumped there at Waring's feet, I thought . . . I feared . . ." He didn't finish the sentence, his voice breaking on the last words. His glowance swirled with turbulence, but it was warm and comforting, radiating shades of gold, pink, and blue. Marlie's heart squeezed pleasantly with the realization that he cared for her.

She reached over, wrapped her hand over his arm, and gave him a warm smile. "I'm okay," she said hoarsely. "A little mangled, perhaps, but okay."

Carvelle took her hand and sandwiched it between his own. He leaned forward earnestly, his voice low so only she could hear. "We need to talk," he said. "I'm sorry for all the—"

Marlie silenced him by placing two fingers against his lips. "Later," she whispered. "We can talk later. Right now, I just want to get out of here. Besides," she added with a wicked smile, "for now, your glowance tells me all I need to know."

epilogue

Marlie, Carvelle, and Damaris stood in the tunnel along with the rest of the news crew from WKAL. As the technicians busied themselves with the lighting and sound settings, Marlie pulled Damaris off to one side.

"Here," she said, handing her assistant a slip of folded paper. "This is for you. My way of saying thanks for saving my life."

Damaris blushed. "You don't need to thank me," she said. "I was just doing my job."

"And damned well at that," Marlie said. "If it hadn't been for your sharp investigative work, I wouldn't be standing here right now. I'm curious, what made you decide to call Carvelle after all the investigative work I had you do on him? You had to know I was suspicious about him."

Damaris nodded. "I knew, but it was something you said to me that helped me to decide."

"Something *I* said?"

"Yep. You told me that instinct was one of the most important aspects of this job and that I should always trust mine. And my instincts told me Carvelle was one of the good guys. It also told me he cared a hell of a lot about you."

Marlie gave her a wry grin.

Damaris unfolded the paper Marlie had given her and stared at it, a puzzled expression on her face.

She held it up. "I'm sorry, I don't understand," she said with a smile.

"That's the name, current address, and phone number of your birth mother," Marlie said. "I had Dennis find her for you."

Damaris gaped at her. "I . . . I don't believe it. Really?"

Marlie smiled and nodded. "Really," she said. "Just do me a favor and don't tell anyone where you got it from. I don't want to get Dennis into trouble."

Damaris stared at the paper for several long seconds, speechless. "Has he contacted her?" she asked finally, her voice soft with shock.

"No, I only asked him to dig up the information. The rest is up to you. And her," Marlie added with a nod toward the slip of paper. "I hope it all turns out the way you want."

"This is incredible," Damaris said. She shook her head, as if she still didn't quite believe it. Suddenly, she flung herself at Marlie and gave her a huge hug. "Thank you, thank you, thank you!"

Marlie laughed with delight and hugged her back. "You are quite welcome," she said. Then, stepping back, she added, "And thank *you*. Now, quit dilly-dallying and get back to work."

"Aye, aye, Captain," Damaris said smartly, and she slipped away to join the other crew members.

Marlie was still watching her, an expression of fond affection on her face, when Carvelle walked up behind her and slipped his arms around her waist, pulling her against him. "She looks like one happy lady," he observed. Marlie felt his breath stir her hair as he spoke, and she leaned into him, relishing the warmth of his body along her back.

"I hope she stays that way," Marlie said. "She's a great kid, and one hell of an investigative reporter to boot." She twisted around then, so she was face-to-face with Carvelle, their noses only inches apart. "You could take lessons from her in self-confidence, you know."

"How long are you going to hang that over my head?"

"Forever, I hope," Marlie said suggestively. "I still can't believe that a big tough cop like you is so insecure about his looks. You know, I could tell there was something bothering you after I had the surgery. You were so distant, so aloof. Even your glowance showed it. It was always narrowed and gray, drawn in and locked down, as if you were afraid, or hiding something. I imagined all kinds of reasons for it, but I confess, insecurity about my first laying eyes on you wasn't one of them."

"Sure, you say that now, but you still can't see all that clearly. Trust me, no one I've ever known has called me handsome."

"Then let me be the first. I think you're incredibly handsome."

"Yeah, like that's going to make me believe, coming from a half-blind woman," Carvelle teased.

Marlie slapped his arm playfully.

Carvelle sighed, gazing down at her. He raised his hands up and plowed his fingers through her hair on either side of her head, "You are so beautiful," he said. "I was attracted to you from that first time I saw you in the hospital. Why the hell do you think I kept up the pretense of investigating that warehouse explosion when it was obvious we didn't have a thing to go on? I couldn't stand the idea of giving it up and not seeing you anymore."

"I figured it was because you knew I was holding something back about why I went there that night in the first place."

"You mean that police corruption thing?"

"You knew?" Marlie said, aghast.

"Of course I did. One of the first things I did when I started the investigation was ask to see the files you had at the station so I could find out what you'd been working on. I found the one on your police corruption story, though it didn't have much in it other than some quickly jotted notes about the anonymous phone call. I confess, I took it with me, even though your boss told me I couldn't."

Marlie shook her head, smiling wryly. "I was wondering what happened to that file," she said.

"I'd been hearing rumors down at the department about suspected corruption from my first day at work there. I never was convinced those junkies hiding out in the house where I shot Phillips weren't a setup by some of our own guys. Phillips was doing some undercover work for IA, you know."

Marlie nodded. "I found that out."

"There's times when I think Phillips would have died that night even if I hadn't been the one to shoot him. That whole setup stank. Something wasn't right. Unfortunately, I think I played into someone's hands when I accidentally shot Phillips myself. We've finally managed to finger a couple of guys who we now know are dirty and they were there that night. But you can bet they're never going to cop to that setup."

Marlie shook her head in disbelief. "I thought you were one of the dirty cops," she said. "All the lies you told me—"

"I never lied to you, Marlie. I just didn't tell you all the truth."

"Why not?"

He sighed heavily. "I don't know. I guess I was afraid it would color your opinion of me and I didn't want to risk losing you. I felt like I had a good thing going with the fact that you had no idea what I looked like. It made everything so much easier. It gave me a level of confidence I've never had with women before."

"What about your wife?"

"Lisa? I always believed she had to have been crazy to love me. I kept telling myself how lucky I was to find her, though technically, it was she who found me. I never would have had the courage to approach her. She was the aggressor, right from the get-go."

Marlie saw how his glowance turned a pale shade of blue as he spoke. "You really loved her, didn't you?"

"With all my heart," he said softly. "When she died, still carrying our unborn child, I thought I'd go nuts. I swore I'd find the bastard who killed her, no matter how long it took me. It took me years to track that false ID Denver had when he was working at the bank back to the people who gave it to him, although even they didn't know his true identity. I managed to follow Denver's trail here, but then I lost him. He and Waring might have been identical twins, but you never would have known it from the few pictures we had of Denver back then. He was much thinner than Waring, wore colored contacts, and had dyed his hair blond. Even then he was plotting, covering all the bases. You know, I hate to admit it, but he was one smart son of a bitch."

"He was a sick son of a bitch," Marlie said with disgust. "I can't believe I didn't see through him sooner. The clues were there. The way his glowance was so different from anyone else's. You know, I think his glowance was a reflection of his sociopathic personality. It behaved just like he did, charming and mesmerizing me, its light hypnotic. His true self only came through when he was unable to mask his murderous thoughts, like that night at the political dinner when he was startled to see me there. Even then, he managed to recover pretty quickly."

She shook her head in disgust. "I was so stupid. I should have picked up on that business with the spleen. I can't believe I missed it. Hell, Ronni figured out Waring's true nature easily enough. Why didn't I?"

"Don't beat yourself up over it," Carvelle told her. "We all make mistakes. That was one of the other reasons I related so well to you when we first met."

Marlie gave him a puzzled look.

"Your remorse over Chris, your sense that you were responsible for his death," Carvelle explained. "I felt the same way about Phillips, although in that case, I was directly responsible, much more so than you ever were with Chris. Yet somehow, watching you deal with your own guilt about Chris helped me to work through mine. It helped me to understand why it happened. You and I were both victims of fate and a moment's worth of bad judgment. You were actually much better therapy for me than that damned shrink the department made me see."

"Then I strongly recommend a continued course of therapy. Indefinite, in fact." Her eyes shifted from his face to the broad, warm light of his glowance. "As for me," she said, raising her hand and wafting it through the light, waggling her fingers in it, "this is all the therapy I need."

"Okay, people," the director yelled. "Let's do this."

Carvelle brushed his lips over Marlie's forehead. "You best get to work," he said.

"Yes, I suppose I should," she said with a sigh. Reluctantly, she moved out of his arms and headed toward the camera.

"Ten seconds," announced the director. The news crew huddled against the walls of the narrow tunnel on either side of the cameraman, hushed and vigilant. All eyes focused on the woman with the microphone who stood a few feet away, her face confident and assured. A trio of bright lights cast a pox of shadows along the tunnel's floor and walls, revealing its dark and dismal interior. Though they had originally planned to do a live feed, the thick walls of the tunnel blocked their signal. So they were shooting film instead.

The cameraman held one hand up and ticked the last five seconds off with his fingers. "Three, two, one, aaannnndddd go!" He punctuated the final instruction with a chopping motion of his arm. In the hushed silence, one voice rang out, clear, steady, and confident.

"We're standing here in the underground tunnel where Sam Denver held his final showdown with police just a few days ago. Denver, who some six years ago killed and assumed the identity of his twin brother, Richard Waring, was shot to death here on Monday night after he charged at police officers with a knife. This tunnel, part of a maze of underground passages used to help slaves escape during the Civil War, was well known to Denver, who spent his childhood in the house built over the secret entrance. While these passageways may once have offered new hope to an untold number of slaves, this particular leg of it bears the mark of death. The skeletal remains of Denver's brother and his adoptive parents, Ed and Carla Denver, were found just a few feet from where I'm standing."

She turned slightly, gesturing toward the end of the tunnel behind her, her expression tragic and grave. "According to police, Denver dumped the bodies of his victims here, gaining access to this underground maze through a vertical shaft carved into a cliff at the tunnel's end. Police have also determined that it was Denver who murdered WKAL reporter Ronni Cumberland, because she had uncovered the truth behind his deception. Ms. Cumberland's strangled body was found at the base of a cliff not far from the shaft, and police have speculated that Denver intended to return to the scene of his crime and stash her body here in the tunnels along with those of his other victims. Those plans were thwarted when police arrived on the scene before Denver had a chance to return."

She turned and faced the camera head-on again. "Police investigators have also tied Denver to the murders of Walter and Mary Waring, the couple who raised Richard Waring, as well as Martha Springer, Denver and Waring's birth mother. In addition, Denver has been linked to a bank robbery that took place in Canton, Ohio, nearly seven years ago, which resulted in the death of two of the banks' employees, including the then-pregnant wife of the detective who was responsible for finally apprehending Denver.

"People everywhere are still reeling from the magnitude of Denver's duplicity, which allowed him to assume his brother's identity and hide his heinous deeds and evil nature so well that he became one of the most popular politicians of our time, even coming within an arm's reach of the governor's mansion. But in the end it was the truth from a timeless adage spoken by another beloved politician that led to Denver's eventual decline: 'You can't fool all of the people all of the time.'

"This is Damaris Dedulonus reporting for WKAL news."